CIRCLE

of

GRACE

CIRCLE

of

GRACE

PENELOPE J. STOKES

RANDOM HOUSE
LARGE PRINT

Copyright © 2004 by Penelope J. Stokes

All poetry contained herein is the original work of the author and may not be used without permission.

All rights reserved under International and Pan-American Copyright Conventions. Published in the United States of America by Random House Large Print in association with Doubleday, New York, and simultaneously in Canada by Random House of Canada Limited, Toronto. Distributed by Random House, Inc., New York.

The Library of Congress has established a Cataloging-in-Publication record for this title.

ISBN 0-375-43368-6

www.randomlargeprint.com

FIRST LARGE PRINT EDITION

10 9 8 7 6 5 4 3 2 1

This Large Print edition published in accord with the standards of the N.A.V.H.

ACKNOWLEDGMENTS

With grateful appreciation to:

My agent, Claudia Cross,

My editor, Michelle Rapkin,

and

My own dear Circle of Grace—
Cindy, Kay, and Kirstin.

You have challenged my preconceived notions,
walked with me through the dark night of the soul,
opened my heart to new hope,
and inspired this novel.

Good friends and noble women all,
Thank you.

CIRCLE

of

GRACE

PROLOGUE

THE PROMISE

Asheville, North Carolina
Thirty years ago

*I*n a dim-lit corner of Kelso's Restaurant, four young women sat around a large circular table littered with the remains of dinner, half-filled coffee cups, and a couple of empty wine bottles. Diplomas in cardboard folders were propped open against one of the bottles, and black graduation gowns lay haphazardly across the back of an empty chair. The animated laughter and conversation from the table drew narrow-eyed glares from surrounding patrons.

"Ladies," the waiter interrupted with a half-smile. "Forgive the intrusion." He

produced a bottle of inexpensive champagne and a silver-plated bucket from behind his back as if by sleight-of-hand.
"Compliments of the manager, with our
congratulations."

The cork released with a pop, three of
the women cheered, and the waiter vanished.

A long-limbed, tanned blonde in a flow-
ered sundress rose to her feet. "A toast!"
she said, raising a glass.

"Come on, Lovey, don't you think
you've had enough?"

The blonde looked down her nose.
"Don't be a party pooper, Grace. I know
you don't normally drink, but you've lived
with the three of us for almost four years
now. I'd think by now you'd learned to
whoop it up a little." She glanced at the
other two. "Liz? Tess? Help me out here."

Liz and Tess exchanged a glance. "It *is*
our graduation," Tess said.

"Yeah," Liz agreed, louder. "And given
the state of the world, we might as well enjoy ourselves while we have the chance.
Kennedy's dead. King's dead. Nixon's in
the White House. We could all be blown to
kingdom come before our first reunion."

"On that cheerful note—" Lovey made a face in Liz's direction. "Can we forget the politics just for tonight? Now, how about that toast?"

Grace relented with a shrug and a half-smile. "All right, all right." She eyed the champagne bottle. "Maybe just a little."

They stood and raised their glasses. "To all of us," Lovey said, her hand a bit unsteady as she lifted the bubbling flute. "First, to Liz Chandler, a woman destined to change the world."

Liz grinned and nodded. "For the better, I hope. It sure needs changing."

Lovey turned toward Tess. "And to Tess Riley, future recipient of the Nobel Prize for Literature."

Tess laughed. "Well, maybe just a puny little Pulitzer."

Liz pointed her champagne flute in Tess's direction. "Don't forget us when you're famous."

"Last, but not least, to Grace Benedict," Lovey went on. "Our resident Truth Teller. The one who has kept us honest. You've shown us the way—even when we haven't followed it."

"Wait. We're not done yet," Liz interrupted. "To Amanda Love. Beauty queen. Cheerleader. Most Likely to Succeed—"

"Cut it out, Liz." Lovey ducked her head.

"And the best friend anyone could have," Liz finished.

Lovey smiled. "Thank you." Her glass sparkled in the light of the candle. "To us. To friendship. To the future."

They clinked glasses, drank to one another, and resumed their seats around the table. Tess reached into her bag and pulled out a small square package wrapped in gold paper. "I have a present for all of us."

"We said no gifts," they protested in unison.

"This is different." Tess handed the gift to Grace. "You do the honors."

"Are you sure?" Grace looked around the table.

"Open it," Lovey insisted.

Grace pulled the ribbon off the corners and carefully slit the paper at the back.

Liz rolled her eyes. "For pity's sake, Grace. We're not keeping the paper for posterity."

"You don't know." Grace pulled a face and adopted her drama-queen voice. "This could be a historic occasion. This paper could be worth money someday, as a memento of our last night together. Why, at auction it could—"

"Just *open it.*"

At last she got the wrapping off, opened the box, and held the gift up for all to see. It was a small leather-bound book, dark green, with a line drawing in gold on the front—a small park bench flanked by a lamppost and a bubbling fountain. "It's a journal."

"It's a *circle* journal," Tess corrected. "We're all going different directions now that graduation's over. I wanted us to have a way to stay in touch. Everybody writes in it, you see, about what's going on in their lives, and then we send it around the circle so we can all read what the others have written. It becomes an ongoing record of our lives, and keeps us connected."

Silence fell over the group, as if Tess's words had brought to the surface what all of them were thinking. For nearly four years they had lived together, sharing each other's tragedies and victories. They had fought and made up, pulled all-nighters, read each other's term papers, evaluated each other's boyfriends. Together they had grown from insecure teenage girls to independent young women.

Four golden years. And now it was over.

"I want us to promise," Tess said, "that we'll all write in the journal and send it on. Promise that we won't lose touch."

"And promise that no matter what happens," Grace added, "we'll always be honest with each other. That we'll always be best friends."

Lovey refilled their glasses from the last of the bottle the waiter had brought. "Friendship like ours comes once in a lifetime," she said. "We'll never lose it."

Again they held their glasses to each other, to the bond that held them together.

And this time Grace didn't sip at the golden bubbles. She drank the champagne down, right to the bottom of the glass.

PART I

GRACE

Whatever Truth may be,
she does not dwell in dreams,
in fabrications of a longing heart
or burning fables from a fevered mind.

What has been is a mist upon the mountains.
What might have been swirls just beyond our reach,
mirage within the mist.

What is
and what is yet to come
may bruise our souls,
but holding to the grand illusion
shatters us
beyond all hope of healing.

The Persistence of Memory

Present Day

Grace Benedict was fifty-two years old, and she still hated going to the doctor. Avoided it at all costs. But this time she had no choice. Two weeks ago a long-overdue mammogram had revealed a suspicious spot on her right breast. Probably nothing, the doctor assured her. Most likely just a cyst; women got them all the time. After a needle biopsy and a battery of other tests, they had called her back in to discuss the results.

No, they couldn't talk about it on the telephone, the nurse had said. Better for her to come in and see the doctor personally. They scheduled the appointment for her lunch hour, promising it wouldn't take more than thirty minutes.

"Have a seat, Mrs. Benedict," said the young woman behind the glass-paneled counter. "The doctor will be with you shortly."

Not Mrs., Grace thought. But she didn't bother to correct the receptionist. Instead, she left the counter and parked herself in a cracked vinyl chair in the corner of the waiting room. To her right, a bubbling aquarium, its back wall lined with a garish shade of blue, housed several brightly colored tropical fish.

Grace picked up a dated, dog-eared copy of *U.S. News* from the coffee table and tried to ignore the whining child a few seats away. ELECTION RESULTS STILL IN DOUBT, the cover proclaimed, the words superimposed over photographs of George W. Bush and Al Gore. And in smaller letters underneath: *What went wrong in Florida?*

Grace tossed the old magazine back onto the table, but her eyes continued to fix on the words: *What went wrong?*

She pondered the question—one that had haunted her for nearly three decades. And there was only one answer, which was no answer at all: *Everything.*

Thirty years ago, she could never have envisioned the future that awaited her. A future riddled with mistakes and heartbreak and—

Well, better not to think about that.

She shifted in her chair and watched out of the corner of her eye as the frazzled young mother tried in vain to comfort her daughter. The little girl, who was perhaps five or six years old, curled up on her mother's lap and whimpered fretfully. "It'll be all right," the mother shushed, pushing back a damp strand of hair from her daughter's forehead. "The doctor will give you some medicine to make it all better."

Grace bit her lip and averted her eyes. If only there were such a medication, something that would "make it all better." But no wonder drug could fix a life, and even if such a miracle had existed, she wouldn't have been able to afford it.

A nurse wearing pink scrubs with Beatrix Potter bunnies printed on them came to the door with a clipboard and looked around the waiting room. "Mrs. Bennett?"

"Benedict," Grace corrected, then turned to the young mother. "Unless your name is Bennett?"

The woman shook her head. "Whitlock," she said.

Grace got up and went toward the nurse. "I guess you must mean me, then. Grace *Benedict*." She forced a smile. "Like the traitor."

"Whatever." The nurse looked at her blankly and shrugged. "Follow me."

Grace followed to Examining Room 3. "Have a seat," the nurse said. "The doctor will—"

"I know. The doctor will be with me shortly."

The second attempt at humor fell as flat as the first. The nurse shoved the clipboard into a plastic holder on the wall and pulled the door closed.

Almost as soon as the door clicked shut, a soft knock sounded. The doorknob turned, and a man entered. He was small and dark, with dense, close-cropped black hair and deep-set eyes. The name *Sangi* was embroidered in red over the pocket of his white lab coat. Grace had never seen him before, but a lot of physicians served the clinic, and it wasn't unusual to get a different one every time.

"Good afternoon, Mrs. Benedict," he said, his words clipped and precise. "I am Dr. Butahali Sangi." He flipped through her chart. "We have your test results."

"Grace. Please call me Grace."

He smiled. "Grace, then. Kindly sit, if you will, upon the table."

Grace complied, scooting onto the high examining table. The protective paper made a crinkling sound under her thighs.

Dr. Sangi eased down onto a rolling stool and drew up close. For a moment or two he said nothing, concentrating instead upon reading the records in front of him. At last he raised his eyes—large, dark, liquid eyes that reminded Grace of some vulnerable little forest creature.

"You recently had a mammogram, that is correct? February 15th?"

Grace nodded. "Yes." Something in her stomach fluttered, a caged bird beating the bars. "Is anything wrong?"

Sangi gazed at her for a full minute.

"There is no easy way to tell such news."
He shook his head.

She exhaled heavily. "The lump. It
wasn't just a cyst."

The doctor laid the medical chart aside
and touched her wrist with squared-off
brown fingers. "There is no one I should
call, perhaps? A husband? A friend?"

The contact was brief, gentle, but Grace
felt as if she had been brushed by a live
electrical wire. "No one." She drew in a
breath and raised her head. "Just give it to
me straight, Doctor. All of it."

"As you wish." He pulled back and ran
his hand through his hair, then retrieved
the chart and read: "You have what we believe to be a stage IV metastatic tumor
with intrusion into the chest wall and in-
tercostal muscles. We suspect significant
lymph node involvement as well, but cannot know for certain until surgery is ac-
complished."

Grace's hand went instinctively, protec-
tively, to her chest. She looked down at her
fingers cupping her breast, and an image
rose to her mind—a dark and menacing
squid, its body lodged inside her, its inky
tentacles spreading out to invade her torso,

slithering toward her internal organs. She shuddered.

Dr. Sangi waited while she composed herself.

"Stage IV," she said at last. "How high do the stages go?"

"Four."

"What about treatment?"

"I have already taken the liberty of speaking with a specialist. We can indeed attempt to remove the major portion of the tumor," he said. "At this stage it is unlikely, however, that surgery would be successful in a total removal of the cancerous cells. There are additional options. Intensive chemotherapy. Radiation, perhaps. Bone marrow or stem cell transplants."

The squid tightened its grasp, and for a moment Grace felt as if her lungs had collapsed. "But you can cure me," she said when she could breathe again.

"In such cases as yours we do not speak of cure," Sangi responded with a sigh. "We speak of containment. We speak of time gained."

"How much time?"

"You wished me to be direct," Dr. Sangi said. At Grace's nod, he went on. "At best, a year. Perhaps two. Perhaps not so much. We cannot know for certain until more tests are done." He turned his hands palm upward in a gesture of surrender. Grace noticed that although the tops of his hands were brown, his palms were pale pink. For a moment she felt as if she had glimpsed some private part of him, and she flushed with embarrassment.

"And what would that year—if I had a year—involve?"

"Radical chemotherapy, certainly. If we could shrink the tumor a bit, then surgery. Additional chemo afterward. As well as the other options I mentioned."

"A mastectomy, months of chemo and radiation, in and out of the hospital," Grace translated. She had seen it before. She knew the symptoms all too well. "Constant nausea. Hair loss. Depleted energy. And no guarantees."

"I fear you are correct." Sangi nodded.

"And if I elect to have no treatment?"

The physician's face went blank. "I beg your pardon?"

"If I walk out of here and don't treat this—no surgery, no chemo, no radiation. How long would I have then?"

A look of comprehension sparked in his eyes, an expression akin to respect. "It is impossible to determine. A few months, perhaps less."

"A few months without pain, without being turned into a voodoo doll, cut and poked and prodded and filled with drugs."

The doctor nodded. "You would likely have little pain until the very end. As a physician, certainly, I could not recommend—"

"Of course you couldn't." Grace slid down from the examining table and put a hand on Dr. Sangi's shoulder. "Thank you for your candor, Doctor. I appreciate it more than you know."

"You are indeed welcome." He smiled then, showing even white teeth against dark skin.

"I need a little time to think," she said. "I'll call you."

"Soon," the doctor warned. "We have no time to waste."

Somehow Grace managed to get through the rest of the day on autopilot—sorting through the return bin, shelving, cataloguing new books that had just come in—without thought or intention. No one at the library knew she had skipped lunch to go to the clinic. No one had a clue that anything might be wrong. Grace Benedict, the faithful stereotype, the unobtrusive librarian gliding through the stacks in silence, like an apparition.

But driving home at five-fifteen, Grace couldn't keep her mind from spiraling around the question Dr. Sangi had asked: *"Is there no one I should call?"*

Curiously, she felt no sense of imminent loss at the news that she was dying. On that count, she floated above the scene like the soul of a patient hovering between this world and the next, watching it all with a dispassionate eye. For the first time in years, she experienced a clarity of vision and an infusion of strength, a flood of adrenaline to the veins and endorphins to the brain. She knew without question that she would not submit to the "procedures" Dr. Sangi had described.

She did, however, feel an overwhelming sense of loneliness.

No, there was no one to call. Not a single friend or lover, no husband or parent or child, no one who might help her bear this moment of crisis.

How had her life come to this?

Grace's heart knew the answer even as her mind formulated the question. In the far reaches of her memory, she could hear the echo of a door slamming and bolts sliding into place—the clang of a vault being locked after the robbers had already come and gone. How absurd, to guard an empty soul with such tenacity. And yet she knew no other way to survive, to keep at bay the onslaughts of life's inevitable pain.

It hadn't always been this way. She'd once had friends, had once been in love, had once harbored wistful dreams of the kind of life other people seemed to live. She had trusted, had laughed, had opened her heart. But that had been a long time ago.

It had been more than twenty years since Grace Benedict had been in love, and then the fires of passion had brought not warmth and comfort but a raging conflagration that left her scarred and terrified of getting close enough to be burned a second time. On a few occasions in the past she had met someone nice and determined to try once more, only to shy away after the first date or the first kiss.

But she *had* had a best friend. Jet. Evelyn Jetterly.

They had met in the library, liked each other, and began meeting for coffee to discuss books. Gradually their intellectual companionship ripened into something more personal, the kind of friendship and belonging Grace hadn't known since college. For almost ten years they laughed together, cried together, told each other everything—almost. The two of them were closer than sisters, and Grace was happy.

Until Jet, too, was snatched out of her life.

Grace could still feel the frail bones of Jet's hand gripping hers, see the skeletal face with its wide eyes and dry, cracked lips. In Jet's case it was cervical cancer, and it took her so quickly that neither of them had time to adjust. She was just . . . gone.

Grace tried in vain to push Jet's dying image out of her mind. She didn't want to remember her friend that way, but the picture stayed with her. Now it was her turn, and there would be no one sitting by her bedside, holding her hand, when she passed.

How long had it been, she wondered, since she had gazed at another human face across a dinner table? Months? Years? Sometimes, in the shaded picnic area under the trees beside the library, she shared a brown-bag lunch with the part-time library assistant, Marge. But that hardly counted as socializing. Marge talked nonstop about the weather or quitting smoking or her current diet or her teenage kids, and she rarely let Grace get a word in edgewise. Not that it mattered. Grace never revealed anything personal about her own life anyway, and Marge never seemed to notice—or care—that their conversations were one-sided.

As she looked back over the years since Jet's death, Grace was hard pressed to account for how she had spent her time. She worked, took drives up into the mountains, watched TV, read four or five books a week. On weekends she went to bargain matinees and sat alone in the darkened movie theater, eating Wal-Mart popcorn she brought in a plastic bag from home.

Sometimes she'd walk through the mall and window-shop. Have coffee at the food court. Chat with people she knew by sight but not by name.

Now Dr. Sangi had asked the question, and Grace had been forced to face the answer. There was no one to call. She could vanish from the face of the earth tomorrow, and no one would know she was missing until someone called the city to complain that their local branch library hadn't been open for a week.

Grace pulled into the gravel driveway beside her house, got out of the car, and crunched across the rocks to retrieve the mail. The late-afternoon sky was a glorious blue, and in the distance beyond the housetops she could see the peaks of mountains touched by the western sun. Gray and green and purple, projecting up like—

Like breasts, her mind interjected without warning. Like firm, young, healthy, noncancerous breasts.

Grace turned her eyes from the view and busied herself with emptying the mailbox.

Bills. Always bills. A second notice from
Carolina Power. A bank statement that, she
knew without looking, would not show a
sufficient balance to cover all she owed.
And a credit card. A brand-new Visa,
stamped with her name.

When had she applied for that? She
couldn't remember, and couldn't believe
anyone would actually issue a credit card to
someone who made less than $25,000 a
year—every dime of which went to rent,
food, auto repair, and other necessities of
life.

For years she had lived from paycheck to
paycheck, always feeling the hot breath of
poverty on the back of her neck, always
worried that the money wouldn't stretch
through the month. Once in a great while,
when she had little extra in her purse, she
would stop along the roadside and give a
dollar or two to one of the homeless folks
who spent their days under the bridges and
their nights in the local shelters.

She understood, and didn't fault them for
their plight. It would only take a month—
two at most—to put someone like Grace
herself on the streets. A layoff. A downsiz-
ing. An illness . . .

She shook her head and pushed the unwelcome reality out of her mind. She always told herself it didn't pay to dwell on
the what-ifs. And now the biggest what-if
of all had come to call—not just to visit,
but to take up residence with her in her
shabby, cramped little house.

She gazed, disbelieving, at the Visa card,
shoved it back into the envelope, and
climbed the two broken concrete steps to
the front door.

The day had been warm, but inside, the
house was dark and chilly. Grace turned on
a couple of lamps, then went into the
kitchen, dumped the mail on the counter,
and opened the refrigerator. Half a loaf of
wheat bread, a couple of eggs, a third of a
quart of milk nearly a week past its prime.
A bag of salad greens, brown and slimy
around the edges.

She opened the cabinet above her head
and took down a can of cream of broccoli
soup—the cheap generic kind, a store
brand. Tears sprang to her eyes, and she
slammed the can down on the countertop.
Ridiculous. Less than six hours ago she had
been diagnosed with cancer, and here she

was, crying because she couldn't afford real soup!

"Damn," she muttered to the empty house. "Just once, I wish—I wish—"

What did she wish? That she could have things *nice*. A house with freshly painted walls and a wallpaper border. Furniture that wasn't sagging and scarred. A real dinner in an upscale restaurant, with flowers on the table and candles and white linen.

Grace emptied the soup into a saucepan, added some of the milk, which smelled all right despite its expiration date, and put two slices of bread in the toaster. When the meager meal was ready, she took it to the kitchen table and sat down with the rest of the mail.

Bills, unopened, went into one pile. She'd deal with them later. The bank statement she set aside to go over after dinner. The usual assortment of catalogues and advertising flyers went straight into the trash can. And there, on the bottom of the stack, lay a padded manila envelope.

Grace pushed the soup bowl aside and picked up the envelope. The return address was from Arlington, Virginia. The handwriting seemed vaguely familiar, but it had been so long. More than a year, she thought. Or was it two?

She wiped the buttery knife on a paper napkin, slit open the envelope, and removed the contents. A small bound book, ragged and faded, its spine broken and its corners bent. On the front, stamped into the green leather, a barely visible image of a park scene—a bench, a fountain, a lamppost.

The circle journal had made its way back to her again.

Grace finished her lukewarm soup and sat fingering the journal as darkness gathered outside the kitchen window. She glanced into the glass, and a reflection stared back at her. An ordinary-looking middle-aged woman with salt-and-pepper hair, badly cut, and lines of weariness fanning out around her eyes and mouth. Who was this woman? Not the person she imagined herself to be. Certainly not the girl she once had been—so sure of everything, so full of hope and dreams.

"*Promise that we won't lose touch,*" she heard Tess Riley's voice echo in her memory.

And her own girlish response, full of feeling and purpose: "*And promise that whatever happens, we'll always be honest with each other.*"

So much for good intentions.

She shoved the book aside as bitter tears stung her eyes. She didn't want to read what was in it, didn't want the reminders it carried of the life that could have been. Didn't want to resurrect that sense of warmth and belonging, those feelings she would never know again.

Yet the memories persisted. Even without reading the words or letting her eyes linger on the familiar handwriting that filled its pages, the journal called her back. Back to the person she had been thirty years ago. Back to the friends she had promised to be faithful to.

And so, as night fell in the mountains and the lamp above the kitchen table spilled a yellow pool of light onto the pages, Grace Benedict took the circle journal in her hands and let herself remember.

2

PILATE'S QUESTION

Fall Semester
Freshman Year

"*What is truth?*" Professor Alberta Wall intoned in her intense, gravelly voice. "That is the question before us, a question that has baffled philosophers and theologians for millennia."

She gazed around the classroom, frowning, her eyes squinting behind round little wire-rimmed glasses. "So." She pushed the glasses back up her nose with a bony forefinger. "You *will* be answering this question—or attempting to do so. But never fear, you will not be alone in your frantic groping for coherent thought. We will be doing this as a team assignment."

Grace glanced surreptitiously around the classroom. A team assignment. Lovely. None of the girls in her dorm, none of the people she hung out with, were in Dr. Wall's Intro to Philosophy course. Grace knew some of the students by name and had laughed and joked with them over the professor's eccentric habits—like erasing the blackboard with the palm of her hand and then rubbing her nose. But who would she pick to do a class project? She didn't really know any of them well enough to decide.

Grace hadn't really wanted to come to UNCA in the first place. She was a small-town girl better suited for a small campus. She'd have been perfectly happy living at home and commuting to the local community college. But her mother had insisted.

"College is the experience of a lifetime," Mama had repeated for the hundredth time. "The university will be good for you. You'll have a wonderful time, trust me. Studying, learning, living in a dorm with other girls your age. College campuses are—I don't know. Magical."

Mama's tone when she said this was wistful, euphoric. Grace heard in her voice the echo of nostalgic longing, a reverberation of long-dead dreams and wishes unfulfilled. And, perhaps for the first time in her life, Grace wondered if her mother might have had more in mind for herself than living in the country, being married, and raising a child.

But she hadn't asked.

Grace had never been particularly close to her mother. From birth, practically, she had been a daddy's girl. Mama always seemed remote and distant, an island barely visible on the far horizon. Daddy, on the other hand, was the ground she walked on, the sun that warmed her. He had a charming smile and an outgoing personality and a quick wit that made everyone laugh. He wasn't handsome, at least not by the conventional standard of movie-star good looks. He had a round, boyish face, thinning sand-colored hair, and a dimple in his chin, and when Grace tried to look at him objectively, he reminded her a little of a golden retriever puppy. But even in that he was utterly irresistible. Adorable, clownish, a tad clumsy, and absolutely endearing.

Oddly enough, only her mother seemed immune to her father's charms. Where Daddy was loose and free and easygoing, Mama held herself tight and standoffish, as if she feared that the least bit of levity might shake her atoms loose and she'd fly apart completely. Daddy drew his energy from others, like a direct transfusion, while Mama retreated into her books and endured with grim resignation the company of Daddy's enthusiastic friends.

As a child, whenever Grace had thought about growing up and getting married, Daddy was the kind of man she envisioned falling in love with. She couldn't for the life of her understand her mother's aloofness, and when Mama spoke about the "grand adventure" of going off to college, Grace had gotten the distinct impression that Mama herself would love nothing more than to escape into the academic world and never come out again.

Maybe for Mama, the adventure of intellectual exploration would have been enough to satisfy. But it wasn't enough for Grace. She liked her classes, for the most part, liked the girls in her dorm. They stayed up late, talking and laughing and pretending to study, but there was nobody Grace really connected with yet. She supposed it would just take time.

The main problem was that Grace's friends in high school had mostly been people she had grown up with since kindergarten. She didn't feel like she had to prove herself with them in order to be accepted. She had known where she fit. Now, at college, she was having to start all over again, and it wasn't as easy as Mama had led her to believe.

Grace forced her mind back to the present. The professor was talking again.

"All right," she said, "how many of you have ever read Aristotle? Plato? Kierkegaard? Sartre?"

No one moved. Professor Wall cleared her throat. "As I suspected. OK, let's take it down a notch. How many of you have ever read the Bible?"

Almost everyone raised a hand, but most of the students looked uncomfortable and tentative, as if afraid Wall might call on them to produce a sermon on the spot.

"Yes, well. A fascinating collection of myths." Dr. Wall quirked one eyebrow.

Grace jerked her head up. She wasn't

particularly religious, but she had been born and brought up in the South, squarely on the brass-hard buckle of the Bible Belt, and she had never—*never*—heard anyone refer to the Good Book as a "collection of myths." People swore on the Bible in court, swore by it in the streets, quoted it from the political stump, wrote their wedding dates and babies' names in the front. Some even dusted it off and carried it to church on Sunday. Rarely did anyone live by its teachings, but if they questioned its authority, they kept their heresies to themselves.

And no one in the South ever called it "myth."

Clearly, Dr. Alberta Wall was not from the South.

If anyone else noticed her faux pas, however, no one spoke up, and the professor went on.

"Perhaps this story will seem more relevant to you than Aristotle or Plato." She picked up a battered black book from the desk and thumbed through it. "Anyone ever hear of Pontius Pilate?"

A few hands went up, and one pimply-faced boy in the second row responded.

"He was the, uh, the governor or judge or something—the one who sentenced Jesus." The boy ducked his head. "I think."

"Right. The story goes that when Jesus stood trial, his judge Pontius Pilate raised a rather significant question. Pilate asked him, 'What is truth?' "

She snapped the book shut and dropped it on the desk with a resounding *wham*. All heads jerked to attention, and someone in the back let out a nervous laugh.

"What is truth?" the professor repeated, narrowing her eyes and looking around. "Pilate asked the question, but Jesus didn't answer. And still the question resounds through centuries of philosophical debate." Her voice dropped to a whisper, and she articulated each word: "*What—is—truth?*"

She held up a typed list, then walked over to the wall and thumbtacked the paper to the bulletin board next to the door. "That's your assignment between now and next Tuesday," she said with her back still turned. "I've divided you into groups of four—and, no, Mr. Jacobs, you cannot be in a group with Miss Summers."

Everyone tittered. The budding romance between Cal Jacobs and Evelyn

Summers had quickly become the stuff of legend around campus. Grace had even seen them making out in the back row when Dr. Wall turned her back to write on the blackboard. Apparently Dr. Wall had seen it too—or had a mole in the class.

"In fact, I've deliberately grouped you with people you most likely will not know," she continued, facing the students once more. "Philosophy is born out of a divergence of opinion, not out of agreement. For the next few days, you will work together with others in your group, and you will come up with an answer to Pilate's question. Beginning next Tuesday, each group will have ten minutes to report its process to the class."

Someone waved a hand in the far corner of the classroom. "You want *us* to answer a question *Jesus* couldn't answer?"

"Exactly." Dr. Wall gave a devious little smile. "It shouldn't be that hard—there are four of you, and only one of him."

A nerdy-looking girl in the front row frowned down at her notebook. "Next Tuesday's supposed to be the midterm exam."

Professor Wall crossed her arms and

produced that same wily smile. "This *is* your midterm exam. It's worth twenty-five percent of your grade. So be serious about it."

Amid a general buzz of disbelief, she picked up her briefcase, stuffed the Bible inside, and walked out the door.

At a rectangular table in the conference room of the library, Grace sat with her hands in her lap and her eyes fixed on the scarred wooden tabletop. Someone had scratched *Pete loves Ginger* into the varnish.

Around the table sat three other students from Dr. Wall's class. By the looks of them, all were definite Gingers—girls who could inspire vandalism as a declaration of love.

"OK," one of them said—a willowy blonde coed, a real stereotype. "Let's get this thing started. I've got cheerleader prac-tice at four."

Grace had always harbored the secret suspicion that natural blonde hair allowed brain cells to escape by osmosis. The theory explained a lot. Now she had verifiable evidence.

"I think we should get to know each other first," a second girl said. "My name is Tess Riley. I'm going to be a lit major, with a minor in creative writing."

Tess was attractive, Grace noted, but not in a blonde-bombshell way. She had rich auburn hair and brown eyes, and wore jeans and a blue UNCA sweatshirt so new it still had creases down the sleeves.

"Liz Chandler," the third said by way of introduction. "I'm double-majoring in political science and psychology—or will be once I declare."

Liz, dressed in black slacks and a black turtleneck, had short dark hair and shocking blue eyes behind wire-rimmed glasses. She reminded Grace of a beatnik from the fifties, someone who ought to be out on the Pacific Coast Highway riding motorcycles with Jack Kerouac.

All eyes turned toward Grace, and she introduced herself. "I'm Grace Benedict. Haven't decided on my major yet," she said. "I love literature, too—" She cast a glance in Tess's direction. "But I'm not a writer, and can't quite imagine myself as a teacher. I'll end up in library science, probably."

The blonde rolled her eyes. "OK, if we've had enough of the tea party chitchat, can we get this done?"

Tess shot a look toward Grace, grinned, and winked. Grace felt a warmth spread through her, and she smiled back. "Don't you think *you* ought to introduce yourself?" Tess said to the blonde.

The girl did a double take, as if she couldn't believe there was a soul on campus who didn't know who she was. Then the facade cracked, and she gave a self-deprecating laugh. "Sorry. Didn't mean to come across as such a bitch. I'm Amanda Love. My friends call me Lovey."

Liz let out a snicker. "You can't possibly be serious."

Grace half expected Lovey to be insulted, but instead she giggled. "I'm afraid so. Awful, ain't it?"

Tess shook her head. "I can beat that. *My* real name is Contessa."

"No!" Liz stifled a snorting laugh.

"Yes."

"What *was* your mother thinking?"

"I have no idea," Tess said. "Maybe that I'd grow up to look like Lovey and become the next Princess Grace." She chuckled.

"We all have to live with our little disappointments, I suppose."

Everyone laughed. Howled until their sides ached and the librarian appeared at the door to ask them in a whispered, condescending voice if they could work more quietly, please.

Tess wiped at her eyes. "Grace, you have to swear you won't become *that* kind of librarian."

Grace put on her haughtiest expression and pinched her mouth into a sour-lemon pucker. "It's genetic, I fear," she said in a breathy voice, aping the librarian dead-on. "Diagnosed at birth. We all have it, and if we don't, we're given injections during the first semester of graduate school."

The girls dissolved in laughter, the kind that reached out and drew her in. And in their laughter was the promise that she *did* have some of Daddy in her, and that college might turn out to be a grand adventure after all.

If nothing else, the week-long discussion of the Pilate question served to emphasize the diversity of perspectives in their little study group. Grace began to think of them as the Four Corners, or the Compass Points.

Tess was North, with her head in the stratosphere, up in the thin air of creativity and metaphor. "Beauty is truth, truth beauty," she quoted from Keats. "That is all ye know on earth, and all ye need to know."

Lovey was South, realistic and practical, her roots in the red Georgia clay. She had turned out to be not nearly as much of an airhead as Grace had expected. "What on God's green earth is that supposed to mean?" she said. "Truth is what's real, what's . . . well, true. Truth is what you can see and feel and know. It can't be defined."

"But we *have* to define it," argued Liz, the dissident. Grace thought of her as West—the pacifist, the radical, as far left as you could get. "Truth is within us," Liz asserted, "not something on the outside. Truth is about what we do with our lives to make a positive impact on the world. It's different for everybody. There's no such thing as absolute truth."

And Grace herself—East on the compass, right on the political scale—chimed in,

"What's that quote, something about knowing the truth and the truth setting us free?"

Liz began muttering under her breath, and Grace thought she caught the words *superstitious drivel*. But Tess looked into Grace's eyes with interest. "What do you think that means?"

This time Liz didn't bother trying to cover up her disdain. "Without the mumbo-jumbo, please."

Grace turned. "Hey, Dr. Wall quoted Jesus, and you didn't accuse *her* of superstitious drivel."

Liz grinned. "I know, but she holds the grade book. Besides, she didn't quote Jesus, she quoted Pontius Pilate."

Grace rolled her eyes. "Right. So, when you run for president, you quote Pilate and see how far you get."

This time Liz laughed out loud. "OK, I give in. What *do* you think it means, Grace? The stuff about knowing the truth and being free."

"Maybe it means that truth enables us to become the people we were created to be."

"That's it!" Tess grinned. "That's our point of compromise!" She began scribbling on a legal pad. Then, after a couple of minutes, she put up a hand and began to read:

"Truth is the core of human experience, the center point which keeps us balanced and aligned, the hub which connects us to all we value. It goes by many names—faith, beauty, love, justice—but whatever we call it, however we experience it, it is the source of meaning and purpose in our lives."

She sat back and exhaled heavily. "Does that do it?"

Liz took the page and studied it for a moment, then nodded. "Sounds good to me, especially the image of the hub which connects us to what we value. It specifies the importance of truth without limiting it to a particular religion or philosophy."

"I like the many-names part," Lovey agreed. "It leaves room for people to get to their own truth through various means— spiritual, artistic, social, personal—and yet acknowledges that at the center there is a shared reality that joins us together."

Tess handed the pad across the table. "What about you, Grace? Can you sign on to this definition of truth?"

Grace read it over a few times. "I'm in." She looked around the table. "This has been quite an experience. I've never come across points of view that are so different from mine. Especially yours, Liz."

"I know. I'm just a dyed-in-the-wool infidel."

Grace chuckled. "Right. And you're very good at it, too." She turned toward the others. "It's been fun. A challenge."

"That's great to hear," Liz said. "Because I think *you* should be the spokesperson for our group. And I think *you* should write up the process we used to get to this definition."

"Why me?"

Liz grinned. "Because Tess wrote the statement, and Lovey and I don't have the faintest idea of how we got there."

Grace typed out Tess's definition and thumbtacked it to the bookcase over her desk. She spent three hours writing up the report. When midterm grades came out, all of them had received A's.

But more important to Grace than the

philosophy grade was the connection the four of them had made. They might have been compass points, each aiming in a different direction, but some magnetic force held them together. And when, at the end of the term, Lovey found a small house within walking distance of campus and invited them all to share the rent with her, Grace said yes without a moment's hesitation.

3

THE DUMP

The first week of January, the tiny house three blocks from the university received its new tenants. Grace and the others had pooled their meager resources and bought some used furniture from the Goodwill store, and with four of them sharing rent and food and gas for Liz's ancient Volkswagen Beetle, the cost was considerably lower than living on campus.

Grace's father, however, was less certain about the arrangement.

When he and Mama first arrived, he had flirted shamelessly with the girls and, as usual, made everyone except Mama laugh. Grace could tell her roommates loved him, but that was nothing new. She was surprised, however, at what he said when he got her alone.

"Are you *sure* you want to live here?" he asked between heaving breaths as he lugged a trunk up the stairs to the dormer room Grace would be sharing with Tess. "You could still change your mind, come live at home and attend the community college. This place is kind of a dump, you know."

The "dump" was a story-and-a-half cottage on Barnard Street, across the creek and up the hill from campus. Grace thought of it as a "grandma house," with its rocking-chair porch and twin second-floor gables that gave it an expression of perpetual surprise. Actually, it *had* belonged to someone's grandma—an elderly woman who had lived here since nineteen-thirty-something. When she died, her grown grandchildren decided to rent it rather than put money into it to make it fit for sale.

The cramped living room had matted green shag carpeting and bright yellow walls, and the two downstairs bedrooms—assigned to Lovey and Liz—were little more than oversized closets, barely large enough for a bed and dresser. Grace and Tess would have to share, but Grace secretly thought they were getting the better end of the bargain. The dormer room upstairs ran the whole length of the house. It was spacious and airy, with windows at either end and built-in storage closets and drawers under the slanting eaves.

When Grace tried to look at the place through her father's eyes, she acknowledged that the faucets dripped and the rooms needed painting and the kitchen was a throwback to the thirties. But she couldn't have cared less. "It's great, Daddy," she said. "We'll fix it up. It'll be absolutely perfect."

What was perfect, although it took Grace a while to articulate it to herself, was the sense of freedom and belonging she felt. She had always known her parents loved her—Daddy demonstrated his love lavishly, and occasionally even Mama would break down and show a little warmth, enough so that Grace learned to believe what she didn't always feel. But there had always been an underlying tension at home, something she sensed but couldn't name.

Now she was in her own place, with a group of friends who liked her and accepted her. They had jokingly dubbed her the Truth Teller—not just because of the Pilate project but because she was the only one of them who could use humor to challenge and pacify Liz when she was being especially bullheaded. Grace was beginning to understand a little more why her mother was so enamored with college life.

If her father had raised the issue last semester, Grace might have jumped at the chance to flee Asheville and go home. Now there was no question of leaving. She fit here. These were her friends.

"No, Daddy," she said when they paused to rest at the top of the stairs. "I miss you, but this is where I need to be."

He dragged the trunk across the room and dropped it at the foot of her bed. The upper room was so chilly, she could see little puffs of white mist as he sank down on it, panting. "All right, Kidlet." He smiled self-consciously at his use of the old nickname, held out his arms, and gathered her in. She inhaled his familiar scent and remembered the feeling, all the way back to early childhood, of being warm and safe in his arms. As long as he loved her—as long

as he was Daddy—nothing could touch
her.

"I miss you too," he said, kissing the top
of her head. "I guess it's kind of hard for
your old dad to realize you're not my little
girl any longer, to let go and let you grow
up."

Grace lifted her face and grinned at him.
"I'll always be your girl, Daddy. Not so little anymore, but—"

He laughed, and as he hugged her
tighter, two tears leaked from her eyes onto
the front of his shirt.

When they got back downstairs, Mama
was in the kitchen, unpacking the box of
old pots and pans Grace had raided from
home. Her mouth was set in a thin line,
and she was opening and shutting cabinet
doors with a vengeance, as if testing the
strength of the hinges.

Grace took one look at her and knew
immediately what was wrong. She was
eyeing the carton of cigarettes Liz had left
on the kitchen table. Mama heartily disap-
proved of smoking.

"They're not mine," Grace said before
her mother could speak.

"I realize I've been telling you that college is a grand adventure, Grace, but I just hope you know better than to be influenced by—"

"Mama, please."

Her mother slammed the last cabinet shut and turned, her arms folded across her chest.

Grace rolled her eyes. "Mother, why can't you just be happy that I've made friends?"

"I *am* happy."

If this is happy, Grace thought, *I'd hate to see what miserable looks like.* But she knew better than to say it.

"I simply want to be sure you know what you're getting into. People can—well, sometimes they can turn out to be different than you expect them to be." Mama lowered her eyes and studied the scarred linoleum on the kitchen floor as if it contained the answers to all life's inscrutable mysteries.

"I'm fine, Mama. Everything's fine."

Daddy had followed Grace down the stairs but had been hanging back in the doorway. Now he stepped forward, and he and Mama exchanged a look Grace caught but did not understand.

"We'd better get going," he said with a smile that seemed uncharacteristically strained. "Don't forget us, Kidlet. Come home to visit now and then."

"Of course I'll come home to visit." Grace swallowed the lump that was growing in her throat. "It's only an hour and a half. It's not like I'm moving to the Outback."

"Come on then, Ramona. Our empty nest is waiting." Daddy hugged Grace one last time and reached out a hand toward his wife. She pretended not to notice, gave Grace a quick, dry peck on the cheek, and headed for the car.

Every Friday evening just before dinnertime, Daddy called, regular as clockwork, to hear about Grace's week and ask how she was getting along. Sometimes Mama would get on the phone for a minute or two of dutiful exchange, but they had little to say to each other, and both of them seemed relieved when Mama handed the telephone back over to Daddy. Grace felt guilty about it, but she had to admit she much preferred her father's easy banter and welcome laugh to her mother's stilted, formal attempts at conversation.

"What's with your mother?" Liz said when Grace hung up the kitchen phone. "I can always tell when you're talking to her instead of your dad."

Grace squeezed around Liz and began dishing up spaghetti from a pot on the stove. "I don't know. I've never known. But I can never talk to her without feeling like I've done something wrong. Like I've disappointed her."

"It's that mother-daughter thing," Liz said in a voice that brooked no argument. "Freud right down the line. You're your daddy's girl, and your mom is jealous. You suppose they still have sex?"

Grace let out an exaggerated sigh. Liz could be counted on to speak her mind, usually without any censorship whatsoever.

"Honestly, Liz, I don't spend much time speculating about my parents' love life. Not an image I particularly want to carry around in my head on a daily basis. Besides, they're pretty old—in their forties already."

"Do you think he loves her?"

Grace slopped spaghetti sauce onto the stove top. "What?"

"Do you think your father loves your mother?" Liz repeated. "And do you think she loves him?"

"Of course they love each other. They're married, aren't they?"

"Sure, but if you think marriage necessarily equals passion, you really are naive. Nobody understands what goes on inside a marriage except the two people involved. And sometimes *they* don't even get it."

Grace mopped up the mess and threw the dishrag back into the sink. "What's your point, Liz?"

She shrugged. "Maybe I'm pointless. But it seems to me they're an odd match, your mom and dad. He's so alive, so funny and cute. She's a black hole of depression."

Grace narrowed her eyes. "You're taking psychology this term, aren't you?"

"Yeah. So what?"

"So quit analyzing everybody, for God's sake."

"But it's fun. And insightful, too. Don't you ever wonder about your folks—what attracted them to each other in the first place, what their relationship is really like, when nobody else is around?"

"No." Grace bit her lip. "Well, sometimes."

"See? You have to admit you think about it."

"I've thought about it all my life—well, at least since I was old enough to notice things. And I'm not any closer to an answer. All I know is that Daddy is everybody's favorite person, and Mama doesn't seem to be impressed with his popularity. But I know she loves him. And he loves her."

Liz took the plate Grace was holding out to her and set it on the table. "You keep on telling yourself that, and maybe someday you'll believe it."

"Just drop it, OK? Go dissect somebody else's family."

"All right. Forget I said anything." But of course, she didn't drop it. Instead, she leaned over the table and pushed back the curtains. "Good thing Daddy already called his precious daughter tonight. If this snow gets any worse, we may lose both power and phone lines."

Grace stifled a biting comeback. "Make yourself useful and get the others in here to eat, will you?"

"Lovey! Tess! Dinner's ready!" Liz yelled, not moving an inch from her spot by the table.

"Shoot, Liz, I could have done that. I meant go get them. Ask them to come to the table with some kind of courtesy."

Lovey appeared from the living room, and Tess poked her head in from the back doorway, where the stairs went up to the dormer. They crowded around the small kitchen table, and Grace put a bowl of salad greens and a plate of garlic bread in the center.

"Who was that on the phone?" Lovey asked.

Liz reached for the bread. "Grace's daddy. You can set your watch by him. We were just having an interesting conversation about her parents' sex life when y'all came in to dinner."

Tess speared her with a reprimanding look. "Be nice, Liz."

"Me?" Liz sprayed crumbs of garlic bread across the table. "I'm nice."

"Sure you are. Making rude comments about Grace's parents is just the way you show affection."

Lovey jumped into the fray. "Tess is right, Liz. Grace cooked this lovely meal for us. I'd think you'd be grateful—at least grateful enough to get off her case for five minutes."

"I *am* grateful." Liz lifted her hands in a show of mock ecstasy. "Hallelujah! I'm *really* thankful Grace can cook."

"That's more than we can say for you." Tess arched her eyebrows. "When it's your turn, we get peanut butter sandwiches."

"I'm telling you, I'm *grateful.*" Liz folded her hands, closed her eyes, and bowed her head in an exaggerated show of piety. "O great powers of the Universe," she intoned in a drawling voice like a traveling evangelist, "thank you, thank you, *thank you* for this *won*-derful spaghetti, and for the hands that prepared it. And for the salad. And for the bread. And for the garlic and the butter on the bread. And for the dessert—" She peered through her fingers. "Is there dessert?"

Grace suppressed a laugh and nodded. "Lemon meringue pie."

"Oh, yes, halle-*lu*-jah for the lemon pie. And for the evolution that has brought us tomato paste and kitchen appliances and opposable thumbs. And—"

"Amen," Tess interrupted.

"I wasn't finished," Liz complained. "There's a lot more to be thankful for. Evolutionary development took a very long time, you know."

"Right," Lovey said. "But the spaghetti's getting cold."

THE STORM

*T*he storm gained force. By eight o'clock four inches of snow had piled up on the front steps, and huge flakes still drifted down in the light of the streetlamps. Traffic ceased to pass by on the main street down the hill. The whole city grew white and silent.

Lovey shut the front door and came into the living room stomping off her shoes, her hair plastered with wet snow and her cheeks red with cold. "Tomorrow's Saturday," she said. "Let's go play in the snow."

They all layered up, put on boots and coats, and retrieved empty packing boxes from the basement crawlspace. The hill in front of the house made for perfect sliding, and the flattened cardboard served as a pretty good makeshift sled. They careened down the street and trudged back up, over and over again, laughing and shouting and skidding into one another. When the cardboard got soggy and began to fall apart, Tess initiated a snowball fight, and they pummeled each other until they were all panting, exhausted, and soaked through.

Grace had never had so much fun. She whooped and hollered louder than any of them, wrestled them to the ground and pushed snow down their necks. And when they all trooped into the house, changed into flannel pajamas, and sat around drinking hot chocolate and telling stories, Grace suspected the warmth that filled her veins wasn't entirely from the flannels or the cocoa or the flickering fire.

A little after ten, the power went out and the phone lines went dead. The loss was barely an inconvenience, since the little house had a gas log fireplace in the living room and a gas stove in the kitchen. They lit candles, dragged blankets and pillows into the living room, and sat on the floor around the coffee table.

Tess leaned against the sofa and pulled a blanket around her. "This is like the sleep-overs we used to have when we were kids." She sipped at her cocoa. "Who made this? It's great."

"I did." Liz raised a hand. "See, I *can* cook."

"If you want to live on hot chocolate and peanut butter."

Lovey laughed. "So, shall we stay up all night talking?"

Liz lit a cigarette and blew smoke toward the ceiling. "Sounds good to me. Tell us about small-town life, Grace. Come on."

Grace stared into the shifting blue haze from Liz's cigarette. "Well, there's not much to tell. We live in a farmhouse out in the country between Greenville and Spartanburg. My dad owns a hardware store— not a chain store, but one of the old-fashioned kind with big aluminum bins of nails and nuts and bolts. People come from all over the county to do business with him. Well, you've met him; you know. With his personality he could sell ice cube trays to a polar bear. When I was little I used to sit on the floor between the aisles and play with the bolts, pretending I was a princess and this was my treasure."

Liz chuckled. "You *were* a princess, honey. At least in your daddy's eyes. That's why your mother—"

Grace threw up her hands. "Do not—I repeat, *do not*—start psychoanalyzing my family again."

"Ignore her," Lovey said. "I want to hear about your mother."

"Mama stayed home and took care of me and Daddy. I guess you'd call her a housewife, except that she never quite fit the stereotype. She didn't like housework much—I learned to cook out of self-defense—and she always had her nose in a book. Until recently, I hadn't thought much about it, but I get the impression she would rather have been doing something else."

"What kind of something else?" Tess asked.

Grace hesitated. She had little experience talking about herself, and even less speculating about her mother's unfulfilled dreams.

"I'm not sure," she said at last. "She reads

a lot of fiction—not potboilers or romances, but real fiction—classics like Tolstoy and Dickens and Victor Hugo, and modern writers like Faulkner and Flannery O'Connor and Carson McCullers. She keeps all these notes on what she reads—pages and pages, whole notebooks full. She's never said so, but I think she might have wanted to be a literature professor."

"But never got the chance," Liz said. "She got married and had you instead."

"Yes. She passed on her love of reading to me, but not much else. On the inside, at least, I'm more like my father. Or maybe I just *want* to be like him. Everybody adores him. He's so funny."

"So are you," said Lovey. "You just never had Liz for a comic partner before."

Liz stubbed out her cigarette and wrapped her hands around her mug of chocolate. "Yeah, that's us. Abbott and Costello. George and Gracie. Rowan and Martin."

Grace cut her a glance. "Jekyll and Hyde."

"Which one am I?" Liz asked, then held up a hand to put a halt to Grace's response. "Never mind. Don't answer that."

"You were telling us about your father," Lovey prodded. "How everybody adores him."

"Including you, right?" Liz nodded in Grace's direction. "And you're still his little girl, even now, when you're all grown up."

"Is that so bad?"

Liz shrugged. "I don't know. People can let you down. When you put them on a pedestal, and they fall off, you can get beat up pretty bad from the flying debris."

No one responded right away, but everyone was listening. At last Tess said, "You're not talking about Grace's family anymore, are you, Liz?"

"I guess not." She grew pensive, chewing at her lower lip. "My folks split when I was just a kid. My mother left, ran off with—with someone else. Took us to school one morning, waved good-bye, and disappeared. I never saw her again, except once, a year later, when we had to go to court for the custody hearing. My dad got me and my brother and sister, and did OK raising us, too. But it broke him. He wasn't the same afterward. He loved us, I suppose, but he never really got over it. He was physically there but emotionally absent."

No one was laughing now.

"How does anybody get over being abandoned like that?" Tess said.

"You go on," Liz answered, her voice low and fierce. "You find strength inside. You learn not to base your self-image on what other people say or do." She blew out a pent-up breath. "You guard yourself."

Tess leaned forward. "But if you guard yourself too much, you never let anybody close enough to love you."

"Could be." Liz stared into the fire. "But love is pretty much overrated in my book. Love is just a chink in the armor, a place for the knife to slip in." She ducked her head. "Let's talk about somebody else for a while."

Lovey came to the rescue. "My parents are divorced, too. My daddy is a farmer, and apparently it wasn't the life my mother wanted. They broke up when I was in high school—couldn't live with each other, but couldn't quite live without each other, either. They both married other people, and somehow managed to stay friends through it all. At Thanksgiving and Christmas, it's kind of like an extended family reunion, with four parents and half a dozen grandparents and all the kids and stepkids. Even a couple of step-grandkids, since my stepfather has a daughter in her late twenties."

"*Leave It to Beaver*—only with a lot more people in the house," Grace quipped. She glanced in Liz's direction to see if she was OK. To her relief, Liz nodded and winked in her direction, then lit another cigarette and blew a perfect smoke ring toward the ceiling.

"What about you, Tess?" Lovey asked. "What's your family like?"

Tess swirled the chocolate in her cup and drained it. "The last functional family in North America," she chuckled. "Boringly normal. My father is an Episcopal priest."

"A *priest*?"

"Yep. A bishop, actually."

Grace gaped at her. "Your father is a bishop, and you never told us?"

"It's no big deal. He runs the diocese, just like your father runs his hardware store."

"Not exactly the same thing," Grace said.

"Isn't it? Everybody has a job to do. When you grow up seeing the church from the inside out, you don't get caught up in the pomp and grandeur of the purple robes. A bishop isn't some untouchable holy person. He's a troubleshooter, a manager. A referee sometimes. Do you know what my father does mostly? He goes around to the churches in his diocese trying to settle petty squabbles between priests and parishioners. I think he was happier when he was just a parish priest, before they made him a bishop. He really likes being a pastor. And he doesn't get to do that much any more."

"What about your mother?" Lovey asked.

"Mom is—well, she's a bishop's wife. That's a whole job in itself. Now that my sister and I are grown and gone, she does a lot of work with the church women—"

"You mean hosting teas and needle-pointing pew pads?" Liz's voice carried a sarcastic edge, and Grace flinched inwardly at the insult.

Tess, however, seemed unruffled. "Not exactly. She went to seminary, too—that's where she and Dad met. She has an M.Div. and a Master's Degree in psychology. You'd like her, Liz. The two of you would have a lot in common. She spends a good deal of her time counseling women—mostly the wives of priests. She conducts seminars on family dynamics and spirituality. To tell the truth, she's more of a pastor these days than my dad is."

"So," Grace ventured, "you sound like you love both of your parents, and respect them. But you—"

"Avoid church like the plague?" Tess gave a wry grin. "You could say I'm on sabbatical. I've spent my life in the church, was practically born in the nave and weaned on communion wafers. I could recite most of the Eucharist service by the time I learned to read 'See Jane run.' And in many ways I love the church. But I need to take some time off to do a little evaluating of my own faith, figure out my place in the church—if there is a place for me."

"And your dad's OK with that?"

"He'd be happier if I still went to church while I was doing my evaluating," Tess admitted. "But it's a matter of conscience."

"Wait a minute," Liz interrupted. "Are you saying your *conscience* is keeping you from going to church? Damn. That's a first."

Tess fell silent for a minute. At last she

said, "I can't support a church that refuses to ordain women."

Grace stared at Tess. "Where I grew up no one would even raise the *question* of whether women could be ordained. That would be heresy. Men are the preachers and women are their wives. Period."

Liz made a face but said nothing.

"Well, at least *men* would say that." Grace went on. "Preachers in particular. Men have the power. Women care for the children and make coffee and organize Vacation Bible School and coordinate potluck dinners. Nobody questions it. That's just the way things are done."

"Maybe it's high time somebody *ought* to question it," said Lovey.

"Tess," Grace asked after a momentary lapse, "is this because—because *you* want to be a priest?"

Tess stared at her for a full minute, then began to laugh. "Lord help us, Grace, *me*? I'm a writer. I might be able to concoct a decent sermon or two. But I don't have the heart for it, don't have the gifts and calling. I'm too impatient; I live too much in my own head. Me, a priest? Not likely."

"Then why is it so important to you?"

Tess didn't answer. Lovey reached out a hand and laid it on Tess's arm. When she spoke, her voice was low and quiet. "Because her *mother* had the gifts and the calling," Lovey said. "Because her *mother* should have been a priest."

"For an agnostic blonde cheerleader, you're pretty insightful," Tess said, her voice almost a whisper. "Yes, my mother should have been a priest. And my father, for all his intelligence and all his love, can't see it."

It was nearly two-thirty when Grace and Tess climbed the stairs to the dormer bedroom. The living room had been warm and cozy with the gas logs blazing, but upstairs it was so cold, Grace could see her own breath. She hoped the power would come on before morning.

She got into bed, pulled up the quilts, and lay on her side staring out the window. The storm was over. The snow had stopped, and as the clouds parted, a bright half-moon shone down, glittering the landscape with pale blue sparkles.

Late as it was, Grace couldn't sleep. She kept rehashing Liz's insistent questions about her family. Did her parents love each other? Was her mother really a black hole of depression? Questions she had never dared to ask, challenges that mauled and twisted her image of family like a string of paper dolls in a hurricane.

Nobody understands what goes on inside a marriage except the two people involved, Liz had said. *And sometimes* they *don't even get it.*

But what did Liz know? She wasn't a psychiatrist. She wasn't married. She hadn't even lived in a two-parent household for most of her life. She was just blowing smoke, regurgitating stuff she'd learned in her psych class.

Nevertheless, Grace tossed in her bed for more than an hour before succumbing to a restless and fitful sleep. In her dreams she heard her father's easy laugh, recalled her mother's tight-lipped silence. She could see their faces, far away, blurred by rain and mist.

And in the dream she was a child again, frantically trying to tread water, to keep her head above the crest of a wave. Forked streaks of lightning split a sky crowded with menacing clouds.

She gasped for air as the billows rolled and pitched around her. For a second or two she could feel the ocean floor beneath her feet—could reach it, just barely, if she stretched and stood on tiptoe. And then the current sucked the sand away and pulled her out into the darkness, alone, adrift on a bottomless sea.

5

THE MORNING AFTER

*E*ven thirty years later, Grace could still recall the vivid details of that dream. The veiled faces of her parents, receding in the mist. The panic of reaching for a place to stand and finding nothing solid beneath her.

She ought to remember it. She had experienced it often enough.

Some dreams, she mused, seem so clear, so significant—until you wake up, and then they slip like water through your fingers and vanish into the pool of irretrievable memory. But others are as real as yesterday's heartburn, returning again and again until they become familiar, if unwelcome, companions.

Such was this dream, a nightmare that

had followed her for years, haunting her sleep and prophesying of things to come.

Now, with the diagnosis of cancer, Grace found herself dragged into the ultimate undertow, the one that would, once and for all, end not with drifting but with drowning.

And the downward spiral had begun during the second semester of her freshman year, the morning after that terrible snowstorm.

Grace awoke to the noise of banging and shouting drifting up toward the dormer bedroom. She pried her eyes open to peer at the clock on her bedside table. A little after eight-thirty. The sun was shining, but the room was still frigid. She pulled on a chenille bathrobe over her flannel pajamas and dragged herself down the stairs.

The living room was warm—apparently Liz and Lovey had slept on the floor in there and kept the gas logs burning all night. Liz, still wrapped in blankets, sat upright with her back to the sofa, looking groggy. Lovey was standing with the front door open, talking to someone.

Grace took a couple of steps toward the door and peered over Lovey's shoulder. It was a man wearing a dark blue down jacket and a disturbed expression.

"Yes, officer," Lovey was saying, "she lives here. Yes, we're just fine. As you can see, we've got gas, and I'm sure the power will be back on soon."

Officer. Grace blinked against the brightness of sunlight on snow and finally registered the patch on the man's shoulder, the badge on his chest. Beyond him, at the curb, she could see a white pickup truck with a Buncombe County sheriff's logo on the side.

"What's going on?"

Lovey turned. "Grace, hey. Sorry about the noise. This officer was just checking on folks in the neighborhood, I guess." She turned back to the deputy. "We all stayed up pretty late last night—no classes today, you know."

"You're Grace Benedict?" The man peered at Grace.

"Yes." She ran a hand through her hair and yawned.

"Mind if I come in for a minute?"

"Well, I guess so—" Lovey stood back and opened the door a little wider. The deputy stomped the snow off his boots and stepped inside the house. And moved in Grace's direction.

"Miss Benedict, could I speak to you— ah, in private?"

Grace frowned. "There's no need for that, officer. Have a seat, and we'll get you some coffee."

"No coffee, thanks, I—uh—" His eyes darted around the room. "OK, well, here's the thing. We got a call from your mother—"

"My mother?"

"Yes ma'am."

Liz came alive. "Jeez-o-Pete, Grace! The phone lines go down and your parents send out the National Guard? This is too much."

The officer ignored Liz and kept his eyes focused on Grace. "You might want to sit down." When she sank onto the sofa, he removed his hat and perched on the edge of the coffee table.

Grace was fully awake now. She accepted a cup of coffee from Lovey, but her eyes never left the deputy's face, taking in every detail—the circular orbit around his head where his hat had pressed his hair down, the ruddy complexion sprinkled with freckles, the way he twisted the hat in his beefy hands. He was young—younger than she would have expected. Twenties, maybe early thirties. He wore no wedding ring. His lips were chapped, and he kept licking them.

"Officer, is something wrong?"

"Yes ma'am, I'm afraid so."

Grace almost laughed out loud at the incongruity of being called "ma'am" by this fresh-faced deputy, but the inclination came from nerves, not humor.

"Like I said, we got a call from your mother. After the storm hit last night, she tried to telephone you."

"But the phone lines weren't working," Grace said.

"Yes ma'am. That's what we told her."

"Well, as you can see, we're all just fine," Lovey said brightly. "Now, how about that coffee, officer?"

The deputy didn't reply. He just kept staring at Grace.

Grace thought of something, and frowned.

"If the lines were down, how did she get through to *you*?"

"Oh. Well, the storm brought down some pretty big tree limbs," the officer said. "Took out phone lines up on Merrimon and a couple of transformers in this area. Crew's working on it right now; don't know how long it'll take. We still got power and phones downtown."

"So you could call her back, tell her you've seen us, assure her we're OK?"

"I could, ma'am. But—" He scratched his head and looked away.

"But what?"

"Well, ma'am, your mama was calling because—" He sighed heavily. "This ain't easy."

"Come on, spit it out," Liz demanded.

The officer gazed up at her mildly. "Just gimme a minute, OK?" He turned back to Grace. "There was an accident with a semi out on the highway down by Greenville. It jackknifed, and—" He pinched at his lower lip. "Nobody oughtn't to have been on the road last night. But it seems your father—"

"Daddy?" Grace's mouth went dry.

"Yes'm. I hate to be the one to tell you like this."

She grasped at whatever straw of hope her mind could latch onto. "He's in the hospital?"

"No ma'am, I'm afraid not. Both of 'em died at the scene."

Grace felt the weight of a hand settle on her shoulder. She reached up and dug her fingers into Tess's arm. "Wait. What do you mean, both of them? My mother called; she's all right, isn't she?" She didn't wait for the deputy to answer, but rushed on. "The driver of the semi?"

"No ma'am. The truck driver's not hurt bad. A broken leg is all, I think. He feels real bad about it, even though it weren't his fault. There was somebody in the car with your daddy. A woman. Maybe a friend of your daddy's or something." He pressed the bridge of his nose with a broad thumb. "It was a bad night, and they'd been drinking. I'm so sorry—"

Grace felt the room beginning to spin. "Someone was in the car with Daddy," she repeated dully. "Someone else, and—"

Suddenly her mind cleared. "Car, you said. They were in a car."

"Yes ma'am. Some kind of little compact. Didn't stand no chance against a semi."

"And they'd been drinking."

"Seems so."

"But Daddy doesn't drink. And he doesn't drive a car. He drives a pickup, a red pickup with *Benedict's Hardware* on the door." She looked eagerly around at Tess and Liz and Lovey, all of whom wore somber, pained expressions. "There's been some kind of mistake, don't you see? It wasn't my father. It was somebody else. *It wasn't Daddy!*" Her eyes roamed frantically around the room. "I've got to call home. Got to straighten this out."

The deputy hung his head and looked everywhere except at Grace's face. "Listen, tell you what. Why don't you come with me. We can go back to the station and call from there."

"We'll all go," Liz said. "My bug can get through anything."

Grace felt Tess's grip on her shoulder tighten, an anchor in the storm. "Get dressed and go with the deputy," she said. "We'll pack some clothes for you and meet you at the sheriff's office. Call your mother and tell her we're on our way."

The funeral was held two days later at Chapel Ridge Baptist Church, three miles from the Benedict home in rural Spartanburg County. The snow had melted, leaving a muddy slush behind. Grace waited in the back of the church with her mother as the pews filled up and whispered conversations swirled around them. Mama, the unrelenting silent boulder past which the stream of nervous chatter flowed, kept her arms folded and her jaws clamped together. But although Grace felt her mother's presence, her eyes focused only on the dirty footprints that marred the crimson carpet down the center aisle.

Blood and mud.

Her mind conjured up images of her father, lying dead at the scene of the crash. Even though she knew better, the mental image included a picture of his red pickup truck with *Benedict's Hardware* painted on the side, crushed under the wheels of a semi.

But the truck had been found intact in a deserted strip-mall parking lot.

A hundred unanswered questions spiraled through Grace's mind as she waited for the funeral to begin. There had been no mistake. The body recovered at the scene of the accident *was* her father. The crushed and mangled Ford compact belonged to a woman Grace had never heard of before. Mama said she was an acquaintance of Daddy's, a customer.

But why had he gone out in a raging snowstorm to meet her? Why was he driving that woman's car? Why, despite everything Grace knew about her father, did the coroner insist it had been an "alcohol-related accident"? Wasn't the storm cause enough for a car wreck? A slippery road, limited visibility, an eighteen-wheeler spinning out of control?

Maybe the woman had called him for help, not knowing where else to turn. Maybe she was in trouble, her car stuck in the snow. Maybe he had gone to her aid. It was like him, to do something risky to help someone in need. Everybody knew it. Everybody loved him. But when Grace offered this eminently rational explanation, Mama just shrugged and turned her blank, empty eyes away.

Grace hadn't seen the remains of the car, hadn't viewed her father's broken body. The big walnut box at the front of the church was closed, covered by an American flag that marked Harlan Benedict's status as a World War II veteran.

She desperately wanted to open the casket, to touch him, to kiss him, to say goodbye. But Mr. Galbraith, the obsequious owner of the funeral home, didn't think it was a good idea, given the nature of the injuries. All Grace had to go on was her imagination, which was far worse, she suspected, than reality.

The hushed murmurs of the mourners surged around her like a wave, cresting over her and carrying her mind where it didn't want to go. She felt Mama stiffen at her side, and turned to look. A slim, well-dressed woman in her thirties had just entered, slipping past Grace and her mother to take a seat in the back row. The woman's eyes locked with Mama's for just a second, and something passed between them. A chill. A recognition.

Grace was pretty sure she had never laid eyes on the woman before. Most of the people who crowded into the church were

folks she knew by sight if not by name.
Customers from the hardware store. Community leaders. Members of the Chamber
of Commerce. Daddy's friends, all of them.
He had so many friends.

Only a few of the multitude assembled
there were strangers to Grace. The woman
who had just come in. A burly man on
crutches, with his leg in a cast, whom
Grace assumed to be the driver of the semi.
Another lady on the right side. A third one
down the row on the outside aisle. She
didn't know these people. But then, a
grown daughter who had gone away to
college couldn't be expected to recognize
all her parents' acquaintances.

A hand touched Grace's elbow and ushered her forward, to where Tess, Liz, and
Lovey were already seated in the front row.
Mr. Galbraith had also said that the girls
shouldn't sit in the family pew with Grace
and her mother—it just wasn't done—but
Grace had insisted. She wanted them there.
Needed them.

She moved into the pew beside Tess,
scooting over to make room for her mother
on the aisle. Mama held herself taut and
straight, not even allowing her shoulder to

touch her daughter's arm. In her black dress and pearls, Mama looked the part of the grieving widow, but her eyes were dry sockets, devoid of emotion. As usual, she was holding everything inside.

The quiet background music of the organ ceased, and a tall, thin man in a dark blue suit got up and went to the pulpit. The minister. His name was Rogers, Grace thought. Or maybe Roberts. She couldn't remember.

The minister cleared his throat and announced the first hymn, "Amazing Grace." Tess squeezed Grace's hand, helped her to her feet, and held the hymnal out between them.

Grace glanced down the row. Liz, the worst singer on the face of the earth and a self-proclaimed atheist to boot, struggled to follow along. Lovey evidently knew the song by heart—agnostic or not, she was from Georgia, after all. Few others in the congregation seemed to need their hymnals. They sang every verse, loud enough to drown out the organ, but most of the voices sounded choked and strained.

When the final echoes of the hymn rose into the vaulted ceiling and faded away,

Pastor Rogers—his name was printed in the program—went to the pulpit again and began to preach the funeral sermon.

He spoke, as Grace had fully expected, of the glory of heaven, where there would be no more pain and no more tears. Of the wonders awaiting the faithful, and how death was swallowed up in victory.

He acknowledged the presence of Jake Jordan, the truck driver from Augusta who had just been released from the hospital, and made it clear that Jake was in no way responsible for Daddy's death. But he did not mention the woman who had died in the same accident that claimed her father, or the fact that Daddy had been driving her car, or that both of them had supposedly been drinking.

And something else was missing, too. The eulogizing. The personal accolades. The assurance that the dearly departed was being welcomed through the pearly gates even as they mourned him. Pastor Rogers seemed tense. There was a carefulness about him, as if he were weighing every word and holding his breath as he balanced them into place, like stacking eggshells or building a house of spun sugar.

"Harlan Benedict was a man loved by . . . so many who knew him," the minister said cautiously. "A man whose death will make an enormous impact on his wife, Ramona, and his daughter, Grace—" Here he paused and nodded toward Grace and her mother.

Mama didn't look up or acknowledge the condolences. She sat like a statue, her dry eyes fixed on the middle distance between the front pew and the pulpit. Grace followed her mother's gaze to the matching sprays of white lilies at either end of the coffin, their pristine blossoms mingling with the blood-red stripes of the flag. Her eyes burned and watered, and she blinked hard, forcing her attention back to the blurred, wavery image of the minister.

"Harlan was a businessman, a father, a husband, a friend," Rogers said. "A generous member of this community who always offered a helping hand to those in need."

Grace's mind jerked to the woman in the car with Daddy. But she pushed the thought aside and tried to focus.

The pastor continued, sprinkling platitudes here and there into his funeral address. And then he invited people who had known Grace's father to speak about what his life had meant to them.

A sound, like the flapping of wings or the rush of fallen leaves, shuddered through the congregation. Someone coughed. A few people shifted. The waiting went on forever, it seemed, until a gray-haired man from the Chamber of Commerce came forward and mumbled a few words that, to Grace's mind, sounded like jabberwocky. After a while he sat down, and several other people stood in their turn and spoke. No one, of course, mentioned anything about the woman who died in the car with Daddy. It was pretty clear that everyone was trying to dispel the tension that lay like a suffocating blanket over the gathering. But no one succeeded.

Grace's throat closed up and her breath came in short, shallow gasps, but she couldn't seem to cry. And through it all Mama sat with her spine straight as a steel reinforcement rod and her lips pressed into a razor-thin line. In the rustling silences that stretched between the testimonials,

Grace could hear Mama grinding her teeth, a muffled fingernails-on-chalkboard sound that made her cringe.

Finally, when the last of Daddy's friends had shuffled awkwardly back to his seat, the minister offered a final prayer, committed Harlan Benedict's soul into eternity, and motioned for the pallbearers to come forward and remove the casket. Out behind the church, in the muddy cemetery, the coffin was lowered into the rectangular grave and the body was committed to the ground: "Ashes to ashes, dust to dust, in the sure and certain hope of the resurrection."

All the good-byes had been said. There was nothing left to do but go home and try to eat some of the mountains of food people had brought to the house. At last, it was over.

But for Grace, it was only beginning.

6

UNRAVELING

In the wake of her father's death, Grace began to founder. She couldn't think. Couldn't focus. Couldn't keep the dark waters at bay. Her mind seemed incapable of comprehension, and her grades began to slide. Depression set in, weighing her down until she threatened to capsize and sink altogether. It was all she could do to hang on to the floating debris of a shipwrecked hope.

Daddy was gone, just like that—a snap of the fingers, a blink of an eyelash. She kept saying it over and over again but couldn't seem to make herself believe it. Whenever she thought of him, she saw him vital and alive, puttering around in the flower beds or waving from the open window of his pickup truck. She heard his laughter inside her head. He wasn't dead. He couldn't be.

She ought to go home on weekends and look after her mother, but she couldn't bring herself to do it. As clearly as she saw and heard her father in her mind, she also saw the thin line of her mother's lips, heard the stony silences. What could Grace possibly have to say to her mother? How could she bear an hour in Mama's presence, not to mention an entire day or a whole weekend or—God forbid—Spring Break or the Easter holiday?

And so Grace avoided the subject. She didn't offer to come home, and Mama didn't ask.

Mama *did* call—like clockwork, every Friday just before suppertime. But where Grace had once jumped to answer the phone, knowing it would be Daddy, now she dreaded the insistent ringing, the shrill reminder of the voice that would no longer be on the other end. No one would call her Kidlet or tell her the latest joke, or listen to her mundane concerns as if she were the most important person in the world.

Her conversations with Mama were, as

they had always been, short and stilted. Dutifully Mama would ask how Grace's week had been, how her roommates were, how she was getting along. Dutifully Grace would answer. Fine. Fine. Everything was fine. Neither of them spoke about Daddy, both of them resolutely skirting the issue of his death the way you tiptoe around a newly dug grave, scrupulously avoiding stepping on the ground above the coffin.

This particular Friday evening, Liz was in the kitchen charring chicken breasts in the frypan when Grace's mother called. Grace sat down at the kitchen table with her back to Liz, staring at the clock on the wall next to the window and blinking hard to keep from crying. The longer her mother's droning monotone went on, the more she wished for her father's animated voice instead.

The call lasted exactly two minutes and thirty-eight seconds, but it might as well have been two hours. When Grace hung up, Liz cleared her throat.

"Not exactly like the conversations you used to have with your dad."

Grace turned. Smoke was beginning to

emanate from the frying pan, but Liz didn't seem to notice. "Your breasts are burning."

Liz looked down at her flat chest. "You think so? They look OK to me."

Grace began to chuckle, then caught herself and stifled it. It didn't seem appropriate to laugh when her father was dead and she hadn't even cried.

"You want to talk?" Liz turned the fire off and scraped at the black crust on the chicken. She didn't look up.

"About what?"

"About your daddy's death. About your mother. About all the questions that are weighing you down."

"Not if you're going to play shrink, I don't."

Liz came to sit at the table. "It might help to get some of it out. When my mother left, I didn't talk to anyone about it, not for years. But the pain didn't go away because I kept it inside."

"That's different. Your mother abandoned you. My father died in a horrible accident. He didn't leave voluntarily." The words were cruel, designed to hurt. Grace could hardly believe she had said such a thing to one of her best friends.

But Liz didn't rise to the bait. "Yes, it is different. But you still have questions. Lots of them."

"Like what?"

"Like what and why and who and how. What happened that night? Why was your father out in a snowstorm, driving a woman's car? Who was she, and what was her relationship with your father? And most of all, how could your father do such a thing?"

Grace shut her eyes and swallowed hard, trying vainly to push back the lump in her throat. Liz's questions, along with so many of her own, hung out there like loose threads on a badly woven sweater. Pull one, and everything might unravel. And here Liz was, picking at them one by one, as if daring Grace to find out if she would hold together.

"I believe in my father," she finally said, the words coming out with greater difficulty than Grace could ever have imagined. "He was a good man."

"I know." Liz waited.

"I have to believe in him. If I ask too many questions—"

"You might find out something you don't want to know?"

Grace stared at her hands, at the ragged fingernails bitten down to the quick.

"And you might end up blaming him."

"Blaming him for what? For dying?"

Liz shrugged. "Or for doing something stupid that led to his death."

"He was helping out a friend. That's all." Grace tried to sound firm and confident, but her voice quivered.

"And you believe that." Liz raised her eyebrows. "Yeah. Like I believed my mother went out for milk and bread and just never found her way home again."

"It's not the same," Grace persisted.

"It is, and it isn't." Liz's tone was uncharacteristically subdued and cautious now, as if she were walking barefoot across a pit of live coals. "Listen, I'm not trying to be obstinate. And I'm not trying to undermine your faith in your father. You've got a perfect right to believe whatever you want. Believe in the tooth fairy, if that makes you feel better. Just make sure you're being true to yourself. Grieve your father's death. Get mad, if you need to. That's all part of the process. Just don't shut down. Denial never did anybody any good."

"You think I'm in denial?"

"I'd be surprised if you weren't. Maybe it was easier for me, in the long run, to accept the truth about my mother. She betrayed us and left us, but she didn't die. Eventually I had no choice but to face the reality of what she'd done."

"I don't know what reality is where my father's concerned," Grace admitted after a minute. "I know he loved me. And I loved him. But—"

"But what if he wasn't the man you believed him to be?" Liz supplied. "What if—"

Grace held up a hand, and Liz fell silent. "I—I can't," she stammered.

"Can't what?"

Can't shake the doubts, Grace wanted to say. *Can't shake them, but can't face them. Can't find my way back to the surface.*

But she didn't. Instead, she swallowed down the lump, patted Liz's arm, and forced a smile. "I can't accept what you're implying about my father." She shook her head. "I know you mean well, Liz, and I appreciate it, honest I do. But you didn't know him like I did. There's an explanation for the circumstances surrounding his death, and I'm going to find it. And when

I do, I know my faith in Daddy will be justified."

A shadow passed over Liz's face—an expression, Grace thought, of disappointment. Frustration. Disillusionment, even. Then she shrugged. "I hope so, Grace," she said. "For your sake, I truly hope so."

The conversation ended as Tess came into the kitchen. "Am I interrupting something?"

Liz got up. "Grace and I were just talking while I cooked dinner."

Tess peered at the charred chicken in the frying pan. "More talking than cooking, apparently. Mind if I lend a hand?"

"Be my guest." Liz resumed her seat at the table and watched while Tess sliced the burned portions off the chicken, cut what was left into chunks, and deftly created a casserole out of the remains of the meat and some leftovers she found in the refrigerator.

"Someday you're going to have to teach me how to do that," Liz said.

"Why would you want to learn when you can get somebody else to do it for you?"

Liz grinned. "Good point."

By the time dinner was ready, Lovey had

appeared, and they all sat around the table, waiting awkwardly for the meal to begin. Everyone looked to Grace, obviously waiting for her to give thanks, but she avoided their eyes. "Well, let's dig in before it gets cold," Tess said at last, and the icy spell was broken.

"This casserole is absolutely delicious, Tess," Lovey said with her mouth full.

"It wasn't just Tess." Liz feigned a crushed look. "I helped. I cooked the chicken."

"That much I believe." Lovey removed something black and crusty from her mouth, held it up for all to see, then laid it delicately on the edge of her plate.

Liz grimaced. "Oops. Guess Tess didn't get all the burned pieces off. Sorry."

"Never mind. We'll keep it as evidence of you making something that doesn't fit between two slices of white bread."

"Let's change the subject, OK?" Liz said. "Tess, do you have time to proofread my psych paper and give me some suggestions? I've got the research done, but I'm having trouble putting it all together."

"Sure, if you'll quiz me for my English Lit exam."

The conversation continued, discussions of midterms and unreasonable professors and the upcoming Spring Break. Words swirled around Grace like smoke from a brush fire, but she barely noticed.

She felt herself withdrawing, receding, rising above the talk and laughter. No matter how hard she tried, she couldn't dislodge her mind from memories of her father, her declaration of faith in his character, and the troubling suspicion that he might not have been the man she believed him to be.

The dream came again, Grace struggling to stay afloat in a cold, dark sea. Far away, ahead of her, she could just make out a faint light, as if she were looking into a small, misty window that revealed her father's laughing face and her mother's tight-lipped glare. And someone else. Someone laughing with her father, a woman, all her attention focused on Daddy, her back turned on Mama's scowl. It was like watching a silent movie on a fuzzy screen—the mouths moving, but no sound coming out.

The screen receded, as if Grace were drifting backward, out to sea. This time the water was colder, the waves higher. Frantically, she felt for the bottom, but the water was deep and all she had to buoy her up was a battered raft, a few cracked lengths of bamboo strung together with ragged ropes.

The raft shifted, and as Grace flailed for a more secure hold, a portion of the bamboo splintered off and floated away, out of reach. And then she saw the problem.

The rotted ropes that held the raft together were separating. She clung tighter, but it was no use. Piece by piece, the raft was breaking apart. Soon there would be nothing left to hold her up except the dwindling energy of her own will.

She was sinking. The whole thing was unraveling, and she could do nothing to stop it.

7

TRANSFORMATIONS

Grace decided she wouldn't go home for Spring Break, or for the Easter weekend. She felt vaguely guilty about leaving her mother alone, but she simply couldn't stand the thought of having to face that house, so filled with Daddy's presence, so empty with his absence. She invented several semi-plausible excuses—a late term paper, being behind in her Lit readings. Justifications that turned out to be a waste of time and energy.

"That's fine," Mama said when Grace broke the news. She sounded weary and apathetic. "You will be coming home for the summer?"

"I guess so," Grace said. What else could

she do? She had neither a good reason nor enough money to stay in Asheville.

"I'll come get you, then," her mother said. "When does the semester finish?"

"The third week in May," Grace answered. "I'm not sure which exact days I have exams, though. I'll have to look at my schedule."

"All right. I'll plan to pick you up on the Monday after, unless I hear otherwise. You'll let me know if that won't work?"

"Sure." Grace hesitated as remorse kicked in. "Mother, are you sure it's OK for me to stay here during Spring Break? I could change my plans—"

"No, don't do that." Her voice went rigid and steely, and Grace could almost see her facial expression, the thin straight line of her mouth. "I'll call you next week."

Somehow Grace managed to get through the remainder of the spring semester without completely wrecking her grade point average. Two weeks before exams, the nation was stunned by the news that four college students had been gunned down by the National Guard at an antiwar protest in Ohio. Liz went ballistic about the massacre, but Grace couldn't get herself focused enough to manage more than a feeble indignation. While Liz attended protest rallies on campus, Tess and Lovey did their best to help Grace cope—taking on her chores around the house, helping her study for finals. Occasionally one of them would broach the subject of grief, expressing concern that she was keeping everything inside. But for the most part, they just continued to be there, and to keep things as normal as possible.

Grace was grateful to them for not pressing her. She couldn't explain what she was feeling—or more precisely, what she wasn't feeling. All her emotions—fear and grief and anger and longing and a dozen others she couldn't even name—seemed to have congealed inside her, a huge, amorphous mass, a shapeless dark lump at the pit of her stomach. There was no way to sort them out; she didn't even dare to try. The best she could do was endure.

Finally, mercifully, the semester came to a close. Liz and Lovey and Tess had all found jobs around Asheville and would stay in the little house on Barnard Street. Grace had tried to manufacture a reason not to go back to Spartanburg County to spend the summer with her mother, but she'd come up empty. There was nothing to do but grit her teeth and try to get through it the best she could.

What would it be like, she wondered— two months in a house devoid of her father's laughter and filled instead with her mother's depression? How was she possibly going to stand it, day after day?

But the Mama who arrived in a brand-new Cadillac DeVille to pack Grace up and take her back to the country was not the woman Grace was expecting. This Mother was smiling and laughing. She hugged Grace and kissed her on both cheeks—a little awkwardly, but with genuine warmth— then made the rounds to hug Grace's three roommates as well.

"So, do you like it?" she asked, stroking the hood of the sleek sedan. It was green— not a discreet dark forest green, but a cross between spring grass and a Granny Smith apple, with sort of an electric sheen. "The color is called Briarwood Firemist."

"It's—it's a *convertible!*"

"I know. What do you think?"

Grace stared at her mother. "Where did you get it? It must have cost a fortune."

"I bought it, of course. The sale of your father's truck paid for it—at least most of it."

"But, Mama, why on earth would you buy a Cadillac? A convertible? When you've got a perfectly good—"

"A perfectly good Chevrolet, I know. I've always had Chevrolets. Usually white. Always used. Your father bought them for me, every five years, like clockwork." Mama shook her head. "All my life I've dreamed of having a car like this. There's nothing like driving down a country road with the wind in your hair. It makes you feel so . . . so *free.*" She turned toward Grace's roommates, who had been standing on the front lawn all this time, listening to the interchange. "You girls want to go for a ride?"

Tess watched Grace out of the corner of her eye. Liz and Lovey grinned at each other. "Yes!" They opened the door and scrambled into the back seat.

"Come on, Grace. I'll let you drive."

Grace got into the front passenger seat. "No, Mother. You drive. It's your car."

Grace soon discovered that the Cadillac was not the only transformation she had to contend with. Their two-story farmhouse out in the country, where Grace had lived for as long as she could remember, had always been white with green shutters like every other farmhouse in the county. Now it was a soft blue-gray with bright white trim and a front door the color of cranberries.

Grace dropped her suitcases in the front hall and stood dazed and disoriented. The old brown living room carpet had been pulled up to reveal the hardwood floor underneath, and a new leather sofa and matching chairs clustered around a deep-toned area rug. The coffee table was an antique wooden sled with a glass top. "Mama, what happened to all the furniture?"

"I bought a few new things," her mother said. "Do you want a snack before dinner? I made beef stew."

"No, I don't want a snack." Impatience

caused Grace's tone to come out harsh and accusing. "I want to know what's happened to you."

"Come sit down," Mama said. She led Grace into the kitchen—also repainted, in a lemony yellow with new curtains at the windows—and took a pitcher of iced tea out of the refrigerator. When she had poured two glasses, she set them on the table and brought a platter of brownies out of the pantry.

Grace pushed the brownies aside. "I'm not hungry."

"Grace, listen—"

Grace's composure snapped. "No, *you* listen. I want to know what's going on, why everything's completely different. There's not a trace of Daddy anywhere in this house. He died in *January*, Mother. Five months ago. And now it's like he never existed." She swallowed hard against tears of fury. "Like you never really loved him at all."

A brief expression of anger flared across her mother's face, then subsided. She bit her lip and reached across the kitchen table for her daughter's hand. Grace pulled back. It was a mean thing to do, but she couldn't help herself.

"I'm sorry you're upset," Mama said at last, drawing her hand back. "I probably should have told you I was making some changes instead of just springing it on you. But—"

"But what, Mama?" Grace interrupted. "The car, the house, the furniture. Go on, explain it to me."

"All right, I'll explain it." She pressed her lips together, and her expression went stony. This was the real Ramona Benedict, the mother Grace recognized, the one she had expected. Not the free-spirited convertible-driving impersonator.

"This is very difficult to talk about," Mama began, "so please be patient with me."

"I'm perfectly capable of being patient," Grace interrupted. "But I want the truth."

"The truth?" Mama closed her eyes and shook her head. "We always think we want the truth, Grace. But the truth isn't always pleasant or noble, and it's certainly not painless."

Get on with it, Grace thought. *Quit beating around the bush.*

"When I married your father, I was just as taken with him as everyone else was. He was bright and funny and sensitive, and for a while we were happy."

"For a while?"

"Yes, for a while. Then things changed."

"*You* changed, you mean," Grace broke in. She couldn't help herself. "I remember when I was little how you and Daddy played with me, and we laughed a lot, and I felt safe." The lump in her throat swelled and tightened. "I haven't felt that way for years."

"Yes, things changed. And maybe you're right. Maybe I changed, too. I'm sorry you had to suffer for it, Grace. But at the time I couldn't do anything about it. You needed your father. You adored him. I thought it would be best simply to try to maintain the status quo. Now I'm not sure I made the right decision."

"What decision?"

"To stay with your father rather than divorcing him. To keep the family together, for your sake."

Grace gasped for breath, but all the air had been sucked out of her lungs. "*Divorce* him?"

Her mother nodded. "I knew I couldn't keep going on this way forever. Now that

you were grown, I thought maybe—" She
hesitated. "Perhaps I should have trusted
you more, Grace. Maybe I was wrong to
keep the truth from you. But then the accident happened, and your father died,
and—"

"And what?"

"And suddenly I was free. Free to be myself. Free not to have to pretend." She
cleared her throat. "But I'm still pretending, Grace. And until you understand the
full reality of what transpired between your
father and myself, I will always be pretending."

Grace's insides shuddered. She didn't
want to hear any more. Didn't want to
know.

"You asked for the truth, Grace. Well,
here it is, and it's not pretty." Mama took a
breath. "Your father was unfaithful to me."

"What?"

"The woman who was with him in the
car the night he died—she was his . . . well,
what do I call her? His mistress."

Grace felt the kitchen spin, and clutched
the table top, trying to steady herself. It
wasn't a totally foreign concept; she had
asked herself the question hundreds of

times since the funeral: *Who was that woman? What was Daddy doing with her?* And always she had come up with the same answer: *She was a customer, a friend, that's all. He was helping a friend in distress.*

It was a rationalization, and deep inside Grace knew it. But it was all she had to hold on to, a flimsy life raft in a troubled sea. If she even considered any other possibility, that would mean that everything—an entire lifetime with her father—had been nothing more than a sham, a lie.

"That's ridiculous!" she shot back. "Everybody loved Daddy. Everybody depended on him. Maybe he was just helping her out, trying to get her home safely in the storm."

Grace looked up. Her mother's eyes, no longer hooded and distant, had gone soft and liquid, filled with pain. "I'm sorry," she said quietly.

"Sorry for what?"

"Sorry I had to be the one to tell you. The one to sabotage your image of your father. I know you loved him. And he loved you, too." She shrugged. "He just didn't love me. Not enough, anyway."

Grace laced her fingers together until the knuckles turned white. "What makes you think I'm going to believe this? Maybe it's not at all the way you paint it. Maybe *you* didn't love *him*. Maybe you were just jealous because—because—"

"Because he had so many friends, and I didn't seem to fit in?"

Grace glared at her but didn't answer.

"Because I always seemed so unhappy and depressed?" She gave a cynical laugh. "And then if he did turn to someone else, it would be my fault, is that it? My fault, for not giving him the adoration he craved?"

This arrow hit its mark, jolting Grace to the core. Mama was right: Daddy *did* crave attention. He thrived on it. Always the center of every group, always making people laugh. Approval intoxicated him; he imbibed it like a drunk on a three-day bender. But that didn't mean—

"Just because Daddy liked attention doesn't prove he—" she paused, groping to put her thoughts into words. "And even if he *did* make a mistake, couldn't you forgive him?"

Her mother leaned back in the chair and

massaged her temples, as if trying to re-arrange things. "A mistake? Yes, I see what you mean. Unfortunately, it wasn't *a mistake*. It was a *lifestyle*. It was twenty years of successive mistakes."

Grace's eyes scanned the lemon-colored walls, the new kitchen curtains, the linoleum floor—anywhere except her mother's face. "What are you saying?"

"Practically from the beginning, your father had other women in his life. He was usually discreet enough not to get caught, but I knew. For a while I pretended not to notice, accepted his excuses when he came home late or wasn't where he told me he would be. I was desperate to keep my marriage intact, at any cost.

"Every time we'd have a confrontation about it, he'd seem so sorry, so broken-hearted, and he'd swear he'd never so much as look at another woman again. Things would get better for a while, and I was naive enough to believe his empty promises. And then, when you came along, I had another compelling reason not to leave him."

"You're telling me that all during your marriage, throughout my entire childhood, my father was having affairs with other women?"

"It's the truth, Grace. At times I thought it would kill me, all the sham and pretense. Ironically, in the end it was your father's unfaithfulness that killed *him*."

The ice in Grace's tea had melted, leaving a watery layer on top, and she jiggled the glass to mix the water in. Something was happening inside her stomach—a churn of acid, a fire blazing hot and white. She felt the burn lick up from her gut to her chest. It was like breathing in ash and smoke, and for a minute she thought she was going to be sick.

Her mother reached for her hand again, and Grace snatched it away. "I couldn't tell you, no matter how much it broke my heart to see you gravitate toward your father and away from me. I understood, but it hurt nevertheless." She bit her lip and let out a long, ragged breath. "I wasn't a very good mother, was I? I'm sorry. I was too absorbed with just trying to keep from going to pieces."

Grace slammed back in her chair and stood up so quickly that it clattered to the floor. "And what about me?" she yelled. "What the hell am I supposed to do? How am I supposed to feel?"

She had never sworn at her mother before. She leaned forward and pounded a fist on the kitchen table, rattling the tea glasses and the brownie plate. "You've purged this house of any remnant of Daddy without even asking my opinion! Did you even *think* about me when you were making all these changes? Did it occur to you that I might want some of his things, to remember him by?"

"There's a box in the attic I've saved for you—" her mother began, but Grace cut her off.

"Fine. I'll cherish his cuff links," she spat out. "Meanwhile, you tell me he was a liar and an adulterer, and that everything I've believed about him has been a deception, and you expect me just to take your word for it, to accept it without question? Well, Mother, I *don't* accept it!"

She flailed a hand, and the remainder of her iced tea went airborne. As if in slow motion, she watched the tea fling out in a fluid arc. Glittering shards scattered across the kitchen floor like water from a fountain. When the crash was over, Grace stared at the debris. One curved section of glass spun in a slow circle near the sink.

"Go to hell," she muttered. Then she turned her back on her mother and stalked out of the room.

8

Shadow of Doubt

*A*ll the windows were open, and through the curtains a warm late-June breeze blew in, laden with pollen and grass and dust and the sound of a tractor rumbling across distant fields.

The house was silent as—

Grace shuddered as the image dropped into her mind. *Silent as a tomb.*

Mama had gone to the grocery store, and Grace had declined the invitation to ride along. She welcomed the solitude, the opportunity to seclude herself and not have to be pressured into conversation by this strange, cheerful alien who had taken the place of her real mother.

She couldn't deny it: Mama was happy. For the first time in years, her mother smiled and laughed and looked her daughter in the eye. Liberation hung about her like a shining golden cloak, reflecting in her eyes and lending a glow to her pallid skin.

Grace had dreaded coming home for the summer to face two months of her mother's melancholy gloom. How could she have known that delight could be every bit as painful as depression? Clearly Mama had tried, for Grace's sake, not to flaunt her newfound freedom, but the truth was undeniable: Ramona Benedict had been resurrected the day her husband died.

Grace lay sideways across the bed, second-guessing her refusal to go to the store with her mother. She had thought she wanted to be alone, but now the silence pounded in her ears, closing in upon her, suffocating her.

She lifted her eyes to the open window, where the gauzy curtain stirred and drifted on the breeze. Beyond the screen the rolling foothills stretched to a cloudless, bright blue sky. A sky so close she could almost touch it.

She reached out one hand. Her fingers brushed the filmy fabric. And in her mind she saw herself lying on the hillside looking

back at the house, stretching her arm
toward the open window with its wind-
blown white curtain.

The image came from a painting she had
once seen—Andrew Wyeth, she thought.
Or maybe N.C. Wyeth. One of them, it
didn't matter. What did matter was how
profoundly the artist's work had affected
her. That posture, reaching toward the
house—her father's house—with that im-
ploring gesture. It raised in her a bitter-
sweet longing, a yearning she did not
understand. And a nameless sense of futility.

Tears pricked her eyes and caused the
scene before her to shimmer like a mirage.
She had not yet cried for her father. And
these tears were not for him, either. They
were for herself, mired and flailing in a
quicksand of uncertainty and doubt. Sinking fast, and with no idea how to get out.

The truth will set you free. She had quoted
that to her friends, accepted it, believed
it—at least theoretically. But so far the
truth—Mama's version of it, anyway—had
done nothing but bog her more deeply in
the swamp of her despair. Reality had
shifted, and everything she had founded
her life on, the firm bedrock of Daddy's

character and his love, had slipped from beneath her feet. Mama's accusations, the specifics of her father's death, the still-unanswered questions, all snaked around her like the tentacles of some malicious plant, binding her, strangling her, releasing its poison into her pores.

She could still see the open window, still reach a hand toward her father's house, still call out for help and comfort. But no one was home.

Grace struggled to wakefulness. The doorbell was ringing.

She lifted her head, ran a hand over her face, and felt the impressions of the bedspread imprinted on her skin. The sun had shifted, and now the rolling fields outside her window were dappled with late-afternoon shadows.

How long had she slept?

The ringing continued. *Ding-dong*. Pause. *Ding-dong*.

She rolled off the bed and fumbled with the laces of her tennis shoes.

Ding-dong ding-dong. Somebody was

growing impatient. Probably Mama, her arms full of grocery bags. *Ding-dong.*

"Sheesh! All right, hang on." She kicked the shoes aside, ran down the stairs in her bare feet, and pulled the door open. "Sorry, Mama, I was—"

She stopped with one hand on the screen door. It wasn't Mama. It was a woman—in her thirties, probably—slim and petite in designer jeans and a pale lilac cotton sweater. One of those perfect women, with never a hair out of place, even on a warm summer Saturday afternoon. Flawless makeup and discreet gold hoop earrings. Just being in her presence made Grace feel frumpy, dressed as she was in sweat pants and an oversize T-shirt.

Grace had never seen this woman before. Or had she? Something about the woman's eyes seemed familiar—a hooded, detached quality, yet with fierce emotion simmering below the surface.

"Can I help you?"

"This is the residence of Harlan Benedict?"

The name caused Grace's stomach to lurch. "Ah, yes. But he's—"

"He's dead, I know. You're his daughter?"

Grace nodded.

"Is your mother at home?"

"No, she's—she'll be back soon. What time is it?"

The woman frowned at this non sequitur and glanced at her watch. "Four-thirty."

"Would you like to come in and wait?" Grace pushed the screen door open and stood back a little.

The woman hesitated, looking around as if she were searching for something. And at that very moment, Mama's green Cadillac pulled into the gravel driveway, skidding to a stop as a small child came running around the side of the house and darted in front of the car.

"Emmy!" the woman screamed. But Mama had stopped in time, and the little girl dashed onto the porch, her chubby fist clutching a handful of wildflowers. "Emily Ryerson, you could have been killed! You *never* run out in front of a car. Never!"

"I'm sorry," the girl mumbled, and took refuge behind the woman's knees.

Mama, meanwhile, had jumped from the

driver's seat and bolted toward the porch, leaving the car door hanging open. "Is she all right? I didn't see her—"

"She's fine. I was more scared than she was, I think."

Mama clutched at her chest and exhaled heavily. "My stars, I thought I'd hit her." Then she looked up, and Grace saw her expression change. "You. You're—"

The woman nodded. "I'm Bette Ryerson. You know who I am?"

They exchanged a glance, and Grace remembered. The funeral. This woman had been at her father's funeral.

"Honey," her mother said, "please get the groceries from the car and go inside the house."

Grace was still holding the door open. She came out onto the porch and let the screen bang shut behind her, but the woman put a hand on her arm to stop her. "Wait," she said, not to Grace but to Mama. "She needs to know, too."

A sick feeling churned in the pit of Grace's stomach. She looked from the Ryerson woman to her mother and back again. "What's going on?"

Mama didn't answer. She narrowed her

eyes at the woman. "This has nothing to do with my daughter."

"Oh, but it does." Bette Ryerson went over to the porch rocker, where the little girl now sat swinging her legs and sticking the wildflowers into her hair. She took the child's hand and pulled her to her feet. "I'd like you to meet Emily," she said, nudging the girl in Grace's direction. "She's four."

Grace looked down at the little blonde urchin. She had clear blue eyes and freckles scattered across her nose, and a swipe of dirt on her chin. "Hello, Emily."

"Remember your manners, Emmy," the woman said. "Say hello to your sister."

Grace felt as if her entire brain and body had been injected with novocaine. She moved sluggishly, putting oatmeal in the freezer and ice cream in the pantry, then realized what she had done and had to go back and start over again.

Mama and Bette Ryerson eyed each other from opposite ends of the kitchen table, talking in low tones and glancing periodically at little Emmy, who sat on the kitchen floor weaving a clumsy necklace from her wildflowers.

At one point the child got up and tugged on the tail of Grace's T-shirt. "Are you really my sister?"

Grace looked down. "No. Absolutely not." But even as the denial left her lips, she knew.

"Aunt Bette says you are. But you don't live with us. Families are s'posed to live together, you know?" Her blue eyes turned somber. "I used to live with Mommy. Now I live with Aunt Bette."

Grace kept silent. Her hands were shaking and she felt cold and clammy, even though the afternoon was warm. Emmy went on talking. "Mommy lives in heaven now. She went there when her car wrecked. Did you know my mommy?"

"No." Grace tried to focus on putting the groceries away. The girl's very presence was rubbing her nerves raw, and it took a monumental effort to keep from screaming at her.

The little girl sighed. "Daddy went there, too. Did you know my daddy?"

Grace balked. She wanted to say a firm,

unequivocal no, but in the face of this child who looked so much like him, a negative answer felt like a denial of Daddy himself. "I—uh, maybe. I don't know. Yes."

The admission pierced Grace's soul like a sword. This little girl wore her father's smile, his round face, his eyes, even the dimple in his chin. Harlan Benedict in girlish miniature.

Mama knew it too, but she did not seem the least bit surprised. "I've been expecting you to show up before now," she was telling Bette Ryerson. "But if it's money, we don't—"

The woman shook her head in protest. "No. I don't want money, and I'm not looking to make trouble." Her icy composure was gone now, and she ran a hand through her perfect hair. "I'm not sure why I came. Vindication, maybe. Connection with somebody who was willing to admit the truth."

"I admitted the truth about my husband a long time ago." Mama shrugged. "But I hadn't really considered *this*—" She waved a hand in Emmy's direction. "Even when you believe you've faced all the painful realities life has to throw at you, there are some things you're just not willing to believe."

"My sister was far too trusting," Bette said. "I tried to warn her, but she wouldn't listen. Until the day she died, she was convinced he was going to divorce you and marry her. He was so charming, so persuasive."

Grace watched over Emmy's head as her mother lifted her eyebrows and nodded. "Indeed he was."

"I'm sorry," the girl's aunt said. "I—I was just so angry when Marian died. Angry at your husband. Angry at the world, I guess. It didn't occur to me how much pain you've been through all these years."

Mama scooted closer and patted the woman's hand. "It's all right. I understand the anger, believe me."

Bette Ryerson's eyes drifted from Mama over to her niece. "Do you suppose—" She hesitated. "Is it possible there were more?"

"More women, certainly," Mama said matter-of-factly. "More children? Not that I know of."

Emmy butted up against Grace's leg, pulling her attention away from the conversation. "Can I have some of that ice cream?"

Grace blinked and gazed down at the child. She glanced over to the table. "Is it all right for Emmy to have a bowl of ice cream, Mrs. Ryerson?"

Bette Ryerson looked up. "Miss. It's Miss Ryerson. I'm not married. But call me Bette. And yes, just a small bowl."

Grace dished up two bowls of ice cream and handed spoons to the child to carry. "Let's take this out on the porch, OK?"

"OK." Emmy followed along, perched herself on the steps, and ate her ice cream while she watched butterflies flitting around the flowering bush at the edge of the porch.

Grace sat in the swing, observing the child as she stealthily moved a hand in the direction of a bright blue butterfly, then laughed with delight when it settled on her finger. It wasn't Emmy's fault that her father was a philanderer, that her very presence in this house spoke of his infidelity and deception. The little girl was just an innocent victim. Like her mother. Like Grace's mother. Like Grace herself.

And like Bette Ryerson. A single woman

committed to raising a child who was not her own, a child who was the illegitimate offspring of her sister's affair with a married man. She could only imagine how difficult that road might turn out to be.

All because Grace's father, whom she had adored and trusted, hadn't been nearly the man he pretended.

She had wanted the truth.

Next time she'd be more careful what she wished for.

THE FACE OF TRUTH

*E*ven now, thirty years after the fact, Grace vividly remembered what it felt like to look into Emily Ryerson's innocent face and see Daddy gazing back at her. The memory made her stomach churn with anger and her shoulders slump with the burden of shame.

He had betrayed them—all of them. Mama, Marian Ryerson, little Emily, even Grace herself. The shame was his, not Grace's. She knew this intellectually, but had never been able to persuade her emotions to come over to her brain's way of thinking.

And she carried not only her father's shame but her own as well, deeply buried but never quite dead.

She had believed him. She had allowed him to dig a chasm between herself and her mother, who had only been trying to protect her. She had given him power—power not only to rewrite her entire childhood into a bizarre and painful fiction, but to plot out the course of her future as well.

How many people, Grace wondered, held to the prevalent belief that yesterday was fixed, done and over with, immutable? But she knew from experience that what had already happened could be changed. When she looked over her shoulder, she saw two pasts, vastly different. The rosy hue of her childhood as she once thought it to be, imbued with the laughter and warmth of a loving, faithful father, and the darker, more sinister reality that had dominated her life since the summer of her freshman year.

Truth was not an abstract concept for Grace. It had a color, a taste, a smell. A dark red hellish light, a bitter burn like acid on her tongue, a scent of smoke and ash and the rotting remains of half-cremated dreams.

And truth had a face. The guileless, winsome appearance of a child, distorted by leering, nightmarish adult features that flickered just below the surface.

It had been years since Grace had thought of little Emmy. Even when Dr. Sangi asked if she had family she could call on to support her, her own half sister hadn't come to mind.

But of course, she hadn't kept track of the child—no, not a child, she realized with a jolt. A woman. Emily Ryerson would be in her mid-thirties by now. Where was she? What had her life been like, growing up fatherless and motherless under a cloud of death and illegitimacy, with only a single aunt to raise her?

It was too late to find out now. One twisted strand of DNA wasn't a strong enough thread to bind strangers together.

Besides, what else might she discover if she lifted that rock to see what was underneath? Other bastard children her father had left behind? More truth that would cut like a razor and drain whatever drops of hope remained in her veins?

Grace didn't know, and didn't want to know. Long ago she had quit believing that the truth would set you free. It manacled

you instead, chaining you hand and foot
and heart and soul and leading you places
you never intended to go.

During the summer break, Grace had gotten together with a few of her old high
school girlfriends. They went shopping,
shared a pizza, forced themselves to laugh
and talk and pretend everything was normal. It was a charade, and they all knew it.
With her father dead, and Grace in the pit
with the great secret hanging over her like
a razor-sharp pendulum, nothing would
ever be normal again. She endured the
company of her friends and tried to ignore
the pitying glances, the whispered conversations behind her back. But by the time
August finally rolled around, Grace was
more than ready to return home.

Home. Compared to her mother's farmhouse, the little place on Barnard Street
was dated, drafty, and, as her father had
once remarked, dumpy. Yet it had become
home. The place where she belonged.

Tess had called her several times in the
past two months, and Liz and Lovey had

gotten on the phone as well, hinting that they'd all like to come visit for a weekend, but Grace had let the suggestion drop. She wasn't prepared to face them yet. She was too afraid that her raw edges would show, that they'd ask questions and she would unintentionally let the truth about her father slip out.

And she had no intention of telling them the truth.

They were too important to her.

Now that Daddy was gone—more to the point, now that her *image* of her father was blasted beyond recognition—all Grace had to hang on to was her friendship with Tess and Liz and Lovey. They were the only remaining buoys that kept her afloat, and she couldn't—wouldn't—risk that their view of her might change.

Tess would smother her trying to be supportive and nurturing. Lovey would attempt—unsuccessfully—to keep things light and uncomplicated. And Liz? Liz would have a field day psychoanalyzing the information, and whether or not she actually said the words, the implication would hang over Grace like a shroud: *I told you so.*

No. Grace couldn't take the chance. All

summer she had been preparing herself, pushing down the anger that simmered below the surface, perfecting an attitude of cheerful normalcy in front of the mirror, making jokes.

Grace tried out her act on Mama, telling stories about Lovey's awful attempts at cooking and Liz's outrageous, irreverent table prayers. Not since childhood had she seen her mother smile so broadly or laugh with such abandon. It almost felt like having a friend.

But, of course, it was a sham. Mama might be happy, but Grace was thoroughly miserable. She couldn't wait to get out of the house, away from memories of her father, away from the possibility that she might run into Bette Ryerson and little Emily. Back to Asheville, where she could create for herself the kind of life she wanted. Back to Tess and Liz and Lovey.

Besides, Grace thought as she packed suitcases and boxes of books, she had it all planned. She would tell them how she had struggled to come to grips with her father's death, how she had reconnected with her mother. How she had finally grieved, and had come through the period of mourning stronger because of the suffering she had endured. She would confide in them up to a point, and that would be enough.

"We've got so much to tell you," Tess said as they crowded around the tiny kitchen table for dinner. "It's so good to have you home."

"For more reasons than one," Liz agreed, eyeing the casserole suspiciously. "Who made this stuff? Has it got tuna in it?"

"I made it," Lovey said. "And it's chicken."

"Looks like tuna." Liz gingerly touched her tongue to her fork. "Tastes like tuna. Since when is chicken gray?"

"Since Lovey started learning to cook," Tess said. "Just eat it."

Liz made a face. "I hate tuna."

"Forget the tuna, will you?" Tess turned back to Grace. "We want to hear all about your summer. You doing OK?"

"It's not tuna, it's chicken," Lovey said.

Grace began to laugh. "I knew I missed you all, but I hadn't realized how much. It was good to get your letters and phone calls. I'm sorry it didn't work out for you to come to visit. It was just rather . . . complicated."

"Well, we all kept pretty busy this summer," Lovey said. There was a glint in her eye and an overtone in her voice. Grace wondered what she wasn't saying.

"That's true," Tess said. "I worked almost every weekend. Liz went to Raleigh for a civil rights demonstration. And Lovey— well, Lovey has some news of her own, which I'll let her tell. We wanted to come, but we gathered maybe you needed some time on your own, with your mom. Are the two of you getting along better now?"

Grace nodded. "Yes, we are. And I'll tell you all about it. But first I want to hear your news."

"Liz got thrown in jail," Lovey said.

"What? When?"

"Just overnight." Liz shrugged. "A bunch of us went to a sit-in on the Capitol steps. It wasn't like Selma, or Birmingham. Nobody got sprayed with fire hoses or attacked by police dogs. But some of us did get arrested." She sighed. "I'm not sure it did any good. Sometimes it seems like the whole movement has fallen apart since Dr. King was killed."

"Let me see if I've got this right," Grace jibed. "Becoming a felon is now the fashionable way to make changes happen?" She meant it as a joke, but her attempt to cajole Liz out of her black mood clearly wasn't working. "Maybe folks need to just give it a little more time," she ventured.

"Time?" Liz exploded. "It's been six years since the Civil Rights Act was passed—long overdue, I might add. And with Tricky Dick in the White House, who knows how far into the dark ages we'll slide?" She narrowed her eyes. "He's a crook. And he's already stepped up the bombing in Vietnam."

"But we elected him, and—"

"Elected authorities need to be held accountable," Liz interrupted. "Look at the invasion of Cambodia. Look at what happened at Kent State. Or maybe you don't give a damn that our civil rights, and the rights of people all over the world, are being violated." She got up from her chair, squeezed past Tess, and went into the living room.

"She's not really mad at you," Tess said. "She's been wired up like that since the beginning of summer."

"She'll be all right," Lovey added. "And now, do you want to hear my news?"

Grace took a breath and tried to forget about Liz's animosity. "Sure," she said. "Let's have it."

"Well—" Lovey leaned forward, her voice hushed and whispery. "I think I may have found the one."

Grace blinked. "The one what?"

"Oh, for Pete's sake, Lovey, don't be so dramatic." Tess arched her eyebrows. "Lovey's got a new boyfriend."

"No kidding? What happened to What's-His-Name?"

"Vince?" Lovey let out a derisive snort. "Ancient history. He's a boy. Bo is a real man."

"Bo?"

"Bo Tennyson." Lovey's eyes unfocused. "He's a football player—"

"Who'd have guessed?" Tess grinned.

"He's wonderful," Lovey went on, unfazed. "He's tall and blond and gorgeous and really smart, too. He plays tight end at Chapel Hill. He's a business major. *And* he's twenty-one. The long-distance thing is a bummer, but at least he was red-shirted as a freshman, so we'll graduate at the same time. And probably get married right after."

Grace tried to take all this in. "How'd you meet him, Lovey? And when?"

"About a month ago. He was in Asheville part of the summer doing something—oh, I don't know what. Some kind of job. We met in a bar downtown, where my cousin Sylvia and I went when she was in town visiting."

"You picked up a guy in a *bar*?"

"Well, it was a *nice* bar, not a dive."

Grace shook her head. "Let me get this straight. You went to a bar, got hit on by some hunk, and now after dating him for a month you think he's going to marry you?"

"I wouldn't call it dating, exactly. Dating is for teenagers."

"You *are* a teenager, Lovey."

"Only technically."

"Your birthday is in June," Grace corrected her. "You're barely nineteen."

"Well, nineteen is almost twenty. Twenty is a woman." She turned her brightest smile on Grace. "You'll meet him next weekend—it's his last free weekend before football practice starts. You'll adore him."

"OK," Grace said. A nagging thought prodded at the edges of her mind. "Lovey, when this Bo Tennyson comes to town, where's he planning to stay?"

"Well, here, of course."

Grace turned to Tess for help but didn't get it. "I don't know, Lovey. This house is pretty small, our couch isn't very comfortable."

"Who said anything about the couch?"

"You mean—"

"He'll stay with me, in my room. I know it will be a little more crowded, especially with only one bathroom and all, but it'll only be for a few days."

Unbidden, a shadowy image flashed across Grace's mind. Her father, laughing drunkenly and pressing himself against a woman who was not her mother.

She felt her face flush, and Lovey laughed. "Don't look so shocked, my innocent little hothouse flower. It's not the first time, and certainly won't be the last. Besides, he's not likely to be here very often. Most of the time I'll be going down to

Chapel Hill—assuming that one of my wonderful roommates will lend me a car." She took her plate from the table to the sink. "Liz was right—this stuff is awful. I really will have to work on learning to cook. Maybe you could help me, Grace."

"Sure," Grace mumbled. She could think of nothing else to say.

"Since I made dinner—even though it was terrible—you two get the cleanup." Lovey flung a salacious grin over her shoulder as she left the room. "I've got a long, juicy letter to write."

By the time the dishes were done, Liz had recovered from her snit and was sitting on the couch with the UNCA catalogue and registration papers spread out across the coffee table.

Grace sat down beside her and peered over her shoulder. "Didn't you preregister?"

"Yeah, but now I'm rethinking everything. What kind of college doesn't offer classes in passive resistance or the civil rights movement? And Gandhi. There's not a single course about the politics and principles of Gandhi."

Tess sat cross-legged on the floor next to the fireplace. "Liz, you could *teach* courses in passive resistance and the civil rights movement. I've seen your bookshelf. If your collection is any indication, you've already memorized most of Gandhi."

"I know. But it would be great to have some real discussion about his work." Liz shook her head. "Sometimes I feel like I'm way out in left field, all by myself."

Grace nodded. "I know what you mean."

"Yeah," Liz said, "except you're in *right* field all by yourself." She stuffed her papers into the catalogue and set it aside. "So, tell us about your summer."

Grace shrugged. "Lots of changes."

"Change is good." Liz arched an eyebrow. "A step in the right direction. Or, dare I hope, a step to the *left*?"

"I haven't become a raving liberal, if that's what you're asking," Grace said. She chuckled at Liz's crestfallen expression. "But I did face some things this summer. You'd have been proud of me."

Tess leaned forward. "Tell us more."

Grace launched into her carefully rehearsed account of what had happened since the Monday after exams, when her mother showed up in the Cadillac DeVille convertible.

"So, it wasn't an easy summer," she concluded. "But Mama and I are doing much better. She's come around, isn't so stiff and distant anymore. Toward the end we actually had fun together." Grace ducked her head and pulled at a loose thread on the arm of the sofa. "I guess I owe all of you an apology. I was pretty upset when my father died. And yes, Liz, I do realize that anger is one of the stages of grief, but it still made me—well, made me feel like a heretic—like I was being disloyal to my father."

"Hey, I love heretics," Liz said.

"I know. But I stuffed everything down, and sort of withdrew. I was really afraid of losing my grip, and I didn't know how to talk to all of you about it, since—"

"Since *we're* a bunch of heretics." Liz threw back her head and laughed. "Grace, you should know you're safe with us. Despite our differences, we've always tried to accept each other and be real with each other."

Grace's stomach twisted. *OK, here's some reality for you,* she thought. *My father was unfaithful to my mother. The woman who was killed in the wreck with him was his mistress. He has an illegitimate daughter.*

Safe, Liz had said. But how could Grace know for certain, unless she took the risk to utter the words, that she *was* safe here, that her friends could accept her without condemnation and love her without judgment? The truth burned to be spoken, a corrosive in her gut trying to bore its way out.

But the words lodged in her throat and gagged her. The risk was too great, the shame too strong. And so, deep inside, like a rat chewing its way out of a locked room, Grace's truth continued to gnaw at her, trying in vain to break free.

LOVEY'S CHALLENGE

Bo Tennyson arrived the following Friday afternoon, skidding to the curb in an old yellow Triumph Spitfire convertible with a large sports bag tied on the back. Even from this vantage point—peering between the living room window blinds—Grace understood immediately why Lovey had fallen for him.

He was tall and muscular, with wind-blown blond hair and eyes more vivid than the blue of his Tar Heels jersey. His upper torso looked as if he had forgotten to take off his shoulder pads. And although Grace was pretty sure being a tight end didn't have anything to do with the shape of his butt, he certainly filled out his jeans nicely.

She watched, with Liz and Tess jostling behind her for a better view, while Lovey ran to the street and jumped into his arms. He picked her up and whirled her around and kissed her, then turned and waved, grinning, in the direction of the living room window.

Grace scrambled backward, tripping over Tess and Liz in her haste. They all fell in a heap on the carpet, giggling and gasping for breath.

The front door opened. "Hello, ladies," he said.

"What on earth are y'all doing?" Lovey demanded. "You're spying on us!"

Bo set his bag down and held out a hand. "Let's see, you must be Grace." He helped her up from the floor. "And this is Tess, and that's Liz."

When they were all on their feet, he took a step back and put an arm around Lovey. "I'm Bo Tennyson."

"We know," Liz said.

He laughed easily and turned to Lovey. "Want to put that away for me, hon?" he said, pointing to his bag. He moved over to the sofa, sat down, and propped his feet on the coffee table. "And then maybe get me a beer while I get acquainted with your roommates."

For the next forty-five minutes, Bo Tennyson regaled them with football stories. Third and long with a minute to go. A blocked punt taken in for a touchdown. The flea-flicker. The double reverse. A game-winning Hail Mary in the last five seconds of the division championship. Grace had seen a few games but was fuzzy on the details, and for the most part she didn't have the faintest idea what he was talking about. Still, she had to give him credit for being entertaining.

But so was Daddy. She watched, as if in slow motion, as Bo Tennyson downed one beer and then another. He wasn't drunk by any means, but by the third beer he had become more animated and less inhibited about touching Lovey in ways that made Grace feel as if bugs were crawling under her skin.

One thing was absolutely clear: Lovey adored him. She sat next to him on the couch with one hand on his thigh, watching his eyes, laughing and throwing glances at them as if to say *Didn't I tell you he was wonderful?*

Finally the beer was gone and the football stories wound to a close, and Bo and Lovey left to go out to dinner. The door had barely shut behind them before the postgame analysis began.

"Well, he *is* gorgeous," Liz said. "I'll give him that much."

"Yes, he is," Tess agreed. "But what was all that bull about 'getting acquainted with us'? He never once asked any of us a single question about ourselves."

"Ha," Liz said. "Even if he *had* asked, he never stopped talking long enough for anyone else to get a word in edgewise."

Grace went into the kitchen. The others followed her and continued the conversation around the table while Grace put pork chops in the skillet to brown.

"Doesn't he know *anything* but football?" Liz said.

Tess rolled her eyes. "A man who looks like that doesn't have to know anything about anything."

Liz retrieved a brick of cheddar cheese out of the refrigerator drawer and a box of crackers from the cabinet. "I don't get it," she said, sitting down at the table again.

"How can Lovey fall for a guy who has nothing on his mind but sports?"

Grace turned from the sink and set a pot of potatoes on the back burner. "I don't think that's the *only* thing on his mind."

"You got that right," Tess said. "Look at him. Look at her. And tell me this has to do with some kind of intellectual compatibility."

Liz handed a cracker and a slice of cheese to Grace. "So it's just chemistry?"

"I doubt if Mr. Tight End knows diddly-squat about chemistry." Grace left the chops to finish cooking and came over to the table to sit next to Liz. Lovey's new boyfriend had stirred up the cauldron of unwelcome thoughts and memories inside her. She needed to frame her response carefully, to keep things light, so she wouldn't reveal the anxiety that surged through her veins. "I have to admit, he *is* handsome—and charming, if you like jocks. But are we really comfortable with the idea of them sleeping together—right here in this house?"

"What difference does it make if they're doing it here or somewhere else?"

"Probably none," Grace said. "It just feels—I don't know. Wrong."

Liz grinned at her. "Are you telling me that if a hunk like Bo Tennyson came into your life and swept you off your feet, you wouldn't have sex with him?"

"Well, for one thing, Lovey's Bo is not the kind of guy I'd be attracted to," she said. "But even if I *were* in love, I wouldn't sleep with a man before marriage."

"Even if it meant losing him."

"If it meant losing him, then he wouldn't be the kind of person I'd want to be with."

"Damn, Grace, haven't you ever heard of the sexual revolution? You're still living in the nineteenth century!"

"Maybe so." Grace got up and went back to her pork chops. "But as I recall, Liz, you once defined love as a chink in the armor where the knife sticks in. Sex outside—I mean before—marriage is risky. Lovey could get hurt. She could even get . . . pregnant." She speared one of the chops with a vicious stab of the fork and flipped it over.

"So tell me," Liz muttered, "where'd you come by all this omniscience? Do you *always* think you're right?"

Grace forced a smile. "Of course I always think I'm right," she quipped. "If I didn't think I was right, I would think something else."

Liz let out a snort of derision. "What about you, Tess? What's your take on having our little house turned into a love nest?"

Tess shrugged. "I have to admit, I'm with Grace on this one."

"You're kidding!"

"I think you need to have a real relationship, a commitment, before you get into that kind of intimacy. And even though Lovey *says* they're already talking about getting married, they haven't known each other long enough to make a decision like that."

"Besides"—Grace tested the potatoes with a fork—"people aren't always what they seem to be."

Liz cut a glance at Grace, and she averted her eyes. "So, Tess, you want to be the one to tell her that she and Mr. Tight End need to rent a room?"

"No." Tess shook her head. "As much as I'd prefer that Lovey would think this through more, I'm not her mother, and I can't go laying down the law to her." She turned and looked at Grace. "And neither can you, Grace. We may wish she'd make wiser decisions, but we can't be the celibacy police for her."

Grace nodded and pretended to concentrate on mashing the potatoes. But she didn't agree with Tess. Not by a long shot.

Grace lay awake in the dormer, listening to the sounds coming from the bedroom below. Tess was snoring softly on the other side of the room.

Once in a while, Lovey had said. *Bo wouldn't be here very often. Just now and then, when he could manage to get away.*

Grace didn't know how he did it, between classes and practice and weekend football games. But he was there at least once a week, sometimes two or three times. He would roar in at ten or eleven at night and get up the next morning just in time to take a shower and use up all the hot water.

It was bad enough having his clothes and play books and beer cans scattered all over the downstairs. Pizza stains on the couch and shaving scum in the bathroom sink. But for Grace, the worst of it by far was what she endured after the lights went out.

For weeks it had been like this. Night after night, grunts and moans and muffled shouts from the two of them downstairs. The headboard slamming against the wall, and Grace upstairs trying to shut out the images that came to her in the darkness. Because in her mind's eye, Bo and Lovey weren't the primary players. It was Daddy, and that Ryerson woman.

She felt a little like a voyeur, straining her ears in the darkness. She didn't want to listen, didn't want to know what they were doing, what Daddy had done with that woman—and how many others? But her imagination wouldn't leave her alone.

Every time she heard them having sex in the bedroom below, a seething rage rose up in her—anger at Lovey for letting Bo take over their house, fury at her father for his infidelity. She'd had enough. And yet, much to her dismay, the noises also brought up unsettling feelings in her, longings she couldn't seem to conquer.

She shifted in bed and tried to force the

unwelcome pictures from her mind. At last the house grew silent, and she dozed.

At four A.M. she awoke to the sounds of someone moving around in the kitchen. Grace certainly didn't want to confront Bo in the middle of the night, probably in his boxer shorts—or worse. But if it was Lovey, this might just be the chance she had been waiting for.

She sneaked down the stairs on bare feet. The kitchen lights were off, but when she peered around the doorpost, she caught a glimpse of a seersucker bathrobe, pale blue in the light from the refrigerator.

"Lovey!" she hissed.

Lovey turned, looking rumpled and sleepy. "Grace! What are you doing up?"

"I heard a noise."

"Sorry. I woke up and was hungry. Is there anything left from dinner? Bo ate most of my steak."

"I made chicken and spinach pasta," Grace whispered. "There, on the third shelf, in the small glass dish."

"Thanks. Want to join me?"

"No. I think I'll just have a glass of milk and a couple of cookies."

Lovey spooned some of the leftover dinner into a pan and set it on the stove. "Should I add water?"

"Maybe a little, to keep it from sticking."

Lovey waited until the pasta was heated, then came to sit with Grace at the table. "You OK, Grace? You seem—I don't know. Funny."

"I'm fine. But I'm glad I found you here—alone. I want to talk to you about something."

Lovey took a bite of the chicken. "This is fabulous, Grace. Really good."

"Thanks."

"OK, go on," she said around another mouthful of pasta. "What do you want to talk about?"

Grace took a deep breath. "You and Bo."

A faraway look filled Lovey's eyes. "He's wonderful, isn't he? He's so—"

"Yes, he's so *everything*," Grace interrupted. "But, Lovey, have you really *thought* about this? About you and him, I mean?"

"What's to think about?"

Grace felt her pulse begin to quicken. "I don't know how to say this, but—" She paused. "What you're doing with Bo is *wrong*."

"Wait a minute." Lovey held up a hand. "If this is about me sleeping with Bo—"

"Yes, it is." Grace rushed on before Lovey could protest. "I know you don't want to hear this, but you have to listen to me. You don't know this guy. You think you do, but you don't."

"What's gotten into you? You're acting crazy."

To tell the truth, Grace was *feeling* a little crazy. Her heart was thudding painfully against her rib cage, and she felt as if some kind of explosion was building up inside her. She couldn't control it; it was going to break out—

"People can deceive you, Lovey," she said in a rush of conviction. "They can hurt you and betray you in ways you can't even begin to imagine. Bo is handsome and charming, all right, but if he's sleeping with you, what makes you think he's not sleeping with other girls? Or what if he becomes an alcoholic? He already drinks a lot. What if he turns into a drunk and continues sleeping around when—"

"Stop it!" Lovey slammed her fist down on the table. "Grace Benedict, don't you DARE try to undermine my relationship with Bo! You're jealous, that's what it is. Jealous because I've got a boyfriend and you don't. We're friends, Grace, and if you want to keep it that way, you'll mind your own business and not meddle in mine. Bo loves me, and I love him. We're planning to be married. But in case you haven't noticed, the whole world isn't required to live up to your standards."

"Jealous, am I?" Grace gritted her teeth. "You think I'd *want* somebody like Bo Tennyson? Someone who looks good on the outside but is rotten to the core? Someone who'd ruin my future and—"

"What gives *you* the right to determine what my future should be?" Lovey interrupted, her voice tight and strained. "Who appointed you the moral lawgiver for the rest of us? *Who died and made you God?*"

Lovey pushed her chair back and stood towering over Grace in the dim light.

"Let's forget this conversation ever happened," she said, her voice low and laced with ice. Then she shook her head. "No, let's not forget. Let's *act like* this conversation never happened. Let's go on and be friends and never speak of it again. But remember this night, Grace. Remember it for a very long time. And when *you've* been in love and faced this question for yourself, come back and tell me how your standards worked out for you."

Then she stalked out of the room, leaving Grace alone in the early morning darkness.

IN TOUCH WITH YESTERDAY

Alone in the dark, with the circle journal still unopened in her hands, Grace marveled at how clear the memories were. She didn't need to read the journal to recall those days, to relive the feelings.

She had never told anyone the truth about her father. And now, thirty years later, Lovey's challenge still echoed in her ears. *When you've been in love and faced this question for yourself, come back and tell me how your standards worked out for you. . . .*

Grace *had* faced the question, finally. And she had failed the test—failed it miserably.

Pride. Fear. Shame. An impossibly high tripod setting her up for a spectacular fall.

Grace opened the journal, thumbed through a few pages, and began to read the

entries from their fourth year after graduation. Tess had gone off to Iowa to attend
the famous Writers' Workshop there. She
was loving it, she wrote in the journal—she
had finished her degree and was finding her
voice, reveling in the creative high that
came to her when she was writing.

Liz had moved to Atlanta to work with
Coretta Scott King at the Martin Luther
King Center, founded shortly after King's
death in 1968. Her entries were filled with
hair-raising descriptions of protests, con-
frontations with the law and even the Klan,
jail time, philosophical musings on methods
of nonviolent action. Liz was in heaven.
She was making a difference.

And Lovey. Lovey had married Bo, and
the two of them were obscenely happy. She
had pasted in a copy of his rookie photo,
looking handsome and disheveled and ma-
cho in his purple Vikings uniform. It was
unlikely he'd get to play much during the
regular season, Lovey said in her distracted,
rambling way, but the money was great and
their house was beautiful and he loved the
attention, and she was beginning to make
friends with some of the other players'
wives, and she thought she might be preg-

nant. The Minnesota winters could freeze the quills off a porcupine, she wrote, but their love would keep them warm.

Grace could practically recite this litany by heart, so often had she read it. And every time she had the same reaction—an inner trembling, like an attack of hypoglycemia.

She knew what came next. Her own entry, in the flourishing handwriting of her youth:

You'll never believe what has been happening in my life since I wrote last. I've met the most wonderful man—a handsome, intelligent, gentle soul. He comes into the library almost every afternoon, and I've been helping him do research for a new book he's writing on religious beliefs and practices of Native American Peoples. He's a historian, a professor at the university. He asked me out to coffee when my shift was over, and ever since we've been seeing each other regularly.

At first our conversations centered mostly on his research, and then gradually we began to talk about other things—more *personal things. He has this deep, rich baritone voice, and this way of using his hands . . . well, I could listen to him for a lifetime. And he's handsome, too, in a professional sort of way. He's got dark hair with just a touch of silver at the temples, and incredible blue eyes that seem to look into my very soul. I think he's in love with me. I <u>know</u> I'm in love with him.*

But you can't rush these things. We both need to be sure. He's older than I am— almost fifteen years older—and has had some heartbreak in his life that keeps him from opening up to love. And yet the spark is there. More than a spark. More like a wildfire.

His name, by the way, is Michael.

There was a space, and then a new date— three weeks later.

Michael and I were married yesterday in a small ceremony in a chapel up in the mountains. I'm keeping my own name— Michael wants me to feel like I'm my own person and not just an adjunct to him. He's so amazing.

I wish I could've had all of you there as

*my bridesmaids, but there simply wasn't
time. Once Michael decided to ask me,
everything moved so fast. He said he didn't
want to take the chance that I would
change my mind (as if I'd let someone like
him get away!), and didn't want to spend
another moment apart. He is so very
romantic, and so loving. The kind of
person I've always envisioned meeting.
Mama adores him. And I think that,
finally, all my dreams are beginning to
come true. . . .*

Grace stared at the page, wondering how
on earth she could have written anything
like this, even thirty years ago. This stuff
was several notches above Lovey in the De-
partment of Nausea, the kind of postpubes-
cent tripe you'd expect in a Harlequin
romance. She could almost see the cover—
the muscular, steel-jawed hero grasping the
lithe, golden-haired heroine by the shoulders, leaning down to kiss her.

Besides, that wasn't the way it happened
at all.

Grace looked up from her post at the circulation desk to find a man standing there with a pile of books in his arms. He was smiling, but his eyes—bright blue with crinkles around the corners—looked sad. A description leaped to her mind: ocean-deep, fathomless eyes.

She pushed the sentimental thought away and stood to her feet. "Checking these out?"

"Yes." He heaved the pile onto the counter and fished a library card out of his wallet. "I'm Dr. Michael Forrester. And you are—"

"Grace." She pointed to her name tag. "Grace Benedict."

"Well, Grace Benedict, I'm happy to meet you." He shook her hand, holding on a little longer than was absolutely necessary. "You're new around here?"

She nodded and began to sort and stamp the books. *Bam. Bam. Bam.* "I've been here a few months."

"I haven't seen you," he said. "I'd have remembered."

His voice was low and deep, smooth as oil and heavy as honey. She didn't dare look up. "I'm a research librarian, so I mostly spend my time in the stacks. One of the circulation workers is off sick today."

"A researcher, hmmm?" He leaned on the counter, and she noticed that there were suede patches on the elbows of his tweed jacket. He dressed like a college professor, smelled like cologne and pipe tobacco. She generally didn't approve of smoking, but this scent was intoxicating.

"Miss Benedict? It is *Miss,* isn't it?"

She jerked her head up. "Yes."

"But *Miss Benedict* is so formal. Mind if I call you Grace?"

"Of course not." She ducked her head again and resumed her task. "Dr. Forrester, these two are restricted noncirculating books, for library use only. I'm sorry, but—"

He chuckled. "If I'm going to call you Grace, the least you can do is call me Michael." He leaned closer, pointing at a list taped to the lower level of the counter. "I'm on the special permission list, as you can see."

"Oh. Yes. All right." His nearness upset her equilibrium, and she stammered like a schoolgirl. "OK. I'll just—ah, sign them out to you, and—"

"Grace." He laid a hand on her arm. "I don't bite. Really I don't."

"Of course." She let out a nervous laugh. "These are due back in two weeks, and—"

"I'm in here every day," he said. "I won't let you down."

The unexpected intimacy of his words caught her off guard, as if he were making a solemn vow, a personal promise. Her hand shook as she returned his library card.

"Grace, I need to ask a favor." He grinned, showing white teeth that over-lapped slightly in the front. A charming, youthful smile. "I'm doing research for my new book—"

"Oh? You're a writer?" Grace cringed as the words came out high-pitched and childish. How stupid could she possibly sound?

"I'm a history professor, actually, but I'm currently on sabbatical. My new project is a study of the religious practices of Native Americans, and I was hoping you might be able to help me."

"Help you?" she said idiotically. "Me?"

"You *are* a reference librarian, right?" He sounded as if he couldn't believe anyone would give such an important job to such a feebleminded girl.

Grace swallowed hard and took a deep breath to regain her composure. "Yes. Of course. What can I do, Dr. Forrester?"

"Michael," he corrected. "If we're going to be working together, I insist on first names." He smiled again, that same expression tinged with sadness. "I need someone to assist with my research on a regular basis, someone who can get up to speed and know the background of what I'm doing."

"I'd be glad to help, Dr.—ah, Michael. But I'm surprised you don't have a research assistant."

The smile faded, but the sadness remained. "Actually, I did have an assistant. My—my wife. But unfortunately, we're in the process of divorcing, and she is no longer interested in continuing the work." His face clouded. "Or our marriage, it appears," he added as if to himself.

So that was the source of the unhappiness behind his eyes. Grace felt a surge of empathy for him. She knew what loneliness felt like. She could imagine him in some kind of transient bachelor apartment, sitting on rented furniture and staring out a curtainless window.

"I couldn't give my exclusive attention to you during work hours——" she began.

"Of course. I understand that." His voice held hope and excitement, almost like a little boy's. "I was thinking that after work——" He paused and shook his head, his enthusiasm deflating. "But surely you have family, friends. Other things to do with your time off besides spend it with a stodgy old academic."

Grace nearly laughed out loud. Michael Forrester wasn't that old, and he certainly wasn't stodgy. Not tall, but good-looking, with broad shoulders and appealing little laugh lines at the corners of those beautiful eyes. She felt drawn to him, the way you'd be drawn to an abandoned pup on the side of the road. And yet that wasn't right, either—he wasn't the helpless type. It must have been the eyes that put her in mind of a lost puppy.

"I'd pay you well for your time," he said. "How does ten dollars an hour sound?"

"It sounds more than generous. You don't have to——"

"Yes, I do." He dropped his voice to a

whisper. "I'll tell you what. You keep track of the time you spend on my project while you're at work, and I'll pay you for those hours as well."

"Double pay for the same work?" she said. "That doesn't seem right."

He shrugged and did a little flickery thing with his eyebrows, up and down again, so fast she almost missed it. "I'm sure your salary here is not nearly what you're worth."

"How do you know what I'm worth?"

"I've got a sixth sense about these things." The eyebrows arched again. "Trust me."

"All right. When do we start?"

"How about tomorrow? Will you be here?"

Grace nodded. "I get off at four."

"I'll pick you up then," he said. "We'll go for coffee, and I'll fill you in on my project." He patted her hand, hefted the stack of books into his arms, and headed for the door.

She watched him go and realized she'd been holding her breath.

Tomorrow. She'd see him again tomorrow.

It wasn't a date, of course. It was a business appointment. But that didn't stop Grace from feeling a little like Cinderella stepping into the magic pumpkin. She'd wear her sky-blue sweater, the one everybody complimented. She'd wow him with her research skills. And maybe, just maybe . . .

12

Second Thoughts

*B*y the next afternoon, as four o'clock drew nearer, Grace was having second thoughts about meeting Michael Forrester for coffee. Not second thoughts, really. Thirds. Fourths. Hundredths.

She hadn't been able to focus all day. Hadn't been able to stop thinking about him. An idea jiggled at the back of her mind, demanding attention. A small, insistent voice, oddly like a miniature version of her own, repeating that she shouldn't be doing this, shouldn't even be thinking about it.

But what could possibly be wrong with it? He wanted her to help him with his research, that was all. A simple business arrangement. He valued her, believed she could aid him in his work.

She heard a click, looked up at the enormous clock as the minute hand jerked and settled on the twelve. And then he was there, standing in the shadows between the high stacks.

Her heart jumped in her chest. He hadn't waited for her up front, by the doors. He had come looking for her.

"Are you about ready?"

The voice was warm, smooth, and entreating. She couldn't see his face, just the dusky silhouette of him as he leaned casually with one hand on the vertical end of the bookcase.

"Yes. I just—almost." Grace shelved the last of the books and turned. "Let me punch out and get my things."

He followed her to the circulation desk and waited as she went into the small office behind the counter to retrieve her purse and sweater. When she came out lugging an overstuffed canvas book bag, his eyes widened.

"What's all that?"

Grace ducked her head. "I—ah, I ran across a few things I thought might be helpful to you. Mostly from interlibrary loan. I pulled up your records, and it didn't seem you had checked any of these out, so—"

"You got all these today?" He took the bag from her and peered into it. "Interlibrary loan must be faster than it used to be."

Grace felt herself beginning to blush. "Well, I—I had some errands to do anyway. It was no trouble. I picked them up on my lunch hour."

"Did you now?" He gazed at her, an expression of amazement on his handsome face, then smiled and held out his arm. "You know what, Grace Benedict? I have the feeling this is going to be the beginning of a beautiful relationship."

He meant their *working* relationship, of course. What else could he mean? Still, the phrase replayed itself over and over in her mind: *a beautiful relationship.*

They strolled down the street to the Haywood Park Hotel, then turned right and walked partway up the hill to a small European coffee shop in the middle of the

block. It was a glorious day, so Grace settled at a sidewalk table while Dr. Forrester—*Michael*—went inside and bought
coffee and chocolate-covered eclairs.

By the time he came out, she was chatting with an athletic-looking college girl at
the next table and making friends with the
girl's companion—a gentle, smiling golden
retriever.

"So, you like animals, do you?" Michael
asked as he set the coffee and eclairs on the
table.

She frowned at the apparent non sequitur. "Animals?"

"Sure." He pointed toward the table
where the young woman had been sitting.
"You seemed to be getting on rather well
with that golden."

"Oh, yes. I love dogs—and cats, too.
When I was little I had a sheltie named
Toby and a Himalayan we called Velvet.
They used to sleep curled up together at
the foot of my bed."

He stared absently into the distance.
"Cynthia would never allow animals in the
house."

Grace picked up her coffee cup and
leaned forward a little. "Dr. Forrester—

Michael, I mean. I don't want to overstep any boundaries here, but do you need to talk about your wife? I'm willing to listen if you do."

Michael smiled at her—a genuine smile, full of warmth and appreciation. "You mean it, don't you?"

"Of course I do. Sometimes—" She paused, trying to find the right words. "Sometimes it's just good to get feelings out in the open. You're separated, you said."

He nodded. "Yes. I always thought my marriage would last forever. Naive, I suppose."

"I don't think it's naive at all," Grace said. "Monogamy. Longevity. Love." She sipped her coffee and watched him over the rim of her cup. "Lots of people think *that's* naive. Old-fashioned."

"Believing in love, you mean? Or in marriage?"

Grace thought about the question. "Both, I guess," she answered after a pause. "When I was in college, I lived in a house with my three best friends. They all thought I was a throwback to the Victorian era."

He chuckled and reached across the table

to wipe a bit of custard cream off her lip. "I think it's nice," he said, his eyes gazing deep into hers. "I think it's very nice."

They dined that evening at The Flying Frog, a small, dim-lit restaurant across from the library. Grace had never set foot in the place even though it was ten paces from where she worked every day. When she saw the prices, she tried to convince Michael to take her somewhere else. He insisted they stay, however, and treated Grace to the Island rum filet—a steak so tender she could cut it with a fork—and for dessert, the most luscious crème brûlée she had ever tasted, with homemade fudge sauce.

"You deserve a treat," he said, his eyes reflecting the candlelight as he spooned up a mouthful of the crème brûlée. "You've put up with my rattling all afternoon."

Grace wouldn't have called it rattling. True, they had not even discussed their working arrangements, but that hardly mattered. She had learned so much about him, so much that fleshed out her initial impressions of Michael Forrester.

For one thing, she discovered—without ever having met the woman—that she despised his estranged wife, Cynthia. How could any woman in her right mind let a man like this get away? But then, Cynthia was not in her right mind apparently.

It wasn't that Michael had said anything derogatory about her—at least not directly. Yet as he talked, Grace pieced together a portrait of a haughty, demanding, petulant woman who could never be pleased and who always wanted more than they could easily afford. Clearly, she didn't understand him, and didn't make much effort to try. Instead, she berated him, belittled him, and in the end walked out on him—or, rather, pushed him out, keeping the house on Town Mountain and the Mercedes and leaving him with little more than a ten-year-old Volvo and the clothes on his back.

Now, if *she* had been Michael Forrester's wife . . .

Grace couldn't stop the images rushing at her, filling her mind: Michael in a spacious, book-lined study furnished with burgundy leather chairs and a large walnut desk. Coming to him as the early afternoon sun slanted through French doors that opened onto a stone terrace, bringing him coffee and a sandwich. Sitting close to him on a sofa in front of the fire, listening and commenting as he read the latest chapter of his book.

She would have been a supportive, loving, encouraging wife. She would have granted him the space and time to do his writing and research, without complaint. She would have been proud of his career as a professor rather than nagging at him to take a job that paid better. She would have given him what he needed rather than making demands of him.

Michael was watching her, his deep-set eyes reflecting the flickering candlelight. "Listen," he said, "I'm sorry I've taken up so much of your time. We haven't even had a chance to talk about the research. How about—"

The waiter appeared at his elbow, presenting the bill, and he handed over an American Express card without taking his eyes off her. "How about if we get together this weekend and finalize things? Say Saturday around noon? Come to my house, and I'll make brunch for us. I'm a very good cook."

The insistent little warning voice in the back of Grace's mind spoke up again, but it seemed farther away now, muffled and indistinct. "Yes," she said, ignoring it. "I'd like that."

He took a business card and pen out of his jacket pocket, scribbled on the back, and pushed it across the table to her. "That's my address, and my home phone number. Call me anytime. Anytime at all."

She reached to take the card, and their fingers touched. His hand was warm, and he left it there, gently stroking her forefinger with his thumb.

Grace had never been in love before, so she hardly knew what to expect. But she hadn't anticipated being so . . . so mixed up. She couldn't sleep, and the feelings that assaulted her in the dark reminded her vaguely of that night so long ago in the house on Barnard Street, when she had lain awake in the dormer and listened to the sounds coming from Lovey's room below. She awoke from those restless nights clutching her extra pillow, seeing Michael Forrester's face in her mind and hearing his low, silky voice echoing in her ears. She went through her work in a daze, making stupid mistakes a first-year intern would have caught. Except when she was working on Michael's research, of course. Then she was fully focused.

The "beautiful working relationship" hadn't turned out quite the way Grace might have predicted. She was helping him with his new book, but she didn't think of it as a job; it was a labor of love. The way she would have done if she had been his wife instead of his assistant. The way she would continue to do, she told herself, when she *became* his wife.

For miracle of miracles, Michael Forrester had fallen in love with her, too.

It was utter chaos. And it was wonderful.

For six months now their Saturday brunches had been a regular occurrence, with Grace arriving promptly at noon at his small house on Chestnut Street. Converted years back from a carriage house behind one of the old Victorians common to the area, the place was quiet and private, hidden from the street, with a small yard flanked by a buffer of trees.

The main room was one large square with vaulted ceilings, floors of wide-plank pine, and a rough stone fireplace. In the back left corner away from the door, Michael had created a study area, separating his desk from the rest of the room by an arrangement of tall bookcases and oak filing cabinets. To the far right, a serving bar divided the compact kitchen from the rest of the room. Beyond the kitchen, a door led to the single bedroom and bath.

The first time Grace had entered the carriage house, she had been struck with a new awareness of Michael's creativity. Rather than try to downplay the fact that his home had once stabled horses, he had used history to his advantage. One weathered wall held a collection of brass bridle ornaments on a long leather strap. A well-oiled English saddle doubled as a footstool next to the fireplace. Stable lanterns hung on the rafters, and a large antique feed box served as a coffee table. The whole place had an air of shabby elegance, right down to the worn leather sofa and secondhand Oriental rug.

On this particular Saturday morning, Grace arrived ten minutes early. The door was open, and she peered in through the screen. As usual, the house was extremely clean and neat—Michael liked things tidy, orderly. She could see a bowl of eggs set out on the kitchen counter, along with a quart of milk, a block of cheese, a basket of mushrooms, and what looked like a cluster of green onions.

But where was Michael?

Grace opened the screen door and stepped inside. Then she heard his voice, sounding hushed and urgent, coming from behind the bookcases that separated the study from the living room. He was on the phone.

"No, I can't. Not today," he said. "I'm behind schedule and swamped with work and have an appointment. Tomorrow, yes. Six-thirty. I promise."

She wasn't deliberately trying to eavesdrop, but she felt stupid standing at the door, waiting for him. Now she wished she had stayed outside. Wished she had been late. Wished she had been anywhere except here, overhearing this one-sided conversation.

White-hot acid churned in her stomach, and her mouth went dry and cottony. Iago's words from *Othello* sprang to her mind: "O beware, my lord, of jealousy; it is a green-eyed monster that doth mock the meat it feeds on."

Michael was supposed to be having dinner with *her* tomorrow night.

"I know, I know," he murmured in a consoling voice. Grace could see his legs now, a flash of blue denim stretching out beyond the bookcase barrier. He was obviously sitting in his office chair, facing away from the desk. "Yeah, OK. Tomorrow. Me too. Bye."

He hung up and came around from behind the bookcases. When he saw Grace standing there, his face went white for a second or two, then he grinned and came over to take her in his arms. "You're early!" he said as he bent down to kiss her. "Sorry about the delay; I was on the phone."

She peered into his eyes. "Is everything all right?"

"Sure, everything's great." He grasped

her hand and led her over to the corner kitchen. "How about cutting the veggies for me while I stir up an omelet?"

Grace sat down on a high stool with the bar between them and began slicing the mushrooms.

"Listen," he said as he broke eggs into a bowl and poured in milk. "I can't have dinner tomorrow night like we planned." His voice was airy, nonchalant.

The bottom dropped out of Grace's stomach. "Oh. All right."

"Aren't you going to ask me why?"

Grace studied him. His eyes crinkled at the corners as he smiled, but something in her gut twisted all the same. "I don't suppose I have the right to ask you anything," she said, fighting to maintain a casual facade. "I don't own you."

He stopped beating the eggs, set the bowl on the counter, and came to her side of the bar, turning her to face him. "Grace Benedict, how many times do I have to tell you? I love you. We belong together. We're a couple."

"We're not a couple as long as you're still married, Michael."

He cupped his palm around her cheek

and stroked her temple with his thumb. "I didn't want to tell you until I was certain," he said in a whisper. "But I was just on the phone with Cynthia. I can't have dinner with you tomorrow evening because I'm meeting her to finalize the divorce agreement." He grinned broadly. "Now this will finally be over, and you and I—"

Relief surged through her, a cooling, cleansing wave. She had nothing to be jealous about. Michael loved her. And now, soon, they could be together—forever.

It was just as she had dreamed it would be. Well, almost. Certainly, marrying a divorced man hadn't been on her wish list. But then, falling in love with Michael had changed her perspectives on a lot of things. After all, Cynthia had left him, not the other way around. He was the wounded party in this separation, the one who had been wronged.

Everything was all right. No, more than all right. Perfect. Completely, totally perfect. Grace knew it for a certainty. She felt it—a sense of absolute peace, of confidence. No longer did she hear that nagging voice inside her head warning her to be careful. She was on solid ground.

Michael leaned down and kissed her, a sweet, tender kiss at first, then increasing in intensity. She clung to him like a woman drowning, felt herself going under. The flash of heat she had experienced before came again—not jealousy but passion, rising up and overtaking her.

"How do you feel about omelets for dinner instead of brunch?" he asked, his voice husky and laced with meaning.

Then, still pressing against her, he reached behind her, opened the door, and led her into the bedroom.

And this time, her only second thought was to wonder why she had waited so long to give herself to the man she loved.

13

MICHAEL'S GIFT

Grace closed the circle journal and stared unseeing at the kitchen table, which still bore the remains of her frugal supper and the pile of mail. Even though it had been more than twenty-five years, she could still feel the fire in her veins, the passion of Michael Forrester's kiss, the breathtaking wonder of that first time.

With a loud and insistent "Mrrow!" a pale shadow leaped onto the table into the pool of light from the overhead lamp and began lapping at the cold soup that had settled into the bottom of Grace's bowl.

"Get down, Snookums," she said automatically, pulling the cat into her lap. "You know you're not allowed on the table."

The cat pushed its head under her hand

and gave a purr that sounded like the rumble of an idling car engine. Grace scratched under its chin, and the purring increased to the level of a motor scooter with a hole in its muffler.

"Sweet girl," Grace murmured. "You're hungry, I suppose. Let's get you some real food."

She went to the cabinet, pulled down a plastic canister half full of cat kibbles, and shook some into a small bowl while Snookums continued to purr and wind around her ankles. Grace set the bowl on the floor next to the refrigerator and leaned against the counter, watching as the cat ate.

This was Snookums III, actually—granddaughter of the original Snookums. The Himalayan characteristics had been only minimally diluted by the questionable genetics of a couple of unidentified fathers, and with the exception of a white chest and small white mittens, Snookums still retained most of her grandmother's beauty and all of her sweet-tempered charm. She had lush fur, a light grayish-brown with darker tips on the ears and tail, and a magnificent ruff around her neck and chest. Her head was round, her face short but not squashed like a Persian's, and her eyes were Caribbean blue, rather like . . .

Like Michael's.

Why, Grace wondered, had she never been able to get Michael Forrester out of her mind, out of her heart? Why, after all these years, was he still so much a part of her life?

But the question was irrelevant. She knew why.

For several months after she and Michael made love that first time, Grace was in heaven. She bought brides' magazines and pored over them, made elaborate wedding plans, picked a color scheme and then changed her mind again. She didn't include Michael in any of this, of course—there would be plenty of time for that later on. She didn't want to pressure him right now, or distract him when he was trying to negotiate a divorce settlement.

She probably should find a chapel—preferably a small, intimate one—where the ceremony could be held. The problem was, she didn't have a clue where to begin.

She hadn't set foot inside a church in years. During college and graduate school, she always had research papers and projects and exams taking up her weekend hours. Later, when she went to work at the library, she often had to work on Saturday, and Sunday was her only full day off.

Now she worked with Michael on weekends, checking his research or reading his latest chapter. He liked to write on Sunday mornings when everything was quiet and he wasn't likely to be disturbed.

Not that she would have attended church services even if she'd had the time. In truth, the very idea exhumed long-buried memories of the last time she had been inside a sanctuary.

The day of her father's funeral.

Besides, she knew what religious people were like. If they got wind of her relationship with Michael, they would condemn her without a second thought. She knew the argument all too well. She had even leveled that same accusation at her best friend once—a very long time ago, it seemed.

No one else could possibly understand. They didn't know what it was like to be that much in love. And besides, she and Michael were practically engaged. As soon as his divorce came through, they would be married. Of course a lot of religious folks—what Liz used to call "the brethren and cistern"—would disapprove of the divorce and the marriage as well. They might even call her a home wrecker.

But that couldn't be helped. Once she and Michael were husband and wife, she would be able to hold her head high and not worry about what anyone said.

She wasn't about to let other people's opinions get in the way of true love. Better to stay away from church altogether. And so every Saturday—and usually a couple of times during the week as well—she would arrive at Michael's for what he jokingly called "research sessions." Grace had to admit he *was* teaching her things she'd never dreamed of. When she laughed with him about being his "love student," a shadow stirred deep inside. It was only a vague feeling, something she couldn't quite get her mind around, but it disturbed her nevertheless.

Then one Saturday morning she arrived at his house for brunch to find his Volvo missing and a note on the door that said: *Come on in. Be back shortly.*

She went inside and found the feed-box coffee table nearly hidden under a crystal vase bearing a dozen red roses. She sat down on the scarred leather sofa and breathed in the heavy fragrance, fingering the tiny white blossoms of baby's breath placed between the rosebuds. A tiny card on a plastic stake bore a single word: *Grace.*

She looked around, half expecting him to jump out of some hiding place, but the house remained silent. Opening the card, she read his message, scrawled in black ink: *Happy Birthday, My Darling. Further surprises to come. All my love, Michael*

Her birthday. Grace had almost forgotten. But Michael, bless him, had remembered. She smiled and pressed the card to her lips, then jumped, startled, as she heard a car door slam.

He was home. It felt almost . . . normal, the way she went to the door to greet him. Like a wife awaiting the return of her husband after a long day.

Grace stood there, watching through the screen door as he got out of the car and came toward the house, bouncing on the balls of his feet like a little boy with a secret. In his hands he carried an enormous box and a couple of huge plastic bags.

"Oh, good—you're here!" He shouldered past her and heaved the box onto the kitchen counter. "Did you find your roses?"

"Yes, Michael, they're beautiful. Thank you so—"

As soon as his hands were free, he swung her into an embrace, kissing her on the lips, the nose, the eyelids. "Ah," he said dramatically, stepping back to look at her. "But that's not all." He pointed to the sofa. "Sit. And close your eyes."

Grace sat and waited, hearing him scuffling around in the direction of the kitchen.

"OK, hold out your hands."

She extended her arms and cupped her palms. Something warm and soft and wriggly was lowered into her outstretched hands.

"Open your eyes," he commanded, "and meet Snookums."

Grace looked. It was a living ball of fluff, soft as fleece. A Himalayan kitten, with wide blue eyes and nearly white fur. Its paws and ears and tail were the color of milk chocolate, and it mewed once before climbing up Grace's chest and nuzzling against her neck.

"To keep you company when I'm not around," he chuckled, leaning down to pet the cat and kiss Grace simultaneously. "She's eight weeks old." He lowered himself to the couch beside Grace and scratched the kitten's ears. "I also bought kitten chow and a bed and a litter box and a couple of toys."

"She's the most wonderful gift," Grace murmured. "I'd forgotten how small they are as kittens, and how beautiful. I had a Himalayan once when I was a girl."

"I know. Her name was Velvet." At Grace's stupefied expression, Michael shrugged. "I listen. So sue me." He pulled her into his arms, kitten and all, and kissed her until she couldn't breathe. At last he straightened up and looked at her.

"I'm taking you out to dinner later," he said in a low, quiet voice. "But first I have another gift I'd like to give you." She saw a smoldering longing in his eyes, and felt her own veins ignite. Slowly, very slowly, he took the kitten and set it on the rug, then reached out for her.

Grace sat on the floor in her small apartment as the sun set and twilight closed in. She ought to get up and turn a lamp on, but she had neither the energy nor the motivation. In the half-light, Snookums pawed at the laces of her tennis shoes. The kitten, now six months old, was in a lanky spurt, her legs so long that she looked as if she were walking on stilts. She grabbed one shoelace in her teeth and ran with it, tumbling head over tail when she reached the end of the tether. As if expecting a laugh or at least a nod of affirmation, the kitten turned back toward Grace.

But Grace simply slumped with her back against the sofa, picking at the carpet and staring into the gathering darkness. Snookums marched back across the room and into Grace's lap, curling herself into a ball and batting her sheathed paws at Grace's fingers.

It was late autumn, with crisp, clear days and cold, starry nights that held a breath of winter. The furnace kicked on with a whining whir, and warm air poured out of the vent. But no amount of mechanical heat could overcome the chill in Grace's soul.

Pregnant, the doctor said. Probably about two months along. Grace had never kept up very well with her cycles. She thought she just had the flu. A little nausea now and then, she had told the nurse when she called for an appointment. No, not much fever. Just generally lethargic. She had expected to get a prescription and feel better in a couple of days.

She exhaled heavily. She'd have to tell Michael, that much was certain. She didn't know how he'd respond—they hadn't yet gotten around to talking about having a baby. Given the fact that he and Cynthia had never had children, she hoped he would be excited about it. It would throw a monkey wrench into plans for a real wedding, of course—she could hardly walk down the aisle of a church in a maternity wedding gown. It would probably mean a hurry-up civil ceremony the moment the divorce papers were signed. But that might not be so bad. She and Michael could get on with their life together that much sooner if they didn't have the complication of arranging for an elaborate wedding ceremony.

They'd likely need the money they would have spent on a wedding, anyway. Babies were expensive. And although Grace's job at the library didn't bring in a lot, they wouldn't even have that once the baby arrived. She couldn't possibly work; a mother's place was at home, raising her child.

Her mind spun out of control, shifting once again to the now-familiar scenario: Michael writing in his book-lined study, with Grace beside him. Only this time a little baby Forrester was crawling around the thick Oriental carpet, pulling up on its daddy's legs. She could almost hear Michael laughing at the baby's antics as pudgy hands grabbed his papers and scattered them around the room. . . .

She picked Snookums up and cradled the cat in her arms, relishing the warmth of the furry little body. "OK," she muttered to herself at last. "I ought to do this now, before I lose my nerve." She got to her feet, sank onto the couch, and retied her shoelaces. "I'll be back later, Babycat," she said, rubbing the kitten's head. "Be good while I'm gone. No jumping on the counter."

She retrieved a jacket from the hall closet, grabbed her purse and keys off the kitchen counter, and put a hand on the front doorknob. "Please," she whispered toward the dark ceiling. "Please let him be glad."

The lights were on when Grace pulled up to Michael's door. Good. He was home. Her hand was shaking as she opened the car door, and she willed it to be still. There was nothing to be so upset about. Michael loved her. She loved him. They were going to be married. What difference did it make if the child engendered by that love came a few months early?

"Everything is going to be all right," she told herself as she moved up the sidewalk toward the front door. She reached the door and raised a hand to knock. But her knuckles never made contact.

She could see inside, through the screen, through the wavery glass of the closed

door. Michael, standing in front of the fireplace, prodding at the logs with a black
poker. The fire blazed up, and warm red
light illuminated his face—the face she
loved so. He was smiling.

He turned, as if speaking to a person
who was out of Grace's line of vision. He
laughed, and someone else came into the
picture from the direction of the kitchen—
a short, curvaceous woman with flaming
red hair. She walked over to him, slipped
an arm easily around his waist, and stood
there, watching the fire. Together they
gazed into the flames for a minute or two,
and then—

Grace's stomach plummeted, as if she'd
just dropped off the precipice of a roller-
coaster. He was kissing her. Holding her.
Stroking her hair. And the woman was
leaning in to him, as if she had done it all
her life.

She waited with her fist arrested in
midair, not having the faintest idea what to
do. The porch light wasn't on; with the
lights on inside, no one would know she
was there unless she knocked. Should
she interrupt them? Get in the car and

drive home as fast as was humanly possible? Confront him? Pretend she hadn't seen anything?

The redhead let go and disappeared again, and in a flash of determination Grace made her decision. Her knuckles came down firmly on the door frame. Once, twice.

Startled, Michael looked toward the door. He swiveled his head toward the kitchen, shrugged, then strode across the room, opened the door, and peered out. "Grace?"

"I need to talk to you."

He hesitated.

"Who is it, hon?" a voice called.

"It's Grace Benedict." He looked back at Grace, pushed open the screen, and held it for her. "Come in."

Grace's legs buckled, and her breath was coming in short gasps, but she managed to get over the threshold without collapsing. Michael motioned toward the sofa. "Have a seat."

The redhead came into view. Now Grace could see that she was very pretty, with translucent skin and warm brown eyes. She wore jeans and an intricately knitted sweater in hues of rusty brown and pale blue that coordinated perfectly with her coloring. When she smiled, she showed two dimples and even white teeth. She held up a half-filled wineglass. "Would you like some? It's Pinot Grigio. Italian."

"No thank you," Grace said.

Michael turned his back and poked in the fire.

"My husband seems to have misplaced his mind—or at least his manners," the woman said, coming forward and putting her free hand on Grace's shoulder. "I'm Cynthia Forrester. And you would be the elusive genius Grace Benedict."

"Genius?" Grace parroted.

"Don't be so modest, my dear," Cynthia said with a wave of her hand. "Michael's told me all about you. I really don't know how he would have managed these last few months without you."

Grace was about to say that this was the most amiable divorce she had ever seen, when something stopped her. A warning in the distant reaches of her mind, telling her to keep quiet.

"We should have met long before this, of course," Cynthia went on, "but Michael is so protective of his privacy. You must have some very special kind of hold on him. When I encouraged him to rent this place as a getaway for his writing, I had to promise never to show up without calling first. He doesn't like to be interrupted." She moved around the sofa to Michael's side, slipping her arm around him again. "As I said, Michael can't stop talking about you—about what a difference you've made in his work. But he failed to tell me how attractive you are." She let out a warm laugh. "Good thing I'm not the jealous type." She gave Michael an affectionate squeeze. "But then, I have no reason to be."

Still Michael hadn't spoken. He was watching Grace warily out of the corner of his eye.

"I—I think I ought to be going," Grace stammered. She attempted to rise, but her legs failed her and she sank back onto the couch.

"Nonsense," Cynthia said, placing her wineglass on the mantel. "I doubt you would have come if you didn't have something important to talk with Michael about. Besides, I was just leaving. The dogs have been alone in the house for hours; they're probably crossing their legs by now."

She stood on tiptoe to give Michael a kiss. "I'll see you later, darling. Don't let him work too hard, Grace. Half the time he comes home completely exhausted." She picked up a coat that had been slung over the saddle next to the fireplace and breezed out the door.

Grace heard a car door shut behind the house, an engine revving, then tires crunching across the gravel driveway. She couldn't have moved if the place had been on fire. She felt petrified, as if her heart and flesh had turned to stone.

At last Michael quit assaulting the logs in the fireplace and turned toward her.

"I wish you hadn't heard all that," he said quietly.

"I'll bet you do."

"No, it's not like that. I wanted to tell you myself. You see, Cynthia isn't ex- actly—well, rational. She's in denial about the divorce. Doesn't want to admit—"

For a moment Grace caught a glimmer of hope. Then the truth crashed in upon her, an echo of Cynthia Forrester's voice in her head: *I encouraged him to rent this place as a getaway for his writing. . . . Good thing I'm not the jealous type. . . . The dogs have been alone in the house for hours. . . .*

"Stop it!" she shouted. Adrenaline rushed into her veins, and she jumped up from the couch. "Not another word. Not another lie!"

She felt feverish and shaky, and as she stood there, staring at him, his features quivered and seemed to change. He became not the man she loved, but a stranger. And yet not a stranger either.

"Grace, sweetheart—" He moved toward her, reaching out for her.

"Get your filthy hands off me." She pulled away from him and threw her arms up, a barrier between them. "How could I have been so *stupid*? I fell for it all, every word. *'Cynthia doesn't encourage my work. Cynthia doesn't allow animals in the house.'*" She paused as the pieces fell together in her mind. "There's no divorce. There never was. You lied to me, you bastard! You— you *seduced* me!"

"*Seduced* is a pretty harsh word," he said.

"What word would *you* use?"

He shrugged and turned his most charming smile on her. "I don't know. These things—just *happen*."

The fire in her veins turned to ice. "Well, something else *just happens*, too, when you can't manage to keep the horse in the barn."

All the color drained out of his face. "Meaning what?"

"You're the intelligent one. You figure it out." She put a hand to her belly.

"You're *pregnant*?"

"Very good, Dr. Forrester."

"That's what you came here to tell me."

"Yes." Without warning the energy tap turned off, and Grace felt completely drained. She propped against the arm of the sofa, unable to hold herself up any longer.

For a moment he said nothing. Then: "What are you going to do about it?"

"You'd suggest a back-alley abortion, I suppose. Something quick and painless— for you anyway—so you wouldn't have to be embarrassed."

"Actually, no." He had an odd look on his face, almost like . . . amusement.

Grace frowned. "What do you mean, no?"

"I wouldn't want you to have an abortion, even if you could find a reputable doctor who would do one. This is my baby, too, and I have an obligation to it. You can't possibly raise this child on your own, Grace."

"Don't you think I know that? I can barely get by on what I make at the library."

"Then let me help."

The words burst through, a ray of hope in a dark tunnel. The sweetly domestic images of the two of them married and happy had dissolved like a soap bubble, but now Grace thought that at least he might admit the truth and stand up and take responsibility like a man. Still, she didn't dare let herself trust again. She narrowed her eyes. "What kind of help?"

"Have the baby. I'll pay for everything. Then Cynthia and I will adopt it." His voice grew wistful. "We've always longed for a child, and never been able to have one."

Grace stared at him incredulously. "Have you completely lost touch with reality? No woman in her right mind would accept an arrangement like that."

"What makes you think Cynthia will ever know? If you don't tell her, that is."

He shook his head, and a slow smile crept over his face. "Of course, even if you *did* tell her, she wouldn't believe you. I'm just the kind of person who would go to any lengths to help out a friend in trouble. My lawyer could draw up the paperwork, so everything would be legal, and—"

Grace couldn't believe what she was hearing. The man was insane. He actually thought he could convince her to give up her baby to him, beguiling her with eye contact and sensual movement, the way a snake charmer subdues a cobra. She got up and made for the door.

"Grace, wait," he said, putting a hand on her arm. "Sweetheart—"

"Don't touch me!" She shook him off and began to walk away.

"You'll change your mind, Grace!" he shouted after her. "You'll come back to me when you've had a chance to think about it."

She whirled on him and pointed a finger in his face. "Like hell I will," she said. "You will never see me again. Never. And you will *never* get your hands on this child."

WEB OF DECEIT

Grace had been true to that promise, at least. She had never gone back to Michael Forrester. But she had never completely escaped him, either. No matter how much she struggled to break free, she remained bound to him by invisible chains. The passion she could never quite seem to forget. The child they had created together. The lies she had fabricated and written to her friends.

Except for Michael, Grace had told no one about the pregnancy. Not even her mother, who was preoccupied with her own plans. Finally, after all those years, Mama had decided to go back to college to pursue her Master's degree in American Literature. She had sold the farmhouse and most of the furniture and rented a small place in Chapel Hill, near the university. Her first class was scheduled to begin January 9.

When Grace had gone home that last Christmas, she wasn't showing, and Mama, caught up in her own excitement, didn't notice anything wrong.

And so, while Mama wrote effusive letters about the authors she was studying, the interesting people she met, and what a grand adventure graduate school was, Grace made excuses for not visiting and went through her pregnancy alone. In May, just before her mother's first semester ended, she delivered a robust seven-pound baby girl and signed the papers to give the child up for adoption.

There was one moment, in the hospital, surrounded by a nurse and two social workers, when she almost lost her nerve. The baby, whom she had named Ramona Claire, squirmed in her arms and gazed up at her with wondering eyes. Blue eyes, like Daddy's, like little Emmy's. A fine fuzz of white-blonde hair. A dimple in her chin.

Grace looked down and saw her father, saw her half sister, saw her ex-lover. But she saw something else, too, in that round infant face. Trust, she thought. Absolute assurance that her mother wouldn't let anything bad happen to her.

"I—I don't know," she hedged as one of the social workers thrust a clipboard and pen into her hands. "Maybe I need to think about this some more. Maybe I could find a way—"

The first caseworker shook her head firmly. "Your baby will have a good home," she repeated for the third time. "A home with *two* parents."

"Yes, but I'm her mother!" Grace said fiercely.

"And a good mother does what's best for her child, no matter how much it hurts." The second social worker frowned. "It would have been better not to see her or hold her. We told you."

Grace clutched little Claire so tightly that the baby began to cry. Perhaps they were right. She knew nothing about being a parent, about being responsible for another human being. She had quit her job at the library—couldn't stand the stares and the questions, couldn't bear the possibility of crossing paths with Michael again. So far she didn't have anything else lined up. How could she possibly take care of a baby?

With tears streaming down her face, she signed the papers and relinquished Ramona Claire to the waiting arms of the nurse. The social worker patted her hand. "You've done the right thing," she soothed. "That's the end of it."

But of course it wasn't the end. There had been no end. Never in all these years.

Every day of her life, Grace thought about that little girl. In the early years she cried herself to sleep, wondering if her baby was warm and fed and cared for. As time went by, she scrutinized every child she passed on the street, looking for reflections of her own face, of Daddy's, of Emily's, of Michael Forrester's. Claire would be five now, she whispered to herself as she leaned on a playground fence, watching a blonde-haired girl squeal with delight as her swing went higher and higher. Claire would be ten this month, she thought as she passed a yellow bus full of elementary-school children. Claire would be sixteen . . . and twenty-one . . . and twenty-five.

Where was she? Grace wondered. What

kind of person had she grown up to be? Had she fallen in love, gotten married, had babies of her own? Was it possible Grace was a grandmother without even knowing it?

Snookums, now fed and content, had crawled up into Grace's lap and was purring. Grace stroked the cat's ears absently, then turned her attention back to the circle journal. She hadn't told her friends about the baby, either. She had simply swept it all under the rug, where it lay like a moldering dark lump—hidden but not gone, waiting to trip her when she wasn't looking. Just like her affair with Michael Forrester.

Affair. She cringed inwardly at the word, but what else could she call it? There was no gentler term, no acceptable euphemism that would free her from responsibility for what she had done. She blamed him for seducing her, blamed herself for being so naive, for falling so readily for his charming lies.

And, if she were going to be honest, she also blamed her father.

It didn't make sense, really, but it was true nevertheless. Her mind screamed the accusation: *Why did you do this to me?* She had tried so hard to overcome his betrayal, but her life, her heart, had never been the same since his death and the revelation of his infidelity. The only foundation of love she had ever known had been ripped out from under her. She had kept the shameful secret, pushed it down—so far down that she had been completely blindsided by the very same unfaithfulness when it reared its head again in the person of Michael Forrester.

She had been so furious at Daddy's duplicity, so righteously indignant over Lovey's relationship with Bo Tennyson. And yet she had let herself get sucked in by that impostor. Even let herself get pregnant.

She was a hypocrite, a fraud—no better than her father or her father's mistress or even her own deceptive lover.

Grace hadn't been able to write about all this in the circle journal—the sordidness of her experiences with Michael, the pain of losing her child, the frustration and despair of watching hope slip through her fingers like water. As Lovey had pointed out on graduation night, Grace had always been the Truth Teller, the moral compass for the group. The one who kept her integrity, who stood up for what was right even when the others disagreed with her.

When she had begun writing about Michael in the journal, she hadn't intended to deceive them. She simply wanted so badly to let them know that she had found the love of her life, to tell them about him. She had firmly believed there *would* be a marriage, a happily-ever-after. It was just a matter of time.

But once the initial lie was told, there was no turning back, no reclaiming of the friendship she had once enjoyed. Over the years the other three had made an effort to get together now and then, but she had never joined them. Year five, the year Lovey invited them all to Minnesota, Grace had been pregnant. Year ten, she had been broke. After year fifteen, no one seemed as eager to do it anymore. But they still kept in touch through the journal.

Grace turned the pages, three decades passing by in a familiar blur. The others had written eager, energetic accounts of their lives. All of them were successful and happy. All of them had fulfilled their dreams.

Liz had moved to Washington. Her marriage hadn't worked out, but she was still in D.C., still crusading. Tess had admitted that she might not be cut out to be a novelist, but she had found contentment and satisfaction as a college professor and fallen in love with a colleague at the university. And Lovey was still married to Bo, who had parlayed his brief stint with the Vikings into a career as the owner of a sports-gear chain, making scads of money.

Tess and her husband had adopted a little girl. Lovey had two bright and beautiful children, now grown and on their own.

And then there was Grace, with her world in shambles and her heart scrabbling for something—anything—to live for.

Shortly after the birth of Ramona Claire, while Grace was still trying to recover from postpartum depression and endemic self-loathing, the circle journal had come around again. Humiliated and despairing and unemployed, completely unequipped to deal with her friends' reactions, she had seriously considered chucking the circle journal into the garbage can and being done with the whole thing. She had told them how happy and in love she was. How could she now come clean with her festering secrets, her illicit romance, her misbegotten child, her stupidity and shame?

But Grace didn't throw the journal away. Instead, she wrote:

> *I've decided to give up my research job at the main library. Michael wants me to be at home more, at least until the baby comes. Yes, that's what I said. We're expecting, and we're so thrilled about it.*
>
> *Tess, I hope this isn't too difficult for you, since you've been open with us about your struggles with infertility. But I simply had to share the joy of this new development with my best friends. . . .*

It was just the kind of news her friends would delight to hear. But it was also what

Grace *had* to write—not just for her reputation but for her sanity. It was the life she desperately wanted, needed. The fantasy that would keep her motivated to get up every morning and breathe.

By now she had it all planned out. The most effective deceptions, she had learned from Shakespeare's characterization of Iago, were those that contained as much truth as possible. She could bare her soul about carrying a child within her womb . . . and then losing it. She just couldn't tell them where that child had come from, or where she had gone.

> *This is almost more than I can bear to write, but we lost our baby daughter last month. I didn't know if I would make it at first—sometimes people think they're comforting you when they say, "It's only a miscarriage. You can have another one," as if losing a baby is like losing an earring. Even if I could have another child, it would never replace the one I carried in my womb and had taken from my arms.*
>
> *But there will be no more babies for me. In that, Tess, I can identify with you, and would welcome any wisdom you have to*

*share about how best to deal with a
situation like this.*

Months passed before the journal returned.
Meanwhile, Grace had taken a job at the
Oakley branch library—barely a blip in the
Buncombe County system, capable of supporting only two permanent employees
and one part-time assistant. Her salary was
abysmally low, and she'd had to move to a
smaller place, a dilapidated rental house.

> *I've gone back to work and have been
> promoted to library director. Michael is
> writing his new book, and is up for tenure
> at the university. Please note the new
> address—we've moved to a marvelous old
> brick home nearer the college—a two-story
> with a walled garden and a perfect screened
> porch. . . .*

Eventually, creating the details of this world
of illusion became second nature for Grace.
She knew she couldn't keep Michael
around forever—and didn't want to, for
that matter. Writing about him only served
to remind her of her gullibility. But she de-
bated for a long time before deciding if his

demise would come through death or divorce. It was years after her pseudo-
confession about the baby that she finally
let him go.

*I apologize for holding on to the journal for
so long. I kept thinking I could bring myself
to call you, or write individual letters, or at
least send this on, but I haven't been able to
do it. You see, Michael died last month. We
had been out to a dinner party with some
other faculty members, and had just gotten
home. He sat down in his leather wing
chair to watch the news, and when I came
back into the den, I found him there, still in
his tuxedo, with a photo of me clutched in
his hand.*

*It was a brain aneurism, the doctor
said—he died just like that, a snap of the
fingers, a blink of an eyelash. I was
devastated. It was so sudden, so
unexpected. But now that I've had a few
weeks to get over the shock, I'm trying to
focus on remembering all the wonderful
times we had together.*

*I know you'll all be angry that I didn't
call you, but please try to understand. I do
have support here—my friend Evelyn*

Jetterly has stayed by my side since the funeral and has helped me with all the arrangements.

Fortunately, Michael made certain I would be financially secure. I won't be taking any round-the-world cruises, certainly, but I can keep the house and won't lack for any necessities.

Grace looked down at the entry about Michael's death and smiled grimly. She would have preferred to give him a more violent death—a little blood and gore, and certainly quite a bit of physical agony, particularly around the region of the groin—but she had settled on quick and painless so that she could justify not communicating with Liz and Lovey and Tess until after the initial grief had subsided.

She scanned through the pages: more about the beautiful house she had shared with Michael, the resolution of her grief over his death, the regret that they hadn't had more time. A long entry about the death of Grace's mother and how much Grace missed her. Lots of superficialities interspersed with a few genuine emotions here and there.

And then the description of Jet's death.

She had been my best friend for years, much like the kind of friendship we all had in college. We laughed a lot, cried together when we needed to, told each other everything.

Jet was divorced and lived alone, and after I was widowed, the two of us became inseparable. We thought alike, finished each other's sentences, knew instinctively when to talk and when to listen. She knew everything about me. . . .

But Jet *didn't* know everything, Grace mused bitterly. She never knew about Michael, or about the baby Grace gave up for adoption. She never knew about Daddy, or how devastating his betrayal had been. All Jet knew of Grace was what Grace let her see.

By the time she died, she had been through so many rounds of chemo, so many doctors, so many experimental treatments. But nothing they tried worked, and it all

made her so sick. At last she said NO—
no more—and prepared herself to die.

The end came quickly after that.
Mercifully, I might say, except for the
eighteen months of hell that came before
the end. As much as I loved Jet, as much
as I miss her now, I can't help wondering if
the true mercy would have been a natural
death from the cancer instead of an
unnatural death from the treatments.

She died holding my hand, thanking me
for the gift of our friendship. And yet I
know that I was the one who received the
greater gift.

All of this was accurate, one of the few authentic bits Grace had written in the circle journal. And yet, even about Jet, she had lied by omission, and what she left out was the most important part of all.

"So few people in this world have the ability to be honest and open about themselves," Jet said near the end. "I am so thankful I can go to my grave knowing that in my life I had one true friend."

As the memory washed over her, Grace bit the inside of her lip and tried not to cry.

She had never been honest about herself, not in thirty years.

How had she pulled it off? Through her father's adultery and illegitimate daughter, an affair with a married man, a pregnancy and adoption, a lifetime of broken dreams, Grace had fooled them all—even Jet. Tess would be proud of her if she knew how good Grace had become at writing fiction. At living it.

She ran a hand over the pages and found that her fingers were trembling. These three women had once been her friends. Besides Jet, the best friends she had ever known. What would her life have been like, even in the midst of all her doubt and struggles and moments of despair, if she had only had Liz and Tess and Lovey to support and comfort and encourage her?

Jet was dead, but the others were alive. Grace could still try to reclaim that connection. She could still make it right.

But how? How could she go back? How could she humble herself to tell the truth at last, to confess that she'd been avoiding them, lying to them all these years? Lying about the seminar in the Caymans, about the European sabbatical, about the house renovations. Even about Michael's death.

The lies had been endless.

Her throat began to burn and her eyes stung. A painful knot of longing rose up inside her. She *needed* them, these friends who had given her a sense of security and belonging so many years ago.

Needed them as Jet had needed her.

She had nowhere else to turn.

By the time Grace had washed the dishes and cleaned up the kitchen, she had settled on a plan. The answer had come to her when she finally got around to sorting the rest of her mail.

The Visa card.

Shiny and compelling, with its holographic logo and its $5,000 credit limit, that card held the answer to her dilemma.

She would write to Liz and Lovey and Tess—not an entry in the journal but a personal letter—inviting them to come to Asheville for a weekend at the posh Grove Park Inn. She would book a suite, complete with gourmet meals and a day at the spa. It would be a spectacular mini-reunion, just the four of them—her treat, charged on the bright new Visa card.

She would confess the truth—all of it. She would unburden her soul and trust that they would be able to love her through it all. She would reconcile with the friends who had been so important to her.

And then, when she had made her peace with them and with herself, she would die on her terms, in her time.

Before the cancer got her, she would take her own life.

PART II

LOVEY

*We toss a coin into a fountain,
gazing toward tomorrow,
hoping some god or genie or a twist of fate
will grant the wish,
secure the aspiration,
turn the longing to reality.*

*But no one warns us
to beware such callow optimism.
No one reveals the hidden truth
that dreams fulfilled
may prove a curse
instead of bringing blessing.*

The Invitation

Minnetonka, Minnesota
Early Spring

*A*manda Love Tennyson stared down at the brass picture frame in her hand. It was the hinged kind that opened like a book, with a photo on each side. On the left stood a handsome young man in a light-blue football jersey, his shoulders broad beneath the pads, his blond hair gilded by the sun, his helmet propped on a jutted hip-bone. Opposite him, a girl—also blonde, in a short pleated skirt—held her pom-poms aloft and cast a vivacious grin toward the camera.

Both of the photographs were faded.

"Excuse me, Miz Manda—"

Amanda started, and her fingers clenched down on the picture frame. She heard a snap as the two halves of the frame came apart in her hands. She fumbled with the broken pieces for a moment, then stuffed them under the sofa pillow.

At last she looked up to see Neva, the housekeeper, standing in the doorway.

"I didn't mean to spook you," she said, taking two steps down into the sunken den, "but the mail's come." She moved forward, her crisp gray uniform rustling in the silence of the room. "If you like, I'll take that frame and see if I can get it fixed for you."

Amanda felt herself flush. "Forget it. I'll take care of it." She retrieved the frame and tried to prop it up on the lamp table, but without being joined by the hinge, it toppled and fell over. The girl's picture struck the corner of the table, and the glass cracked into a spiderweb, radiating from the center of the cheerleader's face. "Or maybe not."

She put the picture back on the table, and for a minute or two simply sat there, staring at the housekeeper. Had she never noticed before how beautiful Neva Wilson was? Skin smooth and clear, the color of antique oak. Large, dark eyes. A perpetual expression of . . . serenity.

Neva had to be in her fifties, but she carried herself like a woman twenty years younger—slim and athletic, with catlike grace. The kind of grace and athleticism Amanda had prided herself on once upon a time. A brief surge of remorse and envy twisted inside her.

"The mail, Miz Manda?" Neva was still holding a bundle wrapped in a thick rubber band.

"Thanks." Amanda laid the mail on top of the broken picture frame. "I'll take care of it later."

"Yes ma'am." The housekeeper complied, then stood, waiting.

"Does the cook know we're having four more for dinner tonight?"

"Yes ma'am. She's making a standing rib roast, I believe. And chocolate cheesecake."

Amanda stirred. "Bo's favorites. He'll be pleased."

"Yes ma'am. Mr. Bo always brags on Isabel. Tells everybody how she used to be a chef at some fancy hotel in downtown Minneapolis, until he stole her away."

"I know. I've heard it a thousand times."
Amanda lifted one eyebrow. "Mr. Bo is accustomed to getting what he wants."

Neva's dusky face broke into a wide
smile. "That he is, Miz Manda. That he is."
When Amanda did not smile in return, the
black woman narrowed her eyes. "Excuse
me for asking, Miz Manda, but is something bothering you? You don't seem
quite . . . right."

Amanda gazed out the French doors,
past the screened porch to the woods behind the house. The trees were frosted
heavily with a wet spring snow. "Tell me
something, Neva. Why do we bother having a screened porch when we only get to
use it about three days a year?"

Neva gave a low laugh. "I don't know,
ma'am. But then, I don't suppose I understand lots of things rich folks do." She
stopped suddenly and clapped a hand to her
face. "Sorry, ma'am. Sometimes my mouth
just runs away from my brain."

Amanda let out a mirthless chuckle. "It's
all right, Neva. You know you can speak
your mind with me. Just not with Mr. Bo.
Go on, then—what do you mean, the
things rich folks do?"

Neva glanced down at the old photographs, her eyes tracing the star pattern in the glass. "Well, ma'am, take this house, for instance. It's a beautiful place and all, but wouldn't you think it'd be better not to be right up on the golf course? Mr. Bo's had to replace that big front window three times in the last two years."

"It's status, Neva. The most expensive lots around the country club are those that overlook the fairway."

The housekeeper nodded. "I reckon so. Just seems to me status costs an awful lot in busted glass."

Amanda got up and went to put another log on the fire. "Neva, did I ever tell you where I came from?"

"No ma'am. I know your people are from Georgia. Never met any of them, though. They don't come to visit much, do they?"

"No, they don't. My mama and daddy are gone now, but even while they were alive, neither one of them ever set foot in this house. They divorced when I was fifteen, and both of them remarried. My daddy was a farmer."

Neva's eyes widened. "A *farmer*?"

"Yep. Grew peanuts in the red Georgia clay."

"My, my," Neva marveled. "Just like President Jimmy Carter."

"Not exactly," Amanda corrected. "He wasn't very good at it. We were always dirt poor. I think that's why my mama left—not the kind of life she wanted."

"I expect she'd be pretty proud of you, then, coming up to this, and all—" The housekeeper waved her hand, indicating the opulence of the house.

"I guess," Amanda murmured. "Only—"

"Only what, Miz Manda?" Neva prodded.

"Nothing," she said. "It's just that sometimes I feel so . . . so *old*."

"We're *all* getting old, Miz Manda," she said. "Nothing we can do about it—it's just the way of the world. But like my grandaddy used to say, 'Gettin' old don't seem so bad when you consider the alternative.' "

Amanda shrugged. "That's true, I suppose. But I don't even recognize myself in the mirror anymore. I used to be thin and blonde and—well, beautiful."

"You're still blonde," Neva ventured.

"*Natural* blonde, I mean," Amanda said archly.

Neva ignored this. "And you're still beautiful, too. Everybody says so. Mr. Bo thinks—"

"Mr. Bo thinks I ought to lose forty pounds. As if he hasn't gained twice that much in the thirty years we've been married."

Neva shook her head. "Seems to me a body can use a little extra padding to keep warm in these Minnesota winters. Besides, what's on the inside counts more than what's on the outside."

Amanda shook her head. "Not in my world, Neva. Not in my world."

"Then your world is just plain wrong." She suppressed a smile. "Lord have mercy. There goes my runaway mouth again."

"Maybe you're right." Amanda sighed. "I just wish—"

Neva waited for a minute, but Amanda never finished the thought. "Wish what?"

Amanda hesitated. She had said too much already. Bo had warned her time and again about spilling her guts to Neva. But who else could she talk to? Who else would listen? "Never mind," she said. "It's not important."

The moment of intimacy passed, and Neva was sharp enough to realize it. She fixed her eyes on the floor. "Yes ma'am. I'll be getting back to work, then." She turned to go.

"Neva?"

The housekeeper looked over her shoulder. "Ma'am?"

"I'd prefer that this conversation remain private, if you don't mind."

"Mr. Bo doesn't like you talking about the old days?" Neva asked with a sly grin.

"Let's just say he'd rather not revisit the past."

Neva nodded. "I got it. Not so proud of his own beginnings, is he?"

Amanda smiled. "His were worse than mine, if you want to know the truth. But let's keep that between us, all right?"

"I will, Miz Manda. Besides, I reckon football's as good as brains or money to get you to the top."

She turned and vanished from the room, leaving Amanda with the first good laugh she'd had in a month.

The mail was still sitting on the lamp table in the den when Amanda came downstairs after a long soak in the heart-shaped Jacuzzi tub. She picked it up and began to flip through it, then became distracted by the delicious scents of roasting beef and yeasty rolls emanating from the kitchen.

She tossed the pile back on the table, went into the hallway, and poked her head through the swinging doorway that led to the kitchen. "Everything going all right in here?"

Isabel pushed the roasting pan back into the oven, closed the door, and looked up. "Just fine," she said in a curt monotone. A tall, thin woman with a hawkish nose and bright, beady eyes, the cook bore a striking resemblance to the Wicked Witch of the West, minus the green skin and prominent wart. Amanda was a little afraid of her.

Still, she was the mistress of this house, and she should have the fortitude not to be intimidated by an employee. She went to the stove and lifted a lid on one of the pots. "Can I do anything to help?"

The cook gave her a suspicious look. "No ma'am. Everything's under control. Dinner will be ready at six-thirty. As always."

"What's this?" Amanda sniffed at a double boiler containing something white and thick, picked up a spoon, and dabbled at it.

"Hollandaise. For the asparagus." Isabel snatched the pot lid and spoon out of Amanda's grasp. "Mrs. Tennyson, are you dissatisfied with my service to this house? Because if you are, I can always find other work."

"Of course not." Amanda backed away from the stove, panic rising in her throat. She couldn't afford to offend the cook. Bo would pitch a fit if Isabel left because of something Amanda had said or done. "I— I just—" she hesitated. "Well, a long time ago, when I was in college and living with three other girls, one of my friends tried to teach me to cook." She felt a hot flush rising up her neck. "I wasn't very good at it, I'm afraid. My roommate Liz thought my chicken casserole looked and tasted like tuna."

"Excuse me for saying so, Mrs. Tennyson, but my job is to cook, not to *teach* cooking."

"Oh, I wasn't asking you to teach me," Amanda said quickly. "I was just . . . making conversation." She retreated a step or two in the direction of the door. "How about if I set the table?"

Isabel cocked her head. "I believe that's Neva's job, and it's already been done."

"Well, then," Amanda whispered, "I'll just go make myself useful somewhere else."

"Yes ma'am," Isabel said, forcing a smile that on her looked more like a grimace. Amanda could almost see those terrible flying monkeys circling around her, could almost hear the woman screeching, *I'll get you, my pretty!*

She fled through the kitchen door and ran headlong into Neva, who was just coming in from the dining room.

Neva caught her by the shoulders before she fell. "Miz Manda, are you all right?" She cut a glance toward the kitchen door. "Best to leave Isabel alone when she's working," she warned.

"So I see." Amanda took a deep breath and tried to steady herself.

"She scares everybody," Neva soothed. "Me, I stay out of her way when I can."

Neva ushered her back into the den and settled her in a chair. "Can I get you anything, ma'am? Some tea, or coffee? Maybe a cup of hot chocolate?"

"What time is it? Four-thirty? That gives me an hour until Bo gets home and another thirty minutes after that before our guests arrive. Yes, I'll have time for hot chocolate." *And Bo won't catch me with it,* she thought but did not say.

"I'll get it for you. Take me just a minute or two."

She turned to go, but Amanda called her back. "Neva, are you happy?"

An expression of bewilderment passed over the woman's face. "Well, yes ma'am, I suppose I'm about as happy as any one person's got a right to be."

Amanda considered this answer for a moment. Neva Wilson was a housekeeper, a single mother who had raised three children on her own, supporting them by doing laundry and vacuuming carpets and scrubbing other people's toilets for a living. Bo paid her a decent wage, certainly, but working here had to remind her on a daily basis of all the things she'd never in a lifetime be able to afford. Her husband had

abandoned her years ago. She drove a battered old car and lived in a rented duplex.
And yet she claimed to be happy, hadn't
thought twice about her answer.

"Why?" Amanda asked.

"Why am I happy?" Neva shrugged.
"Why not? I pay my bills. I've got a sturdy
roof over my head and enough to eat. I've
got a steady job, working for nice folks—"
She grinned. "And besides all that, I've got
friends and family who love me, and children who'd make any mother proud." Her
face lit up. "Did you know my youngest
boy, Ajani, is in college now? Got a scholarship—to Howard University in Washington, D.C."

"A scholarship? That's commendable.
Playing basketball?"

Neva cut her eyes to one side. "No
ma'am. He's got an *academic* scholarship.
Full tuition and living expenses, all four
years. He's going to be a doctor."

Amanda, embarrassed by her assumption,
fell silent. She thought of her own children.
Bo Junior—B.J.—living in Europe somewhere. Maybe France now, she couldn't be
sure. He kept moving around, aimless,
writing or calling home only when he

needed his checking account replenished. And Carolyn, out on the West Coast ostensibly trying to become an actress, but mostly partying with other wanna-bes in the Malibu beach house Bo had bought for her as a graduation present.

"Miz Manda," Neva said after an uncomfortable silence, "why are you asking *me* about being happy?"

Amanda didn't respond. How long had it been, she wondered, since she had been truly content and fulfilled? All her adult life she had run the household and supervised the help, entertained her husband's clients and retreated into Junior League and charity projects. But now the kids had their own lives, and the charities had passed to other rich young wives.

She couldn't tell Neva what she had only recently begun to admit to herself—that she sometimes found herself longing for the old days, before Bo, before the wealth and prestige and status. Longing for Asheville, and that drafty little house on Barnard Street, and the friends who had loved her in spite of herself.

And until she had been left with an empty nest, with too much time on her

hands and nothing to give her life significance, she hadn't even noticed.

Amanda gazed over the long expanse of
snow-covered greens and fairways, a gently
rolling panorama that swept downhill to a
small lake in the distance. The snow had
stopped and the clouds had broken, and
now the setting sun filled the sky with pink
and purple and gold and washed the pristine landscape with pastel hues.

But her mind barely registered the
beauty of the snow-covered scene. She was
thinking of another snowy evening, of sliding down a hill in the dark on cardboard
packing boxes, of being pelted with snow-
balls, then changing into flannel pajamas
and sitting up half the night telling stories
around a small gas fire.

She had drunk hot chocolate that night,
too, she remembered. Not this instant low-
fat, low-calorie stuff you microwave in a
cup of water, but real cocoa, cooked in a
pan on the stove, with powdered chocolate
and whole milk and too much sugar. She
hadn't worried about her figure back then.

She hadn't worried about much of anything.

But that had been—what, thirty years ago?

And now, like a ghost from the past, this letter.

The last of the twilight was fading, and the familiar handwriting blurred on the page. Amanda fished her reading glasses out of the drawer, turned on the desk lamp, and held the letter to the light.

Dear Lovey,
It's been a very long time since we've all seen each other. We've kept in touch over the years through the circle journal, but I never had a chance to get to any of the reunions. And so I'm writing to you—and to Liz and Tess—asking all of you to join me the second weekend of April for a few days in Asheville.

I know it's short notice, but surely you haven't forgotten how beautiful the Blue Ridge Mountains are in the springtime. The redbud trees and daffodils are already blooming, and the ornamental pear trees are coming out with their white blossoms.

There's color and life everywhere. I want to share it with the three of you.

Here's what I have in mind—Friday through Monday at the Grove Park Inn. I've reserved two adjoining suites, and made reservations for a massage and spa treatment for all of us on Saturday morning. I'll take care of everything except your flights, and if anybody can't manage a plane ticket, I'll pay for that too.

I really want us all to be together again. I have something important to talk to all of you about, but I need to do it face-to-face and not through letters or phone calls.

Please come. Please.

Love,
Grace

"Lovey, is it?" said Bo over her shoulder. "Nobody's called you that silly nickname in years. Who's this from?" He snatched the letter out of her hands and began to read.

"Bo, give it back!" She stood and reached for it, but he held it over his head, an infantile game of keep-away.

He scanned the letter, then thrust it back into her hands and frowned down at her.

"Grace? That moralistic prude you lived with in college?"

"She wasn't a prude. She was just—well, idealistic. Fervent."

"She was an idiot. Don't you remember how she gave you holy hell about having sex with me?"

Amanda glared up at him. "Well, she certainly wouldn't have to worry about that issue *now*, would she?"

His face went white, then red, and he ran a finger around his collar as if the neckband were too tight. "Dammit, Amanda, don't start with me. This is not *my* problem." His eyes slid over her ample form, and a poorly disguised expression of disgust skittered across his face. "We've got company coming in"—he checked his watch—"fifteen minutes." He adjusted his tie, retucked his shirt, and pulled his belt up under his bulging belly. "You're not going to wear *that*, are you?"

Amanda looked down at the silky black-and-white blouse over flowing black evening pants. She had chosen the outfit because she thought he liked it—simple at-home elegance, not too formal. "What's wrong with it?"

"It makes you look dumpy. These are important clients, Amanda. High-class people. Go change into something more appropriate, will you? I'll mix the martinis."

Amanda sighed and started toward the stairs.

"And one more thing," he called over his shoulder as he opened the bar cabinets and began to set out crystal stemware. "You can forget about going to Asheville to be with those old college pals of yours. A couple of them came here once, and that was enough. They're—"

She turned. "They're what, Bo? Not our kind of people?"

"Exactly." He opened the bar fridge and peered in. "Where are the olives? And the cocktail onions? Don't tell me we're out of cocktail onions."

Nobody can tell you anything, Bo Tennyson, Amanda thought. But she didn't dare say it out loud.

Then, with Grace Benedict's invitation still clutched in her hand, she went upstairs to change.

THE CHEERLEADER

On Monday morning Amanda lay in bed and pretended to be asleep while Bo showered, dressed, and packed for a week-long business trip. This time it was a sweep of the Big Bo's Sports Gear franchises in northern Minnesota—Duluth, Hibbing, Bemidji, and Moorhead.

College draft prospects aside, Bo Tennyson's professional football career hadn't exactly turned out to be the stuff of legend. For a year and a half he had warmed the bench and paced the sidelines at the old Met Stadium, until his big chance arrived one memorable game during his second season. Injuries to the first- and second-string receivers forced Coach Grant to put him in during the fourth quarter. He dropped the first pass and was penalized for offensive interference on the second. And then, on third and long, a miracle happened—the unknown tight end from North Carolina made a spectacular catch in the last thirty seconds of the game, leaping over three defenders and across the goal line for a game-winning touchdown.

It was a career-making moment. Fans in the stadium snatched up discarded programs, desperately trying to connect his number with his name, then sprang to their feet, screaming, "BO! BO! BO!"

If he had just left well enough alone . . .

But he didn't. When the play was over, he caught sight of the TV cameras in the end zone and couldn't resist grabbing a little more airtime. Grinning hugely, he attempted an ill-conceived vault into the stands, fell back onto the field, and shattered his tailbone on the frozen turf. If he'd made it, the move might have gone down in sports history not as the Lambeau Leap, but the Tennyson Leap, or the Old Met Leap. Instead, in the ultimate indignity, the late-season hero found himself cradling his tight end in a donut pillow and watching on television as his team won the NFC playoffs and lost the Super Bowl.

After two unsuccessful operations, the surgeons fused his three lower vertebrae and sent him home, his football career officially over. He couldn't even sit on the bench anymore. The Vikings paid out his contract and let him go.

But if Bo had turned out to be a bad investment for the Vikings, the Vikings had turned out to be a very good investment for Bo. He had parlayed his contract payoff and his short-lived fame into a multi-million-dollar business. Minnesotans were insane about their Vikings; they would drive a hundred miles to get an autograph even from a washed-up rookie who had played only a few minutes of one quarter in his entire career.

His looks didn't hurt, either. His blond hair, handsome face, and boyish grin made for great ad copy. Never mind that he was from a poverty-stricken backwater town on the Outer Banks, he *looked* Norwegian. He'd even dropped his southern accent and taken to saying "Uff da" and "You betcha." And if the twenty-foot photograph on the billboards went back ten years or more, nobody seemed to care. The old charm still worked its magic. He was Big Bo, and everyone adored him.

Bo Tennyson was no longer a tight end. Or a tight stomach or anything else tight, for that matter, Amanda reflected. The gorgeous muscular hunk she had fallen in love with had been absorbed into an overweight type-A businessman whose primary concern was making money—tons of it—and perpetuating the myth of genial Big Bo.

Still feigning sleep, Amanda watched through slitted eyelids as he closed his suitcase, struggled into his tweed sport coat, and left the bedroom, shutting the door behind him. She listened as he lumbered down the stairs. When at last she heard the faint whine of the garage door opening and his Lexus SUV pulling out of the driveway, she sat up, reached into the drawer of the bedside table, and pulled out Grace Benedict's letter.

Unaccustomed as she was to analyzing her own emotions, Amanda had difficulty discerning exactly what sensations the letter brought up in her. Longing, certainly, for the friendships of those college days. Curiosity, as to what was so important in Grace's life that she would pay for a week-end at the Grove Park to get the four of them together once more.

There were other feelings, too. Anger at Bo for his contemptuous mockery of the long-abandoned nickname Lovey. Rebellion over his declaration that she absolutely would not be going to this reunion, that her old friends were not "their kind of people." And underneath those surface impressions, a deep-seated dread at the idea of seeing them all again.

But why should she, of all people, be afraid? She was Amanda Love Tennyson, wife of Big Bo. She had a half-million-dollar house with a million-dollar view of the golf course and lake. Two beautiful—if spoiled—grown children. A housekeeper, cook, and gardener. More money than she'd ever be able to spend in three life-times. What did she have to be ashamed of?

The answer came to her in Neva Wilson's simple response to the question "Are you happy?" Amanda had everything she always thought she wanted, and nothing her soul really needed. She was lonely.

Empty. Friendless, unless you counted the Stepford wives who accompanied her husband's business associates to dinner.

And Neva.

She'd never really thought of Neva as a friend, but the housekeeper was the kind of person Amanda could talk to. The woman never missed a thing, and despite the fact that they lived in totally different worlds, Amanda was certain that Neva understood what it was like to occupy this house and be Mrs. Big Bo. Understood, and sympathized.

Why, she wondered, had the very fulfillment of all her dreams betrayed her so cruelly? Amanda didn't know. But for once she wasn't going to ignore her own instincts. She was going to find out what was missing, no matter what.

The psychiatrist's office was warm and comfortable, a cherry-paneled room with a desk in one corner and massive bookshelves on either side of a brick fireplace. Gas logs flickered in the grate, giving off little heat but plenty of atmosphere. While she waited for the counselor, Amanda leaned back in the leather armchair and stared into the flames. The effect was calming, almost hypnotic. No wonder people so readily bared their souls in a place like this, and paid a hundred dollars an hour for the privilege.

It wasn't the first time she had been to a psychiatrist, of course. Over the years she had seen two or three counselors in town, mostly on the recommendation of other Junior Leaguers. But her sessions had produced little in the way of fruitful insight, invariably resulting in a diagnosis of depression and a six-month prescription for the antidepressant du jour.

Trazodone. Elavil. Serzone. Prozac. She rehearsed the list in her mind, feeling the rhythms of the words: *TRA-zo-done, EL-a-vil, SER-zone, PRO-zac, rah . . . rah . . . RAH!*

The dowager's cheer, Amanda thought glumly. The team chant for bored, rich, past-their-prime women who have nothing more productive to occupy their time and attention.

When she was younger, she had made

fun of them, those gaggles of clucking hens, all dressed by Bob Mackey and Liz Claiborne, all with hair dyed exactly the same color blonde. She would see them gathered around a corner table at the country club, lunching on salads and discussing their latest discoveries in hairdressers and manicurists and shrinks. Now she was one of them. Fifty-something and going to seed, desperately clutching to the last remnants of her youth and vitality.

The door opened, and a man entered the office and crossed over to the desk—a big, jovial-looking man with curly gray hair and a ruddy complexion. This must be Jonathan Whitestone, Amanda thought. She had heard of him by reputation but never met him in person before. And now that she had seen him, she was gripped by an unaccountable urge to run for the door. He reminded her of her husband's business associates, all of them, morphed into a single seething mass of masculinity. She could feel the air around her teeming with testosterone. How could a man like this—or any man, for that matter—possibly understand a woman's angst?

He closed the file folder on his desk,

swiveled his chair in her direction, and rose to shake her hand. "Mrs. Tennyson, is it? All right if I call you Amanda? I'm John. Lucky break, what, having a cancellation when you called?"

She stared at him. He had the oddest voice—not a low, powerful baritone, as she had expected, but a bright tenor, with a bit of the Brit around the edges. His eyes creased at the corners when he smiled, and his two front teeth were crooked.

A leprechaun, she thought suddenly. *I'm going to be psychoanalyzed by a leprechaun.*

He gave a short bark of a laugh, seated himself again, and pulled his rolling desk chair close up in front of Amanda. "Now then, let's get to it, right? Comfortable? You'd not rather have the couch? No? Pinch of the stereotype in that, eh?"

Amanda gazed at him. She opened her mouth to speak, and shocked herself by what came out. "Are you—*Irish*?"

He laughed again. "Lord, no, lovey. Aussie by birth. Come from Queensland, near Longreach. My ancestors were sheep farmers, but in the last twenty years or so they've taken to raising ostriches. Delicious meat, ostrich, but bloody cantankerous birds they can be—"

He stopped and cocked his head, peering at her. "I see tears, lovey. Clearly I've said something that's struck a nerve."

Amanda blinked and bit her lip. "You called me . . . lovey."

"Just an expression," he said. "My granny used to call everyone lovey, and I suppose I picked up the habit from her." He propped his hands on his knees. "Does that mean something to you?"

"My maiden name was Love. Amanda Love. In high school and college, all my friends called me Lovey."

"Ah. And so the name brings back some memories, does it?"

"Not just the name. Other things. A letter—I received a letter yesterday from an old friend. One of my best friends, actually. Four of us shared a house together during college, and we've kept in touch over the years. Occasionally we'd get together—all except Grace, this friend who wrote the letter, who never came to any of the reunions. But we haven't seen each other in almost fifteen years. And now out of the blue Grace has invited us—all of us who lived together—for a kind of reunion. Says she has something she needs to talk with us about. In person. It sounds important." Amanda dug in her bag. "You can read it if you like."

He waved the offer aside. "It's more important what the letter says to you than what it might say to me. How do you feel about the prospect of seeing these friends again?"

"I have mixed feelings. I want to go, in a way. But in another way, I'm reluctant."

"Reluctant?"

"Afraid." She looked into his eyes. "Terrified."

"Why would you be terrified to see old friends? Did you have a falling-out with them? Some rift that needs to be mended?"

"No." Amanda shook her head. "It's just that the last time I saw them—the other two, not Grace—I was caught up in raising kids and doing charity work. And now I'm older, and those things are past, and I'm not—" She could feel his eyes boring into her, and she faltered.

"Go on," he urged quietly. "Say whatever it is that's floating to the surface of your mind."

"I'm not what they expect me to be!" Amanda blurted out.

"Ah. And what *do* they expect of you?"

"I don't know. Sophisticated. Together." She paused. "Happy."

She anticipated the question: *Why aren't you happy?* It was what a psychiatrist ought to ask, after all—the natural segue into a discussion of her life and current woes.

But he didn't. Instead, he asked, "Why do they expect you to be happy?"

She hesitated. "Because—because I'm rich and secure and have everything I ever wanted."

"Yes. Indeed. You're Mrs. Big Bo."

Amanda gaped at him.

"Don't look so shocked, lovey. Everybody in Minnesota knows Big Bo Tennyson. But that's not the issue, now, is it? The real issue is—" He held out a hand, waiting for her to fill in the blank.

"I don't know."

"Sure you do. Don't think too hard. All the answers are inside you, just waiting to come out. The real issue is—"

"How I feel about myself?" She exhaled the tentative question.

John Whitestone grinned broadly, his eyes dancing. "Right you are. And how *do* you feel about yourself? What's the first descriptive word that comes to mind, without censorship?"

"Lost." The word popped out before Amanda could stop it. Tears stung at her eyes. "Blank. Void." She took a deep breath. "Abandoned."

He pounced, but gently. "Abandoned by whom?"

"By everyone. My husband. My children. I would say my friends, except I have no friends. I'm just—just a cheerleader."

John leaned forward. "What does that mean, a cheerleader?"

"It's what I was when I met Bo and fell in love with him. A cheerleader. Pretty good joke, right—the cheerleader and the football hero?" She paused, went purse-diving again, and extracted the broken picture frame, which she had brought along just in case she decided to replace it. "See?" She pointed. "Football hero. Cheerleader."

He cradled the photos in his hands and looked at them, giving particular attention to the smashed picture of the girl. "Throw this against a wall, did you?" He grinned.

Amanda frowned. "It fell off the table. It got broken by accident."

"Interesting. So tell me more about being a cheerleader," Whitestone prodded.

"That's all I've ever been. I've spent my life swishing imaginary pom-poms and doing the rah-rah number for other people. The Junior League. My children, though God knows they've turned out to be less than heroic. But mostly I've stayed on the sidelines, cheering for my husband."

"And yet you're much more than a cheerleader on the inside. You don't belong on the sidelines, do you?"

"Don't I?" She narrowed her eyes. "No, you're right. I *don't* belong on the sidelines. I *am* more than a cheerleader. I have much more to offer than that, even if my husband doesn't recognize it." She felt strength flowing out from her as she said the words, and then returning to her again as she heard them.

He nodded. "And who in your life has recognized that you have more to offer?"

Amanda swallowed against the rising lump in her throat. "My friends from college," she whispered, fingering the letter still clutched in her hand. "Tess and Liz and Grace."

"And yet you're afraid to come clean with them, to let them get acquainted with the woman you've become."

"I don't even *know* what I've become— or how I got this way," she said.

"Then tell me about it, and we'll figure it out together."

She went on talking, rambling about Bo and the kids and her life up to this point. Before she realized it, the hour had slipped away.

"Just talking about it helps a little," she concluded. "But I still don't seem to have any direction."

"Then perhaps we have a little home-work to do," he said. "I'd like to suggest that you spend some time this week evaluating where you are and where you've come from. Start by creating a time line of your life, identifying the important changes and emotional turning points in your life. And in the meantime, think about whether you really want to miss a chance at this reunion with your old friends."

"I can think about it, but it won't do me

any good. Bo's already decided I'm not going."

John leaned back in his chair and folded his arms. "Has he, now?"

Amanda smiled. "Or so he thinks. But maybe I'll have something to say about that, too."

"Could be." He slid the chair over to his desk and opened his appointment book. "Next week? How about Monday?"

"You're going to see me again? You're not just going to give me a prescription for antidepressants and send me on my way?"

He turned and grinned, showing his crow's feet and crooked teeth. "I'm all for better living through chemistry, lovey. But there's something to be said for lancing the boil instead of merely slapping a Band-Aid over the top. It's not always pleasant, of course, not a day in the country, so to speak. But the process has its merits. Are you game to try?"

"Yes, I am," Amanda said.

"Monday at eleven, then." He stood up and ushered her toward the door. "Take care, Lovey."

Lovey. This time he had used it not as a catch phrase, but as a name. Her name.

She walked back to her car with a warmth spreading through her despite the spring chill. It felt like a promise. Like crocuses under the snow.

Like hope.

17

LIFELINE

*A*manda sat on the sofa in the den with the small oak desk from the bay window pulled up in front of her. A fire blazed in the grate, and papers were spread out all over the desktop. For once she was glad that Bo was gone for the week. She had a lot to do, and couldn't stand the thought of him breathing down her neck and hovering over her shoulder, asking questions.

Her mind flitted around an unspoken truth. Being grateful that Bo was out of her hair wasn't a one-time feeling. She often felt that way, if she were honest enough to admit it—relieved to be rid of him for a while, as if a burden had lifted off her back the moment he walked out the door.

But a woman shouldn't feel that way about her husband of thirty years.

She pushed the internal reprimand aside. John Whitestone had made it very clear that Amanda's job was not to give in to the "shoulds," but to deal with the actual emotions that came to the surface, without placing a value judgment on them. *Don't should on yourself* was the way he put it.

All right, she'd simply say it—or at least *think* it—straight out. She was glad Bo was gone. His presence gave her the sense of being hemmed in. Claustrophobic. She loved him, but still . . .

She shook her head. This was very confusing. She *did* love Bo—at least she loved the man he had once been, in the early years before they were married. Before he became obscenely wealthy and famous, when he was still a bench-warming rookie. And even after the Vikings cut him, during his surgery and recovery, and when he was trying to get his business off the ground. He had needed her in those days, had reached out for her.

Or had he? Amanda considered the question but had no answer. Now that she thought about it, the past thirty years with

Bo seemed hazy and distorted, as if hidden behind a translucent curtain.

Had he ever really needed her? Or had she rewritten their history in her mind, desperate to hang on to something, even a fabrication of her imagination? Even an outright lie?

And if he had needed her, what, exactly, had he needed? Was it mostly sex, a warm body in the bed next to him? An ornament for his arm, a trophy to adorn his life and advance his business? Someone to lavish him with consolation and support? Now that she was looking at their relationship with a more critical eye, she wondered: Had there ever been even the tiniest measure of support and encouragement coming her way?

Amanda couldn't quite recall when things had changed between them. She jotted down the questions on a scrap of paper and put it aside. She'd deal with that later. Maybe things would come clearer as she got the rest of her life in order.

Her session with John Whitestone had, apparently, pierced the top crust of a seething volcano of emotions. For three decades a cauldron had been heating up inside her, contained but malevolent, gathering strength in its dormancy. Now it threatened to annihilate every one of her illusions with a single eruption. She could almost feel the searing burn from the red-hot lava flow.

John had spoken of lancing a boil, yet this was much more than an annoying but benign lesion of the heart. This was a deep abscess, whose poison ran through her veins and into every crevice of her soul. At last the top layer had been cut away, and she had no idea how to scab it over again. Or even if she wanted to.

She rearranged the papers on the desk and stared down at them. This exercise felt a little pretentious, creating a time line of her own life, and she had little experience with introspection. Still, she was convinced that there was something important here, if only she could get to it.

She had worked with historical time lines once or twice during her college days, and she cast her mind back thirty years to try to remember how. It was pretty simple really—a chronological chart of important dates and events, an attempt to get the big picture. Plus, for her purposes, a notation of the emotional significance of the moment. She already had the beginnings of her personal time line in place:

1951. June 5—birth.

1957. Age six. Mama and Daddy had a big fight, ruining my birthday party and embarrassing me in front of my friends. My first conscious realization that their marriage might be in trouble. Don't recall what the argument was about, only my humiliation and anger.

1961. Age ten. Mama permed my hair. For six months I looked like I had stuck my finger in a light socket. Kids at school jeered at me and called me Bush Head and Bride of Frankenstein. Seems like this might have been the first time I determined I wanted to be beautiful so no one could ever ridicule me again.

1966. The year my parents divorced. Hated the fact that they split up, but was glad for a break from the tension and fighting. Stayed with Daddy because I thought he needed me more than Mama did. Cooked (or tried to), did laundry and kept the house, and swore someday I'd marry a man who had prospects, somebody who would take care of me instead.

1967. Spring term. Had Miss Parvin for English class. She invited me to her house, helped me learn how to do my hair and makeup. She was the first person who ever told me I was attractive, and the first person I really opened up to about my pain over my parents' divorce.

1967. Fall term. Tried out for cheerleader, and made it. Finally part of the "in" crowd.

1968. Age seventeen. Spring term. Billy Corcoran asked me to the Junior Prom. All the girls worshipped him—he was the quarterback on the football team—but I got him. My

first boyfriend, maybe my first love.
We made out a lot, but didn't have
sex.

1968–69. Senior year. Went steady
with Billy. He was crowned
Homecoming King, and I was
Queen. Billy rented a hotel room and
sneaked in a six-pack. We fooled
around, but when he told me he was
going to Notre Dame for college, I
cried and ruined everything.

Amanda balked. Now that she looked at
them on paper, the events of her early life
seemed shallow and superficial rather than
significant. Yet she pressed on. If John
Whitestone believed this exercise would
help her, she was willing to give it a try.

1969. Fall. Began college at UNCA.
Lots of dates but no real friends. Girls
didn't like me. Made the cheerleading
squad. Dr. Wall's Philosophy class and
the project on Pilate's Question.
Teamed up with Tess and Liz and
Grace.

1970. January. Found the little house on Barnard Street and began living there together. The snowstorm when Grace's father was killed.

1970. Summer. Met Bo and fell in love with him. Finally lost my virginity. The terrible scene with Grace when the two of us locked horns over the issue of me sleeping with Bo.

Amanda recalled her anger that night—the hot metallic taste in her mouth, the burning outrage in her soul. She had been so furious with Grace, so utterly offended that Grace would have the nerve to question her. And yet . . .

She stared into the fireplace, watching the flames shift and dance.

Was it possible—even conceivable—that Grace had been right all along?

If memory was carried in the blood, Amanda had slit a vein.

Perhaps this was exactly what John

Whitestone had in mind when he gave her the assignment. Creating the time line was only a catalyst, like browsing through old photograph albums and reminiscing. The memories flooded out, pulsing and spurting everywhere. Except there was little nostalgia where Bo was concerned.

The bitter truth was that almost from the beginning things had begun to go sour. Once the rice was thrown and the limousine pulled away from the curb, the charm and romance and passion Bo had exuded during their dating and engagement seemed to vanish. All that was left was the drinking and the sex and the interminable repetitions of football glory stories.

Even on their honeymoon in the Virgin Islands—an ironic choice of destinations, Amanda mused—Bo spent most of his time at the beachfront bar with his back to the blue Caribbean, slugging down drinks and regaling other patrons with tales of his college conquests on the gridiron and the fame that awaited him with the Minnesota Vikings.

Everyone was impressed, of course, with the handsome young jock and his stunning blonde wife. Bo was a celebrity—at least a star in the making—and people wanted to be with him. Night after night, for the full two weeks of their trip, they dined with a succession of self-important businessmen and their doting wives. Champagne and bourbon flowed like water, enough to float the massive cruise ships that sat anchored in the harbor.

And then, if Bo was not too drunk to persuade his little soldier to stand at attention, they would retire to their oceanfront suite for ten minutes of sweaty, frantic coupling, after which he would drop into a coma spread-eagled across the bed.

Now that the curtain had been pulled aside, Amanda could remember every detail of that honeymoon. How she went shopping and sightseeing on her own. How she was forced to fend off advances from men on the beach who, oblivious to the wedding ring, homed in like vultures to a lone beauty in a black bikini. How she nearly drowned in an undertow and finally made her way exhausted and gasping to the sand without anyone noticing.

And how, every night after he thought she was asleep, Bo would get up and study the thick Vikings playbook while she lay listening to the crashing surf on the beach below, unsatisfied and unfulfilled.

That honeymoon, which should have been the most romantic, most exciting two weeks of Amanda's life, had set a pattern for the years to come. Bo in the spotlight, at the center of the universe, while everyone else revolved around him, caught in his gravitational pull.

All her life, Amanda realized, she had been drowning. Sucked down into the vortex of her husband's ego. She might have abandoned the marriage long ago, but then Bo Junior and Carolyn came along, demanding and needy and draining her of both the motivation and the means to leave. And by the time they were grown, well, she had become accustomed to the relative ease Bo's money could buy.

An ease of lifestyle, at least. But not an ease of the heart.

The awareness brought a sense of liberation to her soul, but it also unnerved her. How many years had she wasted in the backwash of her husband's wake? She had gone where he wanted her to go, become what he wanted her to be. She had raised two spoiled, coddled children into spoiled, coddled adults, and felt ashamed to bear the name of Mother. Was it too late to redeem herself now, to find her own center, to do something important and significant with her life?

Amanda glanced back over the time line she had written. At the edge of the desk, a corner of Grace's letter stuck out from under the pages. She picked it up, inhaled the scent of ink and paper, and pressed it to her chest.

Somehow, she sensed, Grace's invitation had arrived at just the right moment. Amanda needed direction. She needed friends—even if they were friends she hadn't seen in years.

What might happen in the distant future, she had no clue. But she *would* go to Asheville for this reunion with Grace and Tess and Liz. She would defy Bo to his face if need be.

The letter was a lifeline, thrown out to her just as she was going down for the last time. She grabbed it and held on, and felt herself being pulled toward the surface.

Toward light and air. Toward the faces of people who had once loved her.

And toward a tomorrow that, even if uncertain, had to be better than yesterday or today.

18

THE THING AT THE
BOTTOM OF THE BOX

The following Monday, Amanda arrived at John Whitestone's office with a file folder tucked under her arm. All week she had worked on the time line, giving Neva and Isabel Wednesday and Thursday off, even preparing her own meals. Granted, what she ate was mostly leftovers she found in the huge stainless-steel refrigerator, and Isabel fumed and muttered about having her territory disturbed when she returned on Friday morning, but Amanda enjoyed the peace and quiet and the sense of solitary self-reliance.

By Friday afternoon she had compiled a six-page summary of her life, and had another fifteen pages or so of journaling. It had taken her most of one day to get the hang of the computer, but now everything was neatly printed, the floppy disk tucked safely away in her underwear drawer.

"Excellent, excellent," John said when she showed him the file. "I wish all my clients would take their counseling this seriously." He spent a few minutes perusing the time line, but did not, she noticed, read the journaling pages. "Tell me now, Lovey, what stands out most vividly to you about the emotional work you've done over the past week?" He handed the folder back to her.

Amanda thought for a moment. "The fact that I've been deluding myself for years. About my marriage. About my life."

John extended both hands, motioning for her to continue.

"I always believed that my family life was as good as it gets," she went on. "I made myself believe it because I couldn't imagine anything else."

"Not being married, you mean? Not having someone to take care of you?"

"That's part of it. Bo does take care of me. Lavishly." She paused. "He works hard.

He doesn't fool around. He comes home on time at night. He does drink too much, but—"

John crooked a smile and raised one eyebrow.

"Ah, I'm doing it again."

"Doing what?"

"Rationalizing, the way I've done for thirty years. The truth is, his drinking bothers me more than I'm willing to admit. I've raised the issue to him a time or two, but he always brushes my concern aside. Says it's part of the business, drinking with clients."

Amanda shook her head. "Anyway, I've spent years convincing myself that I should be grateful for what I've got. And I want to be grateful, I really do. But creating this time line and spending a week alone with my own thoughts and feelings—well, I realized that despite the money and the luxury, my life is pretty empty."

"Tell me about the emptiness."

She rubbed her forehead and frowned. "It doesn't make sense."

"Doesn't matter," he said. "Sometimes the sense comes later. Tell me anyway."

"All right." Amanda blew out a long

breath. "I've hidden it from myself, pushed it down, but when I was working on the time line and doing the journaling, I became aware that I've somehow lost myself. Not lost the person I was earlier in my life, but rather lost the woman I might have become if I had chosen a different path."

"Different from marrying your husband." It was not a question.

"Maybe. But I suspect the different path has to do not so much with externals, like who I married or what kind of lifestyle I live. Maybe it's simply that I've taken the easy way, not challenged myself to grow and develop."

"That's quite insightful."

"Thanks for the affirmation. But this process is hard as hell."

John grinned at her. "Indeed it is. Is it worth it?"

"I don't know yet," she answered honestly. "The jury's still out on that one. Why don't you guys just invent a pill that would make people feel better about themselves?"

He threw his head back and laughed. "Oh, Lovey, there are lots of those available. The problem is, most of them are illegal, and they can have some nasty side effects."

"So we just go on slogging through this swamp?"

"I'm afraid we do." He waved one hand. "Please, continue about the Road Not Taken."

Amanda gathered her thoughts. "Where was I? Oh, yeah. Taking the easy way. Well, creating the time line did exactly what you knew it would do—" She fiddled with the corner of the file folder and gave him a wry smile. "It started me thinking about everything—why I married Bo, what my life has been like. I remembered details that had been buried for years."

"Rather like opening Pandora's box, eh?"

"That's from mythology, right? I recognize the reference but don't know the details." Amanda sat back, surprised at this admission. Ordinarily, if she didn't know something, she just pretended and smiled and nodded. She would never ask, for fear of looking ignorant. And this, too, she acknowledged to John Whitestone.

"Pandora," he said in answer to her question, "was, in Greek mythology, the first woman, created from water and earth."

"Like Adam, only female."

"Exactly. The name Pandora means 'all-gifted,' for she had been endowed with many gifts—beauty, music, intelligence, the works. But there was, as always, a catch. Zeus, king of the gods, also gave her a box, which she was commanded not to open under any circumstance. Pandora's curiosity, however, got the best of her. She opened the box to see what was inside, and all the evils of the world escaped and spread over the earth."

Amanda leaned forward, fascinated. "I'm not religious, but I know enough to recognize this as a Garden of Eden story. The box is like the forbidden tree in the center of the Garden. And the woman is always to blame."

John smiled. "It does seem that way sometimes, doesn't it? And yet this story, unlike the Genesis tale, has a bit different ending. Pandora tried to close the box, but all its contents had escaped, save for one thing which lay at the bottom, underneath all the evils."

He stopped and leaned back in his chair. Amanda knew he was waiting for the question.

"What was in the bottom of the box, John?"

He crossed his arms and looked at her, and she felt as if he were gazing into the depths of her soul. "Hope," he said quietly. "After all the evils were unleashed, hope remained."

"Ah," she whispered. "And that's what this counseling process is like, isn't it? Letting all the dark things out of the box, to get to the hope at the bottom."

"I couldn't have said it better myself."

"So where do we find my hope?"

"Perhaps somewhere along that untraveled path. Tell me more about what you discovered when you opened your box."

Amanda bit her lip. "A lot of things I didn't want to face. From the very beginning, my marriage was a mess. I could blame Bo for everything—he's a very controlling man, not just with me and the kids, but with everyone. And his drinking has made it worse. He's got an ego a mile wide, and always has to be the center of attention. But—"

"But what?" John shifted in his chair and waited.

"But I let him do it. I didn't stand up to him. I didn't create my own life, I just allowed myself to be absorbed into his. What do you shrinks call it? Enabling?"

"Precisely," he said. "When one member of a family is dysfunctional, the whole family system regroups and adjusts to the dysfunction. Partly it has to do with comfort—it's just easier to survive without rocking the boat. Easier, but not healthier."

"The elephant in the living room."

John's eyebrows arched in surprise. "I see you've been reading."

"A little," she admitted. "But the image is all too familiar. I've been walking around in that elephant's shit for years." Amanda felt a little electric shock at the language that came out of her, and yet it felt honest. Cleansing. Like a deep breath of cool air after being underwater for too long.

"And now you've finally noticed the stink."

"Right. So what happens when someone in the family opens their eyes and sees a need to scoop up the crap and clean the carpet and chase the elephant back to the zoo?"

"All hell breaks loose," he said with a grim smile.

"Well, that's encouraging."

"For a while," he amended. "It's never a simple matter, making changes in one's life. It's always a risk. But it's worth it."

"I'll have to trust you on that one," Amanda said. "So where do we start?"

"We've already started." He ran a hand through his hair. "Usually in situations like this I recommend individual counseling for both the husband and the wife, and additional couples counseling with both of them together."

"In situations like this?" Amanda repeated. "You've seen this before?"

"More times than I can count, Lovey. Do you think there's any chance Bo might be willing to enter into therapy for himself?"

"I doubt it. But that's not my primary concern at the moment."

"What is your concern?"

"Dealing with myself. Finding the hope in my box. Recovering the self I lost, the woman who never had a chance to exist."

"And how does that translate for you? What does that look like?"

"Not subjugating myself to my husband's expectations, for one," Amanda said. "But more than that—discovering something that will give my life meaning apart from my roles as wife and mother."

"So what would you like to work on between now and next Monday? Do you have anything specific in mind?"

She glanced at the clock; their time was almost up. "What do you suggest?"

He shrugged. "Going back to your time line, perhaps. Identifying moments in your life you might have omitted, times you *did* feel that sense of purpose and significance. Watching the way you interact with your husband this week."

"That sounds like a plan."

He got to his feet and opened the door for her. "Anything else you might think of?"

"Just one more thing—" Amanda gathered up her purse and the folder that held her journaling, and paused in the doorway. "Buying a ticket to Asheville for the second week in April."

In Another Life

Amanda was no writer, but once she had lifted the dam on her emotions and memories, she couldn't seem to stem the tide. She sat at the computer pounding out page after page, adding them to the ever-growing file now contained in a maroon three-ring binder.

Ruefully she looked over what she had written as the most recent pages slid out of the printer like multiple births from a mechanical womb. Tess, no doubt, would be horrified by her lack of organization, her spelling and punctuation errors, her sentence fragments. But she wasn't writing for publication; she was writing for herself.

Writing for her soul.

Writing for her life.

And when that writing might possibly unlock an invisible door to a better future, who could bother with spell-check?

She had, as John Whitestone had suggested, begun with her time line, picking through the events one by one, trying to identify the moments when she felt a sense of purpose, of significance. It was rather like sifting for uncut diamonds in a bin of shattered glass.

And ironically, the memories that warmed her most thoroughly were not the expected ones. Not her wedding day. Certainly not her honeymoon. Not the lavish cruises or the trips to Europe. Not the day she moved into her dream house. Not even, to her chagrin, the birth of her children.

Her fondest recollections went back thirty years, to that crowded little house on Barnard Street. To Tess and Liz and Grace.

I've never been quite sure what motivated me to invite those girls to come and live with me. We didn't know each other very well, actually. We'd only had just that one project together, the one from Philosophy class about Truth. But something happened that semester, something I never expected.

Tess and Liz and Grace seemed to care about me—not about some image I projected, not about the cheerleader or the Prom queen, but about ME.

We couldn't have been more different, the four of us. Tess the intellectual, the writer, the one who had poetry and storys running around in her head all the time. Liz the radical, with her hard edges and her thick bright armor. And Grace, who I called the moral compass, but sometimes she seemed more like the morality <u>police</u>. I never did get that, really. I mean, I know she had her standards, but I couldn't figure out why she seemed so determined— driven, almost—to impose them on me. Still, even when we had our big middle-of-the-night blowout over me and Bo, I got the feeling she wasn't so much trying to control me as to protect me.

And as it turned out, maybe she wasn't so far off. She didn't get it right about Bo running around on me—not with women, anyway. But I guess there are lots of ways to be unfaithful. Bo's been making love to his bourbon and his business for years. Right under my nose.

I got off the track. Back to the girls.

I remember especially the time Grace's father died. Except for cleaning and cooking (well, <u>trying</u> to cook. I never mastered that one, did I?) and taking care of Daddy after the divorce, it was the only time in my life I can really say somebody needed me, that I had something important to offer. But there are different kinds of need—the kind that has to do with duty, and the kind that has to do with loving somebody. And with Grace it was the good kind of need, not Daddy's kind. She needed us—all of us—to support her and help her get through the shock and grief. And though I wasn't always sure I could do anything really to help, I was there, and I loved her.

It feels a little strange to be saying I loved Grace, but I did. I loved all of them. Not the romantic kind of love, but the family, belonging kind. We really were like sisters, the four of us. We fought and disagreed and sometimes got real snotty with each other, but we knew we'd be there for each other. We loved each other.

Sometimes I hate what this world has done to the word LOVE. You can love chocolate or pantyhose or somebody's shoes or a new hair color, but if you apply it to a person of the same sex who isn't kin to you, people look at you funny like you're queer or something. I guess I should say GAY, that's what they prefer to be called.

Anyhow, I don't think any of us ever said, "I love you" to the others, but we did. And I for one knew it—or at least I know it now. When I look back on those years in Asheville, I get the feeling that who I was then was the best of me, and my friends brought it out.

But why was I the best of me then? That's the question that has to do with significance and purpose. . . .

Amanda stared at the page. She had wandered a lot, that much was clear. But she had the sense that some important insight was circling around in her head and just wouldn't land long enough for her to examine it.

She let her mind drift back to the rental house, back to the night of the snowstorm. They had all told their stories that night. And when Tess had talked about her bishop father and her therapist mother, Amanda had known, almost instinctively, that Tess's problem with the church had to do with the fact that the Episcopal Church wouldn't ordain her mother—or any woman, for that matter.

"You're pretty insightful for a cheerleader," Tess had said.

When the memory came, Amanda pounced on it. Lots of people had applauded her for her body, her beauty, her grace and poise—all of which had been deliberately cultivated, created out of the sow's ear of a peanut farmer's daughter. No one had ever praised her for her insight, for her instinct. For her heart.

But Tess had. And John Whitestone had. He had said almost exactly the same thing, had called her therapy work "very insightful" and told her, "You're more than just a cheerleader. You don't belong on the sidelines."

Perhaps, in another life, she could have developed that instinct, honed her insight, and used it to help other people. Like John himself did. Well, maybe not as a psychiatrist, but something a little less ambitious.

She set the journaling pages aside, turned

back to the flashing cursor on the computer screen, and began attacking the keyboard again.

When I look back on that moment, it seems like such a small thing, a tiny flash of intuition, that caused me to say that to Tess about her mother. But it felt right, just as it felt right to support Grace when her father died in that horrible car crash.

And I remember wanting to do more. To sit and listen as Grace poured out her feelings. To be—what do I call it?—a presence. A loving presence. But when she came back after that summer at home with her mother, Grace didn't seem to want to talk about it much, and mostly when she did talk, it was Tess or Liz she confided in. I wonder why.

No, I KNOW why. It was because of Bo. I was so caught up in my infatuation with Bo that I couldn't set aside my own feelings to be sensitive to anyone else's. I was in LUV. I couldn't see past my own raging hormones or Bo's tight end. And so I failed my friends—especially Grace, who had to be having a terrible time coping.

But maybe it's not too late to change.

*Grace has invited us all to Asheville, and
said she has something important to talk to
us about. I'll be there, this time. I'll
REALLY be there—heart and soul and
mind. I'll listen, not just with my ears, but
with everything I've got. And if I have any
instinct or any insight left after all these
years, perhaps it can do somebody some
good rather than just laying around getting
flabby like an unused muscle.*

Amanda scrolled back up the page and
reread what she had written. That was it.
The answer she had been searching for. It
was far too late in life for her to entertain
fantasies of becoming a psychologist or a
social worker or some kind of professional.
But she didn't need a bunch of letters after
her name or an office or a sign on the door
to listen. She didn't need references to be a
friend—a real friend. All she needed was to
get out of the downward spiral of self-
involvement that had brought her to this
place.

All she needed was *heart.*

An image materialized in her mind from
out of nowhere—the Tin Man from *The
Wizard of Oz,* rusted solid from his own

tears and immobilized by years of disuse. He had needed a heart, too, and received it—without realizing what he'd gained—when he risked himself to help a friend find the Wizard and get back home again.

She recalled the Wizard's words at the end of the movie. Everything they needed—the Scarecrow's brain, the Tin Man's heart, the Lion's courage, the power for Dorothy to return to Kansas—all of it was within their grasp, discovered as they committed themselves to each other's welfare.

The whirlwind of being Mrs. Big Bo had snatched her up and transported her here, into a life that no longer seemed her own. Whether her husband acknowledged it or not, she already possessed a heart, a mind, a great reserve of courage. But how could she use them? Where were the ruby slippers that would take her home to her true self?

One thing she knew—this cheerleader role was not the real Amanda Love Tennyson.

In another life, she might have become an altogether different person, a person she could have been proud of. The idea was tantalizing, hanging like a golden apple just beyond her reach.

But there was no other life. Only the life she had chosen for herself—or the one that had been chosen for her.

WHERE THE HEART IS

*A*manda had tried to get the idea out of her mind, but it wouldn't go away.

Home. Home is where you start from, where you go back to when you've lost your way. Home is the place where you can show up unannounced and they'll always take you in, no questions asked.

There's no place like home.

But not for Amanda Love Tennyson.

For more than an hour, since Bo had left for work, she had wandered aimlessly through the house, touching the polished banisters, running her fingers over the custom furniture and designer window treatments. Compared to where she had come from, this place was a palace, a dream, the fulfillment of all her fantasies, even back to the days of her childhood on the farm. But nothing in this house, not a single vase or painting or sculpture or rug, reflected her personality. It was all too . . .

Too perfect.

It could burn to the ground tomorrow, and she would have lost nothing of herself.

A vague sense of emptiness burrowed a hole deep inside her, and she climbed the stairs to the second floor, went into her bedroom, and shut the door.

The room was so vast that even the king-size sleigh bed looked lost and dwarfed on the far wall. A thin veneer of morning sunlight lay translucent and golden over the handmade coverlet. The walls were painted in soothing tones of lavender and taupe, and the floor was thickly carpeted, so that her footsteps made not so much as a whisper of sound when she walked. She felt like a ghost, a spirit come back to haunt the place where she had died.

But a ghost couldn't possibly feel this heavy. Amanda crossed to the sitting area and sank into the velvet chaise next to the window, staring into the middle distance. It was a beautiful room, and yet it seemed foreign to her, like an expensive hotel suite, like a photo spread out of *Southern Living*.

Not like home.

Home. She rolled the word around on her tongue, sampling its bitterness. It tasted like mud and sweat and moldy, humid summers. Like a dungeon, locked and barred, devoid of sunlight and fresh air.

Mama had escaped. And like Mama, Amanda herself had spent most of her adult life trying to break free of the past, to put the poverty and want and shame behind her, to pull her roots out of the red Georgia clay and run like fire in the opposite direction.

She had run, all right. Straight into another cage.

A gilded cage, to be sure—plush and upholstered and furnished with all the luxuries that befitted a rare and expensive pet. But a cage nevertheless.

The past could not be called home. Nor could the present. Where, then? When?

Her eyes drifted to the tall armoire in the corner, its double doors concealing a large television set, VCR and DVD players, and a collection of tapes and books. She got up, sat down on the carpet, and opened the doors.

The bottom shelf was filled with photo-graph albums, all neatly arranged and chronologically organized. A life in pic-tures. Her life. Her memories.

She pulled out the first one and spread it out on her knees, leaning back against the armoire. It did not, like most early photo albums, contain baby pictures or shots of childhood activities. Amanda's life—at least the life represented here—began during her college years, at the house on Barnard Street.

The faded color photos from the sixties showed that her mental images of that time were amazingly accurate. There was the house, with its wide, smiling porch and lit-tle dormer eyes. Grace and Liz playing Frisbee in the front yard. Tess reading in the rocking chair. The four of them—taken by Grace's father the day they moved in, she thought—standing on the steps with their arms around each other. All the trees and bushes were bare, and the sky was a pewter color, so that it almost looked as if this photo had been shot with black-and-white film instead of color.

And then, when spring had come, a pic-ture of all of them standing in a semicircle around Grace's mama's shiny Cadillac convertible, green as the fresh leaves and new grass. This one was taken from the street, so that the blooming dogwood tree and the clusters of daffodils along the front walk made the dumpy little house seem almost charming.

How young they all looked! Amanda peered at her own smiling image. Blonde and lithe and willowy, the way she still remembered herself, the way she still, on rare occasions, felt. But not the image she saw in the mirror every day.

She turned a couple of pages. There they were again, at a table in a restaurant the evening after graduation. Kelsey's? No, Kelso's. A seafood place with a bridge in the middle of the foyer that arched over a shallow stream filled with lazy koi. The waiter, she recalled, had brought them a bottle of champagne and taken this picture while they toasted each other . . . and their friendship.

Now, this felt like home. Like belonging.

And on the opposite side of the page, a formal, posed portrait of herself and Bo. Their engagement photo.

Her heart lurched. He had been so very

handsome then. Lean and muscular and tan, with a strong jaw and a winning smile. Now the muscle had gone to fat and the jaw had dropped into heavy, sagging jowls, and everything she thought she had felt for him swirled in her mind like a vanishing spiral of smoke.

She closed the album and set it aside, going on to another. This one was mostly filled with pictures of Bo in his Vikings uniform. Toward the back she found a shot of him cutting the ribbon at the grand opening of the very first Big Bo sports store, and a few pictures of his grinning younger self staring down from billboards.

It was the third album that caught her up short.

Her babies. There was Carolyn, round and bald in her arms, red-faced and screaming her lungs out. And Bo hanging over the hospital bed, staring at his newborn daughter as if she were the most beautiful thing he had ever laid eyes on.

Amanda focused on his face, the expression of tenderness, of protective longing. This was not just a father, a sperm donor. This was a *daddy*.

And two years later, when B.J. came

along, a similar expression of joy and pride and an uncharacteristic softness around her husband's eyes. She remembered, almost to the minute, when the smiling nurse had taken this photograph. The day after his son was born, Bo had brought little Carolyn to the hospital to meet her new brother, and they had all crowded onto the bed, oohing and ahhing over his tiny toes and fingers.

She flipped the page, and her eyes began to sting.

These were the formal portraits of mother and daughter, mother and son. Soft and furred around the edges, like a dream. And in both pictures, a beautiful blonde young woman gazed down with wonder and awe at the miracle she held in her arms.

What had happened to those feelings? Not just Bo's but Amanda's as well? When had the children she carried and birthed become a nuisance, two spoiled, demanding voices clamoring for attention—

For love?

Amanda could not deny that Carolyn and B.J. had grown up to be self-centered, indulged, coddled adults. She had always blamed Bo, always accused him of controlling them with money, of buying their love—with toys at first, and later with clothes and cars and unlimited checking accounts. But in this moment she realized something else too—that spoiling his children might be the only way Bo knew to show his affection, to make up for the time he spent away from his family, building a business that would support them in luxury.

Certainly, his priorities had been in the wrong place. Amanda herself had never wanted more than a happy, comfortable family life. She hadn't longed for riches or status—only love and faithfulness. But perhaps Bo, coming from a past even poorer than her own, knew only one way to demonstrate love—by assuring that his wife and children would never want for anything.

Amanda looked back at the pictures of herself and her babies. She had failed them by letting those feelings of love slip away. By allowing Bo to give them whatever they wanted. By retreating into herself, into the misery she was only now, more than two decades later, beginning to acknowledge.

She thought of John Whitestone and smiled grimly. Next Monday she'd be sure to tell him how mental health wasn't all it was cracked up to be.

Amanda closed the album and cradled it in her arms like an infant, rocking back and forth as the tears began to fall. And as the salty wetness rose up and spilled over, something else welled up in her as well. The warmth. The love. The remembered feelings she thought were gone forever.

This was home. Not the house, not the money, not the status. Not the lifestyle, but the *life*.

And if she intended to be true to her vow—to be there with all her heart and soul and mind for the people she loved, to listen with everything she had—this was the place to start.

She only hoped it was not too late.

"Carolyn? Honey, it's me. It's your mother."

Amanda heard Carolyn's voice, groggy with sleep. "Mom? What time is it?"

"It's ten here. That makes it"—she did

some quick mental calculations—"eight, California time?"

"Eight o'clock. In the *morning*?"

"That's right. Were you asleep?"

"Yeah, uh—"

Amanda could hear rustling around. A click. A whoosh of air through the receiver as her daughter exhaled smoke from a cigarette.

"OK, I'm awake. Sorry about that. Late night last night." She cleared her throat. "Is something wrong?"

"Why should anything be wrong?"

Carolyn let out a hoarse laugh. "Mother, you never call unless there's an emergency. Is Dad all right?"

"Your father's fine. I'm fine. I just—" She hesitated. "I just wanted to talk, that's all. To find out what's going on with you. To tell you—" The words stuck in her throat. "To tell you I love you."

Silence and a faint static came over the line. Amanda felt her palm beginning to sweat. She shifted the receiver to the other ear.

"Yeah," Carolyn said. "Well. I'm, uh—I'm doing all right. Got an audition for a commercial tomorrow afternoon. And my agent is working on a friend of his to get me a small part in a soap. He thinks I've got a good shot at it."

"That's wonderful, honey," Amanda said. Even to her own ears, the words echoed hollow and false. She had always been adamantly opposed to her daughter's obsession with becoming a star. It was Bo who insisted on supporting her, letting her have her way.

But now that she thought about it, acting was probably the perfect profession for Carolyn. She had inherited natural blonde hair and striking looks from both sides of her genetic stream. She had Bo's drive, and a flair for the spotlight that no doubt came from her father as well. As a child, everything from a broken toy to a broken heart had been high drama for Amanda's eldest.

She took a deep breath and decided that the time had come to set her own apprehensions aside and try to be honest.

"Carolyn," she said, "I've been thinking about a lot of things lately, and I want you to know that I'm sorry for not supporting you the way a mother should. You're a beautiful, talented young woman, and you can do anything you set your mind to. If what you want is to be an actor, I'll not only accept that, but encourage it."

More silence. Then, "Mom, are you *sure* you're all right?"

"Of course. I'm perfectly fine. Why wouldn't I be?"

"I don't know. You just sound so . . . strange. Like somebody else." Carolyn let out a breath. "Have you been to the doctor lately?"

The humor of the situation suddenly struck home, and Amanda laughed. "Honey, I'm not dying. I simply needed to hear your voice, needed to say that I love you."

The words came easier the second time. Amanda felt lighter, as if she had shed that forty extra pounds overnight.

"Thanks, Mom. I—uh—I love you, too."

Amanda knew it was a response that issued from discomfort and confusion, but she didn't really mind. "Let us know how the auditions turn out," she said. "Oh, and by the way, do you happen to have your brother's phone number in France?"

"Yeah, I got it here somewhere." Amanda heard noises that sounded as if

Carolyn were rummaging in a drawer. "Here it is. He's in Paris now. I got a letter from him a few weeks back. Something about painting, I think he's taking lessons from some artist."

She listened as her daughter repeated the long string of numbers twice, jotting them down on a pad from the bedside table. "Thank you, honey. Keep in touch, all right?"

"All right. And, Mom—thanks for calling."

"Sorry I woke you. Take care. I love you."

"You too," Carolyn said, and hung up the phone.

Amanda lay back across the bed and gathered her strength and determination for a similar conversation with her son.

She had some very wide chasms to bridge. A few words of affirmation and a couple of I-love-yous wouldn't solve everything.

But at least it was a beginning.

PART III

Liz

Noble dreams,
like the ghosts of long-dead lovers,
haunt the soul's house,
refusing to be exorcised
by prayers or promises
or good intentions.

Nothing will drive them out
except a faithful heeding,
however late,
of the heart's true call.

GRACE'S GIFT

*L*iz Chandler sat on the sofa, pinching her lips together with the fingers of one hand. In the other she held a letter from Grace Benedict. An echo from the past. An invitation to come to Asheville.

"Liz, say yes. It'll be good for you," Serena said.

Liz looked up. Serena Marchand was a wise and perceptive woman, and Liz almost always heeded what she had to say. But this was different.

"Look, I've already done this. I've gotten together with them a couple of times over the years. But not this time. I'm not going, and that's the end of it."

"Ah. The final word from the queen of stubbornness." Serena paced across the liv-

ing room and back again, then sank down
next to Liz. She sat there silent for a moment or two.

"Let's talk about this," she said at last.

"There's nothing to talk about." Liz
looked away. She *was* being bullheaded,
and she knew it, but Serena couldn't understand—nobody could—why accepting
Grace's invitation was such an impossibility.

"Come on, Liz. Talk to me. Look at
me."

Liz relented, letting her eyes rest on the
face she knew so well. Serena was in her
early forties, ten years younger than Liz.
But she still looked like a college kid. She
could easily be mistaken for a country club
lifeguard or a cruise director. But the
youthful appearance was deceiving. Liz had
never met anyone quite as insightful as Serena, or as devoted to the people she cared
about. And Liz knew herself fortunate—
blessed, even—to be counted in that number. Despite herself, she smiled.

"That's better."

"You know I can't stay mad at you." Liz
shook her head. "And you take full advantage of it every chance you get."

"It's one of my most disarming charac-

teristics." Serena laughed. "I look trustworthy."

Liz rolled her eyes. "You *are* trustworthy.
That's what makes you such a good counselor. I just wish you wouldn't use your
shrink tricks on me so often."

"The joy of living with a psychologist."

"Joy? Funny, I thought it was a burden."

Serena grinned. "You're not fooling me
with these red herrings. Let's get back to
the subject." She extended her hands and
counted off a list on her fingers. "First, you
say you can't go to Asheville for this little
reunion because your caseload is too heavy.
But you can reschedule your individual
therapy sessions, and since we now have
four other very capable counselors in our
practice, someone else can take your
groups."

"I guess so."

"You know so."

"Yeah, well—"

"Second," Serena went on without waiting for Liz to finish her objection, "you say
the flights are expensive and connecting in
Atlanta is a hassle. You tend to forget I know
how much money you make, and a round
trip to Asheville isn't going to break you."

"But—"

"No buts. Let me finish. Third," she concluded victoriously, "you say you don't have any interest in seeing these friends of yours again. But I've heard you talk about them. Those relationships have been something special, and I know you're curious about what your friend Grace has to tell all of you. You want to go, admit it."

Liz reared back. "Oh, now you can read minds?"

"I can read yours. Your face, anyway. Your body language. Your eyes."

"All right." She exhaled heavily. "Part of me does want to go."

"Which part?" Serena asked with a glint in her eye. "The rational part, or the irrational?"

"I have no idea." Liz leaned her head against the sofa cushions and closed her eyes.

"Why are you making this so hard?" Serena's voice was quieter now, tugging at Liz's heart and mind, gently reeling her in. No wonder the woman was such a successful therapist.

Liz sighed. "The last time I saw them—

Tess and Lovey anyway, Grace wasn't there—I was in Memphis, working at the King center. A lot has changed since then."

"Yes, but you've kept in touch with them. You've written in the journal." Serena stopped suddenly and peered into Liz's face. "You *did* tell them about Tim, didn't you? They don't think you're still married?"

"No—I mean, yes." Liz wiped a hand over her eyes. "No, they don't think I'm still married. Yes, I told them about Tim—at least about the divorce."

"But you didn't tell them all of it."

"I couldn't find the words. I didn't know what to say. Or how to say it."

"You're a therapist, Liz. How would you advise a client in this situation?"

"I'd probably tell her exactly what you're trying to get me to say. That being honest about yourself is the only way to have a real relationship. That in order to love and be loved, you have to let yourself be known, and that involves the risk of being rejected. I'm aware of all that. But—"

"But what?"

"But I don't know them any longer," Liz said. "And they don't know me—not really. It's been so many years. A lot of water has gone over the dam."

"Water over the dam?" Serena let out a cynical chuckle. "Let's see, how many more clichés can we come up with? Time flies. Life goes on. No use crying over spilled milk. The old gray mare ain't what she used to be."

"Enough already." Liz flagged her to a halt. "One time, shortly after we moved into that little house near UNCA, the four of us had a long talk—about families, mostly. I remember telling them that love was just a chink in the armor, someplace to stick the knife in."

Serena smiled. "That's a charming image. I'm glad you've changed your perspective."

"Of course I have, but that's a different matter entirely. The first time I let my armor slip was with Tim, and if it hadn't been for you, I wouldn't have gotten through that experience in one piece. To this day I'd be clanking around in my chain mail, protecting myself from anything that might hurt me."

"Well, I'm glad to know I've been a positive influence." Serena squeezed Liz's shoulder. "Look, I'm aware that revisiting the past can be painful, and that the idea of seeing your friends again might be a little intimidating, but I still think—"

"I know what you think," Liz interrupted with a grin. "You've made yourself perfectly clear. I just need some time to evaluate the situation, all right?"

"Fine." Serena raised both hands in a gesture of surrender. "I won't say another word about it." She grinned. "Well, maybe one more. Or two. First, being honest about who you are is always difficult, and usually scary and painful. Don't run from the feelings, Liz. Grappling with this will make you a better therapist. And second, while you're thinking, think about this: What you've been given in this invitation from Grace is a gift."

"A gift?" Liz frowned. "What kind of gift?"

"The gift of a friendship that has endured for thirty years, for one thing. And for another, the opportunity to find out whether that friendship can hold up under the weight of truth."

Alone in the study after dinner, Liz thought about what Serena had said.

Much as she hated to admit it, Serena was right. She needed to do this. Needed to see Lovey and Tess and Grace again, to be honest with them about what her life had *really* been since the last time they'd been together. No one else knew what she had been through—no one except Serena. And although she could rationalize her reticence as privacy, she couldn't help recognizing the feeling. She had certainly seen it often enough in her clients, and even in herself: *shame.*

Her therapist's mind kicked into overdrive. The rational part of her brain told her she had nothing to be ashamed of, but somehow that affirmation didn't help. Her emotions were in the driver's seat, and her gut twisted into a knot at the prospect of trying to explain to Lovey and Tess and Grace—especially Grace—how she had come to be divorced.

Besides, all of *them* were happily married—Grace, of course, was widowed, but still she had, like the others, been a poster girl for emotional stability and family values. And although Liz had told them in the circle journal that her own marriage hadn't worked out, she had omitted a few crucial details.

Well, more than a few. To be honest, she had left out most of the details and almost all the pain.

It was one thing to write in the journal, to be able to think through what she was going to say and word it carefully. It was quite another matter to face them directly, when they could see the expression on her face and look into her eyes. If she went to this little reunion Grace had concocted, she was convinced they would know something wasn't right. Even after all these years.

And they were bound to ask questions.

REBEL WITHOUT A CAUSE

*A*ll the next day, as she listened to clients and facilitated group sessions, Liz couldn't seem to shake a shadowy sense of foreboding. Grace's invitation—what Serena called "the gift"—had stirred up unwelcome memories like algae at the bottom of a pool, and now her mind was clouded and confused. If she just kept quiet, maybe the muck would settle again, and she wouldn't have to face the issues that were floating to the surface.

She tried to tell herself what she told her patients—that you could, eventually, get beyond the pain and change the patterns. Still, the mind stored experiences in a kind of moving spiral, and when some unexpected event triggered the recollections, you needed to confront the situation head-on and deal with it again. Emotional health seemed to be a "three steps forward, two steps back" proposition. Revisiting old traumas didn't mean you weren't getting better—it simply meant that you weren't quite as finished as you thought.

Liz's last appointment of the afternoon—her three o'clock, an inflexible, unhappy woman who blamed her husband for her personal neuroses—had canceled. Serena wouldn't be done until five. They usually drove together unless one of them had an evening session, so Liz had a couple of hours to herself.

She ought to be typing notes or transcribing group session tapes or reviewing files for tomorrow's appointments, but instead she cleared her desk and sat listening to the faint noises that came through the walls and the closed door. The click of the secretary's computer keyboard, the ringing of the telephone, muffled voices from Serena's office next door.

She leaned back in the desk chair and shut her eyes, her mind still circling around the memories that had been haunting her all day. The paperwork could wait. She needed to figure out what she was really feeling about Grace's invitation, about her reluctance to return to Asheville, about the shame that had descended on her when she thought about making the trip and facing the three of them once more.

During graduate school, Liz had discovered that if she just centered herself and let her brain take the lead, confusing or disorganized ideas would eventually align themselves into some kind of order and bring her to the clarity of perspective she was seeking. It was rather like defragmenting a hard drive. She simply had to wait a bit, and the data files would shift around to where they belonged.

Faces floated behind her closed eyelids. Serena. The new therapists. Current clients, and past ones. Her roommates in Asheville. Tim. Voices echoed in her ears—snatches of conversations, comforting words, angry shouts.

The chaos began to take on an order, and then, as the fog began to dissipate, a series of memories pressed in upon her.

❧

Halfway through the joint fund-raiser for D.C. area nonprofit organizations, Liz caught a glimpse of him across the crowded hall—a tall, rangy man with sand-colored hair and a wide, winning smile. Young Clint Eastwood meets young Robert Redford.

Over a dozen heads he caught her eye, then grinned and nodded and began to thread his way through the mob in her direction.

Liz had never been a romantic. She had always shunned the idea of love at first sight—or love of *any* kind—as nothing more than juvenile fantasy, hormone infatuation. But at this moment, much to her chagrin, she could hear a faint echo in the back of her mind, a string quartet hidden in some distant alcove, playing a romantic interlude.

She shook her head sharply, and the music screeched to a stop, a needle sliding across a record's grooves. "Get a grip, Liz," she muttered under her breath.

But he was still coming toward her. Now she could see that his eyes were a clear pale blue, and that a smattering of freckles peppered the bridge of his nose. He closed the gap between them, smiled down at her, and won her heart with his very first words:

"Do you hate these gatherings as much as I do?"

Liz nodded mutely and felt his hand seize her elbow. She let herself be ushered out the double doors onto the deck, and sank down in a wrought-iron chair. The splendor of the city spread out before her—the lighted monuments, the clear, starry night overhead—and behind her, the babble of conversation, indistinct, like the gabble of geese on a lakeshore.

"Ah, that's better." He sank down in the chair next to her and leaned his elbows on the glass-topped patio table. "I'm Tim Delancy."

She shook his outstretched hand. "Liz Chandler."

"I know." He didn't let go. His grip was warm and strong and oddly familiar. Liz had a sudden rush of déjà-vu, the eerie feeling that she had been sitting there, holding hands with him, all her life.

"You know?" she parroted idiotically. "How—?"

"I do my homework," he said with a shrug. "You're maybe new to D.C., but as far as I can tell, you're the best thing that ever happened to this town."

"I wouldn't say—"

"Of course you wouldn't. That's what separates you from ninety percent of those do-gooders in there." He motioned with his head toward the party, still in full swing behind them. "Most of these people are here to salve their conscience with their checkbooks. I'm not complaining, mind you. Your work—and mine—couldn't go on without the guilty scruples of the Washington elite. I'll take their money without a qualm, and gladly. But we both know that money isn't the primary moving force of social justice. Passion is."

Liz gazed at him, mesmerized. Then she came to her senses and frowned.

"And exactly what do you know about my work?"

"Everything." He rested his chin in one hand. "I know that in college you majored in psychology and political science. That you worked with Coretta Scott King in Atlanta. That you've been arrested on several occasions for nonviolent protests. That you currently serve as crisis counselor and free therapist for the Sexual Violence and Domestic Abuse Center." He grinned slowly, seductively, revealing white teeth with one slightly overlapping incisor. "And that you probably don't have the faintest idea who I am or what I do."

Liz nodded slowly. A flush crept up her neck. "I'm sorry."

"No need to apologize." He waved her concern aside. "I'm currently working with the Fair Housing Council, but I'm getting ready to take on the directorship of a new program, the Hope House Coalition. It's an umbrella effort to coordinate a number of nonprofit organizations, to minimize duplication and consolidate services. We'll be overseeing the city's food banks and homeless shelters, and—if I can get the funding—starting up a new venture called the Payback Project, to help lower-income families buy homes without cash equity."

"It sounds wonderful," Liz said out loud, but her mind said: *He's wonderful.*

Tim smiled and drew his chair closer, as if he'd read her thoughts. He captured her hand again.

"It always strikes me as ironic," Liz said—babbling, she knew, but she couldn't seem to help herself—"how in this city, in the shadow of the wealthiest and most powerful government in the world, people still sleep under bridges and raid food from garbage cans. It's a travesty. A mockery of this nation's claims of equality and justice."

She sounded like an idiot. Silently she cursed herself, stumbled to a halt, and fought for air. He was so near, so close she couldn't breathe. Her mind was starved for oxygen, that was it. She was losing brain cells by the thousands. If only he wouldn't concentrate all his attention on her—

"Go out with me," he said in a whisper.

"Excuse me?"

"Go out with me," he repeated. "I want to get to know you better."

"When?" she said stupidly.

"Tonight. Tomorrow. The day after that. All the days of my life."

Six months later they were married at the Lincoln Memorial, on the steps where Martin Luther King had given his "I Have a Dream" speech, with the reflecting pool at their backs. The Great Emancipator gazed mutely down at them from his enormous chair, and—fanciful as it might seem—Liz almost felt him nod and smile, as if pronouncing a benediction on their union.

On the day she said *I do,* Liz was thirty-five years old. Never had she expected to marry a man like Tim Delancy—if truth be told, she had never expected to marry at all. Where most people had personal boundaries, Liz Chandler had counties, multiple square miles of private space separating her from others. She knew Tim loved her and she loved him—as much as she was able to love, anyway. And she respected him enormously, yet nevertheless it proved difficult for her to trust his love for her.

But he was gentle and compassionate and undemanding, both in the bedroom and out. Eventually she was able to tell him about her mother's desertion, and he held her while she wept over the betrayal. At last his tender declarations of love and commitment broke through her walls, and she gave herself to him, heart and soul and mind and body.

Even if she had been searching, she couldn't have found a more perfect life partner than Tim. He was exactly what she had been looking for all her life, without even knowing she was looking. A man of integrity and authenticity, intelligent and persuasive, generous and compassionate and . . . good. A man whose calling to equality and social justice equaled her own. Tim Delancy knew what he believed, and lived it, no matter what the cost.

Liz had never before understood, even theoretically, what a glory it could be to love completely and be loved in return, to be in harmony with another human being—spiritually, intellectually, emotionally. Under the warmth of Tim's affirmation and affection, she blossomed, a tight-budded rose finally opening its face to the sun. Her characteristic cynicism faded into the background, and she was happy, totally and unreservedly happy, for the first time in her life.

Liz soon discovered, however, that love and shared values were not enough to build a life together. She spent long and grueling hours at the abuse crisis center, a job whose rewards didn't show up in the monthly paycheck. Tim was working equally hard to get the Hope House Coalition off the

ground, and being paid a similar pittance—
what he jokingly referred to as "bringing
home the bacon bits." They were behind
on all their bills, eating macaroni and
cheese four nights a week, barely scraping
by. But the struggle was worth it for the
difference they were making.

Then the eviction notice came. They
were required to pay their back rent and a
month in advance, or in thirty days they'd
be out on the street. Liz checked their as-
sets: They had exactly two hundred sixty-
nine dollars and thirty-two cents in their
checking account. If something didn't
change—and soon—they were likely to
find themselves homeless and destitute, on
the receiving end of their own services.

"I have an idea," Tim said that night over
a dinner consisting of their last two cans of
clam chowder and a fifty-cent loaf of day-
old French bread. "It's a last resort, but I'm
afraid we're there."

"Let's hear it," Liz said. "I'm fresh out of
options."

"All right, here it is: If you were to
switch to private therapy, you could make
enough money to support both of us."

Liz let out a heavy breath. "Leave the abuse center?"

"I know private counseling isn't your idea of making a difference, but you'd still be contributing to the causes we're both passionate about—just not directly." He took her hand across the table and stroked it. "I'd do it, babe, but I don't have the salable skills you have. The only thing I'm trained to do is run a nonprofit agency."

Liz hated the idea of giving up nonprofit work for private practice, but something had to give. They couldn't go on this way. And so, with a sinking heart, she conceded. While he was out in the trenches, fighting for the rights of the poor and disenfranchised, she resigned her position at the sexual violence center and went to work at Brook Green of Virginia, an upscale counseling clinic, charging eighty dollars an hour to listen to the recurring neuroses of upper-class society matrons.

At first it was sheer torture. But her reputation as a therapist grew, and after a while Liz finally did attract some clients who genuinely needed her help. She began to feel a little better about herself once she was actually doing some good. And having a decent paycheck coming in was easy to get used to.

Still, being on the fringes of the battle against injustice gnawed at her. All her adult life she had been passionate about being a voice for those who had been silenced—the weak, the poor, the abused, the ostracized of society. Now she could only sit on the sidelines and applaud her husband's work. She was no longer part of the solution, simply the financing behind the solution. One of the do-gooders with a checkbook.

Her impotence galled her, but there wasn't much Liz could do about it. At Tim's insistence, they had bought a small arts and crafts bungalow in Arlington and were in the midst of renovations. It wasn't an opulent place by any means, but real estate in the D.C. area was obscenely expensive, and in addition to the mortgage, the plumbers and carpenters and electricians had to be paid. The bills kept coming in, and the expenses kept rising.

Liz felt trapped, and she chafed at the bit to get out of private practice and back into the fray again. But as time passed and the renovation costs were paid off, she grew to love the Arlington bungalow, the old neighborhood with its towering trees and safe sidewalks, the sounds of children playing in the park at the end of the street. She grew accustomed to being the primary breadwinner, rationalizing that she was, after all, contributing to the cause of social justice by supporting Tim in his work.

And eventually she no longer bothered with any rationalization at all. . . .

Liz paused in mid-thought, opened her eyes, and straightened up in her desk chair.

That was it—one part of it anyway. One of the reasons she was so reluctant to accept Grace's invitation and go to Asheville for her little reunion.

In her college days, and long afterward, she had been uncompromising about social issues. As Tim had noted the first night they met, she had protested the war in Vietnam, had put herself on the line for civil rights, had even been jailed a time or two for civil disobedience.

She had loved Gandhi, had read every

word he had written—some of it three or four times. She had been fervent about his principles of passive resistance. She had practically idolized Martin Luther King, and at one time had even declared herself willing to sacrifice her own life for the principles she believed in.

Instead, she had sacrificed the principles.

Not really, a voice inside her head argued. *The clinic operates on a sliding scale, and you do a good bit of pro bono counseling. You're still contributing, just not in the same way you once were.*

It was true, all of it. She still cared, still did what she could. But what a pittance it seemed in comparison to the all-consuming fire that once blazed in her veins.

And how would it look to Grace and Lovey and Tess, who had listened to her blustering about civil rights and the plight of the poor? They had bailed her out of jail, supported her as she tilted at windmills, even toasted her at graduation as the one among them who would change the world.

But the world hadn't changed. Prejudice and poverty, intolerance and injustice, violence and corruption and the abuse of power—all the evils that existed thirty years ago still blighted the emotional and political landscape. The System still prevailed, exploiting the weak and oppressing the outcast and bringing no solace to the helpless.

Her logical mind told her that there was only so much one person could do. And yet Liz still felt like a failure. The crusader who had copped out. A rebel without a cause.

A Meeting of Minds

A soft knock sounded on Liz's office door, and Serena poked her head in.

"You busy?"

"Not really. I was just doing some thinking." Liz arched her eyebrows. "Vastly overrated, the value of contemplation. Makes my head hurt."

"Take two aspirin and call me in the morning." Serena grinned. "My four o'clock's just arrived. I should be able to clear my desk by five-thirty or so. You want to go out for dinner?"

"That'd be great. I don't feel much like cooking."

"Me either. Let's go straight from work. Karin Buckley called in for an emergency session at noon, so I didn't get any lunch."

"What's the big crisis?"

Serena chuckled. "Her mother's coming to visit."

"Oh yeah, that definitely qualifies."

"I'll buzz you when I'm done. See you later." She shut the door behind her, and Liz listened as her footsteps receded down the hall.

All things considered, Serena Marchand was the best thing that had ever happened to her.

Four years after Liz went to work at Brook Green, the posh counseling center was pulling in so much new business that the practice branched out. Money flowed like the Potomac River at flood stage. The entire facility underwent extensive renovation, supervised by an eccentric and outrageously expensive decorator. Another suite of offices was added, and three new counselors hired.

One of them was a slim, dusky-skinned young woman, fresh from her Ph.D. program and newly licensed, looking like a teenager with her blue jeans and tennis shoes and spiky dark hair. The younger clients adored her, and by the end of her first six months she had become the resident—albeit unofficial—expert on neglected little rich kids, problem students referred by private school headmasters, and angst-ridden adolescents.

Her name was Serena Marchand, and as it turned out she was not quite as young and certainly not as inexperienced as she looked. She turned thirty the same week Liz hit forty, and in the break room, dividing up their shared birthday cake, she asked Liz to go out to dinner with her to celebrate.

"I've just moved to D.C. and don't have any friends here," Serena said bluntly. "And you seem like the best candidate."

Her candor took Liz off guard, and she accepted the invitation. Tim had another fund-raiser, anyway—he was rarely home for dinner these days—and Liz didn't even bother to leave him a message telling him where she'd be. She simply went, lightened by an unfamiliar sense of liberation, almost as if she were single again.

Their birthday dinner, at a Japanese

restaurant where the chef juggled razor-
sharp knives and cooked everything at a
grill built into the table, turned out to be
much more comfortable than Liz had anticipated. They talked nonstop about the
clinic, about problematic clients, about the
outrageous cost of mental health care and
how underprivileged people needed counseling, too. And they laughed—a lot.

"So what on earth is someone like you
doing at Brook Green?" Liz finally asked.
"Forgive me for saying so, but you just
don't seem the type."

Serena balanced a piece of grilled shrimp
between her chopsticks and waved it in
Liz's direction. "And what type am I, pray
tell?"

"Well—" Liz hesitated. "You seem much
too sensible, too grounded to be working
in such a classy place."

"So you don't think I'm classy?" She
feigned a wounded look and dropped the
shrimp into her teacup.

"I didn't mean it that way. I meant—"

Serena laughed. "I know what you
meant. I take it as a compliment, believe
me." She fished the shrimp out of the tea

with her fingers and popped it into her mouth. "Why am I at Brook Green? Two words: *educational debt.*"

"Ah." Liz nodded. "Not the scenario you painted for yourself in grad school, I take it."

"You got that right. Even therapists have to make enough money to live, but in my opinion it's unethical to cater to the rich and fleece people simply because the market will bear it. Seems to me that we also have an obligation to give something back. As soon as my school loans are paid off, what I'd really like to do is establish my own counseling center, with a sliding fee scale depending on the client's ability to pay."

"And with time built in to give free sessions to those who can't pay at all," Liz added.

"Absolutely."

"And none of this unnecessary opulence like custom-made furniture and expensive antiques." Liz was on a roll now, feeling that old fire surging through her veins. "I simply cannot justify investing that kind of money in decorating when those dollars would be better spent on client services."

"Exactly." Serena grinned, a sly, knowing look. "Now it's your turn."

"My turn for what?"

"To confess why *you* work at a place like Brook Green."

Liz ducked her head. "When my husband and I first met, we both worked for nonprofit agencies. I did crisis counseling and free therapy at the Sexual Violence and Domestic Abuse Center."

"Very noble."

"Not really," Liz said. "At least, I didn't think of it that way. It was emotionally exhausting work and very long hours, but I loved it. I felt like I was making a difference."

"So what happened?"

"Tim was trying to get his Hope House Coalition off the ground, and—"

"Tim Delancy? You're married to Tim Delancy?"

"Yes. You've heard of him?"

"Who hasn't? His face is in the news almost every day." Serena took a sip of her shrimp-flavored tea and grimaced. "But your name is Chandler."

Liz nodded. "I kept my maiden name

when we married. That's a rather nonfeminist construct, isn't it—one's *maiden* name."

Serena laughed and motioned her to continue.

"So, anyway, when Tim and I married, neither of us was making any money. That's all right when you're single, I guess, living in a studio apartment, driving a beater, and eating beans out of a can. But somehow being penniless didn't work so well for a couple trying to build a life." She paused. "When the eviction notice came, we gave in and decided one of us needed to get a real job."

"And you drew the short straw."

"Not really. It was a mutual decision." Liz said the words with conviction, but in her heart she knew better.

And so did Serena, apparently. "I find that hard to believe."

Oddly enough, the straightforward reply didn't offend Liz in the least. "Well, let's just say that I was the more marketable one. It's a temporary situation. I hope. Like your need to pay off your school debt."

"And if you could do things differently?"

Liz considered the question carefully before she responded. "I've just turned forty, you know. Right around the corner from my dotage. And so I think that at this point in my life, what I'd really want is to be part of a counseling center like the one you're describing."

"I was hoping you'd say that." Serena arched her eyebrows and held up a slice of mushroom. "Have you tasted the shiitakes? Take one. They're luscious."

Liz scooped up one of the dark rich mushrooms from Serena's plate. "Mmm, you're right," she said. "It's wonderful."

And unaccountably, an old memory pushed to the surface of her mind—that instant of recognition when she had held Tim's hand and thought, *He's wonderful.*

Because of her natural reserve, because of her history with her mother's abandonment, because of a hundred reasons she had articulated only to herself, Liz tended to keep to herself. In large groups, at parties, she always found herself withdrawing to the fringes, her eyes roaming the crowd to identify a familiar face, someone—anyone—she could talk shop with. A colleague, someone who worked with Tim, someone who could rescue her from the agony of small talk. These were acquaintances, people she regarded as casual friends. But since college, and those days with Tess and Lovey and Grace, she'd never really had a *best friend*.

In her mind she held a number of images for such a relationship. The person who would always welcome her company and make time for her. The person she could call if she had a crisis at four in the morning. The person who, in a room full of strangers and nodding acquaintances, would watch for her to come in the door and gesture her to a chair reserved especially for her.

And here she sat with Serena, talking and laughing as if they had known each other for years. It wasn't just the shiitake mushrooms that were wonderful. It was the connection that was taking place, the invisible cable that had begun to stretch between them.

They stayed in the restaurant until all the tables except theirs were empty. When the manager came by for the fourth time to ask if they wanted more tea, Liz glanced at her watch, and a little thrill of shock ran through her. They had been there nearly four hours.

Looking back on the evening, Liz wasn't quite certain how it had happened. Neither of them, to her recollection, had actually asked the question "Are we ready to commit to this?" But by the time they had paid their bill and walked out into the parking lot, the two of them had planned the counseling practice they would build together. They had discovered one another in a shared dream, in common values. They had drawn together, not just in a meeting of minds, but in a merging of souls.

They had become . . . friends. Best friends.

And Liz, for her part, had experienced a renewal of something she thought she had lost forever.

A sense of passion.

24

TIM'S SECRET

"*W*hen hell freezes over," Tim said when she broached the idea to him.

Liz felt her hackles rise. "What kind of response is that—'When hell freezes over'? I'm not a child, Tim, that you can lay down the law to me and expect me to just roll over and take it. I'm your wife."

"And I'm your husband."

"So you know best, is that it? I can't believe we're even having this conversation."

He ignored her anger and went to browse in the refrigerator.

"Don't walk away from me, Tim." She stalked into the kitchen behind him. "This discussion is not finished."

"It's not a discussion," he said with a calm superiority that enraged her even more. "A discussion is when two people speak rationally and come to a compromise about their differences." He closed the fridge and popped the top on a can of cola, surveying her with half-lidded eyes.

Liz fought to maintain her composure. "What has gotten into you? It's not like you to be so . . . so dogmatic. We're not planning to do this tomorrow. It will be a couple of years, at least, before Serena will be able to finish paying off her school loans. We'll have to save up for the down payment on the clinic—that could take another two or three years."

"Liz, we agreed," he said smoothly, "that you would do your counseling at Brook Green and I would continue with Hope House Coalition and the Payback Project. This is important work, work we both believe in."

"And I'm not asking you to give it up," she countered. "I'm only asking for a little equity, a chance to realize *my* dreams." She followed as he went back into the living room, feeling a little like a reprimanded puppy trying to get back in its master's good graces. "Besides, I don't recall that we 'agreed' about my leaving the sexual violence center to take on private practice. Seems like you made the decision and I capitulated."

He flopped into the easy chair and put his feet on the ottoman. "Since when have you had this big dream of your own practice?" he asked. "I don't remember ever hearing you talk about it."

"Well, I—" Liz paused, buying time. The truth was, she *hadn't* really considered it before. As she and Serena discussed it, it just came together. The plan simply dropped into her mind, fully formed, and she embraced it without question. It just seemed . . . *right.*

"I see," he said when she didn't answer his question. "This isn't your idea at all. It's *her* idea, and she needs you to help her fulfill it. You've had one dinner with Serena Marchand, and now you want to throw everything we've worked for out the window and stake your future—*our* future—on some half-baked harebrained scheme?"

"Serena's not like that," Liz protested. "She's smart, and she's a wonderful counselor. She's trustworthy—"

"Right. She's a Girl Scout."

"Don't be cynical, Tim. You don't know her."

"Yes, I do. We've met." She watched his expression change, a door slamming shut. When he spoke again, his tone was distant, detached. "Face it, Liz. You're naive, easily swayed. This woman may be persuasive. She may even have good intentions. But establishing a new practice will cost an arm and a leg, and if it doesn't work out—"

"It's about the money, isn't it? It's not about my welfare, or my dreams, or what kind of work I could do, what kind of good I might accomplish by leaving Brook Green and going in with Serena Marchand on our own counseling center—a clinic based on ethical choices and concern for others. This is about dollars and cents."

He rolled his eyes. "Damn right it's about the money. Your income supports us, supports Hope House and Payback. Gives us the wherewithal to be involved in other nonprofits as well. Even if this idea proved to be successful, it would be years before you could bring in the kind of money you make at Brook Green—if ever."

"So never mind my need to do what I believe in, what I have passion for."

"We all have to make certain sacrifices," he said mildly. "We agreed to this arrangement. You can't go changing the rules midstream."

"Stop." Liz held up a hand. "If this conversation continues, I'm going to say something I'll regret later."

"Fine." He switched on the lamp, picked up a book from the table, and began to read.

❦

Tim was wrong, Liz thought as she thrashed in bed, unable to sleep. Wrong about so many things.

Wrong about Serena. Wrong about their plans for the counseling center. Wrong about Liz herself.

The more she thought about it, the angrier she got. No one, ever, had accused her of being naive or easily swayed. Tim knew better. But he also knew what would push her buttons, what would gall her the most. He'd been baiting her, trying to get her to lose her temper. Determined to win. But why?

Well, if his ultimate aim had been to get Liz to doubt her own mind, to doubt Serena, he had failed.

Objectively speaking, it was true she hadn't known Serena long enough to trust her. And yet, Liz *did* trust her. They had connected. And in that moment Liz's walls had come down, and she found herself opening up in a way she had never done before. Not even with Tim.

Trust your gut, she often told clients who were struggling to find their way. *Listen to your heart.*

It was time she started taking her own advice.

The interoffice phone on her desk buzzed, and Liz picked up the receiver. "Yes?"

"Hey, it's me." Liz heard the voice as if in stereo—clearly, distinctly, over the telephone at her right ear, and faintly, an echo through the wall, in her left.

She glanced at the clock. It was five-forty. "Why are you using the phone? Are you done? Ready for dinner?"

"Not quite." Serena sounded tired. "I'd have come to your office, but I'm buried under a pile of paperwork. Cisco's got to take his mother in to the hospital for some tests tomorrow morning, and he asked me to take his CD group. They meet—get this—at seven A.M."

Liz groaned. "Better you than me."

Cisco—Francisco Morales—was one of the newer therapists in their group. He was a genius when it came to dealing with troubled teens, and around the office his clients were affectionately referred to as CDs—Cisco's Delinquents. Mostly referrals from the counselors in the school system or juvenile judges and parole officers, these problem kids responded more positively than anyone could imagine to Morales's direct, no-nonsense approach to guidance. He loved them, and although they rarely admitted it, they reciprocated. Cisco was . . . *cool.*

"Anyway," Serena went on, "they have to meet before school, which means I need to go over their files before I leave tonight. You know how I am in the morning."

"Totally useless, at least until you've had two cups of coffee," Liz said.

"Right. So I'll need another thirty, maybe forty-five minutes. I'll try to make it quick."

"No problem," Liz assured her. "Take your time."

She could almost hear Serena smile. "Thanks. You're the best."

"So are you. Taking the CDs practically qualifies you for sainthood."

"Saint Serena. Has a nice ring to it." She chuckled. "See you in a bit."

Liz hung up the phone and sank back in her chair. Well, she had wanted some time alone, time to evaluate her unwillingness to accept Grace's invitation to come to Asheville. And she had gotten it. Unfortunately, her thoughts had taken her places she hadn't quite expected to go.

Still, the mind had its own path to get to the truth. She was a good enough therapist to recognize that, even in herself. And now it occurred to her that perhaps she should be writing some of this down, so that she could see the whole picture without forgetting the details.

Her computer was asleep, but not turned

off. She hit a key at random and waited for
the screen to appear, then jotted down a
page or two of notes from her earlier musings. She could go back and fill in the details later. For the time being, she wanted to
keep moving forward.

Where was she? Oh, yeah—the argument with Tim about her and Serena setting up their own practice . . .

*As it turned out, it took almost three years
for Serena to pay off her college loans, and
another two for us to put aside enough
money for a down payment on our own
offices and the necessary renovations.*

*Five years. And in all that time, Tim
never changed his mind either about the
plan or about his preconceived notions of
the kind of person Serena was. He didn't
trust her, and he made that perfectly clear
every chance he got.*

*But he did change in other ways, ways I
couldn't understand at the time. As plans
for the clinic solidified, and especially after
we closed on the property and began the
renovations, he became silent and
withdrawn. In public he presented the
same energetic, passionate presence that*

*drew me to him in the first place, but in
private he was brooding and
uncommunicative. It was as if he were
living two lives, existing as two radically
different people—his public persona, and
the face he showed to me when we were
alone together.*

*I couldn't comprehend it. Hope House
was flourishing, and the Payback Project
had taken off from the start. Local banks
and lending companies were lining up to
participate, and already a dozen or more
low-income families had been approved for
home loans. Tim Delancy was everyone's
Golden Boy, one entire wall of his office
covered with appreciation plaques and
nonprofit awards.*

*And yet he seemed . . . secretive. When
I would try to talk to him about the success
of his ideas, he gave one-syllable responses
and discouraged questions. I tried to
communicate how proud I was of him, but
even those affirmations fell on deaf ears.*

*For months we went on that way, never
really connecting with each other—
although I attempted to get him to open
up. We lived in the same house but passed
like ghosts in the darkness. Something was*

eating at him, and he couldn't—or wouldn't—tell me what it was.

Suddenly, almost overnight, he changed again. The gentle, affectionate, compassionate man I had married didn't completely return, but I had hope. At least he quit criticizing Serena in my presence. On the rare occurrences when the two of them crossed paths, he made an effort to be civil to her, and she did the same—for my sake, no doubt. He didn't show up for the grand opening of the Arlington Counseling Center, but he did manage to keep his negative opinions of the venture to himself.

And then, a few weeks after the center opened . . .

The memory pressed in upon her, invited but unwelcome.

A vicious flu bug had been floating around that winter and had finally landed on Liz. Achy and feverish, she canceled her last two appointments, left the center early, and drove home.

Tim wouldn't be there, of course. He never was this time of day, and most likely he wouldn't show up until nine or ten o'clock at the earliest. She'd just fix herself a bowl of soup and fall into bed. Or, considering the way her stomach was beginning to feel, maybe she'd skip the soup altogether.

She put the key in the lock, opened the door, and staggered in, wrenching her back as she slipped on a pile of magazines and envelopes that lay on the floor under the mail slot. Groaning, she bent to gather up the mess.

And then she saw it.

A thick, heavy, cream-colored envelope that bore an unfamiliar logo and the return address of a Virginia law firm. She picked it up and went into the kitchen, dumping her briefcase and the rest of the mail onto the counter.

It was addressed to Tim. She frowned and fingered the envelope. And then the world shifted, and she felt a block of ice fall into her stomach: *divorce lawyer.*

A few months ago it wouldn't have surprised her. But lately things had been getting better—not back to normal, really, but closer. At least they were talking again.

Surely he wouldn't consult a divorce attorney without letting her know. Still, she was a psychologist, and she couldn't sup-

press the nagging awareness that sometimes a person who had been depressed or
withdrawn would undergo an unexpected
improvement after deciding to leave a relationship—or even commit suicide. The
change wasn't necessarily a sign of overcoming the depression, but merely the relief of having taken action.

She hesitated for a moment, thinking,
trying not to think. Normally she wouldn't
even consider opening Tim's mail. They
respected each other's privacy. Still, he *was*
her husband, and if—

Before she had consciously made the decision, as if her fingers were moving without regard to neural synapses, she pried up
the flap of the envelope and unfolded the
letterhead inside.

It *was* from an lawyer, but not a divorce
specialist. A *defense* attorney. The letter was
long and detailed, and apparently referred
to papers that had already been served. Isolated words floated across her vision, coming into focus as if lit with a laser beam.
*Criminal charges. Summons. Kickbacks. Abuse
of power. Misappropriation of funds.*

No. There had to be some kind of mistake. Tim would never do these things. He cared too much, was far too passionate about helping those who couldn't help themselves. He was a good man, a man of integrity. *He was her husband.*

She sagged against the counter, trying to breathe, her brain squealing its resistance as she tried to get her mind out of neutral. Her stomach churned, and acid rose up in her throat.

She leaned over the sink and gagged, bringing up nothing but a little bile. She spat into the sink, then took a clean glass out of the drainer and filled it with water. Just as she lifted the glass to her mouth, she caught a glimpse of movement out of the corner of her eye.

The hair on the back of her neck prickled. The glass slipped from her fingers and shattered against the drain. She whirled, clutching the papers to her pounding chest.

It was Tim.

He shut the door behind him and set his briefcase on the tile floor of the entryway.

"Are you all right?" he said. "You look flushed."

She took one slow-motion step back,

and then another, until the handle of the refrigerator pressed into her spine. "I—ah, I think I'm coming down with something."

He approached her with a curious look on his face. "Bad bug," he said. "Everybody's getting it. Maybe you should take something and go to bed." He drew nearer, his gaze fixed on the lawyer's letter she still held grasped in one hand. Gently, he pried it out of her clenched fist and put a palm to her forehead. "You've got a fever."

"I—I'm all right."

He looked down at the letter. "Ah."

That was all, just "Ah."

Tim took her trembling hand, led her into the living room, and settled her under an afghan on the sofa. Then he went back to the kitchen, poured a glass of orange juice, and returned with the glass and two small green gelcaps. "Take these," he said, holding out his hand. "They won't cure the virus, but they'll make it more bearable."

Liz washed down the pills with a swallow of orange juice and watched him over the rim. Her head was swimming and her eyes felt gritty.

He pulled the ottoman away from his

easy chair, rolled it over to the couch, and sat down in front of Liz. Smoothing the pages across his knees with his hands, he read through them quickly.

"I should have told you, I suppose. I didn't want to worry you."

The old Tim was back—gentle, entreating, considerate. He reached out and pushed the hair back from her eyes. "You've had a lot on your mind lately, getting the new clinic off the ground."

Liz blinked and squinted at him. "Is it true—what they say you've done?"

"You know me better than anyone. Do you think I'm guilty?"

She shook her head and looked down. "I don't know what to think. Things between us have been so . . ." She shrugged.

"I know. I'm sorry." He bit his lip. "It's my fault, Liz. This has been building for a while now, but I thought I could handle it without getting you involved." A heavy sigh escaped him. "I know I haven't been myself. I've been . . . preoccupied." He looked up. "Can you forgive me?"

"Tell me the truth."

"All right. The truth is, there *have* been kickbacks—from the banks and loan companies associated with the Payback Project. There *has* been abuse of power and misappropriation. I didn't know about it at first. Not until Eric started shifting the blame my way."

"Eric? You can't be talking about Eric Mayhew. Tim, he's practically your *mentor*!"

"I know. He's on the board of almost every nonprofit in the District. Got his fingers in all the pies. And apparently he's been taking a slice here and a slice there, until it caught up with him."

"How long have you known?"

"A few months. I've been trying to put out brush fires, trying . . . well, trying to save him. He is—was—a good man. I always respected him." He shook his head. "I tried to confront him privately, to help him figure out how to fix this, to keep him from destroying himself. Big mistake. Once he discovered I was aware of all his under-the-table deals, he—"

"He tried to frame *you*?"

"What better candidate could he have? I'm the director of Hope House, the upfront guy, the fund-raiser. Payback Project was my brainchild."

Liz slumped against the couch pillows. "What are you going to do?"

"That's why I'm home early. I've sent all the evidence—spreadsheets, financial data, everything—to my computer here. With a few hours' work, I can have it ready for the defense lawyer. Eric will go down for this, but that can't be helped. We've been friends and colleagues for years. I like the guy and sympathize with him. But I won't take the fall for him."

Liz looked into Tim's eyes. "I love you," she whispered. "And I believe in you. You know I'll do anything I can to help." She squeezed his hand. "I just wish you hadn't been so determined to go through this alone."

Liz stopped typing and dropped her hands into her lap. Amazing, how vivid and visceral the memories were. She could still feel the nausea, the fever, the initial shock and disbelief, the warm wave of love and relief that washed over her as she accepted Tim's story and felt her devotion and respect for him renewed.

And the shame.

Even now, years later, the shame still burned upon her soul.

Therapy was about dealing with trauma and moving on with your life, she thought.

But some things stayed with you forever.

25

LIES, BETRAYALS, AND UNCLAIMED BAGGAGE

"Corelli's?" Serena asked as she settled herself behind the wheel and clicked the seat belt in place.

Liz nodded. "Perfect." Corelli's Italian Bistro was one of their favorite haunts, a dark little hole in the wall with latticework strung from the ceiling and bunches of grapes hanging down from above. The kind of place, Serena always joked, where the atmosphere kept falling into your food. The scampi, however, was magnificent— enormous shrimp simmered with great chunks of roasted garlic. A heart attack waiting to happen, a redefinition of the phrase *food to die for.* Liz pretended to believe that the garlic, which was supposed to lower cholesterol, canceled out the butter. But even if it didn't, what a way to go.

Giorgio Corelli, the owner, knew the two of them by sight and often came to their table to check on their food and service. This evening—it was six o'clock by the time Serena had finished reviewing the CD files, and nearly six-thirty when they arrived—Giorgio met them at the door with a deep, sweeping bow and a smile like a Cheshire cat.

"*Bella, bella!*" he effused, kissing their hands and ushering them to a corner booth near the fountain. "My two favorite ladies! The usual tonight, I presume?"

Liz slipped into the seat and waved the menu away. "Yes, please. The shrimp scampi and a small Caesar salad."

"Not for me," Serena said. "I think I'll try something different—chicken Marsala with linguini."

"*Perfètto,*" Giorgio said. "And a bottle of *vino bianco,* eh?"

"Iced tea," Liz said.

"Water with lemon." Serena laughed as he gave an exaggerated grimace.

"No wine? *Mìo cuòre.* My poor heart

cannot stand it. You wish to be Italian? You must relish the *vino*."

"Maybe some other time." Liz patted his hand. "Thanks, Giorgio."

He left them, and once their drinks had arrived, Serena leaned forward, fiddling with her silverware. "Is everything OK, Liz? You seem . . . distracted."

"I'm all right," Liz hedged, then decided that honesty was the better approach. "I've been doing some thinking and journaling in the past day or so. About Grace's invitation to come to Asheville, and my reaction to it."

"And?"

A candle in a Chianti bottle flickered in the center of the table. Liz pulled it toward her and began picking off flakes of wax. "It's led me to memories I'd rather not revisit. About those early years."

"About Tim."

"Yes, that, too."

"Come to any conclusions?"

"I'm not finished yet."

Serena leaned back in the booth and smiled. "Well, when you're ready, I'll be glad to listen. If you want me to."

This was one of the traits Liz admired

most about Serena—her patience, her inner peace, the ability to wait, to sense when Liz needed to talk and when she needed to be left alone with her thoughts. It gave her a sense of security, knowing that her privacy wouldn't be intruded upon, that she had the freedom to open herself up—or not— and that Serena wouldn't coerce her to reveal anything she wasn't inclined to share.

Serena had never tried to elbow her way into Liz's soul, never pounded on the door and demanded to be let in. And ironically, Serena's lack of pressure was exactly what had motivated Liz to unlock the gates and pull down the walls around her heart. Serena exuded a calm centeredness, an unconditional acceptance. With Serena, Liz didn't have to guard herself, and after so many traumas and so many reasons not to trust, it was a welcome relief to take off the armor and stand emotionally naked and unashamed with someone who loved and valued her.

A black-vested waiter delivered their salads, and the conversation turned to other things. The issues Serena was likely to face tomorrow with Cisco's group of teenagers. Liz's frustrations with the implacable client she dubbed the Whine Queen—the chronic complainer who had canceled today. An informal evaluation of Francisco and the other new counselors.

By the time they had finished dinner, paid for their meal, and gathered up the to-go boxes, it was almost eight-thirty.

"I'm going to turn in early," Serena said as they pulled up in front of the Arlington bungalow a few minutes before nine. "I'm assuming we'll be driving separately tomorrow."

Liz laughed. "Given that you have to be at the clinic before seven, that's a pretty safe assumption." She waited beneath the porch light as Serena unlocked the door. "I'll put these leftovers in the fridge, then I think I'll go back to my journaling."

Serena was already in bed reading when Liz came out of the bathroom in her pajamas. She poked her head through the doorway. "Will my being on the computer bother you, do you think?"

"Not unless you intend to throw it against the wall."

"I'll try to restrain myself." Liz started down the hall toward the study, then retraced her steps. She waited until Serena sensed her presence and looked up. "I just wanted to tell you how much I appreciate you."

Serena raised her eyebrows. "What brought this on?"

"I was thinking at dinner tonight—how you never force me to spill my guts. How you're always patient with me when I'm trying to work something out. It means a lot."

"Well," Serena responded with a wry grin, "I'm a very patient person. You said it yourself, this afternoon—I'm nearly a saint." Her expression softened, retaining only a dim trace of a smile. "Trust yourself," she said quietly. "You'll find your way."

By the time Liz went into the study and booted up the computer, Serena was already snoring softly in the next room. She had the gift of sleep, Liz thought—the by-product, no doubt, of a pure heart and an untroubled conscience. The woman could fall asleep as soon as she hit the pillow—or the couch, or even sitting upright in a chair with the TV blaring. It was a gift Liz devoutly wished for but never quite seemed to acquire.

When the computer had finished its start-up routine, she slipped her journaling disk into the slot, scrolled through what she had written at the office, and picked up where she had left off.

I loved Tim. I believed in him. I let my guard down, and trusted him completely. Even when the truth finally came out, I couldn't bring myself to accept it.

But the evidence was irrefutable. That night, while I lay on the couch in a fever-induced stupor, he hadn't been organizing his files to give to the prosecutor proving Eric Mayhew's misdeeds. He had been deleting files implicating himself.

Liz felt the anger wash over her again, the hot boil of rage and incredulity. Tim hadn't heard her enter the study. For several minutes she had stood behind him, squinting at the computer screen, her fever-riddled brain desperately wanting to deny what her eyes could plainly see. She had to be mistaken. She was delirious. She was dreaming.

"What are you doing?" she asked.

He turned, and his gaze was cold, calculating. "Working."

She didn't answer, but he could read her face, and she could read his. She took a step closer. "Tim, you can't do this."

"It's already done."

"And how do you expect me to respond? You lied to me. You lied to *everyone*! And you're going to blame this on Eric Mayhew, ruin his career, his life, to save your own skin?"

"I expect you—" He spoke quietly, a cynical smile curling his lip into a sneer. "I expect you to put your Pollyanna attitudes aside and keep your mouth shut."

"I can't keep silent about this, Tim. It goes against everything I believe, everything I've worked for."

"And what about the things *I've* worked for?" His voice rose, louder and more intense. "For years I've sweated and slaved in the trenches, hobnobbing with people who could buy and sell me on a whim, on the off chance that I might be able to make the world a better place. But the world *isn't* better. Wake up, Liz. Idealism died with the sixties. Nobody gives a shit anymore. The only thing these so-called philanthropists care about is themselves, salving their consciences with a donation that for you or me is equivalent to giving a quarter to a bum on the street. There's no sacrifice in that, no self-denial."

"And so your answer is to become one of *them*?"

"One of them?" He gave a snort of derision, and his tone went up another ten decibels. "Like hell. Do you know what I'm going to do with this money, Liz? I'm going to make a difference, dammit. *I'm* going to be the one who determines where this money will do the most good. Hope House was *my* baby; Payback Project was *my* brainchild. *I* raised the big bucks. But do I get to decide what to do with it? Not a chance. I'm subject to some executive-board moron who doles out the dollars according to what's politically expedient. Some senator or congressman or wealthy bigwig who wants a shelter named after him. Some piece-of-crap bank president who's only interested in the PR."

The veins in his neck were bulging now, and his eyes were wide, frightening. "The day of the charity du jour is over, Liz. I'm going to do this my way."

"But—but what you're doing is *illegal*," she stammered.

"And who are you going to tell?" he countered. "You're my wife, and a wife can't testify against her husband." He narrowed his eyes and stared her down. "Besides, if you breathe a single word of this, I'll ruin that precious little counseling clinic of yours. You know I can do it." He laughed curtly. "How long will you last if your loans are called in? A month? Six weeks? You'll go down quicker than the *Titanic,* but without nearly as much of a splash."

Liz gaped at him. "You couldn't. You *wouldn't.*"

"I could, and I would," he replied coldly. "But I don't think I'll have to. Despite the image you project, my darling, I'm betting that deep inside you're not noble enough to sacrifice your dream for the sake of your integrity."

Would *I have been willing to give up the dream I had worked for in order to do the right thing? The question haunted me, even more so because I never discovered the answer. The truth came out before I had to make a decision. Subordinates had been fired. Superiors had been undermined. Funds raised for Hope House Coalition had been funneled into numbered accounts. Bank presidents had slipped cash under the table and jacked up interest rates for the Payback Project. Money, lots of money, had gone into Tim's pocket.*

As it turned out, no one even asked for my testimony. The prosecutor's computer gurus had retrieved all the evidence they needed from Tim's hard drive.

Our clinic was safe. Our dream was intact. And yet the ethical questions continued to plague me. Serena was convinced that I would, in the end, have sacrificed everything for the truth. She had more faith in my character than I did. I have never been certain—even now.

As it turned out, the people Tim claimed to care about were the very ones who were hurt the most. The weak. The helpless. Single moms. Unemployed dads. Kids crowded into underfunded homeless shelters.

*And everyone in the nonprofit
community, it seemed, knew—or at least
suspected—what he had been doing. Even
Serena. Everyone except me.*

*I had been blindsided. The very core of
my being was lacerated by this betrayal,
fractured into a thousand shards that sliced
my spirit apart a piece at a time. My
confidence as well as my heart had been
broken. If I could be so wrong about Tim,
what business did I have being a therapist?
What had happened to my instincts, my
insight, that I had trusted him so
thoroughly?*

*And how could I bear it, to see the
expressions of pity and disbelief on my
colleagues' faces, to watch them whisper
and shake their heads?*

Liz stopped typing. As she reread her confession, a realization began to form in her
mind—one of those coincidental epipha-
nies, a "Eureka!" moment that comes
when you least expect it.

For a while after her mother had left,
during her early teenage years, Liz had become fascinated with jigsaw puzzles. She
would sit for hours at the kitchen table,

challenging herself with the most complicated puzzles she could find. She quickly
learned to do the edges first, the flat-sided
pieces that formed a frame around the picture. And then she would center her attention on one section, one color at a time. If
she got stuck, she would let her eyes go out
of focus and roam aimlessly over the myr-
iad shapes and shades. And it usually
worked—when she wasn't trying so hard,
the piece she was searching for would mag-
ically appear. She would somehow see it
differently, from another angle, and recognize how it fit.

Now, nearly forty years in the future, Liz
could look back on her younger self from a
vantage point of objectivity. The obsession
wasn't about the puzzles at all. It wasn't
even about becoming absorbed in something—anything—that would help get her
mind off her pain.

It was about imposing order on the
chaos, discovering meaning in the broken-
ness. If all those puzzle pieces could eventually fit together into a coherent whole,
maybe the jagged shards of her life could be
reassembled, too.

Liz sat very still, allowing her subconscious to circle around the idea. She had been doing the very same thing all her adult life—letting her mind go, trusting it to find the right angle on the part she needed to complete the picture.

Now the pieces were beginning to shift around and sort themselves out. It was all coming together.

She began to type again:

The trial seemed to go on forever, draining me of every remnant of energy and passion and hope. At last Tim was convicted and sentenced to seven years in a minimum-security prison, one of those places with handball courts and inmate tennis tournaments, reserved for white-collar criminals. To the end he maintained that he had done nothing wrong, that he and only he was equipped to decide who deserved assistance and how the nonprofit funds should be distributed. In his final testimony he even compared himself to Jesus, who healed some but not others.

Through it all, I remained strong, my armor fully in place. But when the divorce papers arrived and I scrawled a shaky signature finalizing the dissolution of our marriage, I broke.

I never liked to admit it, but I went through a total psychic meltdown. And Serena—dear, capable Serena—was my stronghold and support. Not as a therapist, although those skills certainly came in handy more than once, but as a friend.

Almost from the beginning I had counted Serena as my best friend and admired her enormously, but now I began to see her for the amazing person she really was. She stepped in to help me put myself back together, to rebuild my confidence in myself, to find hope for a future I couldn't even begin to envision. She kept giving and giving, asking nothing in return.

Once the crisis had passed and life began to move back in the direction of normalcy, I invited her to share the Arlington bungalow I had kept in the settlement. I needed help with the mortgage, and Serena wanted to get out of her cramped apartment. But it was much more than a move of convenience. The bonds we had forged during my dark night of the soul had grown into a deep devotion and mutual respect. It was the strongest relationship I had ever known, ever even imagined.

Only Serena knew the unanswered questions that still gnawed at my soul.

Only Serena saw the chinks in the armor.

Liz stared at the screen in front of her, and her mind homed in on the truth she didn't want to admit.

When Grace and Tess and Lovey knew me thirty years ago, I was a crusader, determined to change the world, and willing to make any sacrifice to do that. Now I'm a psychologist in private practice, making good money, living like every other upper-middle-class capitalist. In my heart I know that what I do is valuable, that it changes lives for the better. It's a different kind of crusade. My life isn't a cop-out, but it could look that way to them. And trying to explain it simply feels like defensiveness.

But that's not the worst of it. I'm a decent enough counselor to understand— theoretically—that I'm not responsible for the things my husband did, or what he became in the end. And yet the memories continue to bring pain. I have to confess that deep down I wonder if I couldn't have intervened before it degenerated into full-blown megalomania. Even now, reliving that part of the past dredges up insecurities about myself—who I chose to trust, to open myself up to.

Why I didn't see the truth before it slammed me up against a wall?

The answer echoed in Liz's head, a quiet, familiar, imminently rational voice:

Because you're human. Because it's impossible to live up to others' expectations—even your own.

Because no matter how hard you try, you'll never be perfect. *You just have to trust people to love you anyway.*

She gazed at the words she had written, and somewhere deep inside she felt a spark, flint on steel, an answering vibration. This was her unclaimed baggage. And it was high time she took responsibility for it.

"Serena?" Liz whispered quietly.

Outside the window, darkness was beginning to thin into the first gray light of dawn. Birds were tuning up, and somewhere in the distance, a dog was barking a deep, throaty "Woof."

"Serena," she repeated, a bit louder this time. "Wake up."

"Huh?" Serena jerked and groaned. Her eyes opened to slits, and she squinted in the half-light. "Liz? What time is it?"

"Almost time for your alarm to go off. You've got the CDs this morning, remember?"

"Yeah, I know." She struggled to a sitting position and ran a hand through her hair. One side of it was mashed flat to her head, and the other stood up in irregular spikes. "Did you sleep at all?"

"No."

She leaned against the headboard and tried to focus on Liz's face. "What's wrong?"

"Nothing. Everything's fine. I just needed to talk to you for a few minutes before you left this morning." She took Serena's hand and wrapped it around a steaming mug of coffee.

"Ah, you're a genius. What would I do without you?" She blew on the cup and took a sip. "So, what's up?"

Liz settled herself on top of the blankets. "I've made a decision. I'm going to Asheville for Grace's little reunion," she said. "And I want you to go with me."

PART IV

TESS

The story of our genesis—
dust and water, sculpted in the image
of the Great Unknown,
waiting to receive
the kiss of life—
reminds us of clay feet
and holy inspiration.

Child of earth,
can these bones rise and live?
Only with the Maker's breath
exhaled into their souls,
the gift, the call, the sacrament
of passion and imagination
coursing through the blood and heart
like oxygen.

26

INVISIBLE CREATOR

Kendall slung his heavy book bag over his shoulder, closed his locker with a quiet click, and ducked into an empty classroom. He peered through the crack in the door. Someone was following him—a man with a heavy, limping step and a breathy wheeze. The same old guy, Ken guessed, who had stood under the shadow of the bleachers and watched him during football practice yesterday. If the man was supposed to be monitoring Ken's movements while staying out of sight, he was doing a rotten job of it. So far he had turned up once at the mall, twice at practice, and now this afternoon, in the deserted school building. He was getting bolder.

But why was he tailing Ken? What did

he want? Was he dangerous? And was it
possible he knew about—

The telephone rang, jolting Tess out of the
scene and back to the real world. She shut
her eyes, heaved a sigh, and waited. She
ought to let the machine pick it up. With
every new project, she swore she would
begin screening calls. But even the answering machine disrupted her creative process.
She simply found herself stopping to hear
who it was, and her concentration was broken anyway. Voice mail. She really should
get voice mail.

The phone rang a second time, then a
third. At last she jerked up the receiver.
"Yes?" She sounded snappish, and she
knew it, but she did hate being interrupted
in the middle of her writing.

"Hey, C.J. It's Travis."

Travis Jinks, her editor. His voice
sounded as if it might have belonged to her
character Kendall Wright, who had just
turned fourteen. Didn't publishers hire
anyone over thirty anymore? Travis had
proved himself an intelligent, savvy editor,
but just talking to him made her feel about

a hundred years old. After reading the manuscript of her last book, he had actually called and left a message saying, "This is awesome, C.J. You so rock!"

"Travis, how many times do I have to ask you to call me Tess?" Her gaze wandered around the office, and her eyes lingered on a shelf of hardbacks, each one by the author C. J. Kenning. Her persona, a combination of her own initials and her grandmother's maiden name.

"Ah, c'mon," he said in that familiar cajoling tone. "You're the great C. J. Kenning. Why won't you cop to it?"

Ordinarily, Tess found herself mildly entertained by Travis's casual mall-rat lingo. But today it annoyed her. "C. J. Kenning doesn't exist, Travis. I am Tess Riley-Hopkins, remember? Just Tess."

"OK, OK, I'll chill," he said with a laugh. "But lemme tell you this crazy wild rumor I heard about you the other day—"

"Travis," she interrupted. "I don't mean to be curt. But I'm right in the middle of Chapter 9, and if I don't get Kendall out of his stalker's path, he's going to get caught and this is going to be a very short book, ending abruptly with the violent and unexpected death of an exceedingly popular protagonist. So, what can I do for you?"

"Well, we can't have Ken die on us, now can we?" Travis chuckled. It always seemed to amuse him to hear Tess speak of her characters as if they were actual living people with their own minds and agendas. This was one aspect of fiction writing he just didn't get. "So, here's the deal. I've just gotten out of this megameeting with the marketing and publicity dudes, and—"

"Let me guess. Personal appearances."

"Well, yeah, sort of. I mean, it's not like a real long book tour or anything—only a coupla weeks, major cities, all expenses, five-star hotels, the works, you know. The M and P guys think it would jump-start pre-sales on the new book, and—"

"Travis, I've got two Newbery Medals and three Horn Book Awards hanging on my office walls. What more do they want?"

"They want *you,* of course."

"No they don't. They want C. J. Kenning. They want a clone of J. K. Rowling—an outrageously wealthy, sleek, sophisticated, witty blonde who's a natural for interviews with Barbara Walters and spots on *Good Morning America*."

"What's wrong with that?"

"For Jo Rowling, probably nothing. She's good at it. I'm a dumpy Iowa house-wife in her fifties. I'm my readers' grand-mother."

"You're not a housewife," Travis countered. "When was the last time you scrubbed your own toilets?"

Tess noted wryly that he hadn't argued with the part about being fifty and dumpy. "Point taken," she said. "One of the best perks of success—hiring a cleaning person once a week. Nevertheless, the answer is no."

"This would be good for you, C—ah, Tess. They're calling you the Mystery Woman, y'know, and that's not a reference to the genre."

"Travis, how long has it been since you've reviewed my contract?"

"I dunno. A while."

"Then go back and read it again. It specifies that I will under no circumstances do personal appearances, and that my true identity is not to be revealed—to *anyone*."

"Yeah, but—"

"But when we negotiated the contract, no one really expected me to stick to my guns on this clause."

"Uh—right."

"Everybody thought they could convince me otherwise."

He hesitated. "Yeah. I guess so."

"Well, looks like they were wrong, doesn't it?" she said brightly. "You can just go back and tell them they have nothing to complain about and, legally speaking, not a leg to stand on. My sales are great, and everyone knows it—including the directors of marketing and publicity. If they still balk, they can take it up with my agent. Being mysterious is my calling card, Travis, and I intend to keep it that way. Besides, I'm a writer, not an itinerant peddler. Now, is there anything else?"

"Ah, yeah," he stammered. "Just a couple other quick things. The artsy-fartsy guys are finished with the mock-up of the new cover; I'll FedEx a copy to you tomorrow. And the catalogue people want to know if they should include this next novel in the spring releases."

Tess sighed. "Travis, have I ever missed a deadline?"

"Well, no."

"And I won't miss this one. You'll have the book by October first, as promised— assuming I can get a few minutes' writing time here and there *in between telephone conversations with my editor.*" She ran these last words together fiercely, between gritted teeth.

He laughed tautly. "I get your point. Call me if you need me."

"Always a delight talking with you, Travis," she said sweetly, and hung up the phone.

For a while after Travis's call, Tess sat at her desk trying to recover her focus. Next to the stack of research books she kept close at hand were two of her favorite photographs. In the one from their wedding, Tess was flanked by Hal (handsome and distinguished in his tux), her parents (with Daddy in his bishop's robes, beaming) and her maid-of-honor sister, Duck (so dubbed because of the bobbing, splay-footed waddle she had adopted as a toddler). The other, a candid, more casual shot, showed

Tess and Hal and their daughter Claire on a family vacation to the Smoky Mountains the summer after Claire's graduation from college. Some stranger biking along the Parkway had volunteered to take the picture, and had done a good job of it, too. Hal sat on a huge boulder with one arm around Tess and the other around Claire. Behind them, a rushing, rocky stream and thick stand of trees created an artistic backdrop to the photograph.

This is what matters, Tess thought as she ran a finger over the glass and traced the outline of Hal's cheek. Love. Belonging. Family. Not book tours and sales figures and being recognized.

But this essential truth—this treasure hidden in the field, this peerless pearl—had not come without a price.

Tess Riley had just turned twenty-three when she entered her very first fiction seminar at the Iowa Writers' Workshop. She felt numb and a little befuddled, her head swirling with the names of illustrious writers who had been associated with this program—Robert Frost, Steven Vincent Benét, Robert Penn Warren, John Berryman. A shining constellation of stars, and expectations high as the moon.

The stories she had submitted in her admission portfolio must have been all right, though. She *had* been accepted after all. And yet as she looked around the classroom, no one else seemed quite as unnerved as she felt.

Some of the students obviously knew each other. They were chatting and laughing and introducing themselves to the newbies. One fellow in particular appeared completely at ease, not the least bit intimidated by his surroundings. He leaned casually against a desk in the front row, his foot propped on the seat and his backside resting against the desktop. Nice-looking, Tess thought, observing his well-cut brown hair and wide white smile. But no doubt an egomaniac. He threw back his head and laughed at something the girl next to him said. Yes, Tess thought. Definitely a narcissist.

She headed for an empty seat in the back, took a new spiral notebook out of her bag, and opened to the first page. *Fiction Semi-*

nar, she wrote across the top line. *Dr. Harold Hopkins.*

The clock on the front wall of the classroom indicated that it was three minutes after nine, and no sign of the professor. She waited, chewing the cap of her pen. Then, at five after, the handsome student in the front heaved himself off the desk, went to the door, and slammed it shut.

Everyone jumped and turned to face the front.

"Now that I have your attention," he laughed, sticking his hands in his pockets and pacing across the front of the room, "let's get started, shall we?" A portable podium took up most of the horizontal space on the teacher's desk. He dropped it to the floor and slid to a sitting position on the desktop, his brown tasseled loafers making little clicking sounds as they tapped against the wood.

Tess frowned. What a juvenile stunt, impersonating a faculty member. She'd been led to believe that students at the workshop took their education seriously. Well, when Professor Hopkins finally did arrive, this clown would get his comeuppance.

He leaned over the left side of the desk,

retrieved a tan leather briefcase that had been propped against the trash can, and snapped it open. "Let's see who's here." He pulled out what was unmistakably a teacher's attendance book. "I am, as some of you already know, Dr. Harold Hopkins." He made a face. "But 'doctor' is too stuffy, and Harold was my father's name, so please call me Hal." He looked around the room and grinned.

Tess sat back in her chair, blinking hard, her brain clouded with disbelief as Dr. Harold Hopkins—*Hal*—read off a list of ten or twelve names in alphabetical order. When he got to "Contessa Jean Riley," he had to call the name twice before she answered.

"Here," she said, raising her hand timidly. "It's Tess."

"Tess," he repeated. He gazed at her with a curious stare, as if trying to probe the depths of her soul. "Well, that's a relief. I'm afraid I don't have much experience dealing with royalty."

The class laughed, and Tess felt her ears redden.

Two more names, and he was done. He flung the grade book back into his briefcase and closed the lid. "That's the last time I'll be using *that*," he said. "I don't take roll in my classes. You can attend or not attend as you wish. Your grades will be based on what you produce, so let me assure you that if you're deep into writing, by all means do not—I repeat, *do not* lose your momentum by stopping to come to class." He shrugged. "And if I'm the only one who shows up, I'll go to the grill, get a cup of coffee, and enjoy an hour and a half of my own company."

He paused and let his gaze roam over the upturned faces. "OK, circle up. We want to be able to see each other."

Desks scraped across the wooden floor as the students got up and rearranged the furniture into a rough semicircle around the professor's desk. Having lost the protective barrier of the rows in front of her, Tess tried to situate her seat so that she wouldn't feel so exposed, but it was a futile effort. Her choice of the back row now put her clearly in Hopkins's sight line, directly across the circle from him. She busied herself with pretending to look for something in her book bag.

"All right, let's talk about what we'll be

doing here," he said. "The Iowa Writers' Workshop is not primarily about academic achievement or competition or who you know. It's about *writing*—in your case, fiction. Short stories, novellas, novels. It's about the passion and the process. If you have thin skin, I suggest you consult your dermatologist and deal with the condition immediately, because you need to be able to take criticism in order to improve. Most of our class time will be taken up with reading what you have written and listening to comments and suggestions from your peers—and myself."

A few students groaned anxiously, and Tess exhaled a pent-up breath. At least she wasn't the only one who was dreading the evaluations to come.

Hopkins ignored the murmuring. "Writing is both gift and skill," he went on. "I have no power whatsoever to impart the gift—that comes from an entirely different source—God, fate, genetics—take your pick." He looked directly at Tess, and she felt herself flinch and withdraw a little. After a moment his eyes moved on, stopping on one face, then another. "But you *can* learn the skills, the techniques—things like

plot development and focus, effective characterization and viewpoint, dialogue and
pacing. And you can develop the self-
editing eye that enables you to become the
best writer you can possibly be."

He stopped briefly and smiled as if to
himself. "I'm sure most of you have taken
creative writing courses at some point in
your education. What principles have your
previous teachers imparted to you about
the process of writing?"

A hand went up on his left.

"This isn't grade school; you don't have
to raise your hand," Hal said mildly. "Yes?
Miss Reed, isn't it? Elizabeth Reed?" He
pointed to a young woman whose jet-black
hair fell in a thick braid nearly to her waist.

She nodded. "Most teachers tell you to
write what you know."

"Ah, yes. Write what you know. A bit
limiting, don't you think? Especially if
you're a *Star Trek* fan. Or"—his gaze swept
over the class—"if you're only twenty-
something and don't know much yet."

A wave of laughter flitted around the
room, leaves rustling in a sudden breeze.

"Let's make a slight alteration to the

principle, shall we?" Hal jumped off the desk, went to the blackboard, and scrawled in two-inch letters WRITE WHO YOU ARE.

"Surely that doesn't mean that all our fiction should be autobiographical," said a slouchy-looking guy who wore faded blue jeans and a moss-colored T-shirt.

"Surely not," Hopkins agreed, returning to his perch and bracing his hands on his knees. "It means that in order to create fiction that moves people, that compels them to suspend their disbelief and enter into the world and the characters you have created, you have to be *vulnerable*."

"Right. You have to slit yourself open, neck to navel," suggested a blonde girl a few seats down from Tess. "You have to let your guts spill out." She didn't seem the type to come up with such a gory image, but then Tess supposed that Agatha Christie and P. D. James also looked like nice, normal ladies at the tea shoppe.

Hal raised an eyebrow. "Quite a vivid metaphor. But yes. You have to open up, to pour yourself heart, mind, and soul into your fiction. Become your characters—

good or evil, stable or insane, flawed or—"
He broke off with a shrug. "Well, we're all
flawed, aren't we?"

Several students were scribbling notes,
but the majority were simply listening as if
entranced.

"And how do we begin to open up, to
write who we are?"

The black-haired girl, Elizabeth, started
to raise her hand, then apparently had second thoughts and withdrew it again. "It
seems to me that in order to write who we
are," she said, "we first have to *know* who
we are."

"Precisely." Hal pointed at her and gave
her a thumbs-up. "There will be times
you'll feel as if this is Therapy 101 rather
than a fiction seminar," he warned. "Many
of you will go through some difficult times,
coming to the place of understanding and
accepting yourself. The process of writing
can turn over some pretty moldy rocks,
and you're not likely to appreciate what
you find crawling underneath them. But
until you acknowledge and come to grips
with your own dark side, you'll probably
never produce the kind of fiction you aspire to."

"To which you aspire," muttered a voice to Tess's immediate right.

"Ah, yes," Hal said with a grin. "We have a grammarian among us. Mr. Cage, isn't it?"

"That's right. Jack Cage." He crossed his arms over his chest. "Sorry."

Tess didn't think he sounded sorry at all. And he certainly didn't look apologetic. He had a surly air about him, a defiant, challenging demeanor.

"It's all right," Hal went on, ignoring Cage's glare. "We'll get into the proper use of the English language later on. But for now, here's something to think about: *Real people don't.*"

"Real people don't *what*?" Cage asked.

"Don't use proper grammar. This is not to say, of course, that the rules that govern coherent writing do not apply to fiction. It's simply a reminder that each character has his or her own peculiar voice and thinking pattern, and you need to be true to the character's viewpoint."

Hopkins went on talking about what they could expect from his class and from the workshop curriculum as a whole. He talked about voice and passion and the difference between calling and ambition. At last he paused and craned around to look at the clock. To Tess's astonishment, almost an hour and a half had passed.

"Well, I've gone on a bit too long. We'll come back to these questions as the semester progresses. In the meantime, I have some exercises I'd like you to do before we meet again." He rummaged in his briefcase, retrieved a sheaf of photocopied papers, and divided the stack between the students on his right and left, each of whom took one and passed them on.

Tess was the last to leave, since she had been sitting in the middle of the circle and it took a few minutes for the assignment to come around to her. She moved toward the front of the classroom, laid the remaining pages on Dr. Hopkins's desk, and sidled around him, her eyes on her feet.

"It's no good, you realize," he said as she reached the door.

She turned. "What's no good?"

"Trying to be invisible. You're going to be far too conspicuous for comfort before this class is over."

"I know," she said, feeling a bit sheepish.

"Reading my work, listening to criticism. Spilling my guts, and all that."

"All that, certainly." He stood behind the desk now, and surveyed her over the top of his open briefcase. "But not only that."

"I—I'm not sure I understand."

"You'll understand eventually." He narrowed his eyes, and his intense gaze made her feel as if her mind were being probed. "I read your entrance papers, the stories you submitted with your application."

He headed toward the door, and she stood aside to let him out into the hallway. "I was wrong about you, Contessa Jean Riley," he said. "Completely wrong."

Tess's heart thudded into the lower regions of her stomach. It had been a mistake. She hadn't really been accepted to this program. She'd be on her way back to North Carolina before the sun had set on her first day.

Tess stared at him. She opened her mouth to respond, to apologize, to beg for a second chance. But his next words stunned her into utter speechlessness.

"I made a joke about your name back there in class. But in terms of your talent, your gift, you *are* royalty. You may try to fade into the woodwork, stay invisible, hide your light under a bushel. But trust me, invisibility is not an option."

He gave a jaunty salute and moved off down the hall, swinging his briefcase. "Sooner or later, the publishing world is going to know about you," he called over his shoulder. "And unless I miss my guess, it'll be sooner rather than later."

27

RACHEL'S WILDERNESS

*T*wo years to the day after Tess Riley had finished her residency at the Iowa Writers' Workshop and received her M.F.A., she married Dr. Hal Hopkins in a quaint little Episcopal chapel with her father the bishop presiding.

Her family adored Hal. They had been hearing Tess rave about him for years—how he had believed in her, mentored her, made some publishing contacts for her, even spoke to the dean on behalf of her application to teach part-time. She had brought him home to North Carolina last Christmas to announce their engagement, and they had endured a week of informal premarital counseling during which her parents assumed a kind of tag-team analysis, with Daddy fielding the spiritual issues and Mother taking on the role of benevolent counselor.

At the end of the week both Mother and Daddy declared them "perfect for each other," and immediately adopted Hal as the son they'd never had.

About three years in, however, their "perfect" marriage flew into a turbulent storm. It wasn't a question of being in love—Tess and Hal were completely devoted to each other and rarely argued. But they both wanted children, and after two years of trying and a year of fertility tests, the final evaluation came: Tess was unable to conceive.

Hal took the news philosophically enough. His desire to be a father had little to do with male ego or biological parenthood. "We can adopt," he tried to assure her. "There are plenty of children in the world who need loving parents."

But Tess would not be consoled by the prospect of adoption. As she neared thirty, her hormones had been going haywire, her biological clock ticking double time. And now, without warning, it had shuddered to a halt completely.

Hal couldn't possibly understand how it made her feel to be told she was . . .

Barren. Sterile. Empty. Fruitless.

She deliberately used the cruel and anti-quated words to describe her condition, the way a self-mutilator will hide in secret and carve up tender flesh with the shattered shards of a bathroom mirror.

Tess didn't want someone else's child. She wanted her own. She desperately wanted the experience of carrying that tiny, squirming burden, sharing her body's nourishment with the growing life inside her, feeding her baby with warm milk from her own distended breasts.

Having a child was like . . . like writing. Holding the idea inside, nurturing it, feeling it grow until it was ready to break forth painfully into the world, herself and not herself, separate and independent from her, and yet joined to her forever by heart and blood and mind.

The realization dawned upon her as the metaphors moving inside her brain dove-tailed into a single shocking truth. She was fruitless not only in body, but in spirit as well. Void of creativity. Soul-barren.

Hal had told her, years ago, that she

wouldn't be able to stay invisible forever, that the publishing world would know about her. And to some extent, his prophecy had proved true. Several of her stories and articles had appeared in some fairly prestigious journals, to the applause and affirmation of her colleagues. In the publish-or-perish world of academia, she was one of the lucky ones.

But it wasn't enough, any more than mothering another woman's baby was enough. What were a few obscure short stories in comparison with a novel? And not just any novel. A great novel. A monumental novel. *The* Novel. The book that would turn the literary world on its ear.

Anything less was unthinkable.

She recalled with perfect clarity Lovey's toast at their graduation dinner: "To Tess Riley, future recipient of the Nobel Prize for Literature." And although at the time she had feigned humility, deep inside she could envision herself flying to Stockholm for the ceremonies, shaking the hand of the Swedish king, and tucking the bronze medal and diploma under her arm. Her name would be engraved on the golden tablets of literary history, along with the likes of Faulkner and Hemingway, T. S. Eliot and Pablo Neruda.

Tess's early workshop experiences had called that dream into question, certainly. At first she had felt displaced, insecure. But gradually she had regained her footing and come to embrace Hal's confidence in her as her own. And even if the Nobel laureate stretched as far above her as a distant star, she nevertheless clung to the dream of being Somebody. Of being Known.

The next Great American Novel was inside her—she felt it, a seed, an idea germinating in the darkness, waiting for its time to be born.

And yet the wanting, the longing—both for the Child and for the Novel—produced only increasing frustration and self-recrimination, bordering on despair.

"I know this isn't what you expected out of life," Duck said when Tess called yet again. "And I sympathize, truly I do. You want Hal's baby, a child created from the love between you. But Tess, it isn't going to happen. You've got to make a choice—you can let it go, or you can let it destroy you."

Silence stretched between them, a static

tautness over the telephone lines. And then Duck uttered the mystical incantation that made all the pieces fall into place. "You're a writer, Tess. For God's sake, write about it."

It was the answer Tess had been waiting for, the word of redemption from On High. Lance the boil. Open a vein. Bleed out all the pain and desolation and misery and anguish onto the page. Water the desert with your tears. Make the wilderness bloom again.

Out of the depths of her woundedness flowed some hidden source of courage and determination. Tess began to write—frantically, furiously. She could do this. She *would* do it. She would write a book so exquisitely crafted that the mountains would shake and the heavens would weep and the stones of the earth would cry out and shudder with ecstasy. . . .

Day after day she pounded away at her hulking red typewriter, and the stack of rough-draft pages on her desk grew. She turned down the offer to teach fiction workshops again, and while Hal led his classes at the university, she holed herself away, slipping into her character's mind and

heart so thoroughly that she found it difficult to surface again at day's end.

Hal was patient, encouraging, understanding. He prepared dinners, massaged
her aching back and shoulders, soothed her
with conversation that did not require her
full attention—his students, the lives of
friends and colleagues, a *New Yorker* article
he had come across, lamenting the de-
plorable lack of originality in contemporary American fiction.

He did not ask to read what she had
written, did not violate her inner, unspoken need for emotional and intellectual
seclusion. When she wanted intimacy, he
took her into his arms and loved her. When
she wanted privacy, he left her to her
thoughts without complaint.

And then one spring evening, when the
first draft was nearly done, Hal looked at
her across the dinner table and said, "Your
father called me today."

Tess's head shot up. "Did he?" A bolt of
guilt sliced through her. She hadn't seen
her parents and sister in nearly nine
months, had barely even spoken to them,
and when she did, the conversations had

been brief, distracted exchanges of trivial information.

"He——" Hal paused, obviously uncertain how to proceed. "There's a child——"

Tess blinked, feeling as if she'd just emerged from a cave into blinding sunlight. "What?"

"A little girl, nearly four. She went into foster care when she was a baby, and the foster family applied for adoption. But there was some kind of problem in the foster home, apparently, and she was removed, and then got shuffled around while they were trying to sort it all out." He paused and swallowed hard. "Now the red tape is cleared up, and she's ready."

"Ready for——?" Tess still couldn't comprehend what he was getting at. Her brain wasn't operating properly.

"The child services supervisor has worked with your father before," Hal persisted, laying down his fork and staring into her eyes as if willing her to understand. "She trusts him. If we wanted to take this child, she would expedite the paperwork."

"*Take* her?"

"Adopt her," Hal said pointedly. "Childless couples in their thirties are often paired with children in the three-to-six range. If they're open to adopting an older child, that is, rather than an infant."

Tess willed her mind to wrap around this concept. Every day for the past nine months she had been writing about the pain of the empty womb. Now, jerked suddenly back to reality, she realized that she no longer felt barren at all. Her personal agony had been siphoned off into Rachel, her protagonist, a catharsis that had drained her of her own grief and torment. The tomb had sprung open—not after three days, but after three trimesters. She could almost feel the graveclothes slipping away.

"Tell me about her," she said, smiling up at Hal.

"Her name is Clarissa. She's very bright, your father says, short and a little stocky, with curly blonde hair." He grinned. "She loves to make up stories, and the caseworker thinks she'll be reading for herself by the time she gets to kindergarten."

"I still have my book to finish," Tess hedged.

"I realize that. But the semester is nearly

over, and I can beg off teaching during the summer term." His tone was hopeful, his expression eager.

"I don't know," Tess went on, shielding her eyes with her hand and pretending to think. "This raises a lot of questions, but one in particular."

"Go on." He looked deflated.

"Well—*Clarissa*? Hal, really! A mother named Contessa with a daughter named Clarissa?" Tess raised her face and winked at him. "Do you suppose she could make the transition to being called Claire instead?"

His eyes widened. "You mean it?"

"I mean it. It's time." She nodded. "Claire Riley-Hopkins. Has a nice ring to it, doesn't it?"

Claire turned five the same month *Rachel's Wilderness* was released.

Hal had handled the little girl's adjustment to her new home and family with amazing grace and finesse. Clearly born to fatherhood, he had taught her to read, to ride a small pink bike with training wheels, to play catch, to fish with a bamboo pole and big red bobber in the river that ran along the edge of the park.

And to give Tess the peace and quiet she needed when she was writing.

Claire adored her daddy, but held her mommy at a respectful, awestruck distance.

Tess couldn't blame the child, she supposed. The revisions and rewriting of *Rachel's Wilderness* had taken far more time and energy than she had anticipated. It was incredibly difficult, trying to be attentive both to the emotional needs of a precocious toddler and to the intellectual and creative demands of completing a novel.

And this wasn't just any novel. *Rachel's Wilderness* was Tess's debut, the novel that would set the tone and direction for her future career. It had to be perfect.

At last she finished—or abandoned her perfectionism, anyway. Around two hundred pages into the manuscript, she had, with Hal's help, secured an agent who had sold the unfinished novel to a small but prestigious New York house, and now she sent it off in duplicate to both her agent and her in-house editor. She waited, nervous and anxious and battling the postpartum depression that often follows the completion of such a work, as the book made its way through another nine months of editing and production.

It had taken all Tess's self-restraint to keep from spilling the beans to Lovey and Liz and Grace in the circle journal. She had written to them about the Iowa Writers' Workshop, about her romance with Hal and their wedding, about her infertility, about adopting Claire. She had tried to explain about her passion for writing, even though nonwriters rarely understood. But as much as she wanted to tell them how she had, finally, fulfilled her life's dream, she didn't dare jinx the book's release by prophesying its success.

Still, she had done it. *Rachel's Wilderness* would leave its imprint on the literary world, and the name Tess Riley-Hopkins would be on everyone's lips.

The novel made its mark, all right, and almost overnight her name *did* become known in the small subculture of literary fiction.

Riley-Hopkins's debut novel, Rachel's Wilderness, *leaves the unfortunate reader sucking sand from a desert mirage, searching for water but finding only dust,* one critic wrote. *The worst sort of maudlin, predictable, pseudo-literary angst.*

Feminism may be on the rise, said another reviewer, *but Tess Riley-Hopkins clearly lives in the stultifying world of the 1950s, where a woman's sole fulfillment—indeed, her only salvation—comes through childbearing. Rather than answering the call for edgy, razor-sharp contemporary fiction, Riley-Hopkins subjects the reader to a brutal assault with a blunt knife.*

Tess couldn't believe it. They had missed the point entirely. Everything she had written into Rachel's character was true. The torment was real, authentic.

It was Tess herself.

Consumed by horror and a sickening despair, she read the critiques like a condemned traitor facing a verdict of execution: *Self-conscious, contrived, plodding, oppressively unoriginal. An inauspicious beginning that bodes ill for both author and publisher.*

And the final scathing analysis, which chilled her blood as if ice had been injected directly into her veins: *Has no one ever told this woman that she is more than two ovaries and a womb?*

Surrounded by the devastating reviews, Tess slumped across the bed clutching a brand-new copy of *Rachel's Wilderness*. She inhaled the scent of crisp paper and fresh ink, watched the cover shimmer past her unfocused eyes, submerged under relentless tears. Her breath came hard, in racking sobs. Again and again she forced herself to read the clippings, as if her numb and bleeding soul were trying to flay itself into atonement with the scourging words.

Somewhere in the distance she heard a soft rustling sound, and turned to see Claire entering the bedroom on tiptoe, her wide blue eyes fixed on Tess's face. The little girl put a pudgy finger to her lips. "I'll be quiet," she whispered.

"It's OK. Come on." Tess pushed the clippings aside and scooted over to make room on the bed. Claire scrambled up beside her and snuggled her stout little body close, bumping the book out of her mother's grasp as she wriggled into the embrace.

"I know why you're sad, Mommy,"

Claire said softly. "Daddy told me. Some bad people didn't like your book."

Tess kissed the top of her daughter's tousled head and felt the child's warmth seep into her. She smelled like sunshine and fresh grass and toddler sweat, with a faint hint of strawberry jam. "They're not bad people, honey. They're just . . . just critics."

Claire reached a hand up to stroke Tess's tear-glazed cheek with her stubby fingers. She leaned close, as if she were about to reveal a grand and glorious secret.

"You know what, Mommy?" she whispered with a fierce, determined intensity. "Next time—" She beamed up at Tess, and her tangled blonde curls bobbed as she gave a vehement nod. "Next time you can write a story about *me*. And ever'body will love it. Even the crickets."

THE BIRTH OF C. J. KENNING

*T*ess smiled wistfully as the twenty-year-old memory returned. The scent of sun and earth in her daughter's hair. The light in the child's eyes, that determined lift of the chin as she prepared to unveil the utter genius of the idea her five-year-old brain had formulated.

Even now, as an adult, Claire still got that look on occasion. And when she did—when her jaw jutted upward and her expression illuminated from some hidden inner source—Tess and Hal both knew that their daughter had tapped into a deep well of the soul, and that whatever vision or decision proceeded from its depths, it was not to be second-guessed or argued with.

Besides, Claire was not often wrong.

The girl had a gift. She discerned innately, even at age five, how to connect with another's heartfelt longings and dreams, how to bring hope out of circumstances that seemed worse than hopeless.

Tess fingered the photograph on her desk, her mind now miles away from her protagonist Kendall Wright and his fictional dilemmas. "Out of the mouths of babes," she murmured, "come knowledge and insight and understanding."

Seven years had passed since the birth and untimely death of *Rachel's Wilderness*. In all that time, Tess Riley-Hopkins wrote nothing for publication. Not a single word.

Seven long years. Seven lean years. Seven years of drought and famine.

And yet she had rarely felt herself burning with inner thirst or clutching her distended soul in hunger. Her energy and attention had been consumed with a more immediate and infinitely more challenging career direction—learning to become a mother to the little girl she and Hal had adopted.

Tess had missed so much those first few months. Absorbed in the important work of finishing the Great American Novel, she had both physically and emotionally absented herself from her new daughter's life. But when *Rachel's Wilderness* launched and immediately sank before it ever got out into deep water, Tess found her perspectives radically altered—by force, initially, if not by choice.

Aimless and disoriented, she had wandered through the days immediately following *Rachel's* demise like a war refugee suffering from traumatic amnesia. What was she, if not a writer? *Who* was she? And where in God's name was she supposed to go from here?

Stalwart little Claire, with the immeasurable wisdom of a child, held all the answers. Tess was Mommy, and she was supposed to go to the park and play.

And so Tess played. She mastered the seesaw and the jungle gym and the vertigo-inducing curved slide on the far edge of the playground. Tucked her daughter in for afternoon naps. Created wild, floury messes in the kitchen, trying to figure out her grandmother's recipe for homemade brownies. Read *Horton Hears a Who* and *Wind in the Willows* and *The Secret Garden.*

Children, fortunately, tend to be resilient, and this particular child was extraordinarily forgiving. As soon as Tess made the first tentative move toward her, Claire flung herself into her mommy's arms and reached out to haul her daddy into the family hug. The little girl's compelling love drew them all together and held them there, and Tess felt a trickle down her spine, a shiver of understanding. Her icebound pain had begun, at last, to melt.

The humiliating agony of *Rachel's Wilderness,* of course, was no sidewalk scrape that could be healed with a kiss and a cookie. The experience stayed with her, a pulsing, tender scar. Periodically, without warning or premonition, questions bolted abruptly into her mind like forked lightning from a cloudless sky. Had the gift been recalled as retribution for her failure? Was it lying dormant, awaiting the day she would reclaim it? Had the muse deserted her forever, or merely withdrawn for a time?

And the ultimate question, the savage, clawing doubt that invaded her dreams and awakened her shuddering in a cold sweat: *Would she—could she—ever write again?*

But Tess could find no answers, and after a while the questions themselves came less frequently and eventually faded into irrelevance. Gradually the pain subsided and the wound scabbed over, mended partly by time, but mostly by the restorative balm of her husband's steady devotion and her daughter's exuberant affection, easy laughter, and curious mind.

And Tess had recorded it all. On an upper bookshelf in her office—now used primarily as her daughter's "quiet room," where Claire did homework and puzzles, read and thought and spent time alone—stood a series of three-ring notebooks, journals that spanned the past seven years. Filled with funny and tender and loving and heartrending moments, the pages chronicled Tess's life with Hal and Claire, capturing images that might otherwise have been lost to the inexorable passing of time.

On those inevitable random, rainy days when Hal was teaching and Claire was off at school, Tess would spend an hour or two sitting at the window, reading back over the memories the way others might flip through a favorite family album. The words generated recollections far more vivid than any photograph.

And then, one cloudy afternoon in the seventh year after the *Rachel* catastrophe, Tess pulled down the very first journal and opened it at the beginning.

At a time when I thought nothing could comfort me, she had written, *my little girl, just barely five and far too precocious for her own good, gave me a bit of advice about my writing career. "Next time you can write a story about me," she said. "And everybody will love it. Even the crickets."*

Write a story about me, Claire had said.

Something stirred deep in Tess's soul—a longing, a welling-up of desire so powerful, it threatened to overwhelm her. Images rose to her mind—the Secret Garden behind its high stone wall, overgrown with vines and yet burgeoning with unassailable life. A hidden door. A rusted key. A lily blooming beneath the thorns. The indomitable strength of love and faith, collective virtue and common hope.

The muse had returned, infused with fire

and trailing clouds of glory as it came. A vision, a concept so unpremeditated as to seem ludicrous upon first glance.

Tess sat stunned, her eyes unfocused, gazing past the raindrops that had begun to cluster and slide in rivulets down the windowpane. The floor beneath her angled and pitched—the tilting outward of a womb, the shift of heaven's dome when formless clouds transfigure into shapes upon the bright blue sky. A silent film unreeled against the back wall of her mind, and she watched in awe as earth heaved itself up into mountains, down into pastures and valleys. Water pooled to fashion lakes and oceans, rivers running endless toward the sea. From the arc of a wave, a fish leaped toward the sunlight, scattering drops like diamonds from its scales. Wind rose in the trees, and birds exploded into flight on untried wings. Hidden creatures moved through tall new grass—sleek, slithering things and furry, bustling things, predators on silent paws and prey scuttling to safety.

And then a shadowy figure, insubstantial as smoke, knelt and leaned down as if to kiss the earth. . . .

The notebook dropped from Tess's lap

and landed with a dull thud on the carpet at her feet. She gulped a breath, felt oxygen flow into her lungs, and heard the words inside her head:

It is good.

Her soul broke open, paused, and poised itself for birth. It was time. Time to listen to a five-year-old's advice. Time to set aside her fear and embrace a new and unfamiliar courage.

Time to take the risk to write again.

"C. J. Kenning?" Hal gazed at her, his expression a mixture of admiration and bemusement. "The *C. J.* I understand—it's the *Kenning* that puzzles me."

"Kenning was Mom's grandmother's maiden name," said Claire, as if this should be perfectly obvious to anyone with half a brain.

Tess moved the remains of dinner to one side and propped her elbows on the table. "And where on earth did you come by that bit of family trivia, my darling daughter?"

Claire shrugged. "You told me once. And last Christmas Aunt Duck showed me the family tree she had needlepointed for Grandma."

Tess slanted a glance at Hal, and he grinned broadly, as if to say, *Too smart for her own good, isn't she?*

"Well, you're absolutely right," Hal said, leaning across the table toward Claire. "I'd forgotten that Kenning was your great-grandmother's name. But it has another meaning, too. In literature a kenning is a specific type of metaphor, a combined, hyphenated form used in place of a name."

"Such as referring to God as Heart-Mender or Soul-Maker," Tess added. "Kennings often appear in Anglo-Saxon and early medieval literature."

"Like *Beowulf*," said Claire.

"What do you know about *Beowulf*?"

Claire heaved a sigh and raised one eyebrow. "I'm nearly thirteen, Mother, and have been literate for a year or two now. There's a copy in the school library—not a translation, really, but a kids' edition. Obviously dumbed-down a lot, but it's still a great story. And whoever did it kept in some of those words. God is the Heaven-Ruler, the World-Shaper. Grendel's mother is the sea-wolf, the monster-wife who drags

Beowulf, the sword-wielder, down under the whale-road—the sea—into her mere-house." She rolled her eyes. "Apparently this guy thought seventh-graders needed a footnote to tell them that *mere* means ocean. Like we never heard of mermaids. I hate it when grown-ups talk down to kids like that. Anyway, when Grendel's mom dies, the battle-blade melts into icicles, and Beowulf is released from his water-bonds. But it's not done just in epic poetry. I read some stuff by this guy named Hopkins, and he—"

"I see you've grasped the general concept of the kenning," Hal said dryly.

"Cool images," Claire went on. "Very cool. Let's see, my science teacher would be the Bunsen-Dweeb, and Mrs. Vole, the librarian, would be the Hiss-Whisperer, and—"

"We get the point. Can we amble on back to your mother's discussion now?" He turned toward Tess again. "Do you want to tell us more about this idea of yours, or do you need to keep it to yourself for a while?"

Tess, appreciative of his sensitivity around the issue of her writing, sent him a grateful glance and blew a kiss across the table. "It was Claire's idea, really."

"Mine?"

"Yes, yours. Something you said a very long time ago. I wrote about it in my journal, and then stumbled upon it again today. After—" She paused and pinched her lower lip. "After the disaster with that first novel, you told me I should write a story about you, and that everyone would love it."

Claire stifled a gasp. "How old was I, Mom? Four, maybe five? A little egomaniac, from the sound of it. A miniature drama queen." She shook her head. "Mother, *please* tell me you are not going to write about me and embarrass me in front of the entire world."

"Would I do that?"

Claire groaned. "Yes, you would." She flung her head back and screwed her eyes shut. "Help me, Jesus."

"There's no need to be sacrilegious," Hal said.

"I'm not being sacrilegious, Daddy. I'm *praying*." She fixed him with a scathing look.

"Well, you can quit storming the gates of heaven," Tess said. "I have no intention of writing specifically about you. What I'm considering is a series of novels about adopted children."

Claire looked up from her plate. "Now, *that's* a great idea," she said seriously. "I can give you lots of details about how awful it is."

Hal glared at her for a moment, then poked her in the ribs, and both of them dissolved into a fit of giggles.

Tess cleared the table while they regained their composure. When she resumed her seat, Claire had gone to do her homework and Hal was tearing his paper napkin into shreds.

"What?"

He rolled the napkin into a ball and placed it in front of him. "I was just wondering why you feel compelled to use a different name. A lot of years have gone by, and I doubt—"

"You doubt anyone would have the faintest idea who I am?" Tess laughed, a little surprised at how easily the admission came. "Trust me, sweetheart, this is not about leftover shame or public humiliation or some deep-seated fear that I might fail again."

"Are you sure?"

"Yes, I'm sure. I'm assuming a different name because—" She hesitated. "It's hard to explain."

"Take your time. I can be patient."

"You're always patient, my love." Tess reached across the table and twined her fingers in his. "I made a promise today. A promise to do things differently this time."

"Tess, you poured your soul into *Rachel's Wilderness*—"

She squeezed his hand. "Let me finish, all right?" At his nod, she continued. "Yes, I poured my soul into that book. I opened a vein, but what came out wasn't lifeblood. It was poison. *Rachel's Wilderness* was therapy, not fiction. It should never have been published."

"But you're a gifted writer, Tess. I've known that from the beginning."

"Yes, darling. I remember. You told me I couldn't remain invisible forever. It was a wonderful affirmation. But don't you see, that's exactly what I need to be. Invisible."

He waited while she arranged her thoughts. "I've never admitted this, even to you, but when I was in college and first beginning to identify myself as a writer, I entertained this persistent fantasy about becoming a Nobel laureate. Receiving the medal. Basking in the acclaim. Having my name go down in literary history. What I forgot—or perhaps was too young to realize—was that writing isn't about the prize. It's about the process. It's about serving the gift, whether I'm called to write the Great American Novel or a simple story for children."

He was gazing at her now with a look of rapt astonishment. "What changed?"

"*I* changed, Hal. I had—I don't know what to call it. A vision, maybe. An epiphany. A revelation. Not a physical manifestation, but a very detailed picture in my mind. An image of creation, of things coming into being. An image of the Earth-Shaper exhaling life and creativity into the world—and into me."

She ducked her head. "Maybe it sounds silly, but I had the feeling that I was being shown something I'd never seen before—or never acknowledged. Whatever gift or talent I possess is not really mine, but is instead part of the whole creative heartbeat of the universe. That's why I need to be invisible—so I can tell the story without getting in the way. So I can inhale that creative breath and feel it in my lungs and blood and soul. So I can breathe it out into my work."

"And you're not—" He hesitated. "I mean, after what happened with—"

"Afraid?" Tess finished. "Honey, how long have you been teaching fiction? You should know by now that writers are *always* afraid. Every time they begin a new project, they have to prove themselves all over again. With every new idea, they put their souls on the line."

She arched her eyebrows at him. "But invisibility has its perks. This time, at least, I won't be writing for the crickets."

THE CHOSEN CHILD

The Chosen Child.

Tess gazed down at the synopsis of her new book, and a surge of warmth rose up in her veins as her eyes lingered over the title. The time of famine, those seven lean years, had come to an end. The time of abundance had begun.

She had taken as her model her daughter's favorite classic novel, *The Secret Garden,* and she had a vision of creating intelligent, thought-provoking stories that centered around a child's inherent strength and insight and wisdom. Stories that would empower young readers to claim their own truths and trust their own hearts even when life cast formidable obstacles across their paths.

Writing novels for an adolescent audience, of course, thrust her into a completely different genre, with an unfamiliar range of expectations. What was important here was not literary erudition, but a compelling plot line; authentic, believable characters; and an element all too absent from her first novel—*hope*.

For this first book, she had begun with a main character who had completely captured her imagination—a witty, clever, outrageous little protagonist named, not surprisingly, Clarissa. She reread the introduction to her synopsis:

> *Abandoned at the doorstep of a rural parish church shortly after birth and raised by nuns in the adjoining convent, ten-year-old Clarissa is determined to find her mother and father. Beyond all doubt and reason, she is certain that her parents have spent the last ten years regretting the decision to give her up. If she can only find them, the family will be reunited and she will have a place to belong. . . .*

A few chapters into the rough draft, however—just as Clarissa had convinced her best friend, Rudy, to help her escape from the overprotective sisters—Tess began to hear it.

The cricket chorus. The murmuring, discordant refrain of disillusionment.

But this was not an echo of the scathing, caustic criticism from years gone by. This was a new voice. An annoying, persistent chirping from behind the baseboards of her own mind.

Junk. Complete trash. Stupid, puerile, infantile rubbish. She had no idea where this book was going, what Clarissa's outcome might be. Would she find her parents and have a happy ending? That seemed far too simplistic. Maybe she wouldn't find them, or find them only to discover they hadn't regretted their decision and didn't want her. And if that turned out to be the case, where was the hope?

None of this was working. What in God's name did she think she was doing? Why was she wasting her time and creative energies writing a driveling little children's tale that had no redeeming literary value? She was a graduate of the Iowa Writers' Workshop, for heaven's sake—the consummate program for writers of stature. She should be spending herself on something important.

Besides, it wasn't as if she were a novice, starting from scratch. Even if *Rachel's Wilderness* had been an abysmal failure from the critics' point of view, at least it had been a real novel—a novel for *adult* readers, intelligent, intellectual readers. And here she was struggling over a book for children. She should be able to turn this out in her sleep—

"Mom?" Tess turned. Claire stood in the doorway, her head cocked to one side. "Am I interrupting you?"

"No, it's all right." She waved a hand to brush aside her daughter's concern. "Come on in, if you dare."

Claire crooked a half-smile. "Writing's not going well, I assume?"

"It is, and it isn't." Tess shrugged. "See, I've got this terrific story in my head, about a little girl who was abandoned at birth and now, ten years later, is trying to find her parents." She hesitated for a moment. "The novel is called *The Chosen Child*—"

Claire settled herself into an overstuffed chair opposite the desk. "I like that. I remember Daddy explaining my own adoption to me. That's what he called me—a chosen child."

Tess grimaced. "Right. All great authors steal their best material. Look at Shakespeare."

Claire chuckled. "Anything I can do to help?"

Tess gazed at her daughter. Just barely thirteen, the girl was a walking dichotomy—immature at times, giggling and silly and still clinging to her childhood. And sometimes, as now, composed and centered, almost adult, with intelligent eyes gazing out from a fathomless soul. Perhaps it was time to have the conversation she had half dreaded for so many years.

She bit her lip and plunged. "Honey, have *you* ever thought about wanting to find your birth parents?"

Claire lifted an eyebrow. "Is this discussion for the novel, or for us?"

"Both, I guess."

"Well—" She shifted in her chair and dropped her book bag to the floor with a dull thud. "I—I'm not quite sure how I should answer that."

Tess leaned back in her chair. "Honestly, I hope. Go on. You won't hurt my feelings."

"OK then, yes," Claire said. "I have thought about it. It's not that I don't love you and Daddy—you know I do. You've been the best parents I could ever have imagined. But—"

"Please, continue," Tess urged.

"It's like this. I feel kind of a gap, this huge chasm I can't seem to jump over. I don't want to change my life, I just want to *know*. To know who my biological parents were, and why they gave me up. To know where I came from."

"Of course you do," Tess responded, trying to keep a lid on her emotions. It was to be expected, after all, that an adopted child would raise such questions. It didn't mean she had failed as a mother, or was on the verge of losing her only daughter to someone else. "The problem is, you may not be able to get those answers. Birth records are sealed, and until you're eighteen—"

"I know," Claire said. "It may be a mystery I have to live with."

"Still, it's a perfectly natural question." Tess was aware that her voice sounded unnaturally bright, strained. "You want to know who you are, who your real parents are."

At this, Claire gave her mother an incredulous glance and shook her head. "*No.* That's not it at all."

"What do you mean, *no*?"

"Mother, I *already* know who I am. I'm Claire Riley-Hopkins. I'm your daughter, and Daddy's. Don't you get it? You *are* my 'real' parents. It doesn't matter whose gene pool I came out of. Oh, sure, I'm curious about my past, my birth, but having that information wouldn't make any difference. I belong here, right here, in this house, in this family. Family's not about bloodlines, it's about love and acceptance. You become who you are not because of where you came from, but because of where you're going, and who's going there with you."

Tess took in a ragged breath, and something bright and sparkling exploded in the back of her mind. She held up a hand. "Can you give me a minute here? What you've just said has triggered an idea for me, and I'd like to write it down."

Claire grinned. "Sure. I'll go get a drink. We got anything to eat?"

"Yeah, there are some chocolate chip cookies in the pantry," Tess said distractedly. "Bring them back with you when you come. And a glass of iced tea for me, if you don't mind."

"You got it."

Claire left the study, and Tess turned back to her typewriter. She jerked out the half-written page, fed in a fresh one, and began to pound the keys furiously. Suddenly it had all come clear, where little Clarissa's quest was taking her. Not to an answer, but to an understanding. Not to finding her parents, but to discovering herself.

She had typed nearly a full page of notes before she realized that Claire was back in the armchair again with her legs crossed under her. "You done?" She pointed to the glass of iced tea on the edge of the desk and held out the cookie tin.

"Yes. Thanks." Tess took a sip of tea and helped herself to two cookies. "Nothing like chocolate to soothe the troubled soul."

"So, are you going to tell me about the book?" Claire dunked a cookie into her glass of milk and bit off half. "O word-forger, story-crafter, kenning-mother?"

"Cute. Very cute." Tess glanced back over the notes she had written. "What you said about family and belonging was exactly what I needed. You don't mind if I use it, do you?"

"Always glad to help."

"I think it will make a difference. Still—"

Claire peered at her over the rim of her glass. "What's the problem, Mom?"

"It's not easy to explain. It's a writer thing."

"Try me."

Tess heaved a mighty sigh. "All right. I've got this idea in my head, and part of me believes it will work. But it's not coming out the way I want it. Everything I write seems—I don't know. Stupid. Juvenile."

Claire laughed and popped another cookie into her mouth. "Wait, wait—I know it's not funny," she protested when she caught a glimpse of her mother's expression. "It's just that—OK, let me ask you a question. You're trying to write for kids, correct?"

"Yeah," Tess hedged. "Your age, and a little younger."

"So how are you doing it? I mean, what's the difference between writing for kids and writing for adults?"

Tess considered the question and tried to recall the parameters she had set for herself. "Well, it's partly a matter of construction. A book for children can't be a head trip, it's got to have action and movement and clear chronology, and—" She shook her head. "I don't know what I'm doing wrong. I just can't seem to translate my ideas into the proper language."

"Translate?" Claire slanted a glance at her. "Oh, you mean like dumbing it down so your pathetic, ignorant little readers can understand it."

When her mother didn't respond, Claire backtracked. "Sorry. I probably shouldn't have been that blunt."

"Don't hedge." Tess waved her on. "I want to hear what you have to say."

"OK. Here it is. I'm wondering if, deep down, you consider writing for children lower, somehow. Less important. Less challenging."

"Right now it seems *more* challenging, if you want to know the truth."

"Maybe it is. I'm only thirteen, so I

probably don't know much about it, but what I do know is that kids understand a whole lot more than adults usually give them credit for. I read a lot, and the books I like most are not dumbed-down. They're books where the authors—how do I say this? Where the authors *respect* their readers even if they're only kids. And it seems like in those books the authors respect themselves, too."

"And you think I don't respect myself?"

"Until I read what you've written, I have no idea. I just know that the best children's stories aren't only for children. They may have kid characters, but they've got substance."

She fixed Tess with an intense gaze. "Mom, why did you decide to write under a different name?"

Tess thought about this. "So I could be free," she said at last. "Free from the pressure of other people's expectations."

"Hmmm. Seems like your own expectations are the ones you ought to be worried about." Claire unfolded herself from the chair and retrieved her book bag from the floor at her feet. "I've got homework," she said. "But think about something, will you? This *Chosen Child* thing sounds like a pretty good idea to me. Maybe you should just let yourself go. Forget about being a great writer. Forget about trying to translate down to kids. Just write it."

She slung the bag over her shoulder and headed for the door.

"Honey?" Tess called to her retreating back.

"Yeah?"

"How on earth did you get so wise?"

Claire turned and grinned. "That's easy," she said. "I'm my mother's daughter."

THE BEST PRIZE OF ALL

*T*ess turned back to her computer, back to her protagonist Kendall Wright, still trapped in the deserted schoolroom. Sometimes she still couldn't believe how far that first *Chosen Child* book had taken her.

Her eyes wandered to the wall above the computer desk. Three Horn Book awards, two Newbery medals, and numerous less auspicious honors, all bearing the name *C. J. Kenning.* No one knew it was she, Tess Riley-Hopkins, whose books had garnered those awards. No one except her immediate family, her agent, and her publisher.

And displayed prominently in the middle of all of them, an antique bronze plaque bearing the words of William Blake. A daily, hourly reminder: *Imagination is evidence of the Divine.*

Her dear, wise daughter Claire had been right all those years ago. She had touched a nerve, revealed a truth that Tess herself hadn't been able to admit. It wasn't the critics' expectations that threatened to undo her—it was her own.

When Tess had told Hal about her intention to write under an assumed name, she had said that writing wasn't about the prize, it was about the process. It was about inhaling the creative breath and exhaling it again in her work. It was about watching the dry bones of an idea rise up, slip on a cloak of flesh, and live.

It had taken some time, however, for her heart to grasp what her head had instinctively perceived. The goal was not to *be known,* but to *know*—to understand herself, to discern the subtle presence of wonder, to embrace the connection with the universe that came through creativity. Her calling was not to be a prodigy, an intellectual or artistic marvel. Idols shattered; golden calves got ground to dust. Her only ambition, now, was to receive the kiss imparted when the eternal Source bent down and

touched the earth—the image of the Cre-
ator, the pulsing breath of the Word-
Crafter.

Ironically, it had been C. J. Kenning, not
Tess Riley-Hopkins, who in the end became a star. Perhaps not a luminary like
C. S. Lewis or Madeleine L'Engle, or a
polestar like Frances Hodgson Burnett, or a
celestial phenomenon like Jo Rowling, but
nevertheless a clear, bright pinpoint in a
minor constellation.

And behind the name of Kenning, Tess
had been protected, shielded from the siren
song of fame, the seductive lure of ego. She
was the mystery woman. The invisible
celebrity. And she intended to keep it that
way.

Chapter 9 had disappeared again, behind
the screen saver of the Blue Ridge Mountains. Tess gazed at the picture—a sunset
scene, with vivid pink and orange clouds
descending over multilayered pinnacles of
blue and green and dusky purple. The
scrolling photos always reminded her of
home, of Mother and Daddy and Duck, of
growing up surrounded by those magnificent peaks.

She loved her life in Iowa with Hal and

Claire, in what her daughter always called "the not-so-little house on the prairie." But sometimes she couldn't help wishing the landscape here weren't so . . . flat.

A soft tread on the stairs alerted her to the fact that Hal was home. She looked up as he paused in the doorway.

"Am I interrupting you?"

Tess laughed. "Believe me, there's nothing to interrupt."

He entered the study and came over to the desk to kiss her. "Are we having an unproductive day?"

"Not really. I'll get this chapter finished eventually. Travis called, and he always jolts me back to unwelcome reality."

"Your publisher wants a book tour, right?"

"How did you guess?"

Hal grinned and dropped an armload of mail on the edge of the desk. "What else does Travis usually want, unless he's asking about your deadline?"

Tess picked up the pile and began sorting through it. "What are you doing home at this hour?" She kept one eye on her husband as she picked out the bills and chucked the advertisements in the trash.

"And what hour do you think it is?" He gave her a wry half-smile.

She laid aside a large padded envelope from her publisher—no doubt an accumulation of fan mail. "I have no idea."

"It's twelve-thirty. My two o'clock class isn't meeting—they're doing small critique groups today—so I thought I'd come home and get some lunch, then start on that stack of short stories I haven't had time to grade."

"Sounds good," she said, only half listening.

"So, have you eaten?" When Tess didn't answer, he knocked three times on the desktop. "Hello? Porch light on, nobody home."

"Oh, sorry." Her eyes returned to his face, but she kept fingering the cream-colored envelope she held in her hands.

"I asked if you'd eaten. But that's a ridiculous question, isn't it? You forget about insignificant issues like meals when you're writing." He took the bills off the desk and tapped them in his hand. "Listen, I'll go make some chicken salad, and if you want to join me, it'll be ready in ten minutes."

"Hal," Tess said as she slid into a chair opposite him at the small breakfast table, "do you think you can spare me for a few days?"

Hal spluttered into his iced tea. "Spare you?" He tried unsuccessfully to suppress a laugh. "Darling, you know I love you. You're a wonderful writer, a great mother, a marvelous partner. But unless I'm sadly mistaken, I've made more dinners and done more housework than you have in the past twenty years."

"That's quite true," Tess conceded willingly. She took a bite of her chicken salad sandwich. "Mmm. Good."

"What's this about? Don't tell me you've decided to go on tour."

"Very funny. As if Travis wouldn't have a coronary right there on the spot if I said yes." She fished in the back pocket of her jeans, took out the cream-colored envelope, and handed it to him.

He read the letter quickly. "This is the Grace of the circle journal girls?"

"Women," Tess corrected automatically,

then realized he was baiting her, and flushed. "Yes. She doesn't say what it is she wants to talk about, but it sounds important. And it's been ages since any of us have seen each other. I want to go."

"Sure, I don't see any problem with it. Will this interfere with your deadline?"

Tess waved a potato chip in his direction. "I can make up the time when I get back. I've got revision days built into my schedule."

"Then by all means, go, if it feels important to you."

"I probably should stay a couple of extra nights and visit Mother and Daddy, too. They'd never forgive me if I went to Asheville without seeing them—assuming, of course, that they can fit me into their schedule." She took another bite of her sandwich and smiled. "When they retired and moved to Deerfield Village, I was worried about how Daddy would adjust to idleness after being bishop for so many years. But the last time I talked to Mother, she said he was playing tennis three times a week at the Racquet Club and preaching at least once a month for Sunday services at the chapel. Mother swims every day and offers spiritual direction and volunteer grief counseling." Tess shook her head in disbelief. "Hope I'm in that kind of shape when I'm in my seventies."

"I'd settle for being in that kind of shape *now*," said Hal. "So, let's see—" He checked his pocket planner. "You'll be gone April 11th through 14th for the reunion, and then, what—two more days with your parents? That'll get you back on April 17th. Claire's big day is June 9th. That's plenty of time to finalize the arrangements." He looked up from the calendar. "Your parents are coming, right? And Duck?"

"They wouldn't miss this for the world. Mother is wild with excitement, and Daddy, bless his heart, couldn't be prouder."

"And what about you?" Hal asked. "Do you feel like you're about to lose your little girl?"

Tess muffled a snort. "That child hasn't been a 'little girl' since she was about seven. But no, I don't feel as if I'm losing anything. I feel as if I'm witnessing the fulfillment of something I've waited a lifetime for."

The second week of April came upon Tess more quickly than she had anticipated. She was still tossing clothes into her suitcase when Hal came into the bedroom to tell her it was time to go.

She glanced at the clock on the bedside table and groaned inwardly. "It's 8:25, for heaven's sake. My plane leaves Cedar Rapids at 10:40, and it's only forty-five minutes from here to the airport. But of course you always want to be everywhere an hour earlier than we need to be."

If Hal took note of the irritation in her voice, he didn't let on. He sat down on the edge of the bed and waited.

"I can't figure out what to take," she said, holding up a short-sleeve cotton sweater in a heathery lavender tone. "How's this?"

"I like that one. It goes great with your hair color."

"My hair color, as you know perfectly well, is Clairol #613 Dark Auburn." She scowled at him.

"Yes, but it's a perfect complement to your—ah, *original* color."

"*Men,*" she muttered under her breath. "I'm mostly packing nice jeans and light sweaters, and one pair of black dress pants. Think that's OK?"

"Whatever you take will be fine, I'm sure."

"Don't be patronizing," Tess growled.

He held up his hands in a gesture of surrender. "Call me when you're done."

"I'm done." She flung one last pair of jeans into the suitcase, wedged in her hair dryer and makeup case, and slammed the lid. "Let's go."

They bolted down the stairs and through the kitchen to the garage. While Hal put the bag in the trunk, Tess settled into the passenger seat with a sigh.

"Sweetheart," he said tentatively as he backed the car out of the driveway, "is there something you'd like to talk about before you leave?"

"Such as?"

"You seem a bit . . . *edgy.* I thought you were looking forward to this trip."

She pulled down the visor mirror and pretended to check her lipstick. "Edgy," she repeated. "That's a tactful way of saying that I've been a grouchy, irritable bitch."

"You have been a tad grumpy. What's wrong?"

Tess exhaled heavily and twisted around in the seat to face him. "It's the idea of this reunion," she admitted. "Yes, I want to go—at least I think I do. It'll be great to see Grace and Liz and Lovey again, and if Grace's news is bad, I want to be there for her. But—" She paused, frowning. "But what am I going to say to them?"

"Do you let them know, you mean, that you're C. J. Kenning, the celebrated children's author?"

"Something like that. You know how these things go. We'll all catch up on what we've been doing. I don't think it'll be like a big school reunion, where everybody's trying to impress each other. At least I hope we'll be more real than that. Still, I feel torn. If I'm honest with them and tell them I'm C. J. Kenning, it might sound like bragging, and besides, being famous can be a huge ego trap, one I still have to guard against. On the other hand, I don't want them to pity me because it looks like I never fulfilled my dreams."

"And is becoming a successful writer the only dream you've fulfilled?" he asked gently.

"Of course not. There's you, and Claire, and our life together." She shrugged. "Sure, I can talk to them about our family life. But things have changed a lot since the last time Lovey and Liz and I were together. I'm not sure they would understand about the other aspects of my life—the spiritual stuff that has to do with my writing. When they knew me I was on hiatus from the church."

Hal reached over, took her hand, and held it. His grasp, warm and firm and reassuring, filled her with a familiar sense of comfort.

"Trust your instincts," he said. "You'll know what to do when the time comes."

Tess settled herself in 7B, the aisle seat over the wing. She fastened her lap belt and looked again at her itinerary. The first leg of the flight, from Cedar Rapids to Cincinnati, would take a little over two hours. She had a layover in the Cinci airport from one to three-thirty, long enough to get lunch and do a little work, and then another two hours to Asheville. Assuming no unfortunate surprises—which was a big assumption, she realized—they'd be landing in Asheville at 4:30, Eastern Time.

Spending seven hours in crowded airports and in the cramped quarters of a fifty-seater minijet wasn't her idea of a good time. But it wouldn't be a wasted day, at any rate. She had the first eight chapters of her current novel stuffed in her carry-on bag, and as soon as the plane got off the ground, she intended to get to work revising and polishing the manuscript.

Other passengers were milling about, finding their places and stowing gear in the overhead compartments, but as yet no one had taken the seat beside her. *Please,* Tess thought silently, *please . . .*

But her prayer went unanswered. Someone was standing in the aisle, hovering over her, waiting. She looked up to see a beefy, red-faced woman with overpermed blondish hair. A farmer's wife, if Tess's years in Iowa had taught her anything.

"Hey there," the woman said, pointing

to her boarding pass. "Looks like we're gonna be seatmates."

Tess unbuckled her seat belt and stood up. The woman squeezed past her, crammed her bulk into the window seat, and with much huffing and grunting managed to click the belt around her wide hips. "Shoot, don'tcha hate these tin cans?" she said with a grin.

Tess nodded, reached under the seat for her carry-on, and extracted the file folder containing her manuscript. The woman didn't get the hint.

"Name's Jane Seymour," she said, holding out a workworn hand. "Goin' to Cincinnati to visit my daughter and grandbaby."

Tess kept her face lowered and dug in her bag some more, trying in vain to suppress a fit of the giggles. What might the beautiful auburn-haired actress think of her namesake? Tess could almost see the headline of the *Enquirer*—a grainy photo of this Iowa version of Seymour superimposed by a two-inch headline: DR. QUINN'S BATTLE OF THE BULGE.

She fought to get control of herself, turned, and shook Jane's hand. "Tess

Riley-Hopkins," she said by way of introduction.

"Nice to meet you, Tess." Jane gave a self-deprecating shrug. "Yeah, I know. Pretty funny, ain't it? Jane Seymour. Don't I wish."

The minijet revved its engines, taxied down the runway, and took off, its droning whine nearly drowning out the flight attendant's passenger safety instructions. As soon as they were at cruising altitude, heading southeast toward Ohio, Jane launched into a one-sided conversation about her daughter Mary Anne and her successful executive son-in-law William, and how William was a little too snobby and highfalutin for her taste, but how he was good to her daughter and granddaughter and provided well for them, and how she reckoned a mama couldn't ask more than that. Eventually she abandoned the in-law bashing and wandered on to a bizarre story about her husband, who had last year dropped dead from a stroke while tilling his cornfields.

"And that old tractor just kept chugging on in a straight line until it brought him right back to the house and only stopped when it plowed into the silo. I run out to see what the blazes was going on, and there he was, dead as a doornail, still hangin' on to the steering wheel. Holy buckets, it was some kinda sight, I can tell you."

She paused for breath while the flight attendant lurched past them with the cart, setting down cans of barely cool pop and little foil packages of mini-pretzels.

When the attendant had proceeded down the aisle, the monologue rolled on, with Tess half listening and saying "uh-huh" as Jane Seymour spun out her life story. Twice the epic skidded to a halt while Jane flagged down the flight attendant—whom she called *stewardess*—to ask for another can of diet pop and more pretzels. But once the in-flight refueling had been successful, the woman's engines sputtered to life again.

Jane Seymour would make a great character for a novel, Tess thought.

"I see you got yourself a load of paperwork there," Jane said when the attendant had come and gone for the third time. She pointed to the unopened file folder that lay on the tray table in front of Tess. "You a writer or something?"

Tess pasted on a smile. She had been dreading the inevitable question, although Jane's tendency toward nonstop narration had given her a faint, fleeting hope that a two-hour flight wouldn't be long enough to get around to the subject. "Yes," she said reluctantly.

"Well, I'll be jiggered. Never met a writer before." She peered at Tess as if she were some exotic zoo specimen. "What was your name again?"

"Tess. Tess Riley-Hopkins."

Jane frowned and shook her head. "Sorry. Can't say I've heard of you. Got anything published?" She said this with overtones of awe, as if a published writer were an alien who breathed the elements of a completely different stratosphere.

"A few things here and there."

"And what kind of stuff do you write?" Jane gave a furtive glance at the file folder, which still lay closed in front of Tess.

Tess pushed the folder a little farther out of Jane's reach. "I write books for children."

"Children's books. If that don't beat all." Jane leaned over with some difficulty and dragged a large, bulky purse from beneath the seat in front of her. "Looky here. I'm taking this one to my grandbaby." She emerged again, puffing hard from the exertion of bending double. "Her name's Chantell. Now, who'd go and name a baby that?" she asked, not pausing for an answer. "My daughter's high-and-mighty husband, that's who. Never heard of such. Sounds like some kinda hundert-dollar perfume."

She hauled a hardbound book from the side pocket of her handbag and pushed it in Tess's direction. "It's called *The Chosen Child*," she explained as if Tess couldn't read. "See, it's signed by the author and everything."

Tess peered down at the title page. Sure enough, there was her signature—one of the special autographed editions that had been distributed to selected bookstores.

"This book's been around awhile, I reckon, but it's real good. The fella at the store called it a classic. Won some kind of big book award. See that little gold seal there?" She shut the cover and held the book up, displaying the Newbery Medal. "Chantell will be real thrilled to get a signed copy."

"Ah," said Tess. "Wait a minute. I thought you said Chantell was a baby."

"Aw, she ain't really, not anymore." Jane guffawed heartily. "She'll be eleven come November. But she'll always be my baby girl." She leaned forward and lowered her voice to a whisper. "She's real smart. And this is her favorite book. She's adopted, y'know."

"Is she?"

"Yeah," said Jane. "That son-in-law of mine might be vice president of some big bigwig company, but he ain't got swimmers worth spit."

Tess stifled a laugh but managed to refrain from commenting on William's fertility problem. "Adoption is a good choice. I have an adopted daughter myself."

"No foolin'. Well, ain't that nice. How old is your little girl?"

"She's all grown up. Twenty-seven."

"I bet you're real proud." Jane picked up the autographed copy of *The Chosen Child* and jammed it back into her bag. "I s'pose there's something to be said for being a writer like that, rich and famous and gettin' medals and awards and recognition for what you do," she said. "But for my money, there ain't no prize like a simple life and a loving family."

Tess leaned back in her seat as the plane nosed forward for its descent into Cincinnati. "You got that right," she said. "Love is the best prize of all."

PART V

THE CIRCLE

A well-loved signature,
a simple stroke of pen on paper,
transports us
to gilded leaves in autumn,
candid photographs,
spring grass,
old ink—
the long-neglected moments
from a past
we thought we'd left behind.

Memory changes everything—
what was, what is,
and what is yet to be.

TOUCHDOWN

Grace sat fidgeting in the waiting area of the Asheville airport, her hindquarters squashed into an unnaturally curved plastic seat. The clock overhead told her it was nearly five. The arrival/departure board listed Lovey's flight, Delta #4276, connecting through Atlanta, as scheduled for arrival at 4:54 P.M. The sign now blinked the words ON GROUND next to Lovey's flight, but Grace had yet to see anyone emerge from the narrow tunnel leading to the tarmac.

For a small regional airport, the place was uncharacteristically nice—one long, low, meandering front building of natural stone that expanded to two levels on the runway side. The upper level, which serviced the few jets in and out of Asheville, actually boasted an expanding passageway so that travelers could board and exit without going outside. The recently renovated lower level had a long hallway leading to a couple of ground-level gates. Here the flights loaded and disembarked on the runway, forcing passengers to descend from the smaller planes on an open metal stairway and dash, windblown and harried, across the blacktop to the shelter of the building. It always put Grace in mind of the final scene of *Casablanca,* and made her feel as if she had been transported back to the forties.

Grace had intended to wait for Lovey at the gate, where there were comfortable rocking chairs and plenty of room. But since 9/11, the Asheville airport had become strict to the point of paranoia. Security guards swaggered around with their thumbs hooked in their belts, daring anyone to look suspicious. Ticketed passengers only were allowed through the checkpoint to the boarding areas. Family and friends waited out front, milling around in the open space next to the coffee shop and haggling for the minimal seating.

The metal detectors, the luggage searches, the body wands—it all seemed like overkill to Grace. What terrorist in his right mind would bother hijacking a flight from Asheville? Most of these planes were antiquated two-prop jobs that made passengers feel as if they ought to flap their arms or hold up their feet to aid in the liftoff.

Delta #4276, however, had apparently landed without incident, and now travelers began to filter through the passageway in twos and threes. Grace got up and went to stand amid the small cluster of greeters crowded around the doorway.

She felt as if someone had unleashed a colony of live bats in her stomach. For a brief moment she wondered if she had been wrong to avoid those earlier reunions, if having seen Liz and Lovey and Tess in the interim might make things easier now. But then the reality of thirty years of deception came crashing in on her. No. Avoidance had been the wiser move. It was *this* reunion that was pure insanity.

Behind a businessman carrying a briefcase and talking in a loud, animated voice on a cell phone, she caught a glimpse of someone who might be Lovey. Not thin and athletic-looking like the old college Lovey, but blonde, at least, and looking around as if searching for someone.

Grace raised a tentative hand, and their eyes met. The woman veered in Grace's direction, hauling a rolling blue suitcase behind her. She cocked her head and pointed as if to say *You?*, and Grace nodded.

The two of them met in an awkward, one-armed hug. Grace pulled back and peered into the unfamiliar round face. "Lovey?"

The woman gave her a curious look. "No, I'm not Lovey. I just needed a hug after that hair-raising flight." Then she laughed. "Yes, of course it's me. How are you, Grace?"

"I'm—I'm fine," Grace said, flustered. "Can I carry something? Do you have checked baggage?"

"Nope, this is it. You can take my carry-on, if you don't mind."

Grace retrieved the bag, which had slipped down to Lovey's elbow, and hefted it onto her own shoulder. "Tess's flight was supposed to be in at 4:33," she said, "but it's been delayed. Supposedly it'll be here by 5:45 or so." She steered Lovey toward the coffee shop. "Since we're going to have a bit of a wait, I thought maybe we'd sit outside."

She bought coffee and cinnamon rolls at the counter, then led the way to the patio, a small enclosed garden accessible only through glass doors at the back of the coffee shop. A few metal tables and chairs sat adjacent to a large stone waterfall that cascaded into an eddying artificial pond surrounded by early spring flowers.

"Ah, this is nice," said Lovey as she settled into a chair and stretched her legs out. "Whoever planned this garden did a beautiful job, with the flowers and all. It feels miles away from the airport." She tore open a pink packet and stirred the artificial sweetener into her coffee with a stick. "We've still got snow at home."

"I can't imagine." Grace took a sip from the foam cup, then tried to cut off a bite of the cinnamon roll with a flimsy plastic fork. The fork shattered in half, and the handle flew out of Grace's hand. It landed with a splash in the pond, leaving plastic tines still embedded in the top of the roll.

"Fingers," Lovey said, pulling a portion

of the sticky bun apart and plopping it in her mouth. "Mmm. That's really good."

Grace got up, fished the plastic handle out of the water, and dropped it in the trash can next to their table. "So, ah, how was your flight?" she asked as she surreptitiously examined Lovey over the rim of her cup.

"Fine. Long." Lovey took another bite of cinnamon roll. "They say you can't get to hell without transferring in Atlanta." She laughed lightly. "But given what I saw at Hartsfield, Atlanta *is* hell—or purgatory, at least."

They sat in silence for a few more minutes, ostensibly admiring the waterfall, but in actuality scoping each other out—the clumsy, tentative dance of reacquaintance.

Up close, Grace could just barely recognize the old Lovey, the cheerleader. She wore a smart black suit with teal trim, a glittering diamond ring and matching bracelet, and—she cut a glance under the table— very expensive shoes. Her nails were immaculately manicured, and her makeup was perfect, even after a grueling day of traveling. On the surface she looked exactly the way a rich businessman's wife ought to look—content, well-heeled, put together.

Beneath the surface, however, there was something else. Something not quite so *finished*. Her smile was the same, although padded with more flesh through the cheeks and around the jawline. The blonde hair was an excellent color job.

Still, fine lines fanned out from around her eyes and mouth. She seemed . . . *old*. Old and tired and worn.

But they were all old, Grace mused. She had put on a few pounds over the years too—or, if she were to be perfectly honest, a few *dozen*—and her hair was more gray than brown. The metamorphosis had come on gradually—she didn't know when or how—until one day she woke up to realize she had become one of those ubiquitous middle-aged women who haunt the malls and grocery stores, all looking as if they had been cloned from a single original source. Had she not been standing in the airport craning her neck, clearly on the lookout for someone, Lovey probably would have walked right past her.

"Yeah, I know," said Lovey suddenly. "I'm not exactly what you expected."

Grace felt heat creep up her hairline. She had been staring. "Sorry, I—"

"It's all right. After so long, this is bound to be a bit awkward at first." Lovey gave a tight little laugh. "I wish you had been able to come to the other reunions. But, gosh, the last one was, what—fifteen years ago? Doesn't seem like that long. Of course, we've kept up with each other through the circle journal, so it's not like we're starting over from scratch."

"Right," Grace said. The bats in her gut shifted and fluttered.

"And I suppose we ought to save the important conversations for when we're all together." Lovey looked at her wristwatch. "When did you say Tess's flight was supposed to arrive?"

"Quarter to six. What time is it?"

"Five-fifteen. What about Liz?"

"She's driving. She'll join us at the Grove Park." Grace picked at her cinnamon roll. "She's bringing a friend with her."

"Oh." Lovey sounded disappointed. "I—I thought this was just for the four of us."

"It is. Her friend—Samantha? I forget. Anyway, her friend is riding down with her and then will go back up to Blowing Rock for a couple of days. She has a sister or cousin or somebody who lives there."

Lovey frowned. "Isn't that doubling back? I thought Blowing Rock was east of here off I-40."

"It's about ninety miles northeast. And yes, coming here first is out of the way. But I guess she needs the car. And Liz asked if she could have dinner with us tonight—she wants us to meet her."

"Really?" Lovey raised a perfectly arched eyebrow.

"That's what she said. They live together, and apparently have for years, since Liz's divorce."

"Hmmm. Liz didn't tell us any of this in the journal. Do you think—?"

Grace laughed, feeling a bit more at ease now. "I have no idea, Lovey. I guess we'll just have to see when they get here."

"Well, that would be pretty interesting, wouldn't it, if Liz had—ah, switched sides?"

"I don't think people just *decide* to 'switch sides,' as you put it," said Grace. "I think people are who they are. It may take some people longer to discover the truth about themselves, that's all."

"And you'd be OK with that? If Liz turned out to be—?"

"It's Liz's life, not mine," Grace said firmly. "As long as she's settled and happy with herself, that's all that matters to me. I certainly have no plans to interfere."

Lovey's eyes widened. "All right, where's the pod?"

"Excuse me?"

"Whoever you are, you're not the Grace Benedict I knew thirty years ago. That woman once gave me hell about my relationship with Bo."

Grace shrugged. "Yes, I'm afraid I did. And I should have kept my mouth shut." She fixed Lovey with an intent gaze. "This comes years too late, Lovey, but will you forgive me? I was completely out of line. I had no right to impose my opinions on you."

An odd expression flickered across Lovey's face. "That's water under the bridge, Grace. It's been over and forgiven long ago." Her voice lowered almost to a whisper. "You *have* changed, haven't you?"

"I sincerely hope so," Grace said.

❧

"Lord help us," Lovey hissed in Grace's ear as she caught her first glance of Tess. "She looks exactly the same."

Grace watched as the auburn-haired figure in blue jeans and a heathery purple sweater made her way through the knot of jostling passengers in the doorway. "No. She looks *better,*" Grace breathed. "Maybe running around after a child kept her in shape." An old familiar pain throbbed somewhere in the reaches of her stomach, and she fell silent.

"I had two," Lovey countered. "Never did that for me."

Tess scanned the crowd, caught a glimpse of them, and waved. She moved closer, hefted her black bag higher on her shoulder, and caught them both in a hug, an arm around each of them.

"Grace, Lovey!" She grinned broadly. "It is so good to see you both."

"I thought it was going to be good to see you, too," Lovey said. "But I was wrong. I hate you, Tess. You look *wonderful.*"

"I hate you too, Lovey." Tess laughed, and her eyes roved appreciatively over Lovey's designer suit. "You're looking pretty fine yourself." She turned toward Grace. "This was a brilliant idea, Grace. I'm so glad you invited us."

Grace pasted on a smile as they went through baggage claim, retrieved Tess's suitcase, and left the airport. Had this reunion been a brilliant idea? She had thought so when she conceived it. Now she wasn't so sure.

The limousine ride from the airport to the Grove Park Inn seemed to take forever. Grace and Tess sat in the back seat facing Lovey, who had removed her shoes and was massaging her aching feet.

"You're the smart one, Tess," she said, pointing to Tess's leather running shoes. "I should have gone more casual." She gave a self-deprecating shrug. "Who am I kidding? When you're Big Bo's wife, this is as casual as you're allowed to get."

Grace and Tess exchanged a glance. "Big Bo?"

"Long story better left for later," Lovey said. She narrowed her eyes at Tess. "So, come on, out with it. How can you possibly look so good? Plastic surgery? Liposuction?"

"Me?" Tess lifted one eyebrow. "I'm just a dumpy midwestern housewife."

Lovey snorted. "Right. And I'm Cindy Crawford."

"Let's face it, none of us is going to make the cover of *Cosmo*," Tess said.

"Maybe not, but you look fabulous."

"Thanks to Miss Clairol." Tess ran a hand through her hair. "And my husband and daughter, of course. I'm—" She paused. "Well, I'm happy. Really happy."

Lovey leaned forward and put her shoes on again. "How is your little girl?"

"She was a *little girl* the last time we saw each other." Tess crooked a smile. "She's now twenty-seven."

"I should have realized that. Mine are in their twenties, too. Carolyn is twenty-eight, and B.J.—Bo Junior—is twenty-four."

"Makes you feel old, doesn't it, when your kids are grown and on their own?" Grace watched as the expression on Tess's face turned soft and nostalgic. "I seem to spend half my time remembering things Claire said and did when she was a child."

Grace's insides turned over. *Claire.* She

had forgotten that Tess's daughter was named Claire. Just like—

She turned her head and stared out the window of the limo, willing herself not to think.

"She was a wonderful child," Tess went on. "Sensitive and wise and loving. And, fortunately, she's grown into an equally sensitive, wise, and loving young woman. I'm very fortunate. Very proud of her."

Grace barely heard the conversation that swirled around her. Carolyn, the actress. B.J., the budding artist living in Paris. And Claire.

Claire. Claire. Claire. The limousine's tires sped over asphalt patches on the highway, thudding in rhythm with the pounding in her head.

Claire. Claire. Claire.

She shut her eyes and leaned her forehead against the cool glass of the window, praying with all her might that she would have the strength to get through this. The limo ride, the thumping, the memories, the confession. All of it.

She just wanted it to be done.

32

Table for Five

"Samantha, we're so glad you could join us for dinner," said Grace as a waiter in a white tuxedo shirt seated them around a table at the edge of the Grove Park's Sunset Terrace.

Liz felt herself wince, and instead of looking at Grace, she stared off into the distance, at the mountains that rose up in layers of blue and purple against the setting sun. A breeze lifted her hair from her forehead.

"It's Serena," Serena corrected with a generous smile.

"Oh—oh, sorry," Grace mumbled.

"That's perfectly understandable. Serena is an unusual name." She looked around at Grace and Lovey and Tess. "I'm so pleased to meet all of you. Liz has talked about you so much that I feel I almost know you."

"Funny, she hasn't mentioned you at all," Lovey muttered under her breath to Tess.

Liz heard this and shot Lovey a scathing glance.

Tess leaned forward. "So, Serena, how long have you and Liz been friends?"

"Almost thirteen years now. We celebrated our birthdays together—Liz's fortieth and my thirtieth."

"You've lived and worked together all that time?"

"Worked together, yes. We were both practicing at the Brook Green counseling center when we met. I was the new kid on the block. Liz taught me everything I know."

Liz chuckled. "That's not exactly the way I remember it."

"Yes, but you're ten years older, and my memory's sharper." Serena grinned at her across the table. "We didn't live together, of course, until after Liz's divorce. That's been seven years."

"And you have your own clinic now?"

"That's right. It was just the two of us when we started. Now we have five therapists on staff, and a client list of more than three hundred. We also do quite a bit of pro bono counseling, and have a sliding scale for lower-income clients."

"That sounds exactly like the Liz we knew in college years ago," Lovey said. "Always a champion for the underdog."

Serena shot a glance in Liz's direction. "She still is."

The waiter came to inquire about their choice of drinks, and much to Grace's relief, everyone ordered iced tea or coffee instead of wine or mixed drinks. The menu prices were obscene—nearly $40 for a steak, $23 for chicken, $30 for blackened tuna. Twelve dollars for a measly shrimp cocktail appetizer, for heaven's sake. Seven twenty-five for a house salad, and a dollar more for a Caesar. Eight dollars for the Oreo cheesecake everyone had already been oohing and ahhing over. This one dinner was likely to cost her over $400, not including tip.

She requested plain water with lemon, doing some quick calculations in the back of her mind. Twenty-six hundred for three nights in the mountainview suite and adjoining extra room. Four hundred for this dinner, and perhaps half that for the Saturday-night prime-rib buffet and the Sunday brunch. For a day at the spa and a massage, $150 each, not counting lunch.

She'd be lucky if she didn't overspend the $5,000 limit on her new Visa card.

But did it really matter? She had no intention of living long enough to pay it, anyway. And even though she felt more than a twinge of guilt at the idea of running up a bill she did not have the funds to cover, it was the first time in her life she had ever been treated to this kind of luxury.

The first time, and the last.

She might as well relax and enjoy it.

By the time their entrees had arrived, a wine-red sun was descending behind the mountains, spangling the high cirrus clouds with gold and pink and purple. Tess absorbed it all—the multicolored hues of the mountains, fold upon fold stretching to the horizon, the scent of spring blossoms on the breeze, the fresh taste of the cool evening air. It had been too long since she had rested in the shadow of these peaks. After all her years on the prairie, the Blue Ridge still stole her breath and filled her heart.

She took a bite of her crab-stuffed mountain trout, savored the flavors on her tongue, and watched the interaction around the table with the cultivated vision of a writer. All eyes were fixed on Serena Marchand, Liz's friend, who was regaling Lovey and Grace with a story about a group of teenagers she referred to as the CDs—Cisco's Delinquents. Although Serena was careful not to violate any confidences, she had a host of tales about her experiences with them, with herself as the butt of all the jokes.

While the others' attention was occupied, Tess watched Liz watching Serena. Now that the awkward introductions were over and Grace had finally gotten Serena's name right, Liz seemed relaxed and comfortable. Throughout the evening she and Serena had teased each other, finished each other's sentences, and corrected each other with the ease of two people who were secure in their relationship and glad to be together.

Tess could easily understand the attraction. Serena was adorable—energetic, lithe, and vivacious, with dark olive skin, intelligent brown eyes, and short-cut black hair spiked up on the top. She was bright and intense and completely captivating, the kind of person Tess herself would welcome having as a friend.

Grace, however, seemed to be struggling to fit in. Gone was the acerbic wit, the mental swordplay she had once exchanged with Liz. She tried to joke a little, but her humor mostly fell flat. After a few lame attempts, she withdrew, and although she smiled and nodded and injected a comment or two into the dinner-table discussion, her mind was clearly elsewhere. She picked at her food—a chicken breast stuffed with spinach and Asiago cheese that looked absolutely luscious. She twisted her napkin between her fingers, dropped her fork twice, tipped over her water glass, and when Serena attempted to draw her out, had to ask her to repeat the question and never did answer it.

Perhaps Grace's nervous demeanor had to do with the issue she wanted to discuss with them. Everyone was curious, certainly, but given the fact that they were facing three days together, no one would bring up the subject until Grace was ready to talk.

"Well," Liz said at last, "that was delicious, but I simply can't do any more." She pushed her plate back, just slightly, from the edge of the table.

"Yes, I'm done too," said Lovey, whose plate still bore part of her blackened tuna and half a baked potato.

"I think we should ask for doggie bags," Liz suggested. "There's no point spending money for lunch tomorrow when we've got all this left, and a fridge and microwave in the suite."

Tess noticed a distinct expression of relief pass over Grace's face. "That's a good idea," she said, taking one more taste of trout and putting her fork down.

The waiter appeared bearing a large silver pot. "More coffee, ladies? And how about dessert?"

"Oh, no thank you, we're much too full. We simply couldn't manage it," said Tess.

Lovey slanted her eyes in Tess's direction. "Speak for yourself. Being full has nothing to do with it. Anyone want to split Oreo cheesecake?"

"An excellent choice, madam," the waiter oozed.

After a brief discussion, the decision was made—one Oreo cheesecake and one Heath Bar torte, with five forks. The waiter began to gather up the remainder of their dinners to be boxed. Like the feeding of the five thousand, Tess thought. Five loaves, two fish, and twelve baskets of leftovers.

Serena glanced at her watch. "Four forks, actually," she corrected, getting to her feet. "It's nearly nine, and I've still got an hour and a half drive to Blowing Rock. I told my sister I'd be there by eleven."

A chorus of dissent greeted this news, and Tess smiled. Liz's Serena had turned out to be a winner, that much was clear. No one wanted her to leave.

"We've got plenty of room in the suite," Lovey suggested. "Tess and Grace could take the double room, and I could sleep on the Murphy bed in the sitting room. That would leave the king for you and Liz—"

She paused and grinned. "If you don't mind sharing a bed, that is."

Liz shrugged and raised her eyebrows, but Serena would not be swayed. "Absolutely not," she said firmly. "The four of you need time together. I just came to meet you all, and now I'll be on my way."

She gave hugs all around and retrieved her shoulder bag from the back of the chair.

"I'll walk you out," Liz said, then turned back to the table. "I'll be right back. Don't eat all the dessert while I'm gone."

The two of them passed through the Great Hall in silence. The lobby area—indeed, the main section of the entire inn—was built of enormous stones, dry-mortared to look as if they were simply fitted into one another like a huge puzzle. The sitting areas were furnished with mission oak and leather, the arts-and-crafts lights obviously handmade. At opposite ends of the lobby, stone fireplaces large enough to accommodate a Volkswagen rose two stories into the vaulted, beamed ceiling and concealed cleverly hidden elevators in their massive chimneys. Here and there throughout the room, engraved stones in the walls proclaimed quotations from literary and philosophical luminaries.

The entire effect was one of strength and solidity and permanence—as the PR literature proclaimed, the Grove Park was "built for the ages." Quite impressive, and yet it had a homey, comfortable feel about it, like a great estate where people actually lived.

Out front, under the stone archway, Liz sank into one of the oversize porch rockers as she waited with Serena for the valet to bring the car around.

"You OK?" Serena sat down beside her and put a hand on her arm.

"Yes, I'm fine. It just feels a little strange, that's all."

"Like a time warp, with the past and present colliding?"

"Exactly." She nodded. "I care about them, I truly do, but when I'm with them I feel as if they're looking at someone else, not the real me."

"They don't know the real you, Liz. Not the person you are now."

"Guess it's time to get honest with them about myself and my life."

"Isn't that what you came for?"

"I came for Grace." She thought about this for a minute. "No, that's not entirely true. I came for myself, too."

"Then trust them." Serena stood up as the valet tapped the horn and got out of the car.

Liz nodded. "Say hi to your sister and the kids for me."

"I will." She dug in her purse for a tip, then hugged Liz quickly before settling herself behind the wheel. "See you Monday afternoon. Have fun."

Liz walked around the car and stood beside the open door. "Drive carefully. Call me on the cell if you want to."

"You'll have plenty to do without talking to me," Serena said. She shut the door and lowered the window. "They're good people, Liz. They'll understand. Just let them."

With a wave she was gone. Liz watched until her taillights disappeared over the hill, then turned and walked slowly back through the Great Hall toward the Sunset Terrace, dragging her feet all the way.

"She's coming," Lovey cautioned as she caught a glimpse of Liz in the doorway. Everyone fell silent, intent on the desserts that had arrived moments before.

In her brief absence they had all been talking about Liz and Serena, of course. Tess had sternly warned them to keep their opinions to themselves. If Liz wanted to talk about it, then fine, Tess said. If not, it was nobody's business to ask.

"You've got to try this Oreo cheese-cake," Lovey said brightly.

Liz resumed her seat, gamely picked up her dessert fork, and speared a bite of the cheesecake. "That's delicious."

"And the Heath Bar torte is nearly as good." Lovey snatched the plate right out from under Tess's nose just as she was cutting off a bit, and pushed it toward Liz.

"Lovey, really!" Grace retrieved the torte and handed it back to Tess.

"It's OK, Grace. I'm full to bursting any-way." She turned toward Liz. "Your friend Serena is a real find, you know. She's sharp and witty and intelligent—"

"Yeah, she fits right in with all of us!" Lovey added around a mouthful of cheese-cake.

Everyone laughed at the self-serving compliment, and Lovey felt herself blush a little. "Well, you know what I mean."

"Yes," Liz said absently, "she's great." She spoke as if her mind were miles away. Following Serena down I-40, Lovey guessed. Wishing she were still here.

After three more cycles around the table, both dessert plates were empty, and like a genie reappearing from a lamp, the waiter materialized, carrying their leftovers and a leather folder containing their check.

He made as if to set the bill down at Grace's elbow, but Lovey caught his eye and waved him over. Without even looking at the balance, she handed him a platinum American Express card. "Put it on this," she instructed. "My treat."

"Lovey, you don't have to do this. I invited all of you to come, and—"

Lovey shook her head, waving away Grace's attempt at a protest. "I want to, Grace. I can't tell you how wonderful it is for me to be here with all of you again."

And she meant it. These were her

friends, these women who accepted her as she was and made no comment on the fact that she was forty pounds heavier and showing her age. Besides, it was long past time for Amanda Love Tennyson to get a little joy out of life—the joy that came from doing something nice for someone else.

A rush of warmth flooded through her as she noticed Grace's ill-disguised look of relief. But even more gratifying than that was the thought of Bo's reaction when he got the bill.

Things were changing. *She* was changing. Big Bo wouldn't know what hit him.

33

SHRINKING BIG BO

"*W*here is she, dammit! Tell me!"

Bo ran his hands through his hair and paced across the floor of the den. He had come home from Moorhead late last night to find the house empty, Amanda gone, no car in the garage. He couldn't have slept more than an hour, and now felt as if he were nursing the world's worst hangover—a condition he was all too familiar with.

Neva Wilson, the housekeeper, stood next to the fireplace with her eyes downcast.

"Look at me, Neva!"

Her head popped up. Something flickered in her eyes, but Bo couldn't figure out what it meant. "If you know something, you'd better spill it, and quick."

"Mr. Bo," she answered slowly, "what makes you think Miz Manda would tell me something she didn't tell you? You're her husband."

"Yeah, right. But I'm never here. You spend more time with her than I do."

The words leaped out before he had time to consider them, and he saw Neva's eyebrows jiggle up, then down again. "What?"

"I don't know, Mr. Bo. I don't reckon she's been kidnapped, since her car's gone with her."

Kidnapped. Bo hadn't considered this before. He had money, lots of it, and come to think of it, his wealth and celebrity would make him an easy target for a ransom demand.

He grabbed for the phone and knocked it off the sofa table.

"What are you doing, Mr. Bo?"

"I'm calling the police. In case you hadn't noticed, my wife is missing." He fumbled to retrieve the telephone, which had begun to scream its off-the-hook signal, and slammed the receiver back down.

"She was here yesterday," Neva said calmly. "You can't file a missing person report till somebody's been gone forty-eight hours."

Her composure worked a number on his already jangled nerves. "How do you know that?"

Neva shrugged. "I've got cable. I watch *Law & Order.*"

Bo cast a withering glare at her. *Think,* he ordered his brain. *Think.* Where would she have gone? What could she be doing? Why would she just leave like that? He stopped in mid-stride across the den and whirled on Neva. "For God's sake, woman, say something!"

"I don't quite know what to say," Neva said. "Has she ever done anything like this before? Just take off, I mean?"

"Of course not. She's my wife. She belongs here, at home."

"When you want her here," Neva muttered under her breath. "Otherwise you don't pay her much mind."

Bo felt the throbbing in his temples accelerate. "Damn you, Neva! I'd fire you on the spot, I swear I would, except—" He paused. "Except I need your help."

"What kind of help?"

"We're going to search this house." He

bit his lip and squeezed his forehead, trying to make his mind work. "There's got to be something here, some clue to where she's gone and why she left."

"So you *don't* think somebody's kidnapped her?"

The question caught him up short. No, he didn't believe she had been kidnapped. He believed . . .

She had left him.

But he didn't say this to Neva. He wasn't about to bare his soul to the hired help. Instead, he turned and pointed a finger at her. "You check upstairs, in the bedroom. Go through all her drawers, the closet, everything. I'm going down to the study."

As she nodded and turned to go, another thought struck him.

"Neva, wait."

"Yessir?"

"Have you noticed anything different about Amanda lately? Anything she's said or done that's out of the ordinary?"

"Besides leaving, you mean?"

Bo frowned at her. "Come on, Neva, you know what I mean."

"Well, yes, Mr. Bo. She did say something kind of odd."

He took a step toward her. "Do I have to drag it out of you?"

"She said—" Neva paused. "She asked me if I was happy."

Happy, Bo thought as he rifled through the desk drawers downstairs. Why would his wife ask a *servant* if she was happy? Amanda had everything going for her—a fine home, a family, a successful husband, plenty of money. Never had to lift a finger.

Ungrateful, that's what she was. Had everything handed to her on a platter, and now this. Just up and left, without a word to anyone.

He slammed the desk drawer shut and had just begun on the bookshelves over the computer desk when something caught his eye. On top of the bookcase, nearly hidden, lay a maroon notebook, the kind of three-ring binder he used for his manager training program. But this one didn't have the Big Bo logo imprinted on the spine.

He jerked it down and flipped it open. There, neatly hole-punched and inserted into the binder, were pages and pages of computer-generated writing—diary entries, it looked like, each one headed with a date.

Since when had Amanda learned how to use the computer?

The idea that she could master such a skill without his help—without him even knowing about it—nettled him, and a flash of what could only be called jealousy ran through his veins like fire. What had generated this sudden outburst of creativity? And why had she asked Neva Wilson, of all people, about happiness?

A faint, distant nudging in the region of his gut told Bo he ought not to be reading Amanda's journal, but he smothered the thought. She was his wife, dammit, and he had a right to know what she'd been up to behind his back. But as he began to scan through the pages, he started wishing he had never found the notebook, never read a word of it.

Amanda had asked Neva about happiness because she herself was so horribly *un*happy.

He tried to tell himself that this was typical of a hysterical woman, to dredge up stuff from the past and refuse to let it go.

But the more he read, the more he couldn't help seeing Amanda in a way he'd never seen her before. She had loved him, had tried to make excuses for his drinking, his workaholic tendencies, his lack of attention. But she'd been miserable from the beginning, and no amount of success or wealth or status as Big Bo's wife could make up for it.

And then he stumbled across it—the thing he dreaded most. Another man's name.

John Whitestone.

She was seeing him, apparently on a regular basis. The pages were full of him—John said this and John suggested that. It was his influence, the filthy bastard, that had lured Amanda away from him. She was probably with him right now.

"Shit," he muttered. He slammed the book shut and lumbered up the stairs, breathing hard and gasping out the housekeeper's name.

"Neva!" he bellowed again as he reached the landing. "Neva! Get down here!"

She appeared at the top of the stairs with a cream-colored envelope in her hand. "You find something, Mr. Bo?"

"Yeah. What have you got there?"

"Looks like an invitation from somebody name Grace, asking Miz Manda to come to a reunion of some old friends."

A memory swam to the surface of his confused and tortured mind. He recalled the invitation, and just as clearly recalled telling Amanda that she couldn't go. "Forget that. I know all about it." He motioned her to come downstairs. "Anything else?"

"Yessir." She held it out to him—a double brass picture frame that should have been joined at the hinges, but had broken apart. On one side, a photo of him in his college uniform. On the other, Lovey as a UNCA cheerleader. The glass in her frame had shattered, radiating out like a sunburst from her smiling face.

Something twisted in the region of his stomach. Had she broken it deliberately?

He pushed the question aside and faced Neva again. "You know anybody named John Whitestone?"

"Whitestone? No sir, I don't believe I ever heard that name. Who is he?"

"He's the man Amanda has been having an affair with," Bo snapped, all propriety now forgotten.

"Oh, no, Mr. Bo. Miz Manda would never do something like that."

"I've got *evidence!*" he roared. "And I'm going to find him. Both of them. And when I do . . ."

He jerked open the drawer of the sofa table, took out a thick telephone directory, and dropped it on the coffee table. "Whitestone, Whitestone," he muttered as he turned pages. "Here it is. Whitestone, Jonathan. MFCC. Lives in Eden Prairie. What does MFCC stand for?"

"I have no idea, Mr. Bo."

"Find me something to write on," he ordered, but Neva was already rummaging in the drawer and came out with a small white notepad and pen. He tried to write down the address and phone number, but the pen didn't work. Finally, exasperated beyond control, he ripped the page out of the telephone book and stuck it in his pocket.

"Are you going to call him?"

"And give him advance warning?" Bo snorted. "Not a chance in hell. I'm going to go over there and *get my wife back.*"

The Eden Prairie neighborhood where Whitestone lived was nice enough, Bo supposed—an upper-middle-class area of large two-story brick homes, mostly, surrounded by mature trees and landscaped lots. But nothing to match what he owned.

He peered at the numbers painted on the curb and finally came to 1164. Whitestone's house. It was set well back from the street, with a circular driveway and a gaslamp.

He glanced again at the crumpled page from the phone book. This was it.

Bo looked around for Amanda's car but saw nothing but a green Volvo station wagon parked in the garage. The door stood open, and a man came out pushing a lawn cart and carrying a rake.

He looked to be about sixty, Bo noted, stocky, with white hair and a reddish complexion. He wore work clothes—faded blue jeans and a gray Minnesota Twins sweatshirt. While Bo watched, he wheeled the cart to the front porch and began to rake sodden leaves out of flower beds still patched with snow.

This was the man Amanda had left him for? Some old fart who pottered around on a Saturday morning doing his own yard work? Bo couldn't believe it.

He got out of the Lexus, shut the door, and walked up the driveway. When he was almost to the porch, the man looked up.

"G'day, mate," he said in a jovial voice. His accent reminded Bo of Crocodile Dundee. "Can I help you?" Then he stopped raking and shielded his eyes with a gloved hand. "Crikey, you're Big Bo Tennyson."

"So you recognize me, do you?" Bo took a step forward, his hands clenched into fists.

"I expect anyone would," the man said, "seeing as how your face is plastered on half the billboards in the state."

Bo hesitated. The guy had a point. He was well known, after all. He was Big Bo. A brief surge of pride rushed through him at being recognized, but it vanished the minute he remembered why he was there. "You're John Whitestone?"

"I am." He pulled off the gloves and extended a hand. "Good to meet you."

"You can skip the pleasantries," Bo snarled, "and tell me where Amanda is."

"Amanda?" For a split second Whitestone looked confused, then his expression cleared. "Ah. Lovey. Yes."

"Lovey? Is that what you call her?"

"Just a little nickname. Her friends used to call her that in college, I believe. As did you, once."

Bo took another step closer, his anger rising. "You don't know a damn thing about me."

"Ah, but I do. Quite a bit, actually. Unfortunately, anything Lovey has told me is strictly confidential. I can't talk about it."

"Well, you're going to talk." Bo seized him by the neck of his sweatshirt. "How long have you been seeing her? Is she here?" His eyes flitted to the front door, which stood open, but he couldn't see anything beyond the glass storm door.

"Of course she's not here. What would she be doing here?"

"She'd be—uh, being with you, of course."

"And she would be here because—?"

"Because you're having an affair with her!" Bo gave him a little shake.

"With Lovey?" Whitestone laughed, not in the least put off by Bo's show of force. "Not a chance, mate."

"I'm not your mate. And what's the matter, she's not good enough for you?"

"She's a lovely woman. And, I might say, quite a catch for any man. It's just that—" He grinned, showing uneven white teeth. "I believe you've gotten entirely the wrong idea, Mr. Tennyson. Lovey—Amanda—is my *client*. We do not have a personal relationship."

"Client?" Bo repeated. "What do you mean, client?"

"At the center," Whitestone said calmly, as if this should be perfectly clear. "The Minnetonka Family Counseling Center."

"She's been going to *counseling*?" Bo let go of the sweatshirt and stumbled back a step or two. "With you?"

"Right you are." Whitestone eyed him cannily. "As you undoubtedly know, if you've been reading her journaling and discovered my name."

He threw the leather gloves into the lawn cart and motioned to the chairs on the front porch. "Perhaps we should sit down and have a bit of a chat."

Bo followed him onto the porch. Whitestone opened the door, leaned his head in, and called, "Sheila, darlin', would you mind bringing out some coffee? I'd do it myself, except my shoes are muddy." An indistinct voice answered him from inside the house. "Right. Two cups, please. That's a love." He turned back to Bo. "Black?"

Bo nodded, and Whitestone conveyed the message to whoever Sheila was. After a moment, a woman with tousled strawberry-blonde hair appeared at the doorway bearing two steaming mugs of coffee.

"This is my wife, Sheila. Sheila, Mr. Bo Tennyson."

"Big Bo, is it?" Sheila handed a mug to each of them and surveyed Bo from head to foot. He had the strange feeling he was being examined, like a bug on a skewer. "Pleased to meet you." She disappeared back into the house.

"Now," said Whitestone, all business. "Why, exactly, are you at my house on a Saturday morning looking for your wife?"

Bo sighed, deflated. "Because she's missing. No note, no phone call, nothing. Her car's not in the garage. She was gone when I got home last night. Just vanished." He groped in his jacket pocket and extracted the broken picture frame. "I found this."

Whitestone took the pieces of the frame and held them in both hands, examining them as if he found them utterly fascinating. "Ah. And you think I might know where she went, is that it? Where, and why?" A grin played around his mouth. "And with whom?"

Bo nodded. "You were right. I found her diary—journal, whatever—and your name was in it. Also a lot of crap I thought was water under the bridge. About—about our relationship. Old stuff, you know. From the past."

"But perhaps not so old for her." Whitestone took a sip of his coffee and set the mug down on the porch bricks. "You believe she's left you for another man. Why might you think that?"

Bo felt himself bristle. "Don't shrink me, Doc. I'm not one of your clients."

"But you do appear to be in crisis," Whitestone said mildly. "And we can all use a little shrinking once in a while, don't you think?"

"I don't know." Bo thought about this for a minute, and recalled how Amanda had referred to him in the journal—as Big Bo, with a hint of scorn. Well, he *had* been a big man, he couldn't help that, could he? He had once played for the Vikings, made a game-winning touchdown that put them in the playoffs.

And broke your tailbone showing off for the crowd, a nasty little voice inside him added.

Then, after his football career was over, he had become just as big—even bigger, maybe—as the owner of the largest sports gear chain in the state. Whitestone had said it himself: Everybody knew him; a twenty-foot reflection of his face was pasted on billboards in every major town in Minnesota.

Big face, big head, the voice chimed in.

He shook himself to silence the inner criticism and tried to focus on Whitestone's last question. "Why am I convinced she's left me for another man, you asked?" He shrugged. "Because she's gone without a word, that's all. Look at her. She's a wonderful woman. She's loving and smart and beautiful and sensitive, and—"

"Have you told her that?"

"What?"

"That she's smart and beautiful and sensitive." Whitestone arched one eyebrow. "That you love her."

"She knows I love her."

"How does she know?"

"Well, shit," Bo said, "I provide every-thing for her, don't I? I give her whatever she wants."

"And what does she want?"

"What does any woman want?" Bo re-torted. "A home. A good life. A platinum card. A retirement fund. Security."

"Are you certain? Have you asked?"

"I've never been unfaithful to her." But even as he said it, Bo's mind filled with im-ages—partly from his own checkered memory, partly from what he had read in his wife's journal. The traveling. The drinking. The social climbing. Long ab-sences when he barely gave her a second thought. Parties and business dinners she didn't really want to attend. And he wondered, just briefly, if faithfulness might be about something more than sex.

"What's been going on with my wife?" he asked.

Whitestone shook his head. "I can't say."

"You don't know, or you can't say?"

"I can't say. That's a question you ought to ask her." Whitestone paused. "But I will make a suggestion to you. You might consider the possibility that your wife has *not* left you to go looking for another man."

A brief hope flared in Bo's chest. "Not looking for another man? What, then?"

"It's likely she's looking for a woman instead."

Bo's stomach lurched and dropped into his shoes. A man he might be able to compete with, but another woman—well, it was unthinkable.

"Amanda, looking for a woman?" he demanded. "What the hell are you talking about? What woman?"

Whitestone turned an intense gaze on him and held his eyes.

"Herself," he said.

Bo drove home slowly, mulling over the things John Whitestone had told him. Now that he thought about it, the man had said very little, actually. He had asked the right questions, though, and now that the wheels had begun to turn, Bo couldn't seem to stop them.

Why hadn't he noticed that Amanda was unhappy? Why hadn't she told him?

But of course she wouldn't. They hadn't communicated in years, and if her journal was any indication, she didn't feel he was capable of being trusted with any part of her heart or soul.

She had simply endured. And now, it seemed, her endurance had come to its end.

Other questions plagued him, too. Why had it taken her leaving to jolt him to his senses? He wasn't too old to remember the passion, the love that had once linked them together like some invisible magnetic force. Before they got married, they hadn't been able to get enough of each other. They had laughed and played and had fun. They had danced under the stars and written long letters when they were apart. She had cheered him on.

The truth hit him like a three-hundred-pound defensive tackle running full speed. Amanda had been his personal cheerleader, and he had expected the cheering to go on forever.

Half a mile from home, he pulled into a drive-through, ordered a double Whopper, extra-large fries, and a Coke, and sat in the parking lot barely tasting the food as he wolfed it down. When the last few fries were gone, he sat with his head on the steering wheel, staring at the empty cardboard container on the dashboard. BIG. BIGGER. SUPER BIG FRENCH FRIES was printed in bright red on a blue background.

Big. Bigger. SUPER BIG.

That was him. Big Bo. Big Man on Campus. Big Vikings Tight End. Big Successful Businessman.

"We all need shrinking now and then," Whitestone had said.

❦

When he pulled the Lexus into the driveway, Neva Wilson was sitting on the front steps waiting for him.

"What's happened?" he said as he jogged up the sidewalk to the porch. "Did she call?" His big burger and big fries made a big churning in his stomach, and acid rose up into his throat, the bitter taste of bile.

"No sir."

"What then? Why are you sitting outside?"

"Because I know where Miz Manda is," she said.

He grabbed her by the arm and steered her inside. "How? What? Where?" he demanded.

She yanked the cream-colored envelope out of her pocket and thrust it toward him. "Here," she said simply.

He opened it and stared at its contents. This weekend, in Asheville, at the Grove Park Inn Resort & Spa.

"And you think she's gone there, to this reunion, or whatever it is?"

"Yessir."

"What makes you so sure?"

"Because I called information, got the number, and phoned that resort." Neva poked a finger at the writing on the invitation. "She's there, all right. She and those three friends from college." She peered at him. "What are you going to do, Mr. Bo?"

He stared back, his mind racing. A housekeeper shouldn't be asking such an impertinent question, and he, as her employer, shouldn't be answering. Still—

He paced over to the fireplace. "The first thing I'm going to do is call John Whitestone and get an appointment for the two of us, soon as he can fit us in," he said. "Then I'm going to fly to Asheville—right now, this afternoon. I'll rent a jet if I have to."

He balked as an unwelcome thought crowded into his mind. "No. Not today. She needs this time with her friends. Tomorrow morning."

"And when you get there—?" Neva prodded.

"When I get there, I'm going to confess a lifetime of stupidity and ask her to forgive me for being such an ass. And if she gives me a second chance, I'm going to work like hell to become the husband she deserves."

He raised his head and looked at her. "Pardon my language."

Neva got up, sidled over to him, and placed a hand on his arm. He didn't pull away.

"You're a big man, Mr. Bo," she said in a tone of respect he had never heard before. "Yessir, a mighty big man."

IN THE GROTTO

*W*hen Grace had initially conceived of this get-together, she had determined that for once in her life she intended to treat herself—and her friends—to the best of everything. The mountainview suite was magnificent; last night's dinner and breakfast this morning had both been excellent. But until this moment, when she opened the door and stepped from the stairwell into the lower level of the Grove Park Spa, she had not even begun to imagine what kind of pampering awaited her.

Now her jaw dropped, and she gaped around in awe. It was a shimmering dream turned into substance, a fantasy, pure magic. The huge room, constructed with massive stone boulders, resembled an un-

derground grotto. In the center of the entryway, an indoor waterfall splashed from
twenty feet above into a lighted pond. Directly ahead was an enormous mineral
pool, five times the size of an ordinary
swimming pool, with soft amber lighting
glimmering off its clear teal waters. Flanking the mineral pool were two caves cut
into the walls—identical sunken hot tubs
with wide waterfalls plunging into them—
and to the right, in a narrow cavern of its
own with a fireplace flickering to one side,
a lap pool. A high glass wall opened onto a
terrace overlooking the mountains, and
here and there other stone fireplaces—even
one outside, on the patio—danced with
flames.

"It's so quiet," Tess whispered in her ear.

And it was. No blaring radios, no jan-
gling cell phones, no squalling children—
just the peaceful sounds of cascading water
and gentle, calming background music. A
few people were floating in the mineral
pool, and in the corner lap pool one man
was swimming energetically.

They were scheduled for massages later
in the morning, but that was a couple of
hours away.

"Let's start there," Liz suggested, pointing to the roiling waters of the hot tub. She pulled off her robe, flung it onto one of the lounge chairs, and descended the stone steps into the steamy water. "Ah, this is wonderful," she sighed as she situated her shoulders under the coursing waterfall. "Come on in, you won't believe it."

Tess and Lovey followed Liz into the hot tub and sank onto the stone bench that ran below the waterline, but Grace held back. At fifty-something, Tess and Liz were both still slim and fit, and even Lovey, with her additional pounds, was pleasantly curved. Grace felt more than a little uncomfortable about revealing her lumpy, middle-aged body in a swimsuit.

She looked around awkwardly. Someone was just coming out of the mineral pool, a white-haired, matronly woman with heavy, sagging breasts, wide, dimpled thighs, and a protruding stomach. She struggled dripping to the top of the steps, pushed back her wet hair, and smiled. "Isn't this marvelous?" she said as she adjusted the straps of a garish blue-and-purple-flowered swimsuit. "Just what these old bones need."

Grace watched as the woman lumbered

off toward the terrace, not bothering to cover her flabby cellulite with the robe provided by the spa. *If she's not embarrassed,* Grace thought, *I certainly shouldn't be.*

And with a sense of welcome liberation, she dropped her robe and joined her friends in the hot tub.

The morning was relaxing, if not exactly conducive to conversation. They stayed in the hot tub, taking turns under the waterfall, for twenty minutes or so, then decided to try the contrast pools, where you soak in very hot water and then plunge into an icy bath.

"People do this in Minnesota," Lovey panted as she came up breathless from the frigid water. "They sit in a sauna until they're so hot they can't stand it, then run and jump into the lake, through a hole cut in the ice."

"And this is supposed to be good for the circulation?" Liz said. She had just come out of the hot pool and was cooling down with a glass of iced lemon water and one of the spa's frozen peppermint washcloths, which were provided around every corner. "Sounds pretty crazy to me."

"Well, you're the expert on crazy," Grace jibed, purely on instinct.

"Grace!" Tess stared at her.

"Lighten up, Tess. I wasn't talking about *Liz*. I was talking about her *clients*."

Everyone laughed, and a rush of gratification surged through Grace's veins. Finally, this was how she had envisioned it—the joviality, the teasing, the fun. The old gang from Barnard Street rediscovering the friendship that had held them together all these years.

After the contrast pools, the mineral pool was perfect. There the water was warm but not hot, and much to Grace's amazement, the music was piped in under the surface, so that when she put her head back and began to float, soft instrumental sounds came clearly to her submerged ears.

It was like being in a womb, drowsy and comfortable, almost hypnotic.

Was this, she wondered, what death was like? To be suspended and completely at ease, the mind at rest, freed from the confines of flesh?

If so, it wouldn't be so bad. Much better than the prospect of being alive and in pain, riddled with cancer, debilitated.

She opened her eyes and stared up at the cavernous ceiling that arched overhead. The sun was moving higher, and a bright slanting beam came in through a skylight set in the rock. A fragmentary image shot through her mind—a darkened cave, a dewy spring morning, a stone rolled away to let in light and air and the fragrance of lilies.

Grace hadn't yet decided how or when to tell them about the tumor that was eating away at her life. Sunday, she thought. Perhaps they'd take a drive up the Parkway, have a picnic. That would offer the opportunity to talk without a lot of other people around. And since they were leaving Monday afternoon, it would also give them time to digest the news without throwing a shroud over the entire weekend.

Her shoulders tightened with anticipatory stress, but she forced herself to let go again, to take in the quietness, the soft music, the caress of water on her limbs. Yes. Sunday. For now she should just give in to the pleasure of the moment.

Out of instinct, Lovey glanced down at her bare wrist. Her watch was in the locker upstairs, but the rumbling of her stomach told her it was close to one o'clock. The four of them, wrapped in lush spa robes, were sitting around a table on the patio, sipping fruit drinks and admiring the beauty of the Blue Ridge in the distance.

A young woman in khakis and a green polo shirt bearing the Grove Park's lantern logo approached them and presented them with menus. "Ladies, would you care to have lunch brought to you here on the terrace?" she asked in a silky voice.

"How utterly delectable," Tess said languorously, raising her drink in a salute.

Loose-limbed and lethargic from the heavenly fifty-minute massage, Lovey had a bit of trouble focusing on the menu. "What are y'all having?" she asked.

"Didn't take long for your southern accent to resurrect," Liz chuckled. "She's spent thirty years in Minnesota, but two days back in North Carolina and she's saying *y'all*."

"*Y'all* is a perfectly logical second person plural," Tess quipped. She turned to the

server. "How are the croissant sandwiches?"

"Excellent," the girl said. "Big enough to
split."

She looked around for confirmation.
"Shall we do that, then?"

The others nodded, and Tess ordered
one roast beef and Swiss croissant and one
turkey, ham, and cheddar.

"With onion on the side," Lovey added.
"For the roast beef."

"Aw, jeez," Liz complained. "I'd forgot-
ten how much you love those stinkers. And
I have to share a room with Miss Onion
Breath." She made a face.

"Give it a rest. You're not going to be
kissing me." Lovey arched her eyebrows.
"Are you?"

"Not a chance." The waitress grinned
and walked away, and Liz let her eyes roam
around the circle. "OK, who's going to
ask?"

"Ask what?" Lovey said innocently.

"Never mind the dumb-blonde-
cheerleader routine. You know exactly
what I'm talking about."

"She's talking about Serena," Tess said.

"She's amazing, Liz. You don't have to be a Mensa genius to understand why the two of you get along so well. But now that you mention it, why haven't you told us about her before?"

"I'm afraid there's quite a bit I haven't told you," Liz said. "Maybe I'd better start at the beginning."

It was a story Lovey was all too familiar with. Liz had fallen in love with Tim instantly, had thought they were perfect for each other. The cynic surrounded by her thick plates of armor had, at last, allowed herself to strip off her protections and be vulnerable. But vulnerability had cost her. She had trusted him, supported him, defended him. And he had turned out to be not the man she believed him to be.

"You mean he actually did embezzle money from the organizations he was supposed to be supervising?"

"I'm afraid so." Liz nodded. "And once I found out, he threatened me if I exposed him."

"Threatened you with what?" Tess frowned.

"He said he'd ruin the clinic Serena and

I had worked so hard to build. He had a lot of clout, and it was not beyond his power to have our loans called in."

"That's blackmail!" Tess's voice was horror-struck.

"Yes. Well, the truth came out anyway, and he was found guilty and sentenced to seven years in a minimum-security facility."

"He's in *prison*?" Lovey shuddered. Her own situation with Bo was beginning to look better all the time.

"*Was*," Liz corrected. "He got out in four. Last I heard, he had moved out to L.A. and was pretty much living on the streets." She smiled grimly. "I can only hope they have good nonprofit services out there."

"Whew," said Tess. "Talk about poetic justice."

"By the time the trial was over and the divorce was final, Serena and I had known each other for six years or so," Liz went on. "We were best friends as well as partners in the clinic. I had—" She paused. "A meltdown. I thought I had finished dealing with my mother's abandonment, but this experience with Tim exhumed everything I'd buried. All the emotional stuff I had been holding at bay came crashing in on me. Serena was the one who kept my head above water and helped me find a way to heal."

She told about Serena moving into the arts-and-crafts bungalow she had once shared with Tim, how Serena's positive influence had taught her to play, to have fun, to let go of the past, to accept herself without the need to erect walls around her heart. By the time the story wound to a close, their croissants had arrived and they were halfway through lunch.

"Why didn't you tell us all this?" Tess stared at her. "Surely you knew we'd understand."

Liz shook her head. "Forgive me for being blunt, but I knew nothing of the sort. You were my best friends back in college, but even in those days, with the three of you, I was wary of emotional intimacy. Besides, this situation was extremely difficult to explain. I felt shamed—humiliated by what a lousy judge of character I had turned out to be. It took nearly a year of therapy to regain confidence in my instincts about people."

Lovey reached out and squeezed her

hand. "But you were not to blame for what your husband did."

"I know. I tell it to my clients all the time. Still, I beat myself up for months. I felt as if I should have seen it coming. And I certainly didn't know how to be honest with you about my emotional struggles. I was always the self-sufficient one, remember? The one with the impenetrable armor." She gazed around the circle, taking in each face.

This was a different Liz, Lovey thought. Not guarded, with her shields up, but open and unfortified and accessible. Somehow the pain she had endured had both softened and empowered her.

"But I have to tell you," Liz admitted, "I don't think I would have made it without Serena. So, does that make me weak?"

Lovey smiled. "Looks to me like it's made you strong," she said. "Strong and happy and blessed."

After lunch they spent another hour or two moving systematically back and forth from the mineral pool to the waterfall hot tubs.

Liz went off by herself for a bit to swim laps, and while she was gone, the others discussed her revelation in hushed tones.

"She's had so much pain," Grace said. "I'm amazed at how together she seems."

"It's obvious she's done a lot of emotional work over the years," Tess mused. "And I for one am absolutely thrilled for her."

Liz returned from her laps grinning and exhilarated. She sat down on the edge of the mineral pool and ran a hand through her hair. "So, you've been talking about me since I was gone, I assume."

"You assume correctly," Tess answered with a laugh. "The consensus is, we all think you're incredibly vital, whole, and fulfilled. And we couldn't be happier for you."

A little before six-thirty Grace stuck her head into Liz and Lovey's room. "About ready?" she asked. "We have buffet reservations in ten minutes."

At thirty bucks a pop, the Saturday-night prime-rib buffet wasn't exactly economical, but compared to the prices at the Sunset Terrace, it would be a bargain, especially since everything, including nonalcoholic drinks and dessert, was included. *Quit obsessing about money,* Grace silently reprimanded herself. *After all, Lovey paid for last night's dinner.*

After a full day at the spa and a brief nap, everyone was relaxed and comfortable. On the way down to the Great Hall, they chatted easily about the marvelous accommodations at the Grove Park and the award-winning spa services. When the elevator stopped and they emerged from the back of the huge stone fireplace, Liz put a hand on Grace's arm. "I just want to thank you for this weekend," she said. "It's a gift."

"Yes, it is," Lovey agreed, linking an arm through Grace's as they walked. "But it doesn't seem right that you should pay for everything. We could all kick in and split the cost." She craned her neck around at Liz and Tess, now a step or two behind them. "Couldn't we?"

"Of course," the other two said immediately. "We ought to help pay our way."

Grace's eyes stung, and her throat clogged up. Because she had never told them even the slightest inkling of the truth about her dismal, miserable life, they hadn't the faintest idea how little she could afford this weekend. Lovey was rich—incomprehensibly wealthy, compared to Grace's standard of living. Tess was certainly comfortable, if not well off. Liz owned half interest in a thriving counseling practice. Any one of them could have paid for this reunion without a second thought.

But Grace had made up her mind long before any of them had arrived in Asheville. This was her legacy, her final bequest—to them, and to herself. A tribute to the memory of a friendship that had endured.

"No," she said at last. "I appreciate the offer, but it's all taken care of. Consider it my—my swan song."

Lovey jerked her head around and shot a glance over her shoulder at Liz and Tess. But if any of them considered this a curious thing to say, no one mentioned it.

At the doorway of the banquet hall, Grace gave her name to the headwaiter, and he led them to a secluded table in the corner, sandwiched between a potted ficus tree and a burbling terra cotta fountain.

The waiter seated each of them in turn, then circled the table, opening stiff linen napkins with a snap and placing one on each woman's lap. "Tonight's specialty is prime rib," he informed them. "The table on the left"—he waved an elegant hand— "offers a variety of soups, salads, cheeses, and assorted cold foods, including pastas and shrimp cocktail. I especially recommend the she-crab soup. At the table on the right are our excellent desserts—"

"Including Oreo cheesecake?" Lovey inquired.

"Indeed, madam. And a wide array of other delicious choices as well. All created fresh by our pastry chef." He gave a deferential nod. "At the large center table you will find our signature prime rib, hand carved to your liking, along with other meats and vegetables. The summer squash soufflé is one of my personal favorites. In addition to the prime rib, this evening's selections also include a marvelous crisped duckling with orange sauce, crab-stuffed trout—fresh, of course—grilled chicken and creamed spinach casserole, and shrimp remoulade." Finished with his recitation, he gazed placidly around the table. "What else do you ladies require? Wine? Coffee or tea, perhaps?"

They ordered iced tea all around. "Very good. I will return momentarily with your tea. Feel free to help yourselves whenever you are ready."

Lovey took a sip of water and eyed the fountain in the corner. "These folks sure do like running water," she commented.

"It's a soothing sound," said Tess. "I feel like I'm back at the spa again. Makes me think about getting a small rock fountain for my study."

"Makes me think about needing to pee," Lovey said.

Liz poked her in the arm. "You are so classy."

Everyone laughed, and Lovey shrugged. "You can take the girl out of Georgia—"

"But you can never take Georgia out of the girl," the others chorused in unison.

"Well," Liz said, placing her napkin on the table, "I don't know about anyone else, but I'm ready to eat."

They all rose and threaded their way through the surrounding tables to the serving area. The largest of the buffet tables was graced with a glistening ice sculpture in the form of a swan with its wings spread wide. On every exposed space of the white table-cloths, strands of ivy interlaced with fresh flowers. The center of the salad table bore a small mountain of large shelled shrimp, surrounded by a wide moat filled with shaved ice and crab claws.

"I could make out my dinner right here," said Tess as she pushed aside a portion of spring salad to make room for crab and shrimp. "I love seafood."

"Me too," Liz said. "I definitely have to try the she-crab soup."

The four of them returned to their table carrying two salad plates each. "There's only one problem," Lovey said as she picked up a pair of seafood pliers and attacked a crab leg. "After all this and prime rib too, who's going to have room for dessert?"

Liz bit off half of a large shrimp. "Is this a big issue? Someone last night—I forget who—said she was too full for dessert, until the subject of Oreo cheesecake came up." She grinned at Lovey. "Come on, babe. You can do it. We believe in you."

She turned in Grace's direction. "Did

you get any of this soup? It's delicious. Have a taste, if you like."

Grace took a spoon and dipped it into Liz's bowl. The soup was a deep rust color, thick with shreds of crabmeat. It was unlike anything she had ever tasted—rich and savory, with just a hint of sweetness. "Mmm," she said. "They're going to serve this in heaven. I'll need to get my own bowl, or I'll eat all of yours."

Lovey leaned across the table and peered into Liz's soup. "Why do they call it she-crab soup?" she asked. "Does that mean it's only made with the female of the species?"

"Exactly," Liz said with mock seriousness. "You see, she-crabs are much sweeter than he-crabs. He-crabs are too . . . crabby."

Lovey appeared to consider this for a minute, then heard suppressed giggles all around the table and looked up. "Why does everybody always make fun of me?"

"Because you're such a perfect target!" Liz exploded with laughter. "You're so . . . so *innocent*."

"Naive, you mean." She tried to pretend she was in a snit, but she couldn't keep it up for long. Finally she joined in the laughter and gave a self-deprecating shrug. "But you're right, Liz, even if you were pulling my leg. She-crabs *are* sweeter." She gazed around the table. "It's great, the four of us together again, just us girls."

Tess grimaced. "Lovey, we haven't been *girls* for ages."

"Maybe not," she responded. "But being with all of you makes me feel young and alive. As if the past thirty years with Bo never happened."

An eerie silence descended over the table. Grace cut a glance at Liz and saw her raise an eyebrow in Tess's direction. Lovey stared at her plate and fiddled with a shrimp.

"Lovey," Liz said after a moment, "is there something you want to tell us?"

She bit her lip and shifted her head, avoiding Liz's gaze. When she turned back, she had adopted a wide, false smile. "Who's for prime rib?" she said brightly, getting up from the table so fast she nearly knocked her water glass over. "I'm going to try that soufflé—I love squash. The duckling, too, and maybe some of the crab-stuffed trout." The smile persisted, but Grace could see that the light didn't reach her eyes. "By the time this meal is over, I'll probably turn into a she-crab."

They all followed Lovey to the entree table, and when she returned with a juicy slice of rare prime rib heaped with horseradish, Liz made a lame attempt at a joke. "First the onions at lunch, and now horseradish? Lovey, you're going to drive me out of the room."

Lovey laughed—a little too loudly, a little too long—and the others gamely tried to share the humor. For the remainder of the evening, all of them tried to pretend that nothing had happened. But the talk mostly centered on the food—how crispy the duck was, how impossible to decide among all the dessert options. The easy banter and comfortable conversation had vanished.

When the dinner ordeal had finally come to an end, they walked in silence down the corridor back to the Great Hall. Just as Grace stepped behind the fireplace and punched the button to call the elevator, the desk manager came scurrying over to her, holding out a small envelope.

"Pardon me, Ms. Benedict," he said, his eyes darting to the other women. "I am so very sorry. A message came this afternoon, you see, but in the shift change it did not get delivered in a timely manner, and now—"

Grace took the envelope. It was heavy stock with the Grove Park logo in raised ink in the upper-left-hand corner. Across the front were printed the words MRS. AMANDA TENNYSON.

"Lovey?" Grace said. "It's for you."

The manager wheeled. "You are Mrs. Tennyson? Please, I beg your forgiveness for the delay. Such inefficiency is inexcusable."

"It's fine," Lovey said dully. "Don't worry about it."

"But you must understand that this is not the Grove Park way. We pride ourselves on offering the finest service to our guests. May I offer my apologies in a more tangible manner? A complimentary bottle of champagne sent up to your suite, perhaps?"

"That's not necessary."

"Take the champagne," Liz hissed.

"Whatever," Lovey muttered, and entered the elevator before the door had fully opened.

The champagne, artfully arranged in a silver bucket, arrived less than five minutes after the door to the suite had closed behind them. The porter waved off the tip Grace held out to him and bowed out of the room.

"All right, let's all sit down." Liz sank down on the sofa and kicked off her shoes. "Lovey, park yourself and talk to us. This silence isn't getting us anywhere. Clearly something's wrong."

Lovey seemed to be considering Liz's words. She dropped the unopened envelope onto the coffee table and sank into a wing chair. "He's found me," she said, her voice flat and emotionless. "I had hoped to have this weekend—just these few days. But he's found me, and now there'll be hell to pay."

"Who's found you?"

Lovey exhaled heavily. "Bo."

Tess frowned. "What do you mean, Bo's found you? He knew where you were."

"No, he didn't. Not exactly." Lovey shook her head. "I needed to get away. He was gone on one of his trips, and I—well, I just left."

"Let me get this straight," Liz said. "You walked out of the house, got on a plane to Asheville, and didn't tell your husband where you were going or when you would be back."

"I left a note in the upstairs bedroom, on the dresser," Lovey said. "Told him I needed to get away. I didn't want him to know I had come here to spend the weekend with all of you—he'd never let me stay. He'd come and get me if he had to." She turned toward Grace. "When your invitation arrived, he absolutely forbade me to go. I've never defied him before."

Grace got up, walked into the bedroom, and returned with the circle journal in her hands. She flipped through the pages, read a couple of Lovey's entries silently, then turned to face her. "Everything you wrote about you and Bo, your children, your life—it all sounded like the ideal marriage, the perfect home. We thought—"

"You thought what I wanted you to think, I guess." Lovey held up both hands in a gesture of surrender. "Or maybe it was what *I* wanted to think. Perhaps I've been in denial all these years, fooling myself into believing my life was like what I wrote in the journal."

Liz straightened up on the couch, and Grace could almost see her assuming the role of therapist, donning the counselor's cloak like a familiar garment. It suddenly struck her how good Liz must be at her job—available, approachable, understanding, no matter how her past experiences had conspired to shut her away behind patterns of self-protectiveness. This, she thought, was a picture of mental and emotional health—facing one's demons head-on and overcoming them, resisting the temptation to hide.

"Lovey," Liz said, "I tease you a lot, but surely you know I care about you. We all do." Grace nodded vehemently, and out of the corner of her eye she caught a glimpse of Tess doing the same. "Whatever's going on with you, we're here to listen—and to help if we can."

Lovey smiled, and this time Grace saw a flicker of illumination behind her eyes. "I've been in counseling the past few weeks," she said, "and my therapist has helped me begin to come to grips with some issues I've been ignoring for years. I believed I had no other choice but to turn a blind eye to the pain and disappointment and go on slogging down the path I chose for myself thirty years ago."

She picked up the circle journal and ran her fingers over the battered cover. "A long time ago, Grace, you warned me about Bo."

Grace shifted against the uncomfortable pricking sensation that filled her stomach. How self-righteous she had been, appointing herself the morality police for the rest of the world! She had reacted partially out of her own pain and despair over her father's unfaithfulness and deception, certainly, but that was no excuse for demeaning a friend.

"Yes," she said cautiously. "And if you remember what I said at the airport yesterday, I should have kept my mouth shut and my nose out of your business."

"No," Lovey countered. "I couldn't see it then, but I know now you were simply trying to be a friend. You were right. Not about sexual infidelity; Bo's never done that, to my knowledge. But he's obsessed with work, with image, with success. I wonder now if he ever loved me at all, or if I was just another trophy."

She went on then, and as she spun out her story, Grace mused that her confession sounded like the flip side of a fairy tale— football hero marries cheerleader, Prince Charming waltzes into the sunset with his Cinderella. But happily-ever-after was a myth, a fable. Real life went on into the harsh, shadowed world beyond the honeymoon curtain. Even extravagant wealth could not shield a soul from anguish.

On a superficial level, everything Lovey had told them over the years was true—the money, the house, the children, the charities, the travel. But there was a dark underside to this tale of the bright and beautiful. Lovey's sense of emptiness, of insignificance. The loneliness. The disconnection from her spoiled, overindulged children. The death of desire—or, rather, in Lovey's case, the barrenness of never having desires of her own at all.

"We had it all," Lovey was saying. "Fame, wealth, social status." She sighed. "But status costs an awful lot in busted dreams."

Grace squeezed her eyes shut and found

her lashes wet with tears. A realization was stirring within her, an unwelcome awareness of her own self-centeredness. She had lived so long in shame, had been so concerned with the image she projected to these friends. How much love and laughter and friendship and shared pain had she missed, cloistered away in her shell, afraid to admit her failings and reveal herself? How many years of comfort and solace and connection had she denied herself—and denied them, in turn?

It was almost too late—but not quite.

Tonight was Lovey's night. They would surround her with understanding and acceptance, wrap her up in affirmation and love.

Tomorrow Grace would break her own long silence. She would open herself, heart and mind and soul. She would trust them.

And for whatever time she had left, she would give love willingly, and accept it freely.

She would become, at last, a true friend.

THE CONFESSIONAL

Sunday dawned clear, bright, and cool, with the sky overhead a brilliant blue. After an early brunch—another of the Grove Park's signature feasts—Grace and the others went out to the deserted Sunset Terrace and watched the play of morning sun and shadow across the western mountains.

"I thought maybe we'd take a drive up the Parkway today," Grace suggested. "Buy some chicken, have a picnic."

"I hardly think we need a picnic lunch after that breakfast," Tess said. "I can barely button my jeans as it is. But driving up the Parkway is a great idea. My family and I always used to go up to Craggy Gardens when I was young."

"Right," Liz said. "I forgot your parents

live here." She grinned. "Bishop Daddy,
Lord High Pooh-Bah of Black Mountain."

"Bishop Daddy's retired now." Tess returned the smile. "They were in Black
Mountain, but the diocese office has now
relocated in Asheville, over in Chunn's
Cove. Mother and Daddy moved to Deerfield Retirement Village a few years ago."
She frowned briefly. "Just so you'll know,
Grace, my parents usually come to Iowa to
visit. I haven't been in Asheville in years—
otherwise we'd have gotten together long
before now, even though you couldn't
come to the earlier reunions."

A fleeting panic stabbed at Grace. She,
too, had forgotten that Tess's parents lived
here. For three decades she'd made excuses
for not seeing them, and it had never occurred to her what might happen if Tess—
or any of the others, for that matter—
showed up in Asheville. What would she
have said to them? How would she have
explained a life that was so radically different from what she had led them to expect?

But scattered all over the country as they
were, they hadn't come. Her deception had
not been revealed. By some miracle, she
had been able to keep her secret life hid-

den, to be disclosed in her own time. She breathed a silent sigh of relief, and turned back to the conversation.

"We ought to take jackets," Tess was saying. "It won't get really warm up there until midsummer, and it's always windy."

A little before ten, Grace retrieved her car from the garage under the Vanderbilt Wing, pulled around to the valet drop-off, and collected the others. They drove through a burger joint to pick up diet Cokes, then headed north on the Parkway.

Everyone seemed in high spirits. They rolled the windows down, ran their hands in the slipstream, laughed, and chatted to one another. The noise of wind and voices came as a relief to Grace. It gave her an opportunity to keep her eyes on the curving road and her mind on what lay ahead.

If her friends questioned why she drove a ten-year-old car when she could afford to treat them to a weekend at the Grove Park, no one mentioned it. Liz and Lovey seemed especially spirited—relieved, no doubt, of the burden of their own secrets. Grace wondered if she would experience that kind of lightheartedness once she had told her story, or if exposing her wounds to

the light and having them scrutinized
would simply bring a different kind of pain.

She drove on. Here, at the higher eleva-
tions, not much was blooming yet. At a
bend in the road, trees and foliage dropped
away to reveal a broad panorama to the
east, mist-hung layers of mountain peaks all
the way to a hazy horizon. And then, almost without warning, a tunnel cut into
the rock blocked the view and plunged
them into darkness.

"We're nearly there," she said when they
came out on the other side. She cut a
glance to the back seat, where Liz and
Lovey were poking each other and giggling
like adolescent girls. "Do we want to go to
the picnic grounds, or on up to the top of
Craggy?"

"Let's go to the top," Liz suggested. "If
it's too chilly, we'll come back down to the
picnic area."

Grace bypassed the picnic entrance, and a
few minutes later turned left into the parking lot at Craggy Gardens. Here the mountain vista stretched out on both sides of the
Parkway, a breathtaking scope of the Blue
Ridge.

Craggy was not a cultivated garden, by any stretch of the imagination, but a high, rocky outcropping overrun with multicolored rhododendron. At peak season this area would be jammed with sightseers, the trails teeming with hikers. Cars and campers and motorcycles would clog the Parkway and slow traffic to a crawl. A few—the stout of heart—might even assault the ridge on mountain bikes.

Today, however, the crag was utterly deserted. The rhododendron bushes would be magnificent in another six weeks or so, but at the moment the abundant buds that covered the bushes were still tight, hard, and green.

"Ah, good," said Tess as she helped Grace take a blanket from the trunk of the car. "We've got the place all to ourselves."

They climbed a small knoll and settled themselves on a grassy slope overlooking the eastern view. Far below, embraced by a half-moon of dark pines, the watershed glittered in the late-morning sun, a diamond necklace adorning the throat of the mountains.

Silence settled over them. No one

moved. Wind rustled in the trees, a shushing sound, and in counterpoint, birdsong rang out clear on the crystal air.

Grace sensed a subtle shift inside her, a feeling she didn't quite understand. There was something different about this place. A presence, a sanctity. She felt as if she had stumbled into a majestic open-air cathedral—waiting, anticipating some glorious moving of spirit, longing to hear the declaration of forgiveness and restoration that would liberate her soul.

Confession, however, came before reconciliation. What words would be sufficient to unlock the door she had kept bolted for so many years?

How to begin?

But before she had formulated a coherent sentence, Tess began to speak.

"I think it's my turn," Tess said. "Time to tell you some things about my life."

She had been thinking about this all weekend. Liz and Lovey had both confided things about their lives they hadn't told in the circle journal. Grace had yet to disclose

the reason she had gathered them all together, but as she seemed a bit nervous and
preoccupied, Tess was relatively certain she
was planning to do it yet today.

Tess had told Hal that she did not intend
to reveal herself as C. J. Kenning, the
award-winning writer. It would seem like
bragging, she feared, and she didn't want to
come across as the Big Important Person.
Her accomplishments, she reasoned, might
make them feel worse about their own
lives. But the more she thought about it,
the more convinced she became that with-
holding the truth had its roots in pride, not
humility. It was a flimsy rationalization at
best, and the very fact that she had considered it testified to her own unacknowl-
edged arrogance.

These were her friends. They had taken
the risk to be forthright about their own
struggles and pain. Did she really think that
she was superior because she had a fulfilling
marriage, an amazing daughter, a successful
writing career?

Deep down, she knew better. Her marriage had endured and flourished not because Tess had been an exemplary wife,
but because Hal had been extraordinarily

patient while she searched for her life's direction. Claire had been a blessing from another woman's womb, and from the beginning had outstripped her mother both in wisdom and in compassion. Even her creative successes Tess could not wholly claim. Whatever talent she possessed came from another source entirely, and the cultivating of that talent had occurred despite her ambition rather than because of it.

It was all gift, grace, benediction. Unearned and undeserved. All of it.

They were waiting, looking at her expectantly. She inhaled a deep draft of the cool, crisp mountain air and smiled.

"It's Sunday," she said, "and somehow this place feels like a sanctuary to me, a temple."

Liz arched an eyebrow. "Seems I remember you boycotting the church."

"That was a long time ago," Tess said. "I've changed a bit in the past thirty years. The church has changed." She grinned at Liz. "Not as much as I'd like, maybe, but enough to lure me back."

She paused and looked around at them. "Lovey, you and Liz have opened up this weekend, and your honesty is, in part, what motivates me to tell the truth about myself. When I wrote in the journal I was, shall we say, *selective* about what I included. Even on the flight to Asheville, I rationalized that omitting certain facts about my life would be best for all concerned. But yesterday, and last night, as Liz and Lovey bared their souls, I realized that I've missed out on so much because I haven't let you know me. Really know me—the person I've become over the past thirty years."

"Let me guess," Liz said, a note of mockery in her voice, "you're a Pulitzer Prize–winning novelist writing under a different name because you'd prefer to be a hermit."

The comment was clearly sarcastic, a typical Liz joke, but the audacious grin faded when she caught sight of Tess's expression.

"Well, not a Pulitzer," Tess said quietly.

"You mean you've actually been writing?" Liz gaped at her. *"Publishing?"*

"Yes," Tess admitted. "But you were right. I do write under a different name." She shifted, stretching her legs out across the blanket. "It all began with a little novel about adoption called *The Chosen Child.*"

"What?" Grace's eyes widened. "*You're* C. J. Kenning?"

"That's right."

"Hold on a sec," Liz interrupted. She turned toward Grace. "You've heard of her? You know who she is?"

"*Everybody* knows who she is," Grace said. "*The Chosen Child* was a magnificent book—intelligent, imaginative, an instant classic. It was a Newbery winner, and if I'm not mistaken, C. J. Kenning's writing has been awarded several Horn Books, and practically every other honor in children's literature. Most of her books are best sellers even before they hit the stores. But she's a mystery woman—never does public appearances." Grace blinked. "And all the time, it was you."

Tess gazed at her. Grace seemed to be fighting for breath, her eyes bright and watery. "You've read *The Chosen Child*?"

Grace nodded. "Five or six times, at least. It's brilliant. It kept me from—" She stopped suddenly, as if afraid she had said too much.

Tess felt herself beginning to blush. Of course Grace would understand what a Newbery meant. She was a librarian, an avid reader. She would keep up with what was going on in the world of books. But Grace had no children—her only pregnancy had ended in miscarriage. Why would a childless woman read such a novel—not once, but many times?

"Wait a minute." Lovey frowned. "How come we didn't know this? Last time we saw you, you told us that you had determined you weren't cut out to be a writer. And in the circle journal you said—"

"I know." Tess waved a hand. "At the time, it was all too painfully true. But if you'll just give me a chance, I'll tell you the whole story from the beginning."

"Well, let's hear it, then." Liz took a great gulp of her diet soda and leaned back on her elbows.

"My first year at the Iowa Writers' Workshop was extremely intimidating," Tess began. "I had big dreams, but no idea how to fulfill them. I desperately wanted to be invisible, to fade into the woodwork. But Hal believed in me. He taught me, helped build my confidence—"

"I'll bet he did," Liz said with a salacious grin.

Tess chuckled and arched an eyebrow.

"No, this was before we fell in love and got married. He always maintained I was talented, and he finally convinced me. After graduation I published a few stories here and there, taught some introductory fiction classes. But it took a major crisis to bring me face-to-face with my dissatisfaction."

"You couldn't get pregnant," Lovey supplied.

"Right. And I realized my inability to have a baby mirrored—in physical terms—my creative barrenness. I determined to use that pain productively, and began work on a novel that I was sure would shake the literary world to its core. A book about the pain of a woman who could not conceive. I titled it *Rachel's Wilderness*—"

"Never heard of it," Grace said, then lowered her eyes quickly.

"It's all right." Tess bit her lip. "No one else did either. No one but the critics, that is. They called it—let's see—self-absorbed, contrived. Maudlin, predictable, pseudo-literary angst. A brutal assault with a blunt knife."

"Ouch." Liz winced.

"It was devastating," Tess agreed. "And the worst of it was that, in the middle of the book—or rather, right near the end of the writing—we adopted Claire. She was four, and took an enormous amount of energy. I wasn't a very good mother. I was much too absorbed with the novel. Obsessed, really. And then after the reviews came out, I went into a pretty significant depression.

"If it hadn't been for Hal, I would have crashed completely," she went on. "Somehow he managed to keep on loving me, and I can assure you I wasn't very lovable. And Claire—" Tess smiled, remembering. "Claire was a child even I couldn't help but adore. Very loving, very wise. It was because of Claire I stopped writing, and because of Claire I took it up again."

"You mean you decided to spend your time mothering instead of writing?"

Tess shook her head. "I didn't *decide* that, not consciously. But I was humiliated by the critics, and determined not to put myself through that again. The door seemed to be shut. The literary world didn't want me, but my husband and daughter did. I—" She shrugged. "I fell in love with Claire. And when I did, nothing else seemed quite so important."

"Does this have anything to do with you coming back to the church?" Liz asked.

"In a way. My journey as a writer was always about faith, only I didn't know it at the time," Tess said. "A door had been slammed in my face. The path I thought I was destined for was now blocked. It took years before I realized that something else was out there, waiting for me. Something I wouldn't have considered in a million years."

Grace looked up. "Writing for children."

"Exactly. I'm ashamed to admit it now, but at the time I believed that writing a simple story for children was beneath me somehow. That my talent was bigger than that—you know, Nobel-Prize big, or at least Pulitzer big. Those expectations were firmly entrenched in my soul. They ate away at me, possessed me.

"For seven years I didn't write a word for publication. And then, one day, the heavens opened up and I felt a new sense of passion, a new challenge. It was as if someone had spoken to me, uttering a truth I had avoided for years—that creativity was a gift, not an entitlement. That when I hoarded it, tried to control it, it rotted and festered and ended up becoming a curse instead of a blessing.

"Finally, after all those years, I understood. My job was not to produce the Great American Novel, to turn the literary world upside down. Not even to be successful. My task was to serve the gift. To listen to my heart. To write what was in my soul. And to leave the results in more capable hands."

"And that's why you wrote under an assumed name?" Liz asked.

"Yes. At least partly. My motives at the beginning were probably not quite so pure and noble as all that. For one thing, I didn't want the failure of *Rachel's Wilderness* to taint whatever else I might create. But mostly it was a determination to keep my ego out of the process. To open myself to the creative breath of God without the distraction of fame, or the lack of it."

Tess gazed out over the panoramic views of the Blue Ridge Mountains. "I discovered faith again in my writing. In my daughter's laugh and my husband's smile. In the hard-won battle for balance between life and work. The faith I'm talking about has little to do with ritual or liturgy or rules, but it has everything to do with community. Finding my place. Experiencing the presence of the holy. Giving love and support to the people around me, and receiving it as well. Defining success in terms of being true to the gift."

A warmth rose up inside her, and she smiled. "My family, my life, my work—it's all a gift from the original Creative Genius. I feel God's presence in me when I love. I feel God's presence in me when I write."

"You wrote *The Chosen Child* because of Claire, didn't you?" Grace's voice sounded hoarse, strained.

"Yes, I did." Tess peered into her friend's eyes. She could see something struggling there, fighting to get out. "And you read it because—?"

Grace took a heaving, ragged breath. "That's a long story," she said. "A very long story."

Grace had never so much as set foot in a Catholic church. She didn't understand the concept of revering saints, or needing a priest to stand as mediator between God and the parishioner. And yet at this instant, on this mountain, she had caught a glimpse, albeit a brief one, of the power of the confessional.

Tess was right. This was a holy place, a sanctuary. God was listening. But it wasn't enough for Grace to bare her soul to some distant deity who already knew all about it anyway. Such confession was a redundancy, a cop-out. She needed to speak the words to another human being, out loud, where she could hear them reverberate against her own eardrums, watch the reaction on human faces and in human eyes, receive the words of consolation—or condemnation—from human lips.

They sat circled around her, waiting, silent, their expressions a mixture of anxiety and compassion, as if they understood what a monumental decision this was. Grace Benedict's moment of truth.

Getting started was hard, harder than she imagined. "You have all shared things this weekend that you never wrote in the circle journal," she began in a whisper. "Details about your life that you couldn't find a way to explain, or were uncomfortable facing. But I—" Words failed her, and she closed her eyes.

Finally she opened them and turned toward Lovey. "A long time ago I judged you, condemned you for sleeping with Bo before you were married." Lovey nodded. "Well, you told me something that night that you may not remember, but I'll never forget. You said, 'When you've been in love and faced this question for yourself, come back and tell me how your standards worked out for you.' That turned out to be a prophetic challenge, Lovey. Because I *did* face the exact same question, and my standards didn't hold up at all."

As she spoke the words, Grace felt an infusion of strength, as if the telling served as an injection of adrenaline directly into her veins. "I told you about falling in love with Michael Forrester, getting married. But there was no marriage." She frowned. "Well, actually there was. Michael was married, but not to me."

"*What?*" The three voices spoke in unison, and then Lovey's voice, disbelieving, rose above the din.

"You were *never married* to Michael? But you wrote—"

"Please, wait." Grace held up a hand. "I know you've got questions. And I'll explain it all, if I can. But let me try to get this in order."

She paused for a moment, then began again. "I didn't even understand myself why I came across so strong that night," she said. "I was so demanding and controlling, and I couldn't seem to hold back my anger. But I wasn't angry at you, Lovey. I was keeping a secret that was eating me alive."

She turned in Liz's direction. "You tried to get me to see this, Liz, but I couldn't— or wouldn't—accept it. My father *had* been unfaithful to my mother. He even had an illegitimate child. I found out the truth about him that summer after his death, but I could never bring myself to tell all of you about it. I was angry—furious. And I was ashamed—ashamed of him, and ashamed of the hero-worship that kept me blinded to his real character, and how he had hurt Mama. I swore I would never ever be like him, or get involved with someone like him. But I did. Michael was *exactly* like

Daddy—only I was too stupid or dazzled or in love to see it."

"Wait a minute," Lovey said. "Back up a little. Are you telling us that *everything* you wrote about this man was made up?"

"Not everything." Grace exhaled a heavy breath. "He was handsome and smart and charming. He was a professor at the university, and I did start out as his research assistant."

"You just didn't end up as his wife," Liz ventured.

"No."

"And all those details about your wonderful new house, the promotion, his tenure—" Tess prodded.

Grace shook her head. Everything was becoming jumbled, confused. "Give me a minute, will you? I need to sort out my thoughts a little better."

"Yeah, I think we need a breather, too," murmured Liz. "This is a lot to take in all at once."

"It's all right, Grace," Lovey murmured. "Take your time." Grace looked at her and saw something in Lovey's expression that both startled and comforted her. Sensitivity.

"OK, let me try to do this more coherently," Grace said at last. "First, about my father—"

As she spoke, the pieces began to fall into place, and a pattern she had never recognized before began to emerge in her mind. She told them, in detail, about being confronted with the evidence of her father's unfaithfulness in the person of his four-year-old daughter Emily, about how her mother had endured most of her married life with a knowledge of her husband's philandering. The truth had cut deep, and a hard edge of scar tissue had formed over Grace's heart. She hadn't been self-righteous with Lovey out of any deeply rooted religious or moral conviction, but out of her own place of woundedness, of betrayal.

"I was so sure I knew the difference between right and wrong, but all those moralistic tenets I had swallowed whole as a child didn't help me one bit when reality crashed in upon me." She looked straight at Tess. "I've never even imagined the kind of faith you've described, a sense of divine presence, of direction. All I had to support me was a flimsy, insubstantial list of rules and codes, and they didn't work

anymore. By the time I met Michael Forrester and thought I was in love, I had suppressed the painful memory of my father's
betrayal so thoroughly that the parallels
between him and Michael didn't even
register."

"So what we know about Michael from
your journal entries is that he was intelligent, good-looking, charming. Very
romantic."

"All true," Grace said. "As I wrote, he
asked me to become his research assistant,
and things blossomed from there." She re-
lated the incidents leading up to her
surrender to Michael—his smooth, well-
rehearsed deception, his declarations of
love, his lies about his pending divorce.
"I'm pretty sure he targeted me as an innocent, a naive girl who had never truly been
loved, desperate for connection and belonging. And then—" Grace paused.
"Then I discovered I was pregnant."

"Jesus," Liz said, massaging her temples.
"So the stuff you wrote about carrying a
baby and then losing it—"

Grace nodded. "Yes. That was real. I
went to tell him, so sure he would be
elated, certain that he would finalize the di-

vorce and we would be married. I can't believe I was so stupid. He was with his
wife—who, as it turned out, believed in
him utterly and had no idea he was fooling
around. He actually wanted me to have the
baby and give it to him and his wife to
adopt! Can you imagine? He told me she
would never know it was his, and even if
I confronted her with the truth, she
wouldn't believe me."

"You can't be serious!" Liz spat out.
"The dirty, lying son of a bitch! Just like
Tim—"

Lovey put a hand on Liz's arm to silence
her. "Grace," she said cautiously. "Did
you—did you have—?"

"An abortion?" Grace shook her head.
"No. I went through the pregnancy alone,
and gave my baby girl up for adoption. No
one knew, not even my mother."

She dared a glance at Tess and saw something odd flicker in her eyes. Grace had
been feeling it, too, every time Tess talked
about Claire. The timing, the age of Tess's
daughter, had to be about right, and Tess's
father, Bishop Riley, had arranged the
adoption of a little girl from North Carolina. Was it possible—

No. It was much too far-fetched. Grace tried to push the idea out of her mind.

"No wonder you made excuses not to see us," Liz said.

Tess shook her head. "Quite a story. I should have been taking lessons from you, Grace."

"Wait a minute, both of you," Lovey snapped. "All of us have enough exposed glass in our own houses that we ought not be throwing stones—"

"It's all right," Grace interrupted. "You deserve an explanation. I didn't consciously set out to mislead you, at least not in the beginning. My life had simply spun out of control, and I didn't know why, or how to get it back again. I was terribly ashamed. I had set myself up to be some kind of moral paragon, and then failed miserably. All of you seemed to be so happy, your lives so significant and full. So I created this elaborate fiction of who I wanted to be. And once I got started, the thing took on a life of its own. By that time I had told you how wonderful Michael was, and how we had gotten married, and the lies just seemed to snowball from there."

"What happened to Michael?" Liz asked. "Did he—?"

"He's still alive, still married to his wife," Grace answered. "I saw him a few months ago, at a distance, in a parking lot." She shook her head. "He's got quite a pot belly now."

"That's reassuring," Liz said. "Every little bit of vindication helps."

"Yeah. I have to admit that when I wrote about his death, I was very tempted to give him a wasting disease."

"The wasting away of particular parts, you mean?" Liz snickered.

Grace nodded and managed a smile. "Accompanied by an oozing rash and lots of itching."

This time everyone laughed, and the tension among them released.

"I am so sorry," Grace said once the laughter had subsided. "I didn't intend to deceive you. I guess I was looking for a way to save face. I was so ashamed."

"But we could have helped," Lovey said. "We could have supported you. You didn't have to go through all this alone."

"I wish I had believed that at the time,"

Grace said. "You were my best friends in college, but I couldn't imagine that even you would continue to accept me in spite of the spectacular mess I'd made of my life. Since the four of us went our separate ways, I've only had one true friend."

"Jet?" Tess asked. "She was real, then."

"She was very real. But her death was horrible, and I let her go without telling her the whole truth about myself—all the things I've just told you. Since then I've been in a kind of emotional isolation—no real friends, no connection. A miserable, lonely life. Maybe I thought it was my penance, a punishment for all I'd done wrong."

Tess and Lovey exchanged a glance, and Grace wondered if they were adding things up and would confront her about how she had afforded this weekend. But it was Liz who spoke.

"Clearing your conscience? I can understand that. But why now, after all these years? Why us?"

Grace looked into her eyes, then shifted her gaze to Tess and Lovey. "Because I need to trust someone, to find out if I can be loved just for myself alone. Because I want us to be friends again, genuine, honest friends who know and love each other, faults and all." Grace swallowed hard, trying to speak around the lump in her throat. "Because—"

Her breath came in short, shallow gasps, and tears blurred her vision. This was it; the final devastating blow.

"Because I have cancer," she said, "and I don't want to die alone."

GIFTS AND GRACES

*F*or a long time they sat together, just the four of them alone on the mountainside, with Grace gathered into a six-armed hug in the center of the circle. They cried—all of them, sharing their friend's tears, her pain and anxiety, her grief. Into a silence broken only by muffled weeping, Tess offered wordless entreaty for direction and wisdom and guidance.

Perhaps the others were praying, too, in whatever way they understood prayer. Tess didn't know, and didn't think it much mattered whether any of them formulated the right words or not. Tears were the deepest form of prayer, and the one who understood suffering would honor them.

When they were all cried out and stiff

from sitting cross-legged on the blanket, they separated as if by tacit consent. One by one they stretched and turned toward the tableau of multilayered mountains and valleys. The sun had shifted, and shadows from behind them cut long dark crevices into the landscape.

For a moment or two no one spoke. Then Lovey said, "Tell us about your prognosis, Grace. We want to know everything. We want to help if we can."

Grace blew her nose on a shredded tissue and shook her head. "There's nothing anyone can do. The tumor is malignant and invasive. The doctor talked about surgery, chemo, radiation, bone marrow transplant. At best, that would give me a year, and it would be a horrible year. I've decided not to submit to treatment."

Tess winced, but deep inside she understood, and respected Grace's choice. Hal's parents had both died of cancer, and what he had told her about their suffering had convinced her that sometimes the treatment was worse than the disease. Still, it was agonizing to think of Grace dying. Even worse was the prospect of her dying alone.

But most distressing of all, in Tess's mind, was the aching reality that for all these years Grace had *lived* alone. Isolated within her shame and despair, she had endured unimaginable emotional torments—repeated betrayals, the loss of her child, the loss of her *self*. Even Tess's well-trained writer's imagination could not begin to conceive the emotional havoc Grace's experiences had wreaked on her soul.

How often, Tess mused, did well-meaning people try to comfort a suffering loved one with careless words of commiseration. The glib phrase *I understand* more often meant *Stop talking about it. I can't take any more,* and only served to thrust the anguished friend into a deeper and more profound isolation.

No one could honestly say, "I understand." The best you could do was be quiet, and listen, and love.

At least Grace was not alone now. She had, in a demonstration of amazing resolve, reached out to the three of them, taken an enormous risk. There had to be something they could do to make things easier for her. They couldn't save her life, but surely they

must be able to find a way to help heal her
heart. . . .

Lovey held Grace's hand, at a loss for
words, but not at a loss for empathy. She
felt as if her own heart had been mangled
and bruised simply by hearing Grace's confession. Living through it had to be a thousand times worse. Did wounds like hers
ever mend? Or did they just scab over to
form a superficial scar hiding an infection
that lay beyond all healing?

Lovey was glad she had told the truth
about her difficulties with Bo. Everybody's
pain was different, but at least Grace now
understood that Lovey wasn't simply a
wealthy airhead whose worst suffering in
life was a bad haircut or a broken finger-
nail.

She felt Grace's fingers shift in her grasp,
and she looked up. Grace seemed a little
more at peace now. Her tears had abated.
Her face bore an expression of exhausted
relief. And as Lovey gazed into the face of
her friend, something stirred in her soul.

No amount of money could repair Grace's shattered life. Nothing Lovey could do would make it all right.

But she could be a loving presence, a shoulder to lean on, a hand to hold, a familiar face in a hostile world. She could listen. She could *be there.*

"Grace," she said quietly, "I won't pretend I understand all the things you've gone through. Despite my problems with Bo, I've never experienced betrayal like you've had with your father, and with Michael. I've never had to give up a child. I've never watched my best friend die. I've never faced my own mortality."

A surge of affection rose up in Lovey, and she lifted Grace's chin with a forefinger. She didn't know where the words were coming from, only that they emanated from some hidden inner wellspring she had never fully tapped before. She felt empowered, confident, connected—to Grace, to herself, to the universe.

"You're a courageous woman, Grace Benedict. You've dealt with all of this, and you've survived. You haven't gone under."

"But I've made so many mistakes," Grace protested. "I've—"

"You've *lived*. You've found a way to be honest, and to trust." Lovey looked around at the others, who were nodding. "What's important is not the wrong turns you think you've made along the path, but where the road leads you. Somehow it's brought you back to us, and for that I am very, very grateful."

The drive back down the Parkway felt very different to Grace than the trip up the mountain earlier that day. A late-afternoon sun threw slants of green light through the trees and mottled the air with gold.

She had done it. She had owned up to the truth about herself, had told them everything—except the plan to end her life. She felt free, as if heavy chains that had bound her soul had been cast aside. Tess and Liz and Lovey didn't condemn her. They loved her, accepted her. And in their love and acceptance she could almost feel a sense of God's forgiveness.

Almost.

For the first time in ages, Grace wondered how different her life might have been if she'd pursued a real faith like Tess's rather than accepting the stern, shallow precepts she had been exposed to as a child. It wasn't the church's fault, she supposed— she had never made much of an effort to move beyond superficialities to explore the complexities of the divine nature. Surely, as an adult, that much was required of her— not to have answers, perhaps, but at least to brave the questions.

But she had asked no questions. When it seemed that she had been abandoned to the consequences of her bad decisions, it hadn't occurred to her to seek out a light in the darkness. She had simply assumed that she had been deserted to face the hard times on her own.

In earlier days, the harsh moral guardian within Grace would probably have inter- preted the spiritual void as punishment for her many sins. But Tess had offered a dif- ferent perspective—that a door slammed in her face represented not judgment, but op- portunity.

Grace had encountered so many closed doors of her own, endured so many dark nights of the soul. But at last she had faced the truth. If her friends—flawed human beings—could accept her, weep with her over the wounds life had inflicted, embrace her without condemnation or judgment, what made her believe a supposedly loving deity would do any less?

The questions swirled through her mind, elusive as smoke, and there were no answers, no resolutions she could pin down. Still, the internal debate gave her plenty to think about, as well as a faint glimmer, just a spark, of what might be hope.

The shock, grief, and outrage over hearing Grace's story had subsided a bit with the waning of the conversation, and now Lovey couldn't help but think again about the note from Bo that still lay unopened on the coffee table in their suite. She vacillated between anger and chagrin, furious at him for intruding on her time with her friends, yet a little ashamed of herself for flying off to Asheville and leaving only a brief cryptic note behind.

No doubt he was angry with her, too. But it was about time he learned that she was a person in her own right, with her own feelings and needs and desires. If this trip had taught her anything, it had convinced her that she could not be a cheerleader on the sidelines any longer. She had more to offer than that, and if he couldn't appreciate her and treat her with the respect she deserved, then—

Then what? Was she prepared to divorce him, to strike out on her own? At her age, accustomed to a lifestyle of ease and wealth, and with no salable skills whatsoever, starting over as a single woman in her fifties was a terrifying proposition. How would Bo react? What would Carolyn and B.J. think? What would her friends say?

What would John Whitestone say? whispered a small voice inside her head.

And she knew the answer. John would say—or, rather, he would encourage Lovey to say it for herself—that she could not allow fear to become the primary issue. All her life she had given in to other people's expectations, pushing her own dreams and longings to the back burner. Now, thanks to John, and to Tess and Liz and Grace, she had caught a glimpse of a different way to live. Not vicariously, through other people's approval of her, but directly, by identifying her own gifts and developing them. She had barely begun the process of becoming a different kind of woman, but she liked it. Despite the risks, she felt strong and powerful and clear-minded, and she had no intention of going back.

Grace pulled the car up to the valet entrance of the Grove Park. "I'll meet you in the suite as soon as I've parked. Shouldn't take more than a few minutes. We'll change, and then get some dinner."

"Great," Liz said as she got out and held the back door open for Tess. "Brunch was a very long time ago."

Lovey opened the passenger door, then turned back to Grace. "You want me to go with you?"

"No, go ahead," Grace said. "I'll be along pretty quick."

Lovey watched as she made a U-turn in the front lot and drove down the hill toward the Vanderbilt Wing. When Grace was gone, she headed toward the Great Hall, following Tess and Liz.

But none of them made it to the elevator behind the stone fireplace.

Lovey was halfway across the room when she saw a man rise from a leather chair in the lobby and make a beeline in her direction. The Great Hall was dim, and her eyes had not fully adjusted, but she could see that he was big—tall and broad, with blondish hair. Backlit as he was against the open doors that led to the Sunset Terrace, she couldn't quite make out his face. Still, she knew. . . .

It was Bo.

Her heart sank.

"Amanda," he said as he strode across the hall. "Amanda—"

Out of the corner of her eye Lovey saw Liz and Tess turn and come back toward her. They hovered just behind, avenging angels waiting to protect her. She could sense their presence, and feeling them near infused her with a rush of courage and determination.

"What are you doing here?" she demanded. "If you've come to grab me by the hair and drag me back to the cave where I belong, you can forget about it."

He took a step back. "I—I just—"

Lovey frowned at him. Big Bo Tennyson had never, in her exceedingly long memory, been at a loss for words. He averted his eyes for a moment, and when he looked back at her, she saw not anger in his face, but something else. Hurt. Bewilderment.

In one beefy hand he held a single red rose.

"We need—I mean, I need to talk to you," he said. His eyes flickered over her shoulder. "Hello, ladies. Nice to see you again."

Lovey glanced back and saw Liz and Tess waving to Grace, who had just appeared in the hallway coming from the Vanderbilt Wing. Liz motioned her over, and with a perplexed expression on her face, she joined them.

"Liz, Tess, Grace," Lovey said, pointing to each one in turn, "I assume you remember my husband, Bo."

Not a one of them spoke. Instead, they stood with their feet planted and their arms crossed, no longer protective seraphim but obdurate female bouncers eyeing a trouble-making patron.

"Could we go someplace private?" Bo asked in a hoarse whisper.

"I don't think so," she responded. "Anything you have to say to me, you can say in front of my friends."

He took a shuddering breath. "All right."

He pointed in the direction of the bar area, where several leather chairs flanked a low table. "Can we at least sit down, then?"

They all sat, with Bo perched nervously on the edge of his chair.

A young woman in black trousers and a white tuxedo shirt came and asked them if they'd like drinks. Liz and Tess ordered virgin daiquiris. Grace requested Perrier with lime, and Lovey said, "That sounds good. Make it two."

She turned toward Bo, fully expecting him to order a double scotch on the rocks, or at least a pint of draft beer. When he asked for a diet Coke, she stared at him. "Are you sure?"

"Yeah," he said.

They sat in uncomfortable silence while the server whisked away and returned with their drinks. Tess caught Lovey's eye. "We can wait for you in the suite, you know."

Lovey considered this for a moment. A sheen of sweat had appeared on Bo's forehead, and he looked anxious and uncomfortable. For a moment she entertained a perverse desire to make this as difficult on him as possible, but then she changed her mind. As much for her friends' sake as for Bo's, she'd take pity on him.

"Maybe that would be best," she conceded at last. "Why don't you all go freshen up and come back down for me in"—she glanced at her watch—"fifteen or twenty minutes?"

Bo's relief was palpable. When the three of them had taken their drinks and disappeared behind the massive stone fireplace, he exhaled heavily and took a gulp of his diet Coke. Lovey had the impression he devoutly wished it were something stronger.

He shifted in his seat, clearly uncertain where to begin. He fumbled with the rose, pricked his thumb so hard the thorn drew blood, then laid it on the table between them. "This is for you," he said, sucking at the wound.

Lovey glanced at the rose, then back at him. "Why are you here, Bo?"

He bit his lip and looked around the Great Hall. "When I got home and you were gone, I didn't know what to do. I found your journal, talked to John Whitestone. Neva figured you had come here for this reunion, and she called the hotel and confirmed it. I rented a jet, and—" He held up his hands. "Here I am."

"Wait a minute." Lovey narrowed her eyes. *"You read my journal? You spoke to my counselor?"*

"Yeah, I—well, I'm sorry about that. But when your wife leaves you without a word, you have to do *something.*"

"What do you mean, leave you?"

"Well, you were, ah, gone. Just gone. Then, while I was looking for some clue about where you might be and who you might be with, I found the notebook and read about how miserable you were, how you'd never had a life of your own, how you'd just been living out the roles other people set for you. And—" He cut his eyes out toward the terrace. "Other stuff. You know, about me. About us. Whitestone's name was in there, over and over again, and—"

He stammered to a halt, reached into his pocket, and drew something out. "I didn't understand it all, but when I came across this—" The words died away, choked and thick. It took Lovey a minute to recognize what he held in his hands—the double picture frame that displayed their college photos. He had rejoined the frame with a makeshift hinge of duct tape, but the glass on her side was still shattered. "This, I understand."

The truth bore in on Lovey. He hadn't read the note she left for him. He had interpreted the breaking of the picture frame as a deliberate act, not an accident. "You thought I was having an *affair* with John?"

"I did. I went to find him—to find you. To ask you—" He stopped suddenly and ran a hand through his thinning blond hair. "To give me another chance."

Lovey sat back in her chair and swallowed half her Perrier in one gulp. The fizz burned her throat as it went down, and a curious sense of satisfaction swept over her.

He thought she had abandoned him, and he was afraid. Scared spitless, if his expression were any indication. She suppressed her instinctive reaction, the impulse to comfort and reassure him, to tell him about the note, to let him know she'd never intended to leave him for good. But she didn't. For one thing, she wanted to hear what he had to say. And besides, it might not be such a bad idea to let him stew for a while.

"Go on," she said, waving her glass.

"Well, like I said, I found Whitestone and confronted him. He wouldn't tell me a thing about you—confidentiality and all that—other than to deny that his relationship with you was anything other than professional. But he did say some things that got me thinking."

"About damn time," Lovey murmured under her breath. He was on his own; she would give him no help. And she had to admit that she was enjoying this immensely. "Please, continue."

"Yeah. OK. Anyway, like I said, I got to thinking. About us. Me and you." He swallowed hard. "I don't know what to do, Amanda. I don't want you to leave me."

"Why not?"

"Why don't I want you to leave?" Bo frowned and chewed on a hangnail. "What the hell kind of question is that? Isn't it—isn't it obvious?"

"Not to me."

"You want me to say it out loud, don't you? That I love you, and that I've been a horse's ass, and that I'm going to change."

Lovey suppressed a smile. "That would be a start."

He blew out a tense breath. "OK, I've said it. Now what do you want me to do?"

"What do *you* think you should do?"

He puzzled over this question for a minute or two and then looked up at her. "Maybe I ought to quit being Big Bo?" he said tentatively. "Maybe I ought to pay more attention to what I have—and to you."

Lovey arched an eyebrow but said nothing.

"You want to hear my plan?" His expression was eager now, hopeful.

"You've got a plan?" Lovey sat back in her chair and waved a hand. "By all means, let's hear it."

"OK, here's the deal." Bo leaned forward. Now that he had moved out of the realm of feelings and into action, he seemed to be gathering momentum. "I want you to come back, but I know it can't be like it was before. I'll support you in whatever you want to do. I'll cut down on the drinking. I'll shift most of the responsibility for the Big Bo stores to the managers. Hell, I'll even sell the whole chain if you want me to. From now on things will be different, I promise."

"Promises can be broken," Lovey said quietly.

"Yeah." He nodded. "I know. That's why I made an appointment next week with Whitestone, for both of us." He picked up his Coke and swirled the ice cubes absently.

"You did *what*?"

"You heard me right. I know I've always said this shrink stuff is a crock of shit—" He paused. "Anyway. God knows you don't have much reason to believe me, Amanda. But I do love you, and I want us to work on it. If it takes counseling, then dammit, I'll go to counseling. I don't want to lose you."

He looked up, and Lovey was startled at the unshed tears standing in his eyes. In all the years they had been together, she had never seen him cry.

"So what now?" she said.

"I've got a jet waiting at the airport. We can be home in three hours."

Lovey shook her head. "No, Bo, I can't do that. This reunion is important to me.

My friends are important. I need to finish what I've started."

She glanced up to see Tess and Liz and Grace, punctual as a Swiss watch, coming toward them from the elevator.

Bo saw them, too. He fished in his wallet and retrieved two crisp twenty-dollar bills. "All right. I'll take care of the drinks, and then I'll go on home." He gave her a pleading look, his eyes soft and liquid. "But you will come back?"

"Tomorrow," she said.

"I could pick you up in Minneapolis."

"My car's in the long-term lot. I'll drive myself. Barring any flight delays, I should be home by six."

He rose unsteadily to his feet and jammed his hands into his pockets. For a minute he stood there, looking lost and forlorn, an abandoned puppy.

Lovey cut a questioning glance at Tess, who spoke for all of them. "You're welcome to join us for dinner, Bo."

His expression brightened, and he seemed to consider this for a minute. Then he shook his head. "Thanks anyway, but the four of you need your time together.

I'll just get a cab and be on my way." He took a step toward Lovey and extended his arms uncertainly. She hugged him around the waist and stood on tiptoe to kiss him on his fleshy cheek.

"It means a lot that you came," she said. "We'll talk more tomorrow night."

"You betcha." Bo squeezed her hand, walked through the Great Hall, and disappeared into the night.

Closing the Circle

"All right," Lovey said on Monday morning after breakfast, "we need to make a plan."

The three of them—Tess, Liz, and Lovey—were sitting on the terrace, finishing their eggs Benedict and sharing another pot of decaf. Grace wasn't feeling well and had returned to the suite alone. Lovey had protested, saying she'd go too, but she felt relieved when Grace declined the offer of company. Lovey had a different agenda for the morning, one that didn't include Grace.

Liz sipped at her coffee. "What do you mean, a plan?"

"She's sick, she's alone. We're all she's got," Lovey said. "We have to do something."

"She's dying, Lovey." Liz shook her head. "I don't mean to be blunt, but unless you've morphed into Jesus and are ready to perform a spectacular healing, there's nothing we can do."

"Of course there is." Tess brightened. "I know what Lovey means. We can't cure her, but we *can* ensure that her last year will be better than the past thirty."

Liz thought about this for a minute, then nodded. "OK, I'm in. So what do you suggest?"

"Maybe we could take turns having her stay with each of us," Lovey said. "We've got plenty of room, and Bo—" She grinned. "At this point I think Bo would pretty much agree to anything."

"That might work for the two of you, but our little house is pretty crowded already. Besides, I doubt if Grace would agree to come to D.C., or to Minneapolis. She's more accustomed to small-town life. And it seems to me she needs stability right now—a place to belong, as well as consistent health care. I don't know if she'd be offended if we offered what seemed like charity."

"I agree," Tess said. "Still, there might be

a way." She held up a hand, dug a cell phone out of her bag, and punched in a series of numbers. Liz and Lovey could only hear one end of the conversation, but they got the gist of it.

"Good morning, sweetheart. Sorry, I forgot about the time difference. Can you wake up and talk to me? I need your opinion about something."

They listened as Tess filled Hal in on what had been going on—about Grace's confession, and her cancer, something about an apartment and Claire and a research assistant.

"You're absolutely wonderful, Hal. I was sure you'd say that. OK, I'll ask. And I'll see you tonight. Love you."

Tess flipped the phone shut and sat back with a pleased expression on her face. "We have an apartment over our garage—a nice place with a private bath and kitchenette. Claire lived there while she went to undergraduate school. It'll need some cosmetic improvements, but I think it would work just fine. Hal, bless him, is a generous, good-hearted man. He said yes without a moment's hesitation."

Liz frowned. "Yes to what, exactly?"

"For a while now I've been considering hiring an assistant," Tess explained. "Someone to do research, answer mail, proof galleys, that sort of thing. It's right up Grace's alley, and it would free me to write more. She could work when she felt good, and still have plenty of time to rest. She'd have privacy, but also a family to belong to. And it would be a job, not a handout."

"Sounds perfect," Lovey said. "Stability plus independence." This was better than she could have imagined. She turned toward Liz. "What about us? What are we going to do?"

"I was thinking about that while Tess was on the phone," Liz said. "It's all a matter of tapping into our resources. Tess has a place for Grace to live, and a job for her. What do you have to offer, Lovey?"

Lovey frowned. "Money? Time?"

"Exactly. You've got money. I'm doing all right, but I don't have the kind of discretionary income you have. What I've got is contacts."

"Contacts?"

"Yes. Serena and I know people in Washington. We can get things done."

"Such as?" Tess asked.

"Such as tracking down Grace's lost daughter, of course. Finding out if she's willing to see her biological mother."

Lovey saw a shadow pass across Tess's eyes. "Tess? Do you not think this is a good idea?"

Tess blinked, and her expression cleared. "Oh, yes, I think it would be wonderful. It's just that—" She hesitated for a moment. "Claire tried to do that once, find her birth mother, but the records were sealed. When you go back twenty years or more, that kind of information can be hard to find."

"Well, we won't know until we try, will we?" Liz was watching Tess's face closely. "Lovey, can you put up the funds for a private detective?"

"Absolutely. Also the money for plane fare and whatever else we need when we find her." She drummed her fingers on the tabletop. "I can pay for medical expenses too. And as I said, I've got time. I can fly down to Iowa once in a while—if that's OK with you, Tess—and be there for Grace when she has chemo. I want to do more than just foot the bill."

Tess held up a hand. "She said she didn't want treatment, and I don't think we should force the issue. That's her decision."

"All right. But if she changes her mind, the offer stands. I do want to be with her."

"You'd be welcome any time you want to come," Tess said.

"Maybe we could all get together for Thanksgiving or Christmas," Lovey went on, a sense of anticipation building in her. "B.J. and Carolyn live too far away to come home much. It would be like—"

"Like a family," Tess said.

"Right." Liz nodded. "One big dysfunctional family. Sounds like fun to me."

Grace lay on the bed upstairs in the suite, her stomach in knots, an almost unbearable pressure bearing down on her chest. She hadn't lied about not feeling well, but it wasn't primarily because of something she ate, or because of the dark, silent tentacles invading her body.

It was because today was Monday. Their last day together.

This afternoon Tess and Liz and Lovey

would be gone. Tomorrow Grace would return to her old life, her real life. For whatever time she had left—she hadn't made a firm decision about that part of the plan—she would be alone, with no one but Snookums the cat for company. Once she had found a loving home for Snookums, she would give up living, and pass on to whatever awaited her—reward or punishment or nothingness, it didn't much matter.

The process of confession—what Liz called "speaking her truth"—had been good for Grace, a release for her soul, a lifting of the heavy burden her heart had carried for years. And yet now that it was done, now that she had gotten a taste of the love and support and affirmation of friends, she felt worse off, not better. How quickly the sweetness of companionship and understanding could turn bitter on the tongue! For she now had been reminded, much to her dismay, what she had been missing all these years. And what she would miss even more desperately between now and the time she passed through eternity's door.

Perhaps this reunion had been a stupid idea after all. Wouldn't it have been better not to know how things could be? Wouldn't it have been preferable to face death never having lived, rather than experiencing the joy of life for a fleeting moment and having it snatched away again?

Her mind wandered by turns to Liz and Tess and Lovey. Liz had endured such terrible emotional torment, but had come out stronger on the other side, with significant work and a fulfilling life. Tess had made her mark—not the mark she intended to make, but an important one nevertheless—and had managed a wonderful family in the bargain. And Lovey. Who could have predicted the changes that were now taking place in Lovey's life? She had, finally, taken the reins of her own destiny and determined to change. She had learned, had grown, had not allowed herself to stay stuck in the mire of other people's expectations. And now it looked as if Bo, too, would be altered by the new Lovey. Assuming he made good on his promises, their marriage could very well bring both of them to a new level of respect and commitment.

These extraordinary women were her friends. They inspired her, made her feel as if life might be worth going on with after all. But not for long. She was about to lose them again, and this time there would be no more reunions.

Grace heard noises in the hallway, a key being inserted in the lock. She couldn't let them see her like this—curled into a ball of despair, feeling sorry for herself.

She jumped up, ran into the bathroom, and shut the door. She could hear them beyond, in the suite, moving about, talking. But she couldn't make out the words. Probably getting their things together, packing suitcases, preparing to check out.

"Grace?" Lovey's voice came through the thick oak door. "Are you all right?"

"I'm—I'm fine," Grace managed. "I'll be out in a minute." She turned on the tap in the sink, and the noise drowned out Lovey's voice. She splashed cold water on her face to reduce the puffiness around her eyes, then brushed her teeth, took a deep breath to steady her nerves, and opened the door.

Lovey stood at the bed, folding clothes to go in her suitcase. When Grace emerged, she looked up and grinned as if she were about to burst at the seams with an exciting secret. "We've got plenty of time to pack," she said. "Come into the parlor; we want to talk to you."

Grace allowed herself to be led into the sitting room, and she sank down onto the couch. On the coffee table in front of her lay the circle journal with its ragged, faded cover. She picked it up and absently flipped its pages, catching phrases here and there written in four distinctive but very familiar styles of handwriting.

Liz grinned and took the book from her. "Pay attention. We've got a proposition for you."

"A proposition?"

"An offer," Tess corrected. She sat down next to Grace, took both of her hands, and fixed her with an intense, searching look. "We've been talking, and as much as we know you love these mountains—we all do—it seems to us that there's not much holding you here. If you're interested, I'd like to present an alternative to you."

"An alternative?" Grace knew she sounded like a particularly annoying parrot, repeating everything, but she couldn't help herself. She had no idea what they were talking about.

"For a while now, Hal and I have been

discussing my need for an assistant—someone to proofread, do research, answer mail, things like that. But since I work at home, I've been hesitant to invite a stranger into my private space. I was wondering if you might consider taking the job."

"Me? Move to Iowa to work with you?"

"Of course you. It wouldn't be a very high-paying position, but you could keep your own schedule, and we have a garage apartment that's currently going to waste. That could be part of the deal—a place to live, meals with me and Hal—" Tess stammered to a stop. "If you'd want to, that is. It's not a big place—the size of a three-car garage. More like a large studio with a private bath and a small kitchen. But it's very nice, and we'd redecorate it to suit you."

Grace gaped at her. "I—I don't understand. You're offering me—"

"I need an assistant," Tess repeated. "And you—"

Lovey perched on the edge of the sofa and slid an arm around Grace's shoulders. "And you need a family," she said gently. "We've all talked about it, Grace. We want to spend more time with you, to be there for you. We could all come for holidays. In between, I could fly down on weekends occasionally. Or even drive—it's only about three hundred miles."

Tears stung at Grace's eyes, and she blinked them back. "I couldn't accept—"

"Why not?" Liz said.

"You're just doing this because—because I have cancer. You feel sorry for me."

Liz knelt in front of Grace, nearly nose to nose. "Look at this face. Do you see pity in this face?" She gave a curt laugh. "Let's be honest—keeping in touch via the circle journal hasn't exactly turned out to be a rousing success. We've all used it as a shield, hidden things from each other. I think it's way past time we negotiated these friendships in person."

"But you're going back to D.C.," Grace said, "and Lovey's going home to Minnesota. How—?"

"Right," Liz said. "But this is the twenty-first century, and we now have such marvels of technology as e-mail and telephones and airplanes." She peered at Grace. "You *have* heard of those things, I trust."

Despite herself, Grace laughed. "You don't have to be sarcastic, Liz."

"Of course I do. It's a gift. It's my calling."

Grace swiped at her tears and leaned back against Lovey's arm. "You three are really sneaky, you know?"

"Yes, we are." Tess smiled. "But this is for real, Grace. I do need an assistant, and you'll be perfect for the job."

"And I won't have to die alone, is that it?"

No one spoke for a moment. Then Lovey said, "Yes, that's part of it. We're your friends, your *family*. If there's nothing we can do to help you live longer, we can at least be there for you during the time you have left." She blinked back tears. "You know, before this weekend I would never have been this honest about death—especially the death of someone I love."

"But now," Liz added, "it seems utterly ridiculous to be anything less than honest."

Tess nodded. "That's what friendship is all about."

Grace smiled, but a voice in the back of her brain reminded her that there was one minor detail she *wasn't* being honest about—the fact that she had decided to kill herself.

She pushed the thought aside. She would face that issue later. She couldn't tell them—not now, anyway. She had been granted the chance for a different sort of ending, to live whatever time she had left surrounded by people who cared about her, who loved her.

She would take it, and be thankful.

38

On a Clear Day

Grace had paid her rent through June 15, but by the first she was ready to hit the road. Lovey had settled the Visa bill for the Grove Park reunion. Grace had sold her furniture for a little cash, and had traded in her old Civic on a used Nissan minivan. The van was now packed with boxes of books, clothes, and personal belongings. In the front passenger seat next to her, Snookums meowed piteously in her crate.

"It's all right, baby," Grace cooed. "We're almost there."

Geographically impaired as she was, she had pictured Iowa as being straight west, near Oklahoma. Instead, her route had taken her north of Knoxville, through the rolling bluegrass of Kentucky horse country and the farms and cornfields of Indiana. Eight hundred miles of Middle America, and once she had left the Smokies behind at the I-40 exit for Dollywood and Pigeon Forge, not a mountain in sight.

It was a strange and unsettling experience for Grace, traversing these flat lands. She had lived in the Blue Ridge all her life, and had become accustomed to the intimate embrace of the mountains and foothills. As she approached the Iowa border on the second day of the sixteen-hour trip, she realized what was bothering her: She could see for miles.

The metaphor was not lost on Grace. For years her vision had been limited to what was directly in front of her, or only slightly at a distance. The mundane routine of getting up, dressing, dragging herself to a boring job, coming home, feeding the cat, worrying about bills, going to bed, and rising the next morning to do it all over again.

But that life was behind her. She was headed toward something new, something utterly unfamiliar. An abbreviated future, no doubt, but nevertheless a future wide with possibility. She wouldn't be alone. She would have friends, and interesting work, and a place to belong.

A memory drifted into her mind, a movie she had seen long ago, with Barbra Streisand as a young woman with a gift of sight. She could hear the theme song building to a crescendo—"On a Clear Day You Can See Forever." How many clear days, Grace wondered, had she experienced in her lifetime? How many of her fifty-plus years had brought her hope?

Yet oddly, anticipation welled up inside her. The past lay like shredded rubber from a blown tire, left on the shoulder of the highway. The future called to her, beckoning to her from a place called Iowa City. Her heart felt lighter than it had in decades. Whatever she was going to, it had to be better than what she had left.

At a little past four, Grace found her exit, pulled into a service station, and consulted the directions Tess had sent her. "Not far now," she murmured to the cat. "First thing we'll do is get you out of that box."

Tess and Hal lived in a quiet, established neighborhood with mature trees and large lots. She turned into the driveway, shut off the motor, and sat gazing through the windshield at a stately two-story brick Georgian with a three-car garage. Exactly right for Tess, she thought. Distinguished but not ostentatious.

Her eyes went to the three-bay garage, also brick, which had a stairway leading to the upper-level apartment. "This is it," she said with a sigh.

Snookums responded with an impatient "Mrowww."

The front door opened, and Tess emerged, smiling and waving. "You made it!" she said as Grace unfolded herself stiffly from behind the wheel. "Long trip."

"It wasn't too bad," Grace said. "I am a little tired." She went around to the passenger side and unloaded the cat crate. "I think Snookums will be relieved to be out of this thing."

Tess took the crate from her and peered inside, poking a finger in to rub Snookums on the head. "Hello, beautiful," she said. "Come on, let's get you upstairs."

Grace opened the back of the van and pulled out a litter box, a bag of cat litter, and a ceramic bowl with the word *Kitty* on one side. She followed Tess up the outside stairway and through the door into the apartment.

"Once we've unloaded your stuff, you can park in the garage," Tess said as Grace situated the litter box in a corner behind the bathroom door and filled the cat's water bowl. "There's a pass-through hall to the main house from up here, so you won't have to use the outside stairs. It goes straight into my office."

Snookums came out of the bathroom looking decidedly relieved, her chin dripping water, and jumped immediately onto the back of an overstuffed chair near the front window. Grace paced back and forth, stretching her legs, gazing around.

The apartment consisted of one spacious room with a sitting area, a queen-size bed in the far corner, and a small kitchenette hidden behind louvered folding doors. "I'm afraid you'll have to share our laundry room downstairs," Tess was saying. "But you've got a small fridge and sink, a microwave, and a two-burner stove." She pulled open a cabinet door overhead to reveal a stack of colorful plates and bowls, and a shelf lined with pale blue glasses and coffee mugs. "I bought some Fiesta ware, and you've got a few pots and pans, but I hope you'll join us for meals most of the time. Oh, and here—" She went to the other side of the bed and pushed back a pocket door to reveal a walk-in closet. "Enough storage space, I hope. Hanging rods on one side, and shelves on the other."

Just as Tess moved to shut the kitchen cabinet, Grace caught a glimpse of food supplies—coffee and filters, a glass jar filled with tea bags, a loaf of bread, some cans of soup. Real soup with red labels, not the generic store-brand variety she had come to despise. "This is fabulous," Grace breathed.

It was, by far, the nicest place she had called home since childhood. The walls were painted a soft blue-gray, and the floor was hardwood with a blue and rust-colored Oriental rug in the center. Flanking the side windows were two tall wooden bookcases, and between them, a walnut desk with a high-backed leather office chair. There was a nearly new sofa in matching tones, two coordinating armchairs, and a big squashy ottoman, as well as a walnut coffee table and end tables topped by slate-blue ceramic lamps. The bed in the corner was hammered copper, covered by a hand-made star quilt in various hues of blue, cream, and brown.

"Well, as I told you, we can redecorate if you want," Tess said. "Not everybody likes blue."

"I love it. It's peaceful."

Snookums seemed to agree. She had curled up on the ottoman and was snoring softly.

Tess smiled at the cat. "That door on the left goes into my office. And here"—she went to open a door on the far side of the room, next to the kitchenette—"there's a small deck across the back, overlooking the yard. We've got an umbrella table and a couple of chairs, but Hal hasn't gotten them up here yet."

She fished in her pocket and handed Grace a small ring bearing two brass keys. "Here you go. The square key fits our front door, and the round one fits your private entrance. Claire's still got the extra garage-door opener, but it'll be yours once we get it back."

Tess turned to go. "Hal will be home in half an hour or so. He's got a friend coming later to help unload your van." She smiled. "I'm going to go check on dinner. Come down whenever you're ready." She put a hand on the doorknob leading to her study. "And, Grace—"

"Yes?"

"Welcome home."

For a long time after Tess left, Grace sat in the comfortable blue chair—*her* chair— with her feet propped on the ottoman next to the snoozing cat. She jingled the keys absently in one hand and stared in amazement around the apartment—*her* apartment.

Home, Tess had said. And her mind echoed, *home.*

Home is where the heart is, where you belong, where people love you. Home is where you have a tile shower and a sofa that doesn't sag and brass keys and brand-name soup and new bowls for the soup, blue bowls that match the rest of the decor.

Maybe, when she wasn't looking, she had already died. Because this certainly wasn't Iowa.

It was heaven.

It had taken Grace a week to sell her belongings and pack up what she had chosen to keep, and several hours of arranging and rearranging to fit it all into the van. It took Hal and his friend Greg—another professor at the Writers' Workshop, apparently—exactly twenty-eight minutes to unload everything into the garage apartment.

Hal had arrived home a little before five. By quarter to six the three of them had sat down to a meal of crock-pot roast beef with potatoes and carrots, and the most delicious homemade bread, still warm from the oven. Hal, Tess informed her, was the bread baker of the household—one of his many gifts.

Grace liked Hal from the moment she met him. He had kind eyes, and a gentle way of drawing her out that made her feel as if she'd known him for years. She had no doubt Tess had told him everything—clearly, that was the kind of relationship they shared—but he mentioned neither her cancer nor the sordid circumstances of her past. He treated her as a person, not a charity case, and there was no question about his welcome of her into their home, not the least glimmer of reluctance at having a stranger invade the sanctity of their private space.

Still, Grace determined not to make a pest of herself. After dinner, and a dessert of luscious apple crisp, she cleared the table, loaded the dishwasher, and tidied up Tess's kitchen. By seven-thirty she had excused herself and went upstairs to unpack.

For a couple of weeks now she had felt her energy levels declining. The two-day drive had exhausted her, and despite her best intentions to get the apartment in order, she couldn't seem to make herself get up and work.

She sat on the rug in the middle of the room, surrounded by cardboard boxes and crumpled butcher paper. The box marked KITCHEN would be easiest to unload—a few spoons and spatulas, some old stained Tupperware, a ceramic teapot, a popcorn popper. The ancient percolator with its frayed cord went back into the box, along with a mismatched set of battered tableware. Those could be thrown out in favor of the new coffeemaker and bright silverware Tess had provided.

At last she got the kitchen stuff stowed

in the cabinets and turned to the boxes of books—old, much-loved friends that would fill the bookcases on either side of the desk. She didn't have the strength to lift the boxes, but at least she could do a little organizing.

Grace had just begun to arrange the contents of the first box—alphabetically, by author—when a light knock sounded on the outside door. She struggled to her feet and went to answer it, and through the nine-light window with its sheer curtain, saw the form of a young woman waving through the glass.

Grace pulled the door open. The porch light on the landing cast a soft golden glow over blonde curls, and bright blue eyes smiled at her. The young woman wore jeans, a light brown leather jacket, and a navy T-shirt that read VIRGINIA IS FOR LOVERS.

"I figured I'd come up and introduce myself," the girl said. "I'm—"

Grace's exhaustion dissipated like smoke on the mountains. She stared at the girl, her heart pounding, her breath coming in short gasps. "You're—you're Claire."

"Yes." She nodded. "Could I come in before all the moths in the Midwest invade your space?"

Grace found her manners and took a step back. "Of course. Forgive me."

Claire eased into the room and waited while Grace shut the door behind her. "Sorry I missed dinner," she said, extending a hand in Grace's direction. "I'm glad to meet you. Mom's told me all about you."

Grace had the sudden irrational longing to throw her arms around Claire, but she resisted the impulse.

"Dad and I have been telling Mom for ages that she ought to have an assistant," Claire went on. "I think it's great you were willing to come. With your background and all, the two of you will make a great team."

Grace motioned toward the sofa, and Claire sat down. Immediately Snookums jumped up from the ottoman she had claimed as her own, leaped into Claire's lap, and began to purr. "She's gorgeous," Claire murmured, stroking the cat under the chin. "She's Himalayan, isn't she?"

"Yes. Partly, anyway. Her grandmother was full-blood. She's Snookums the third."

"Well, Snookums, you're a beauty. And a lover." The cat butted her head against Claire's hand.

"Would you like some coffee?" Grace asked, moving toward the kitchenette. "It's decaf, I think."

"I'd love some. But I see you're busy unpacking, and I don't want to disturb you."

"Sorry the place is such a mess," Grace apologized as she retrieved the bag of coffee and a filter from the overhead cabinet. She filled the pot and started the coffee brewing, then turned back toward her visitor.

Claire had removed her jacket and was sitting cross-legged on the floor beside the half-empty box of books. "I could help if you like. We could talk while we work." Snookums followed the girl like a lovesick puppy, pawing at the packing paper that lay scattered over the rug and rolling belly-up for her stomach to be rubbed.

"Ah." Claire fingered one of the volumes that lay on the floor beside the bookcase. "My favorite book—and from the looks of it, one of your favorites, too." She held up a worn, dog-eared copy of *The Secret Garden*.

Grace lowered herself awkwardly to the floor next to Claire. "I would have thought *The Chosen Child* would be your favorite." She picked Tess's book out of the pile and surveyed it. "Guess I should get my copy autographed."

"Mom would be honored." Claire emptied the open box and began to alphabetize its contents. "Tell you what. Why don't you sit on the couch and give me directions, and I'll organize and shelve them. That way you don't have to keep getting up and down."

Grace fixed her eyes on the girl's back as she began arranging books on the top shelf. "You know about my cancer," she said.

"Yes," Claire said matter-of-factly without turning around. "Mom told me."

"And what else did she tell you?"

"Pretty much everything, I think." Claire finished the top shelf and came over to kneel next to Grace. "We don't have many secrets."

"So you know about—"

"About the child you gave up for adoption?" Claire nodded, her expression revealing no trace of pity or discomfort. "It was a good thing to do, Grace. I can vouch for that."

"Yeah," Grace said. "You lucked out, getting Tess and Hal for parents."

"I wouldn't call it luck. I was blessed."

They talked as they worked—or, rather, Claire talked and Grace listened. She spoke easily, comfortably, of what it was like growing up as an adopted child, her futile search for her birth mother, her conviction that her parents' love for her had made all the difference in her life. She spoke freely about God and faith and the unexpected directions her life had taken. And the more Grace listened, the stronger she felt a sense of connection between the two of them. There was something special about this re-markable young woman, and although she thought she knew what it might be, she didn't dare verbalize that hope.

Claire finished unpacking and arranging the books and flattened the cardboard boxes for recycling. When the apartment had taken on some semblance of order, Grace poured coffee and discovered, much to her delight, a package of Oreos in the cupboard. The two of them sat on opposite ends of the sofa with the cookies between them.

"So, what's an Iowa girl like you doing with a Virginia T-shirt?" Grace said, trying to keep the conversation light.

"I've just moved back from Virginia, actually," Claire said. "Three years of grad school in Alexandria. Seminary was great. I loved every minute of it—but being that close to D.C. was awful. I'm glad to be coming home."

Grace inhaled a piece of cookie and choked violently. "Seminary?"

"Yeah. VTS—Virginia Theological Seminary. I just finished my M.Div. Didn't Mom tell you?"

"No, we—we really haven't had much of a chance to talk since I got here."

"I've received a call to a small parish in Cedar Rapids, about thirty miles north of here. My ordination service is next Sunday, in the afternoon. I'd love it if you'd come." She arched an eyebrow. "I don't think Mom ever expected to have a priest for a daughter."

Grace gaped at her. "A priest? You mean an Episcopal priest, like Tess's dad, with a collar and everything?"

"A collar and everything." Claire laughed. "But not quite like Granddad. He's a bishop. More like Gran, although she always did counseling and never served as a parish priest."

"Wait a minute." Grace held up a hand. "Your *grandmother* is ordained?"

"Sure. The church began ordaining women back in the seventies. The presiding bishop didn't agree with it, but he didn't stand in the way when the convention voted, and he supported the decision despite his personal opinions. Granddad always respected him for that."

Grace's mind drifted back to a late-night conversation in the house on Barnard Street, during the snowstorm that had taken her father's life. "That helps explain Tess's return to faith. When I first met her, your mother was, I think she put it, 'on sabbatical' from the church. She said she couldn't support a church that refused to ordain women. I'd been surrounded by Southern Baptists all my life, so I couldn't even conceive of such a thing."

"Really? It's pretty common now. The president of my seminary was a woman, and nearly a third of the professors. I had some good role models—including Gran." A wistful expression came over Claire's face. "And Mom. She taught me a lot. She's a deeply spiritual person, you know. Even if she was 'on sabbatical' from the church, I can't imagine her ever abandoning her faith. It's not all about religion or ritual with her. It's about love and compassion."

Claire got to her feet and retrieved her jacket from the chair, where Snookums had pawed it into a nest and was sleeping on it. "I'd better go. Most of my seminary stuff is still crated up in the garage, but I do have a few things yet to pack. I'm moving into the rectory on Friday." She pointed to the pile of cardboard. "You have any use for those?"

"Help yourself," Grace said. "Thanks for coming by, and for giving me a hand with the books. I've really enjoyed getting to know you a bit."

"Same here." Claire tucked the boxes under one arm and went to the door. "We'll do it again. Cedar Rapids isn't far. I'll be around a lot, if Mom has any say in the matter."

After Claire left, Grace took a long, hot shower and sank into bed with a sigh. Snookums curled up next to her with a paw on her pillow.

"Well, baby, this has been quite a day," Grace said to the cat. "And Claire Riley-Hopkins is something else, wouldn't you agree?"

Snookums emitted a loud, rumbling purr of agreement.

Yes, Grace thought. Claire *was* something else. Lovely, intelligent, tender-hearted, full of compassion. Honest. Witty. And spiritual. A woman of faith. A woman who was devoting her life to helping others.

She felt a surge of pride welling up in her. She couldn't say it to anyone—not even to Snookums, not even to herself. But as she drifted off to sleep, the thought crept into her mind and nestled there.

My daughter . . . a priest.

39

PILATE'S ANSWER

*L*ovey was just heading downstairs for breakfast when the telephone rang. She glanced at her watch. Who could be calling at eight o'clock in the morning?

She heard Neva Wilson pick up. "Tennyson residence." A pause. "Yes ma'am, she's here. Just a minute, and I'll get her."

Lovey came around the corner into the den. "I'll take it in here, Neva. Would you mind bringing me a cup of coffee? Bo will be down in a minute. Tell him I'll be in to breakfast shortly."

Neva handed over the receiver. "It's Miss Liz, your friend from Washington."

"You don't have to call her 'Miss,' Neva. I'm sure she told you that." She put the receiver to her chest. "And you don't have to call me 'Miz Manda' either. Amanda will do just fine, or Lovey."

"Old habits die hard," Neva murmured as she went toward the kitchen. "Though it seems like you and Mr. Bo have been killing them off right and left."

Lovey smiled and put the telephone to her ear. "Liz?"

"Yeah, it's me," Liz said. "Sorry to be calling so early."

"That's OK. I'm up. I'm off to the adult day care center at ten, but I've got time."

"Lovey, don't you think adult day care is a little premature?" Liz joked. "I know you've been having your senior moments, but—"

"Cut it out." Lovey laughed. "You know perfectly well I go there to help. Lots of them don't really need supervised care, they just want company. Somebody to listen." She shifted the phone to the other side. "How are you? How's Serena?"

"We're both just fine. Busy. The bigger question is, how are you and Bo?"

"We're good, I think. In counseling, working on our issues. Some days Bo really seems like a changed man. Time will tell, but I'm hopeful."

"That's great."

"Hang on a second, will you? Bo's flagging me down."

Lovey held a hand over the mouthpiece and turned to her husband, who was standing in the doorway, giving her a time-out signal. "It's Liz," she said. "I may be a few minutes here."

"That's OK." He came into the room and stood next to her. "You sure it's all right with you if I go play golf?"

"Of course. It's a beautiful day for it. I've got the senior center this morning anyway."

"I'll go on, then. We tee off at nine. I'll grab some breakfast on the way."

"Tell Isabel before you leave, so the Wicked Witch of the West doesn't get her bloomers in a wad about cooking too many eggs."

"Will do. I should be home by one or so. Remember, we've got counseling at four this afternoon. I thought maybe we'd go out for dinner afterward—give us a chance to process."

"Sounds great. Why don't you give Isabel the day off, then? I'll see you later."

He ran a hand over her hair and bent down to kiss her. "Love you."

"You too, hon. Bye."

When he was gone, she turned her attention back to Liz. "Sorry for the delay. Bo—"

"I heard. Sounds like things are looking up. He actually told you he loved you."

"Every day," Lovey said. "More than once." She chuckled. "At first it seemed contrived, you know, as if he had an index card in his pocket reminding him to say it. But it's become more natural now. He's finally quit bringing me flowers all the time. I swear, for a while the place looked like a funeral parlor."

"That's better than the alternative."

"Very true. He lapses now and then, but for the most part we're making progress. He's in AA. Counseling's going well. I have to admit, though, I'm glad he's lost that hangdog expression. Contrition wears thin after a month or two. We're actually having fun now that he's relaxed a little. Oh, by the way, I finally found the note."

"The note you wrote when you came to Asheville for the reunion? The one he claimed he never got?"

"Right. It had slipped down between the dresser and the wall. I suspect Neva might have had something to do with it getting lost, but I can't prove it. She's pretty sharp. Maybe she thought it would do him good to think I had left him."

"She could have been right."

"Well," Lovey said, clearing her throat. "I doubt you called to hear the play-by-play on me and Bo. Did you get the check I sent?"

"Yes, it came day before yesterday. Thanks. It was more than enough to cover the detective's expenses. For now, at least."

"I assume that means he hasn't found anything conclusive."

"She. The detective's a woman, a friend of Serena's. Very smart. Very savvy."

"Hold on. I wrote the check to an Alex Romanowski."

"Alexandra," Liz said. "She specializes in tracking down missing children."

"So what's happening? Have we got any leads?"

Liz hesitated, and Lovey could hear a heavy breath whoosh through the telephone lines. "Yes, we've got something, but it's not the daughter Grace put up for adoption. Every road Alex has followed on that issue came to a dead end."

"Come on, Liz, don't keep me in suspense. What has she found?"

"Grace's half sister, Emily."

"Oh, boy." Lovey sighed. "And—?"

"And Emily, who's now in her thirties, wants to make contact with Grace. The aunt who raised her passed away about three years ago, and of course her mother is dead. She has no other family. She remembers—vaguely—one visit to Grace's mother's house. Says Grace gave her ice cream, talked to her, was nice to her. She wanted to meet Grace again even before she found out about the cancer, and now that she knows Grace is dying, she's very insistent."

"What do we do?"

"I don't know. For now Alex has put her off, telling her that we'd have to have Grace's permission to bring them together."

"How do you think Grace would react?"

"Your guess is as good as mine. Or maybe better. Have you talked to Grace lately?"

"I called her last Friday, and we talked for half an hour or so. She sounds wonderful—loves what she's doing—living in Iowa, working with Tess on the new book.

Talked nonstop about Tess's daughter, Claire. Apparently the two of them have really made a connection. Did you know that Claire is about to be ordained as an Episcopal priest?"

"No kidding? That must be a coup for Tess."

"Seems Tess's mother got ordained, too—after years of waiting. I'm surprised she didn't tell us at the reunion. Maybe there was just too much going on that weekend."

"Or maybe she was trying to be respectful of you and me. We were pretty resistant toward any kind of religion back in college—the atheist and the agnostic."

"I'm still an agnostic," Lovey said, "if you define agnostic as 'not knowing.' I'll never be the church-going type, but maybe there is some higher power at work in the world. Being a parent certainly gives you cause to ask for help now and then, even if you're not sure anyone is listening. But I'll tell you one thing. That higher power—if there is one—has sure made a difference in Bo."

Liz laughed. "I know what you mean. I'm pretty sure Tess and Grace assumed I was still a confirmed atheist, since they didn't bring up the issue when we were together. They'd probably be shocked to know how much I've mellowed over the years. Everything I've seen—in my clients, and in my own life—convinces me that there has to be a gracious presence in the world, a source of the hope that rises up against all odds."

"And then there's Serena," Lovey prodded, grinning to herself.

"Well, that too." Liz cleared her throat. "Back to business. What do we do about Emily?"

Lovey twisted the telephone cord around her finger. "I say we wait and see how the rest of the investigation pans out before we bring the question up to Grace. Emily's presence might dredge up some very painful memories, especially if we still haven't found the daughter. So far she seems pretty healthy. If her condition declines—or I probably should say *as* her condition declines—we can revisit the Emily question. Can Alex hold her off?"

"I think so. For a while anyway."

"So what's next?"

"We keep looking for the daughter, I guess. But there's something else, which could be a complication. Do you remember what Grace named her baby girl?"

"Ramona, after her mother, wasn't it?"

Liz hesitated. "Not just Ramona. Claire. Ramona Claire."

"Oh, my gosh. You don't think—?"

"No, I don't," Liz said. "Statistically, it would be a thousand-to-one chance. But I'll have Alex check it out. The bigger problem is whether Grace thinks so or not."

Grace had never in her life experienced a church service as beautiful as Claire's ordination.

She didn't understand the Episcopal way of doing things—standing, sitting, kneeling, making the sign of the cross. A couple of times she found herself bolt upright while everyone else knelt, or flipping through the Book of Common Prayer, desperately trying to find her place so she could follow along.

Still, none of that mattered. Something mysterious was happening here, and she felt it. Her mind tried to wrap around the experience, to understand it, but the only word she could come up with was *sacrament*.

Tess's father was present, of course, regal-looking in his bishop's purple. The Reverend Mrs. Riley participated, too, clad in a simple linen alb. Together they moved around the altar in a mystical dance of faith. The bishop's voice rang out clear and strong, but when Claire's grandmother began to pray, her voice broke with emotion. Tess, sitting next to Grace in the family pew, clasped Hal's hand and dabbed at her eyes with a tissue.

At last Claire, also garbed in clerical collar and alb, knelt before her grandfather to be consecrated as a priest. Bishop Riley laid his hands on his granddaughter's head, and his eyes were bright with unshed tears. He repeated the words of consecration from the Episcopal prayer book, placed the stole around her neck, and added his own blessing: "Sanctify her in truth, O God. . . ."

Grace did not hear the remainder of the prayer. Her mind latched on to the word *truth* and spun back thirty years. To the

class project that had first introduced her to
Tess and Liz and Lovey. To Pilate's question: *What is truth?*

And just as vividly, she recalled the answer the four of them had come up with.
Embedded deep in her memory, it floated
to the surface intact:

> *Truth is the core of human experience, the*
> *center point which keeps us balanced and*
> *aligned, the hub which connects us to all*
> *we value. It goes by many names—faith,*
> *beauty, love, justice—but whatever we call*
> *it, however we experience it, it is the*
> *source of meaning and purpose in our lives.*

Everything around Grace seemed to fade
away—the dimly lit church, the people in
the pews, the drama taking place before the
altar. Inside her head she could see images
from the past, grainy and indistinct, like old
home movies. The four of them at the dinner table in the house on Barnard Street,
their romp in the snow. Evenings laughing
and talking around the little gas fire. Her
father's funeral, with her friends at her side.
Graduation, and the years that followed—
years of empty longing, of loss and separa-

tion. Jet's ironic parting words: "I can go to my grave knowing that in my life I had one true friend."

And she could see the circle journal, ratty and tattered, filled with partial truths about all their lives.

Truth had brought them together. Fear of the truth had driven them apart. And now a greater truth—the answer to Pilate's question—had reunited them again.

The hub that connects us. The center point which keeps us balanced and aligned. The source of meaning and purpose in our lives.

She had been wrong. So very wrong. She had not been abandoned, flung out into the universe to fend for herself. The hub had held her fast, connected to these people who cared about her. Love was the center point, the source and fulfillment of all her being.

Grace looked up at Claire, who smiled down at her as she took the bread in her hands and broke it, lifted the cup in blessing. Tess touched her arm, and Grace moved forward with the family toward the altar.

All her senses heightened, and everything seemed to come alive. The warmth from Tess's flesh that seeped into her as they knelt shoulder to shoulder. The affection shining in Claire's blue eyes. The crack of the crust as the loaf broke apart. The aroma of candles burning, and the scent of the rich dark wine. The yeasty fiber of the bread, the tang of the grape on her tongue.

We are the bread, Grace thought, *gathered and sifted together. We are the wine, pressed and mingled and distilled. Whatever we call it, however we experience it, this is the bond that holds us together.*

The taste of love. The palpable flavor of forgiveness and belonging.

40

FINAL FORGIVENESS

*U*nder Shelter #8, near the larger of City Park's two ponds, Grace sat at a picnic table writing. In the distance she could hear the hooting whistle of the small train, the squeals of childlike laughter from the amusement ride area closer to the river.

The sun had dropped lower toward the horizon, and a breeze was beginning to carry away the warmth of the October afternoon. Soon the park would be filling up in anticipation of the Autumn Festival fireworks scheduled to begin at dark. Tess and Hal had promised to meet her here with a picnic, and Grace fervently hoped Claire would come, too. A parish minister, Claire had said, could never be completely certain of her schedule, but the annual fireworks display was a family tradition, and she expected she'd be able to drive down from Cedar Rapids in time for supper.

Grace looked down at the yellow legal pad in front of her. She hadn't gotten very far, but then, there wasn't much to do. On the top line, in bold letters, the words stared back at her:

LAST WILL AND TESTAMENT
OF GRACE ARLISS BENEDICT
OCTOBER 4, 2003

A simple handwritten will was all she needed—not one of those complex, extended documents in incomprehensible legalese. She didn't have much of an inheritance, after all. Her minivan, her books, most of the small salary Tess paid her, tucked away in a savings account.

And Snookums. She wanted to make sure the cat was taken care of. But mostly, she wanted to make a statement, a last good-bye. She wanted to thank her friends. She wanted, in some fashion, to acknowledge her daughter.

Grace had no hard data, of course— nothing tangible to back up the conviction that Claire Riley-Hopkins was, indeed, the newborn she had given up for adoption so many years ago. Only circumstantial evidence—the age, the blonde hair and startlingly familiar blue eyes, the fact that she had been adopted out of North Carolina. Internet searches had turned up nothing.

Nevertheless, her gut told her it was true. The thrill she experienced every time Claire walked into a room. The connection between them. The sense of pride in Claire's accomplishments and in her character. There was no denying the certainty that lay deep in a mother's soul. Claire was her baby, all grown up into the kind of young woman who would bring joy to any parent's heart.

Grace knew. At the core of her being, she knew.

Because Claire had changed everything.

It had happened back in June, the afternoon of Claire's ordination—or at least had culminated on that day. Perhaps it had begun her first night in Iowa, the moment she saw the girl standing at her door, her hair gilded with the soft light of the porch lamp. Maybe it was the easy way they talked, or Claire's compassionate but direct acceptance of Grace's cancer and her guilt-ridden past, or her empathy with the pain Grace had endured, or her understanding of the agonizing decision to give her child up for adoption. Or perhaps it went back even further, to April, to that moment on the mountain when she had opened herself to the love and acceptance of her friends.

Whatever it was, during the ordination service there had come a single clarifying moment. Grace had knelt in her pew, savoring the aftertaste of wine and bread, basking in a freedom she had never felt before, when something shifted inside her. A transformation. A door swinging open.

She wanted to live.

The past six months had proved that to her beyond all doubt.

And a glorious six months it had been. The misery and despair of the past now seemed a dim and distant memory. She had been given a family, and friends, and a place to belong. She had received forgiveness and restoration. She had found hope.

Half a year might seem a pittance to those who enjoyed good health and never gave a second thought to death. But to

Grace, these few months had been worth a whole life.

A year ago Grace would never have imagined herself capable of being so free. No longer was there any deception in her life, any pretense. She now lived openly and honestly with the people who cared about her, bared her soul to them, allowed them to share both her pain and her pleasure. She took joy in each moment, gave love and received it. And delighted in the daughter who once had been lost.

She had discovered—better late than not at all—the fulfillment of being truly known and truly loved. And nothing could take that away from her.

Grace didn't expect a healing, some kind of physical sign. She still had cancer. Some days she felt strong and whole, and some days weak and depleted. Perhaps she only had a few months left. But while she lived, she would *live.*

No matter what physical terrors she might have to face, no matter what toll her disease might take as it gnawed away her life from the inside out, Grace refused to second-guess the wisdom and truth that had come to her. She would not take her own life. She would not leave her daughter voluntarily, or spurn the gift of love and acceptance her friends had offered her. She had determined to stay and see it through to whatever end was in store for her.

She had chosen life.

Perhaps, by some mercy, her time might be extended. But in the meantime she would live with fervor and with gratefulness. Every day was a precious gift. How could she ever have thought to deny even one minute to herself and those she loved?

She stared down at the pad again, and then began to write:

I, Grace Arliss Benedict, being of sound mind and spirit . . .

The legal phrase, she thought, was "sound mind and body," but that wasn't wholly applicable. Her body *wasn't* sound, after all. Yet her spirit had undergone a radical regeneration. Legal or not, she intended to include in her last testament the newfound health of soul that had been granted to her.

She smiled at the phrase and continued:

I, Grace Arliss Benedict, being of sound mind and spirit, do hereby declare my last will and testament.

To the Reverend Claire Riley-Hopkins, I bequeath all my worldly goods, such as they are, including my most treasured possession, my cat Snookums. Snookums adored you from the beginning, Claire, as did I, and I know you will care for her in the gracious way you care for everyone who enters your life.

To Tess and Hal Riley-Hopkins, I offer my eternal gratitude for your love in action, for your acceptance and affirmation, and for opening your home to take me in and make me part of your family. You have restored my faith in human nature, in the world, and in myself.

To Liz Chandler and Amanda Love Tennyson, I extend heartfelt appreciation for being the kind of friends I could turn to in a time of great turmoil. Some things never die, and a friendship like ours is one of them.

Dear ones—all of you—you made life worth living again. You gave me hope and a vision for the future, however long or short that future will turn out to be.

Especially you, Claire. Perhaps without knowing it, you have been the catalyst in a significant transformation, helping me come to peace with myself and with the daughter I never knew.

And now that my time has come, I trust that all of you will be able to celebrate with me a life that was not lost, but regained at the end, and a faith that enables me to move on to whatever awaits me with confidence and expectation.

Grace read back over the words, a bit surprised at the power and personal conviction they conveyed. "How can I know what I believe until I write it?" Tess had once mused. "It's the process of composing that crystallizes my thoughts and ideas."

At the time Grace hadn't understood, but now, in her own last will and testament, she had seen the principle in action. Every word she had written was true. She *could* face death with faith instead of fear. She *had* found peace with the daughter she never knew. She had reclaimed her life, thanks to the love and compassion of these friends.

Alone in the park with the afternoon sun casting golden glimmers across the windswept pond, she signed the document and sealed it in an envelope bearing the words *To be opened on the occasion of my death.*

The breeze stirred her hair, and she could almost feel them standing there, smiling down at her. Liz and Tess and Lovey, the friends who had not failed her when she needed them. Jet, who had accepted her without reservation. Hal, who demonstrated the best of what a man could be. Claire, dear Claire, who had no idea how important her presence was to Grace's life.

In her mind's eye they surrounded her, embracing her.

A circle of blessing.

A circle of grace.

The picnic—fried chicken and potato salad, with Hal's decadent chocolate fudge brownies—reminded Grace of her childhood, when she and Mama and Daddy would go down to the river behind the house and spread a red-checked tablecloth on the ground. For the first time in ages, the memory of her parents brought not despair or shame, but a sense of reconciliation with the past, and Grace wished them both well. Perhaps in the next life tears would be dried and old wounds healed.

After the leftovers were packed away, they moved to the north side of the park, on the banks of the Iowa River. Hal set up lawn chairs for Tess and Grace and himself. Claire tucked a blanket around Grace's shoulders and then sat on the ground in front of her. As the dazzling pyrotechnic display began, she pointed to the colors that burst above in the clear dark sky, and below in the shimmering river.

"I sometimes think that's what spiritual life is like," she said. "The glory we experience in relationships, whatever we know of love and faith, is a reflection of something far beyond our imagining." She leaned companionably against Grace's knees. "And yet it's not merely a reflection. It's a promise."

Grace smiled down at her and pulled the blanket closer around her shoulders. "That'll preach."

"You think so?"

"I can't speak for your congregation," Grace said. "But I sure like it."

Ear-splitting explosions precluded further conversation, and as Grace watched the blazing showers of multicolored stars raining down over the river, she marveled at how Claire's mind worked. The grandeur and magic and mystery of human life, which mirrored, like lights on the water, a greater light.

The fireworks went on for nearly an hour. At last, to a chorus of oohs and ahhs, a climactic final burst of rockets ignited, shot into the sky, and filled the air with fiery blossoms of blue and green and red and gold. No one moved or spoke until the last of the sparks had trailed down the night sky and extinguished themselves in the river.

As usual, they had saved the best for last.

"Are you sure you want to drive home?" Hal asked as he let Grace out in the lot where she had parked. "Traffic's going to be awful. We could all go together, and come back to get your car tomorrow."

"That's too much trouble," Grace said. "Go on ahead. I'll just be a few minutes behind you."

Hal waited until Grace unlocked her minivan and started the engine, then waved and exited the parking lot. She sat there for a few minutes with the motor idling. It had been a perfect day, and she was filled with a sense of well-being—an emotion so new that it still took her by surprise. She could almost feel the dark tentacles inside her chest letting go, exiting her body like smoke, like something evil exorcised and banished.

On the passenger seat beside her lay the legal pad she had used earlier in the day. She pulled her will from its hiding place between the last page and the cardboard backing of the pad. Grace had thought that writing a will would be a morbid, depressing experience, a brutal reminder of her own impending mortality. Instead, it had freed her, somehow, from the fear of leaving this world without saying I love you.

She fingered the envelope and tapped its stiff edge on her thigh. With a little luck— or mercy, she corrected herself—this document wouldn't be needed for a long time.

Traffic was still creeping along, clogged in the parking lot and out onto the main road. Grace put the van into reverse and backed out. Behind her, a driver in a white Buick laid on the horn and shook his fist at her.

The process of getting out of the park was infuriatingly slow. Grace drummed her fingers impatiently on the steering wheel as the line of cars snaked toward the intersection of Park Road.

Finally, after an interminable ten minutes of stop-and-go, she pulled into the turn lane at the light. Park Road was also congested, but at least traffic here was moving. When the arrow turned green, Grace made a left onto the main road.

She heard the squeal of tires, the blare of a horn. As if in slow motion, her head swiveled to the left, and two enormous beams of light, right at eye level, blinded her.

There was a deafening crunch of metal slamming into metal. A scream. The shattering of glass.

Then darkness closed in, a liquid warmth, and silence.

Tess slumped in a chair in the ICU waiting area, and tears stung her eyes. She had known this day was coming. She just hadn't expected it to come so soon—or so violently.

The elevator dinged, and the steel doors slid open to reveal Hal, flanked by Claire and four other women.

"Liz! Lovey!" Tess jumped up and lunged at them, her tears flowing freely now. "I'm so glad you're here!" She caught Serena's eye over Liz's shoulder. "You too, Serena."

Her eyes drifted to the young woman who had arrived with them. She was a bit older than Claire, and stood back from the group, her head lowered, as if willing herself not to intrude.

The girl had strawberry-blonde hair pulled back in a ponytail, and a sprinkling of freckles across her nose that made her look younger than perhaps she was. But something about the eyes seemed familiar. "Is this—" She took a breath. "Is this Grace's *daughter*?"

"No." Liz shook her head. "I'm afraid every lead we had in that direction came up empty. This is Emily Ryerson, Grace's half sister."

"I went to UNCA," Emily murmured

miserably, "and worked in the registrar's office afterward. Lived in Asheville since I was eighteen. And I never knew. She was so . . . so *close*."

"Do you have any other family, Emily?" Claire asked gently.

The girl bit her lip. "Mama was killed in the wreck with Grace's father—*our* father. Aunt Bette, my mother's only sister, raised me, but she passed away a few years back. I wanted to meet Grace again, before—you know . . ."

"Before she died."

"Right. She was so nice to me when I was little, that one time we met, even though seeing me must have been a terrible shock for her. I had thought that with time—" She shrugged. "I'm supposed to be getting married in the spring, although I'm not really sure about it. I guess I kind of hoped we could get acquainted. Like having a big sister to talk to . . ."

Emily's words dwindled off into silence, and Liz turned toward Tess. "How is she?"

"Bad," Tess said. "I asked to sit with her, to let her know she's not alone. But the rules in ICU are pretty strict, and they won't allow me much time."

"We'll see about that," Liz said.

A nurse clad in salmon-colored scrubs came down the hall and paused in the doorway of the waiting area. "You're here for Grace Benedict?"

Liz spoke up. "Yes, and we want to see her."

The nurse scrutinized Liz as if she were a lab specimen. "Family only."

Liz took a step forward and eyed the woman's name tag. "We want to see her . . . *Hildy*," she repeated in a tone that dared the nurse to contradict her. *"Now."*

Despite the tension of the moment, Tess had to suppress a grin.

The nurse peered at Liz. "Are you kin?"

"This is Grace's sister." Liz pointed at Emily. "And we're the rest of her family. We've just flown in from all over the country."

"She's been given a lot of painkillers," Nurse Hildy said. "She won't know—"

"She *will* know," Liz countered. "She'll know she's loved."

The nurse's expression softened. "Maybe you're right. Come on, I'll let you go in. But only for a few minutes."

Hal and Serena stayed behind in the

waiting room while Tess, Liz, Lovey, Claire, and Emily trooped off behind Hildy toward the critical care unit.

"Five minutes," the nurse said in a hushed voice as they crowded into the glass-walled enclosure.

Grace's eyes were sunken, her skin pallid. Her chest rose and fell in shallow, uneven breaths. Hildy inspected the various mechanical devices hooked up to Grace's deathly still form, tapped on the tube coming from the IV, checked the heart monitor. "She's breathing on her own. That's a good sign. But I wouldn't hold out too much hope."

"Thank you, Hildy." Liz lifted an eyebrow. "Underneath all that starch, you're a good person."

"I'm an idiot," Hildy responded mildly. "And if anyone finds all of you in here, I don't know a thing about it. Otherwise I'll be an unemployed idiot."

When the nurse was gone, Claire drew her mother aside and backed into a corner of the room. "I need to tell you something, Mother. In case Grace wakes up."

Tess shook her head. "There's not much chance of that, I'm afraid."

"Maybe not, but still—" She dropped her voice to a whisper. "I'm pretty sure Grace believes—"

"That you're the daughter she gave up for adoption."

"You *know*?" Claire's eyes went wide.

"It's pretty obvious. She loves you like a mother."

"Mom, I didn't encourage this. But then, I didn't discourage it either. I never confronted her about it."

"Of course you didn't," Tess said, linking her arm through her daughter's. "You're much too empathetic and openhearted to undermine another person's faith." She peered into Claire's face. "Do *you* believe it's true?"

Claire shook her head. "No, I don't believe she's my birth mother. Still, if she regained consciousness and said something, I didn't want you to think—"

Tess put an arm around Claire's shoulder. "It's all right. Give her whatever you have to give," she said. "Love her. There's always enough to go around."

Grace tried to move, but the pain was too intense—a throbbing inside her skull, a scalp-splitting agony. One side of her chest was on fire, a razor-sharp sword between her ribs. It took a monumental effort just to open her eyes.

Liz. And Tess. And Lovey.

And someone else—she didn't know who.

"We're all here, Grace," a quiet voice said.

A rush of love and gratitude surged into her, and she turned, just slightly, to see Claire standing to her right.

"There was an accident," Tess said, pushing a bit of hair back from Grace's temple. "But you're going to be fine now."

It was a lie, and Grace knew it. But it was a compassionate lie. Besides, she didn't have the strength to argue.

Lovey held a straw to her lips. Cool water dribbled down her chin. Some of it got into her mouth and freed her tongue.

Her eyes slid toward the one unfamiliar face in the room. "Who—?"

"I'm Emily," she said. "Little Emmy, remember? Your father's—" She hesitated. "Your father's other daughter."

"Yes," Grace slurred. "Gave you ice cream. I was so . . . angry. Betrayed."

"Me too," Emily said fiercely. "At least once I was old enough to understand. I hated him—still do. Hate what he did to you and your mother. Hate what he did to *my* mother, and to me. I met this guy, see, and I want to get married, but I'm afraid—"

Grace finally was able to get her right hand to move, and she lifted it slightly from the bed. "Forgive," she whispered. "Live." She fixed her gaze on Claire. "Help her."

"I will." Claire moved in closer, and Grace saw the truth reflected in her eyes.

She knows, Grace thought. *Knows I'm dying. What she doesn't know is how grateful I am for being given the chance to live. . . .*

"Grace," Claire said, "I feel as if I've known you forever. Like a big sister. Another mother. I love you, Grace. I'll never forget you."

It was agonizing to smile, but Grace couldn't help herself. "I love you too," she said with effort. "You helped me find myself again. Find hope. Find faith."

Tears began to spill down Claire's cheeks. "It's all right," Grace whispered. "There was no time left, no time for all the things she longed to say. How their love, their acceptance, had made life worth living. How blessed she was to have had the past six months with them. How freeing it was to leave this world with no condemnation, no regrets.

She longed to wipe Claire's tears away, but she couldn't reach. "I'm ready."

She looked down and saw Claire's hand squeeze hers, a touch without feeling. The room around her began to dim. A weight pressed in on her chest, pushing her down, forcing the air from her body. She fought back. One minute. One more minute.

"I love you all," she gasped between breaths. "Thank you. Thank you."

Then the light came, flowing over and around her like liquid gold. She could see their faces, haloed by the shimmering glow. Never in her life had she felt so unfettered, so free, so whole. A healing, comforting warmth spread through her as the rays around them grew brighter. She could barely see their faces now, but she knew they were there. They had always been there, these friends. Around her, inside her.

Earth's gravity fell away, a heavy cloak

slipping from Grace's shoulders. Weight-less, her soul rose as if they were lifting her, these friends of hers—not with their arms, but with their hearts. Lifting her to the light.

This was no permanent parting. She knew it as certainly as she knew that she belonged. Love like this was stronger than death, more brilliant than any darkness.

Grace smiled without effort, without pain, as the last pale shadows of those beloved faces absorbed into the light.

She closed her eyes, inhaled one final, liberating breath, and surrendered.

The Last Good-Bye

Claire Riley-Hopkins stood on the crest of Craggy Point and looked out over the watershed valley toward the horizon. Clouds were rolling in from the south, and in the distance the mountains stretched toward infinity. Layer upon layer of October reds and yellows and golds, the ornaments of autumn's glory.

This grass-covered rise was the very spot where Grace had opened her heart and shared her truth with her friends. A sanctuary, her mother had called it. A temple.

Claire had been to these mountains a time or two in her childhood and youth, visiting her grandparents in Black Mountain. But she had never considered, until this moment, how vividly they reflected both divine and human nature. Crevices of darkness, illuminated peaks, shifting shade from the wind-rushed billows—a never-ending spectacle of change in a landscape that had stood immutable for thousands of years.

The sun vanished behind a bank of clouds, and an early-morning breeze lifted her hair and flapped at the stole she wore around her neck. White, a symbol of resurrection. The yoke of Christ. But in this place, on this occasion, it did not feel like an easy burden.

She turned back and gazed at the group assembled there—her father and mother, her grandparents. Liz and Serena. Lovey and Bo. Emily Ryerson and her fiancé, Curt. Heads bowed in prayer or thought or meditation, they clustered silently around the urn that held Grace Benedict's ashes.

This would not be a traditional memorial service. No Burial Rites from the Book of Common Prayer, no petitions for mercy upon Grace's eternal soul. Claire had determined that this farewell would be exactly what Grace wanted it to be—a celebration of her spiritual transformation, a gentle passing to the other side.

Claire had become a priest not because she had all the answers, but because she had a calling, a passion for helping people articulate their questions and find their own way. She had realized, almost from the beginning, that Grace believed her to be the daughter she had given up for adoption so long ago. Claire herself did not share this opinion, and yet she had been content not to challenge Grace's conviction, or to obsess too much about the answer. People needed anchors for their faith, and sometimes those anchors were manifested in flesh and blood.

Grace's death stirred many old dilemmas in Claire's spirit, questions raised during seminary, about how—or if—God intervened in the course of human life. It had taken some serious soul searching to decide what she ought to say at this memorial service.

Everyone was waiting, looking up at her. It was time.

"Grace Benedict knew she was dying," Claire said, "and that realization led her to make a radical decision about her life. She determined that no matter what the cost, she didn't want to die alone and in shame, as she had lived. And so she took a risk—she contacted three old friends from college and set up a reunion with them." Claire inclined her head toward Liz and Lovey and her mother. "That reunion—Grace's honesty, her vulnerability—changed everything."

No one spoke, but her mother nodded in her direction, and Claire continued. "As it turned out, Grace's end came suddenly, only six months after making that life-changing decision—not as the result of cancer, but in an unexpected and terrible accident. We all wish her time with us had been longer, and that her death had come more gently. But because she knew her days were short, Grace was able to summon the strength and will of a person who has nothing left to lose. She opened herself completely—to us, and ultimately to the source of all hope. She let herself love and be loved. She reclaimed her soul and discovered what it means to live in trust. She made a choice. She chose life.

"Those of us who embrace religious faith often talk far too freely about divine will and direction, as if we can push back the curtains of eternity and understand the mind of God. We crawl around in a maze of questions, searching for a way out, looking for someone to praise or blame.

"But life is not a maze; it's a labyrinth. We walk, and keep on walking. Sometimes the path leads us far afield from the center, and sometimes very close. When we come to a turn, we're never quite sure which direction the switchback will take us. But we don't have to worry about finding the 'one right way.' We don't have to figure out the answers. In a labyrinth there are no dead ends. We simply continue on the path in faith that it will bring us to the center."

Claire gazed down at the hammered copper of Grace's urn. "It's human nature to try to find explanations for the inexplicable. We ask why. But we are not given to know those answers. We know only that a diagnosis of cancer became a vehicle of blessing, launching a series of events that brought Grace Benedict to a place of peace and hope and confidence before her days on this earth came to an end."

She took in a breath and cleared her throat. "I believe Grace learned something in the process that she would want us to know. She learned that life is brief—too brief for anything but authenticity. I believe she would want us to open our eyes, to be aware, to embrace every moment, to live honestly in the presence of love."

Claire looked up and saw her father gazing down at her mother. Her grandparents had their arms around each other. Liz and Serena were holding hands, as were Lovey and Bo. Curt's arm gripped Emily's shoulder.

"And so we—her family—gather here on this mountain to celebrate her life, to offer thanks for the fulfillment and joy she experienced, and to covenant with her and with one another that we will not forget the lessons she has to teach us. We will remember Grace Benedict, not by the struggles and pain of her life, but by the faithful way she ended it."

Claire finished speaking, and Tess stepped forward. For a moment she stood looking into her daughter's eyes. The eulogy had moved her deeply, and her heart overflowed with love and pride. She offered up a wordless prayer of gratitude for her daughter's gifts, and then, in a trembling voice, turned to the others and read an excerpt from Grace's last will and testament:

Dear ones—all of you—you made life worth living again. You gave me hope and a vision for the future, however long or short that future will turn out to be. . . . You have been the catalyst in a significant transformation, helping me come to peace with myself. . . . And now that my time has come, I trust that all of you will be able to celebrate with me a life that was not lost, but regained at the end, and a faith that enables me to move on to whatever awaits me with confidence and expectation.

Liz picked up the urn and opened it. One by one, each of them took a handful of Grace's ashes and, with simple expressions of love and thanks, scattered them to the winds that blew over the Blue Ridge.

When the urn was empty, Lovey moved front and center. Clutched against her chest she held the battered, dog-eared journal that had passed from one hand to the next over the past thirty years.

"This journal," Lovey said shakily, "was a

kind of lifeline that bound us together—
Grace and Tess and Liz and me. We didn't
always tell the truth, but in the end this
journal, and our friendship, drew us back
together. And now we bury it. Its job is
done, and we've all agreed that we don't
need it anymore."

Tess motioned to Liz. They joined
Lovey, and three hands grasped the journal.

A little to one side stood a large slab of
rock, wedged from its place and propped
on end with a tire iron. Hal and Bo had
dug out a small crevice beneath it, and into
that shallow grave Tess and Lovey and Liz
placed the ragged book.

After a moment of silence the three of
them stepped back. Tess reached out and
linked hands with Liz and Lovey in a semicircle around the stone.

"This journal will stay here forever,"
she said, "as a monument to a friendship
as strong as these mountains, and as
enduring."

They gazed at the circle journal, nested
below the rock. And then, without warning, the bar slipped, the stone slab crashed
into place over the book, and the tire iron
skittered out from under the stone.

In unison they whooped and jumped back, doing a little improvisational dance as the iron bar flew past their feet. Lovey tripped and fell into Liz, who took Tess down, too—all of them in a heap of arms and legs.

Liz grinned. "Guess Grace is done with that journal once and for all."

Lovey struggled to her feet and tried to brush the dirt and grass stains off her pants. "Seems like she's still here. Something tells me she'd really be enjoying this."

At that moment the sun pierced through the clouds, and a shaft of light streamed over them like a gilded waterfall. Lovey shook her fist at the sky. "Turn the spotlight off, will you—at least until I get the mud off my butt."

Tess chuckled. "She's here, all right. She'll always be here."

She flung one arm around Liz and the other around Lovey. And there on the mountaintop, overlooking the eternal peaks and valleys of the Blue Ridge, they embraced in a circle of sunlight and laughed until the tears came.